WINDYRIDGE

A CLASSIC YORKSHIRE NOVEL

BY
WILLIE RILEY

WITH A NEW INTRODUCTION BY
DAVID M. COPELAND

Windyridge by Willie Riley
first published in 1912
by Herbert Jenkins, London.

This new edition with an
introduction by David M. Copeland
published in 2010
by Northern Heritage Publications
an imprint of Jeremy Mills Publishing Limited

www.jeremymillspublishing.co.uk

Paperback: ISBN 978-1-906600-18-1
Hardback: ISBN 978-1-906600-34-1

All royalties from the sale of this book will be donated equally to the
Bible Society and the Leeds Children's Holiday Camp Association.
Willie Riley supported and championed both of these charities for many years.

CONTENTS

ILLUSTRATIONS

WILLIE RILEY

WILLIE RILEY AND THE 'THREE KINDLY CRITICS' TO WHOM
WINDYRIDGE WAS DEDICATED. LEFT TO RIGHT; ETHEL BOLTON,
WILLIE RILEY, CLARA RILEY, FLORENCE BOLTON

INTRODUCTION

DAVID M. COPELAND

PROLOGUE

WHEN WILLIE RILEY saw his first book *Windyridge* published in 1912, he was already forty-six years old, and for fourteen years had been Managing Director of the Bradford-based firm of Riley Brothers Ltd., an innovative company hiring and selling optical lantern slides and the associated equipment, including an international mail order business. This activity was but part of the family business activities, all of which had been established by his father Joseph, who, after several difficult mill management experiences and positions in West Yorkshire, had gone into business on his own account as a Stuff merchant. It was Joseph who had established the magic lantern business in 1884, and Willie and his elder brother Herbert soon were put in charge of the lantern operation, each becoming a partner in the business when he attained the age of twenty-one. Riley was also a major figure in northern Methodism, and was to be an active and sought-after local preacher for an astonishing seventy-five years. He was a popular speaker and lectured on a variety of subjects. He had a lifelong passion for the Yorkshire Dales and scenery, and the people who lived in these remote places.

Although he had been used to writing in a small way, Riley had never intended to become an author. The way in which *Windyridge* was conceived and ultimately delivered was extraordinary, and the consequences were to be far-reaching for Riley for the rest of his long life.

Within two years of the publication of *Windyridge* his world would be turned upside down, and this middle-aged businessman would have to reinvent himself, and live by his newly-found ability to write popular literature. For the next thirty years or so he would publish on average one book per year. By the end of his long life he would complete a total of thirty-nine books, mostly novels located in his beloved Yorkshire Dales. His last book was published just a month before he died, at the age of ninety-five, in June 1961. Between the two World Wars he was to become a household name and an internationally known author.

His writing output was extraordinary. Most writers publish but a fraction of Riley's achievement, which is the more surprising because he only entered the world of literature relatively late in his life. *Windyridge*, however, always remained his most popular and enduring book. To this day there are houses all over the world named after this famous novel. It was one such house in suburban Newcastle upon Tyne that started me on an absorbing journey of discovery that has lasted over thirty years; that eventually led me to meet Riley's nephew, and to discover an archive treasury containing priceless information about this – until now – totally forgotten Bradford businessman, author, and man of God. In 2009 the trail brought me to the completion of a Master of Philosophy research degree at the University of Bradford on the life, work and legacy of W. Riley. It has been a constant surprise to me how little there is in the public domain about this one-time famous son of Bradford. The purpose of my research has been to restore public awareness of Riley, especially in Yorkshire, and particularly in his own city of Bradford, of which he was very proud.

HOW *WINDYRIDGE* CAME TO BE WRITTEN

IT WAS IN 1911, whilst living in Bradford, that an event occurred which would have a lasting, indeed permanent, effect on Riley. Nearby lived the Bolton family, good friends of Riley and his wife, Clara. There were four Bolton daughters, three of them living with their parents. Two of the daughters at home were delicate of health, sharing this feature with Clara. Early in that year disaster struck the Bolton family. Father, mother and the more delicate sister all died in quick succession. The two remaining sisters, Florence and Ethel, were naturally devastated by this calamity. The Rileys took them under their wing, spending time with them once or twice each week; and in July of that year they went together on holiday to the Alps.

Once back home again, Riley conceived the idea of writing a story, and reading it to the three ladies, chapter by chapter. It was just to entertain, to divert, to keep them all from brooding. It is appropriate to point out here that Riley did not read much fiction; other than some of the classics, and poetry, his tastes were rather for books on philosophy, theology and sociology, and about his beloved Yorkshire countryside and people. Apart from writing the occasional piece for the Methodist weeklies, his only creative writing was associated with stories and text for optical slide sets.

When asked what the story would be about, he admitted, 'I haven't the faintest idea!'[1] He eventually declared that he would bring a girl from London to Yorkshire, and then see what would happen, writing the story from the viewpoint of a woman. The three women derided his plan, saying that no mere man could successfully write from a woman's perspective. He gleefully took up the challenge and eventually wrote the whole story without help from any female.

Riley chose his favourite village, Hawksworth (three miles west of Guiseley), as the place to which his disaffected heroine would come. He made up a name for this tiny village, calling it 'Windyridge' as its situation along the ridge of a hill suggested. The name was inspired. He would think about the storyline while walking to and from work, sitting down in the evening to write. On average Riley finished one chapter a week. He would sit in an easy chair by the fire, with a cloth-covered writing board on his knee, with Clara sat on the other side of the hearth. Each completed chapter was then read to the three ladies on the Saturday night. He wrote in student penny notebooks, which grew in number as the story progressed. He later said of the process, 'Like Mr. Thackeray I took a great interest in bringing characters on to my stage and wondering what they were going to do and to tell me'.[2] Neither the structure nor the plot was preconceived. Indeed there was no particular plot as such. Instead, it took

---

1. Riley, W., *Sunset Reflections*, Herbert Jenkins (1957), p. 98.
2. '*Windyridge* and its Story', a lecture by W. Riley.

the form of a diary of events, recounted by one of the central characters, Grace Holden, in a series of sketches and episodes. He said later, 'Until I had written some twenty chapters and the story had begun to assume the proportions of a book I never looked more than one chapter ahead and had not the faintest idea what was to come. I was writing for fun.'[3] By the time he had finished the tale, the pile of notebooks numbered twelve, and he had completed thirty chapters. Riley now thought his task was at an end, but the ladies begged to differ. To his surprise, they insisted that what was now a substantial novel was so good that it should be published. Riley argued strongly against this idea, declaring that, 'It isn't a book so much as a story written for one particular purpose'.[4]

He pointed out how difficult it had been for so many good authors to find a willing publisher. He told them that he did not want to go through the ignominy of rejection, which even established authors experience; and finally, that he was far too busy running a successful company and had neither desire nor need to seek publication.

At Whitsuntide 1912 the Rileys and the Bolton sisters went together to Grange-over-Sands for a short holiday. This time the ladies read the book to him, and he had to admit that 'it sounded pretty good'.[5] Whilst they were walking one day across the race track at nearby Cartmel, Willie glanced down on the ground and found a 6d coin. One of the Boltons said it would bring him luck with a publisher. By now Riley had made up his mind how to progress: 'I will send the manuscript to one publisher and if refused I shall not send it to any other.'[6] Whilst he had not the slightest expectation of the manuscript being accepted, in that way he felt that honour would be satisfied, and the ladies would cease their insistence once it had been rejected. Upon their return home he typed out a copy, taking the opportunity to make some revisions and corrections. He did this himself because he didn't want to waste money by paying someone else to do what he considered to be a fruitless task.

---

3. *Sunset Reflections*, p. 99.
4. 'How I Wrote *Windyridge*', an address by Riley given at Hawksworth Methodist Chapel, 8th July 1950.
5. *Sunset Reflections*, p. 100.
6. 'How I Wrote *Windyridge*'.

The rewrite was completed in June 1912. His working title for the book was *Windyridge*. Now he had to select a publisher, and to do this he decided to draw lots. He wrote the names of three well-known publishers on slips of paper. Then at the last minute he added a fourth name that he had seen recently in the newspaper, a new publisher who was advertising for material. The slips of paper were shuffled upside down on his desk, and from them Riley's random selection was Herbert Jenkins, the name that he had added last. Accordingly he posted the typescript to Jenkins, with a brief note,

> Sir, I beg to submit my MS. 'Windyridge' and shall be glad to know if you consider it suitable for publication.
> Yours Sincerely, W. Riley.[7]

He did not have to wait long. Ten days later Jenkins replied, addressing him as 'Dear Madam'. The letter continued,

> I have read the manuscript of your novel 'Windyridge' and I should like to see you if you will be in London during the next few days. If not, I shall be glad to know if you have written anything else, and also if you have ever published a book.[8]

Conveniently, Riley and the three ladies were about to go to Broadstairs for another short break, so he took the opportunity to call on Jenkins whilst heading there. Jenkins was very surprised to find out that 'Miss Riley' was in fact a middle-aged businessman. They had a good laugh about this, and Jenkins added that not only had he been deceived, but his professional advisors had also thought that the author was a woman. Before Riley had been with Jenkins for more than ten minutes, they had agreed terms for publication, and *Windyridge* was chosen by Jenkins himself to be the first book from his new publishing house. This was a considerable gamble on his part, but was proved to be a wise decision.

---

7. *'Windyridge* and its Story'.
8. *'Windyridge* and its Story'.

Jenkins agonised over the title, but no one came up with anything better. In fact not only the book, but the title too, was seized upon by the reading public, and 'Windyridge' would soon became a very popular house name, with hundreds of homes bearing that name, soon to be located all over the world. The first such house was built by a wealthy Scottish bookseller, overlooking the Clyde. The book having quickly caught on, Riley awoke soon afterwards to find himself famous.

WINDYRIDGE, THE STORY*

THE STORYLINE OF his first novel was simple and straightforward. Using the places and people familiar to him he created a tale around Hawksworth, located to the north of Baildon, and much loved by Riley. As he had outlined to his amused wife and friends, he brought Grace Holden, a single lady of thirty-four years of age, out of London, where she worked and had lodgings, to experience the country life and ways of a small Yorkshire community. She was at a crisis in her life and dissatisfied with her current existence. Her interest in the Yorkshire countryside came from her late father, who was originally from the county and had often spoken wistfully to her in his latter days of the beautiful north country and 'the call of the heather'.[9] 'Windyridge' was to be the first fictitious name of many that Riley would make use of in his novels, though he clearly described and made use of real places.

Grace comes north from London by train, originally on a whim, to attend a summer music festival in the northern city of 'Airlee'. Filled with a sudden yearning to get away from the busy, stifling city, she then takes a random tram ride to its terminus in the nearby town of 'Fawkshill', itself disappointingly industrial. In order to escape from the sight and sounds of its factories, she walks aimlessly into the adjacent countryside, and soon comes upon a village. She is attracted to a cottage that is vacant and available to let, and she meets the next-door neighbour, an elderly widow, called Mrs Mary Hubbard. This paragon would become her companion, guide and confidante once Grace moved into the adjacent property, renting it from a local farmer.

---

* If you don't wish to discover the plot of this book, turn to the next section on page xvi
9. This is the title of Chapter One of *Windyridge*.

The subsequent chapters tell of her life over the next year or so, as Grace settles into village life, and interacts with the locals. She had believed that here in this tranquil and peaceful spot she could escape from the evils, problems, and negativity of her London life; but Mr Evans, a widower who lives in the Hall, and whom she dubs the local squire, warns her that life is not so simple, and that she should:

> ... beware of the inevitable reaction when you discover the wickedness of the village, and learn that injustice and vice and slander, and a hundred other hateful things, are not peculiar to city life.[10]

She takes up residence, and converts the convenient conservatory at the rear of the cottage into a photographic studio; for she is self-employed, carrying out miniature painting and design work, and photographic commissions, for a number of firms. The postal service is convenient for both receiving commissions and delivering the finished product. Note that Riley chose for her a profession with which he was completely familiar. To augment her income from her usual mail order commissions, Grace advertises her studio facilities, taking portraits of the locals and especially the visitors to the pretty village. (In real life, Hawksworth was at that time a very popular place to visit by foot, especially at weekends, from the nearby towns. There were several tea rooms in the village which supplied the thirsty day trippers. The village and the adjacent Baildon and Hawksworth moors are criss-crossed with footpaths which would often be quite busy at weekends and holiday times when people had few leisure opportunities and spent these precious moments locally and outdoors.) With a means of employment that gives her maximum flexibility of time, Grace now gets to know the district, including the nearby communities of Marsland (Baildon), Fawkshill (Guiseley), Romanton (Ilkley), the famous inn known as 'Uncle Ned's' (Dick Hudson's) and the cities of Airlee (Leeds) and Broadbeck (Bradford).

---

10. *Windyridge*, p. 23.

She spends much time walking in the area, meeting and making friends with many of the local inhabitants. As she gets to know the people better, she learns of the sadness in some of their lives, of death and loss and injustice, as well as the Christian cheerfulness of many of the villagers. She becomes valuable as a friend and benefactor to some in need or at a time of great trouble.

Grace finds intellectual food in the persons of the elderly squire, the vicar, and especially his formidable wife; and clashes deliciously with Philip Derwent, a lawyer who is a friend of the squire, and who she calls 'the Cynic'. You almost know where that relationship is going right from their first encounter, despite his provoking banter and opinionated and irritating demeanour.

Mother Hubbard is a Methodist and a Class Leader. Grace, a member of the Church of England, learns to respect this delightful widow's simple but heartfelt Christianity. Eventually, as well as attending church in Fawkshill, Grace joins her for chapel services in Windyridge.

She experiences a happy Christmas evening celebration at the farmhouse of her landlord Reuben Goodenough, and his extended family. Later she endures the cold and snow of wintertime in the country. Caught out walking in a blinding snowstorm she gets lost and accidentally comes upon Marsland Gap (Baildon Moorside, a small community that now does not exist), and gets to know another strong woman in the person of the widow Maria Robertshaw, who later takes on the mastering of the difficult Simon Barjona Higgins.

In June, she entertains her friend Rose from her former lodgings in London, who is dumbfounded as to why Grace had abandoned the comfort of the capital for a cold northern village; but who is won over, at least in part, when she sees the place and its attractions for herself.

A month later, Grace's friendship with the squire causes her to take a trip to Zermatt, where he has been for some time on medical advice, believing that he is terminally ill. He was intending to end his days there; but she manages to lift his spirits and brings him home. (It is appropriate to remember that Riley, his wife and the two Bolton sisters had been to Zermatt the previous summer.) Riley much later admitted that at one time he had considered letting Grace marry the squire, even though he was old enough to be her father.[11]

A sub-plot has Grace convinced that her friend Rose, having met Philip Derwent whilst she was visiting Grace, is now drawing close to the Cynic, who spends a lot of time in London because of the nature of his legal work, though he actually lives in Broadbeck. In due course, near the end of the book, Mother Hubbard passes away, rather beautifully, whilst taking her Wesleyan class meeting.

A little afterwards, Grace finds herself locking intellectual horns again with the Cynic, as they, in the company of the squire and the vicar's wife, discuss Grace's real motives behind leaving London to come to this tiny village. The Cynic suggests that her flight from London to Windyridge was the result of her 'Inner Self' seeking,

... not oblivion, but enlightenment and preparation. All earnest reformers are driven of the Spirit into the wilderness ... to face the tempter ... to discover the devil's strength, his powers and limitations ... to discover their own strength and limitations too. The first essential in successful warfare is to know yourself and your enemy. It was so with Jesus, with Paul, with Savonarola,[12] with scores of other reformers ...[13]

After a long debate about her motives, and her success or otherwise in coming to terms with herself, the squire says, 'I told her a year ago that the devil was a familiar presence in this village, but I thank God, as others do and have done, that she has helped to thwart him'.[14] At the end of this long discussion about the value of service and gained experience, the Cynic returns to London and Grace receives a letter from Rose. In it Rose

---

11. *John O'London*, 13th August 1954. Marion Troughton interview with W. Riley.
12. W. Riley was particularly interested in this fifteenth century Dominican priest, Florentine and reformer, who eventually was put to death as a heretic. In 1899 Riley had written and delivered a lecture on the life of this controversial martyr, who he considered to be a forerunner and prophet of the Reformation.
13. *Windyridge*, p. 229.
14. *Windyridge*, p. 230.

announces her engagement; but not, as Grace expected, to the Cynic, but to her own boss.

Soon afterwards Grace is involved in a tragic incident in the village. During a fierce autumn storm an old and rickety house collapses whilst she is upstairs in the building trying to rescue a child, Lucy, and her mother Martha. During this time the drunken ne'er-do-well husband Roger Treffit threatens all concerned with a gun. Mother and daughter escape, but Grace is knocked unconscious and trapped upstairs in the building as the roof falls in, killing Roger Treffit. The rescue party includes the Cynic, and after Grace recovers from the experience she refers to him as '*my* Cynic now';[15] and we learn that they are to be married. He reveals to her that the romantic Mother Hubbard had recognised their feelings for each other, and had given her blessing to his endeavour before she died. He tells Grace, 'She bade me tell you how earnestly she had prayed for our happiness, and how fervently she had longed to see us united'.[16]

This, at the end of the book, is also the end of her sojourn in the village of Windyridge. The storm has symbolically completely destroyed her conservatory studio, and there is talk of an early wedding. Grace has come to the final page of her Yorkshire adventure and has brought to an end this happy interlude in her life, but with the bonus of finding her life-partner.

THE IMPORTANCE OF LOCATION, AND RILEY'S PEN-PORTRAITS

IN CONTRAST TO many other authors of his time, for whom the location of a story was merely incidental, Riley deliberately used the geographical setting of Hawksworth and the surrounding district as a fundamentally important element of his story. He already knew, loved, and was proud of, this nearby Dales country and the people who lived there. Locating his book *Windyridge* here, using real settings that were familiar, helped to make his writing immediate, genuine and credible. By giving the various locations fictitious names (as, for example, Thomas Hardy did in his 'Wessex' novels) Riley added an extra attraction to the reader, who could try to identify the real places concealed within the narrative.

---

15.   *Windyridge*, p. 243.
16.   *Windyridge*, p. 245.

In this his first book Riley revealed a rare talent, that he was able to paint vivid and astute pen-portraits of both places and people. His descriptions of the Yorkshire scenery were outstanding and a major attraction within the narrative. He was also equally at ease in carefully portraying and bringing to life the characters that inhabited the novel. It was clear that Riley was an excellent student of the places and people that he came across, that he had both attentive eyes and ears, and that he noted and remembered a great deal of what went on around him. His considerable ability to describe convincingly both places and people in his writing gave an extra atmosphere of reality to his output.

Riley later revealed that his co-heroine, Mother Hubbard, was based on a lady he knew well and respected greatly. Mrs Mary Ann Naylor lived in Batley, and was mother to a number of Riley's friends. He explained that she was, 'really the true heroine of the book – more than Grace Holden herself'.[17] Mrs Naylor was embarrassed at, but truthfully greatly enjoyed, the fame of being a main character of a best-selling novel, and she was highly amused that Riley had killed her off whilst the original was still very much alive and active. As she said to Clara, 'It's just the sort of death I should like, love'.[18]

A favourite story of Riley's was how, when Mrs Naylor's daughter read the graphic description of her mother's death in the book, she was so startled that she darted across to see if all was well.[19] Mrs Naylor had never been to Hawksworth, and Riley eventually took her there by car, several years after publication of the book. When she saw the village and the exterior of 'her' cottage she was thrilled. One of Riley's treasured possessions was a signed photograph of 'Mother Hubbard'. Mrs Naylor's fame was not short-lived; the *Yorkshire Weekly Post* of 5th February 1921 ran a long article about her and her famous alias. When she eventually died in 1925 aged ninety-one the *United Methodist* newspaper of 10th October ran a long obituary, headed 'The Late Mrs. Naylor, of Batley.

---

17. 'How I Wrote *Windyridge*'.
18. '*Windyridge* and its Story'.
19. For example, this is referred to in an article in *The Yorkshire Weekly Post*, 5th February 1921, and the *Yorkshire Evening Post* 14th March 1950.

The Original of a famous Literary Character.' Of her was written:

> She was in real life better and more interesting than even as portrayed by Mr. Riley's skilful pen … In his young manhood, Mr. Riley was deeply impressed with the quiet beauty of her character, and her buoyant confidence in God … Beautiful in face, she was beautiful in soul also, and you might as well try to imprison a perfume as to embody that life in a sketch …

In a tribute to Mrs Naylor after she died in 1925 Riley wrote warmly of her:

> … even when I was a boy I looked upon Mrs. Naylor as an old lady … as the years went by, however I knew that she had the secret of perpetual youth and was the youngest of all my friends – full of fun, mentally alert, abreast of the times. None who knew her would accuse me of exaggerating her gracious qualities and her lovable spirit … a woman who delighted to do good, and was very short-sighted towards evil …[20]

Of the actual character Mother Hubbard, Riley said in one of his lectures that she:

> … although a Yorkshirewoman is not a typical one. She stands apart, yet the lovely rose was grafted upon a common briar, and she was what her religion had made her. I will content myself with a mere sentence from her philosophy of life.
> "Yes, love, He maketh everything beautiful in its season".[21]
> [At the time this was spoken] Grace Holden was in a pessimistic mood but Mother Hubbard was an optimist. To her the world was a good place to live in, in spite of its imperfections, and her large heart made allowance for the imperfections.[22]

---

20. *United Methodist*, 10th October 1925.
21. *Windyridge*, p. 181.
22. 'The Yorkshirewoman at Home', a lecture by W. Riley.

Not only was Mother Hubbard drawn from life, but other characters in Riley's books would be modelled on real people. However, after his first novel *Windyridge* was written he would assert (probably under instruction from his publisher's lawyers) that his creations were generally no more than amalgams of many different people who he had met or knew or had heard of. Nevertheless, some Dales people could identify at least some of his creations as their neighbours.

Riley later provided an illustration of what could go wrong when writing about genuinely fictional characters:

A friendly solicitor stopped me in the street one day and warned me of the danger of painting portraits so true to life as that of Roger [Treffit, a wayward, mainly absent and often drunken husband and father, who owned a performing dog]. It appears that there is or was somewhere about a man of drunken habits who owns a dog that assists him in his profession, and who in every respect answers the description in the book. I said of Roger [in *Windyridge*] that:

It looked as though at some time in his life, when he may have been very soft and putty-like, a heavy hand had been placed on his head, and he had been compressed into a foot less height. What gave reality to the impression was the extreme length of his trousers which hung over his boots in folds.[23]

The solicitor said this was more than a description; it was a photograph, and others beside himself had identified it, yet it was from coincidence, as I have never seen the man, and I hope the reporters won't give me away and cause trouble. No, dozens of people are disappointed when they learn that there is no truth in the statement made by a man (or woman) whose word is to be trusted that they have been told by someone who knows that so-and-so is Grace, and so-and-so is Barjona. Only Mother Hubbard ever existed in the flesh, and she never saw Hawksworth until we took her there one warm summer day four years after the book was published.[24]

---

23. *Windyridge*, p. 188.
24. '*Windyridge* and its Story'.

It is interesting that Riley had never actually seen inside either of the houses where Grace and Mother Hubbard lived, so his descriptions of the interiors were completely made up. It was not until 1949, at the age of eighty-three, when he was visiting the village, that he was invited by the current owner to enter Grace's cottage (which by now was sporting the house name 'Windyridge') for the first time. The press were there to record the occasion, and referred to Riley's novel *Windyridge* as being 'as popular as ever'.[25] Riley said to the reporter:

> It was interesting to go inside today. Of course, the present owner has modernised the cottage, and nobody should go there thinking that it now resembles what I wrote about. But quite honestly, I never had even a ghost of an idea of what it was like inside all those years ago.[26]

The owner, Mrs A. E. Brown, was thrilled to entertain the famous man, and declared that this was the realisation of a long-cherished hope. She said that she 'endeavours to keep the garden a riot of colour, so that it may tally with the description in his novel'.[27]

The later fate of 'Windyridge' cottage continued to be reported in the local press, as it was sold on. Mrs Brown died soon after this encounter with Riley, and in 1950 the cottage was up for sale. This fact was the excuse for a long article and picture in the *Yorkshire Evening Post* incorporating an interview with Riley.[28] After 160 people had viewed the £2,415 property it then passed to Mr and Mrs C. E. Smith, who were reported not to have read the famous book 'yet'.[29]

25. *Yorkshire Observer*, 26th September 1949.
26. *Yorkshire Observer*, 27th September 1949.
27. *Yorkshire Observer*, 27th September 1949.
28. *Yorkshire Evening Post*, 14th March 1950.
29. Undated and un-sourced newspaper cutting, the W. Riley Archive.

The cottage that 'inspired the first and best-known novel by W. Riley' was reported to be on the market again in 1955 for £2,825.[30] By 1961 it was again in the press as 'Riley novel cottage for sale' at the much higher price of £42,000, 'luxuriously appointed', after extensive alterations and modernisation work. The article included the usual reference to Riley's book.[31] As late as 1973 the Bradford *Telegraph and Argus* carried an article by the reporter who had been present at Willie's 1949 visit to the cottage. In it he reminisced about that event. Sixty-one years after the publication of *Windyridge*, the reporter wrote briefly about the book, the author, and then the visit in 1949. He concluded:

> The story appeared in *The Yorkshire Observer* at the time. It was in its way a delightful little 'scoop'. I remember it well. It gave me much pleasure to write it then as it does to recall it now.[32]

Even in as late a date as 1977 the *Yorkshire Post* saw fit to report the sale of 'Windyridge' again:

> … A cottage with a place in literature, Windyridge Cottage, in Hawksworth, near Guiseley, has fetched … about £40,000.

The article would not have been complete without the obligatory reference to Riley:

> … W. Riley, who died in 1961 at the age of 95, used the stone-built cottage, near the centre of the village, as the inspiration for the title of his book 'Windyridge' about Yorkshire life which he wrote in 1912. Since then, thousands of homesick Yorkshiremen have used the name for their own homes …[33]

---

30. *Yorkshire Observer,* 11th May and 21st May 1955.
31. *Bradford Telegraph and Argus,* 22nd April 1961.
32. *Bradford Telegraph and Argus,* 27th March 1973.
33. *The Yorkshire Post,* 8th October 1977.

The reporter was, of course, incorrect; the cottage was named after the book, not the other way round. Even today the cottage is still named 'Windyridge', but has been extended at least three times and much altered since Riley first made it famous.

THE PUBLIC RESPONSE TO *WINDYRIDGE*

WINDYRIDGE WAS PUBLISHED in the autumn of 1912. Riley's dedication in the front of the book reads:

> To the Three Kindly Critics for whose pleasure it was commenced, and without whose constant encouragement it would not have been completed, I dedicate this book with much affection.

The 'three kindly critics' were Clara his wife, and Ethel and Florence Bolton, the two bereaved sisters. However, he was now to experience not only kindly but unkindly critics, once his book was reviewed in the national and local press.

Riley had to face the new and not always pleasant situation of being in the public eye, and being treated as if he were public property. A large number of reviews were soon written. Many were enthusiastic, sympathetic and encouraging, whilst some were dismissive, severe, and patronising. Over ninety newspaper and magazine reviews of *Windyridge* fill a scrapbook which once belonged to Riley and fortunately has been preserved. It is notable that the novel was reviewed from the start in the serious national press, not just local north country papers. Here are some examples:

> It is not often that the first book to be launched by a new publishing house is from the pen of an unknown writer. But the new house of Messrs. Herbert Jenkins (Limited), of 12, Arundel Place, Haymarket, shows signs of being inclined toward novelty and enterprise in publishing, and that in a manner which looks like making for prompt success. The first book to be issued under the new imprint is one easy to enjoy, but hard to classify. Its title is 'Windyridge', and its author's name is given as W. Riley.

The publisher's note settles the question of the author's sex, for it describes him as 'Mr. Riley'. But for this, one might have been led, by sundry flashes of intuition and other features of its text, to have attributed the book to a feminine hand.

Its irony is gentle to the point of tenderness, its sentiment is of the kindliest and most delicate, and the supposed narrator – the book is written in the first person singular – is a woman. Be that as it may, here is a book about which one prophecy may be made with safety: it will be read, quoted, and enthusiastically admired by a multitude of people; and that for the simple reason that it will reach the hearts of a multitude. It is that – sufficiently rare – kind of a book; unpretentious, vitally human, rich in kindly, gentle humour, and withal, mellow understanding. It was originally written, we gather, not for publication, but to cheer and divert friends in trouble. Perhaps that accounts for its direct human appeal. 'Windyridge' will be much talked of and much read this autumn; and its publishers are to be congratulated upon the very auspicious start they have made.

The Standard, 26ᵗʰ September 1912.

Whilst *The Standard* gave a warm welcome to the new book and the new author, the *Manchester Courier* of twenty-seventh of September 1912 was less impressed:

'Windyridge' was written without thought of publication. 'Some friends of his being in great trouble, the author conceived the idea of writing a story that would amuse them and divert their thoughts'.[34] And yet it cannot be said that the novel is very enlightening. Grace Holden, who is by way of being an artist, takes

---

34. These quotations are from the book's dust cover. Against Riley's wishes, Jenkins wrapped *Windyridge* in a dust cover which told the sad circumstances of the writing of the novel, and the reluctance of the writer to seek publication. There was no room left on it to advertise the contents of the book. That information was to be found inside the front cover.

a sudden fancy to a cottage in a Yorkshire village. Mother Hubbard, her neighbour, and Farmer Goodenough, her landlord, at once become her friends, while, in a different social rank, the squire and the cynic claim her attention. As the life of the village revolves around her Grace learns that even here sorrow is not banished, and pathos is rather out of proportion in the story. But the happy engagement of Grace and the cynic may prove consoling to those who find 'the ounce of sweet outweighs the pound of sour'. Mr. Riley allows himself scope for sentiment by writing in the person of his heroine. His power lies in simple characterisation, and his narrative, though disjointed, is pleasing. We can imagine those who weep over the story saying they have enjoyed it very much indeed.

T.P.'s Weekly, at that time an important weekly review, was also unsure whether to welcome the new book or not in its twenty-seventh of September edition. It gave a long review, of which here are some extracts. The reviewer had problems with the book, and with the gender of the author:

... there is nothing revolutionary in the issue of 'Windyridge'; one may even be justified in calling its appearance reactionary, so entirely is the story set on the safe, quiet way of the sentimental, the blandly narrative, and the all-ends-well style of fiction ...

... Not that the novel is of entirely poor quality, or that its writing and construction is without taste and grip. On the contrary, of its kind 'Windyridge' is quite a readable, well-written novel; but there is nothing about it which makes it a 'discovery' ...

... One quality Mr. Riley possesses whereupon all must agree – to his being extraordinary. The book is written in the first person, and the narrator is a woman. So thoroughly is the feminine atmosphere maintained that never once does the suggestion of a masculine pen come to the reader; 'Windyridge' is essentially a woman's, or, rather, a girl's book in its qualities ...

... the sketches of life in Windyridge give the great promise of the book. The people are convincing and natural, and remain permanent portraits for the reader ... insight, humour, a sense of

proportion and character remain with our author as long as the
poorer inhabitants of Windyridge are concerned ...

    ... qualities ... irritate in the book – its inconclusiveness, and
its tendency to windy rhetoric ...

    ... The descriptions of scenery are so good as to justify the
narrator's claim of artist. To sum up, for a first novel 'Windyridge'
gives hope of better things by and by; but rarely has one more fully
deserved the curate's-egg description of good in parts. And I can't
help being suspicious of 'Mr.' Riley.

A broadly approving review in the *Globe* of twenty-seventh of
September, headed 'Notable New Novel', compared the book to another
more famous novel:

> ... It is a novel of that genus to which 'Cranford' belongs, and we
> are not sure that it may not challenge comparison even with Mrs.
> Gaskell's classic ...

The reviewer concluded with an opinion which must have much
amused Riley:

> ... Were it not for some solecisms in the dialect, which, however,
> few Southerners are very likely to detect, we should have judged
> Mr. Riley to be a Yorkshireman himself ...

The *Saturday Review* of twenty-eighth of September took a similar
approach to *T.P.'s Weekly*, with a similar conclusion:

> ... If it were not for the asseverated masculinity of the author, we
> should have said this was an extremely ladylike book; plain,
> wholesome diet thoroughly suitable for growing children ... it is
> all quite simply and genuinely done, as far as the narrative is
> concerned; Mr. Riley's characters act, individually and together, in
> a convincing manner, mixing good and bad as men and women do
> in life. We only regret that they do not converse in an equally
> realistic way; the educated rich characters 'talk like a book', and the

Yorkshire peasants, though they use local syntax and vocabulary, exhibit a literary smack in the way of figure and allusion ... The particular merit of the book is that it is not ashamed to discuss ethics and religion ...

The Outlook, fifth of October 1912, found the book attractive:

... the result is pleasing. That a man can and indubitably does derive pleasure from wholesome fare like Windyridge is calculated to put him on good terms with himself. And this of course implies not only a very great literary skill on the part of the author, but very great acumen on the part of the publisher ... it is all surprisingly interesting. Which brings us to the reflection that though it is a good thing from the point of view of a publisher to give the public what it wants, it is better still to make it want what it is good to have.

Riley had wanted to express the northern way of speaking in his writing, but without making the book incomprehensible to readers unfamiliar with the West Riding dialect. In attempting this, he succeeded well, as several reviewers in 1912 commented. For example, the *National Weekly,* fifth of October, in a brief review approved of the novel:

Cast in the form of a diary account of how a lady artist, sick of the noise and turmoil of London, rented a cottage and lived for a year in Yorkshire, Mr. Riley has given us as sweet and simple an idyll of rural life as one could wish. Truthfully does it portray the longing for the land – 'the call of the heather' – of the Yorkshire moors, and sweetly does the book discourse on human nature, with its foibles, its sacrifices and its goodness. We are told it is the author's first novel: if this is so we congratulate him on his fine piece of work, and the public on its acquisition of a potential source of fresh delight, for Mr. Riley is bound to write more. There is some dialect in the book, but not too much nor too difficult to understand. 'Windyridge' is a charming book, and we prophesy great things of this clever author, who writes with restraint as well as power, and with understanding as well as love of human nature.

In *The Observer* of sixth of October, the reviewer also liked the book:

'Windyridge' has the freshness of a brand-new author and a brand-new publisher upon it. It is a very sweet and pleasing book … a very fragrant, charming book.

The Ladies Field, ninth of October, summed up Riley and his book very perceptively:

… The book has a beautiful serenity that is the possession of the author, and is given by him alike to his characters and *mise en scène*. It is a rare and precious quality, and it places the novel apart from the majority.

The *Liverpool Courier*, ninth of October, carried another favourable review.

… Through the book runs a spirit of simple piety – of the type that Tennison has immortalised in many stanzas of 'In Memoriam'. But the writer's very sincerity saves him from any fear of dullness, and frees him from any charge of priggishness. A remarkable novel.

The *Manchester Guardian*, ninth of October, enjoyed the new novel:

WINDYRIDGE, by W. Riley (Herbert Jenkins, pp 328, 6s.), belongs to a class of fiction that is immensely popular in America. The scene happens to be Yorkshire instead of a New England village, but the treatment is the same; that is to say, there is plenty of the softer emotions, a graceful sentiment, genuine feeling for the country mood, and a number of well-differentiated characters in whom both the pathetic and the humorous notes are apt to go a little too high. Mr. Herbert Jenkins, the latest addition to the ranks of London publishers, suitably presents a new writer, and undoubtedly the author of 'Windyridge' – it is a surprise to read, in a publisher's note of 'Mr.' Riley, for the whole manner of the book suggests a woman's writing – has many of the qualities that lead to popularity. Most people like to have their sensibilities gently worked upon by writers of fiction, and when, in addition to the gift of tears, an author possesses kindliness of outlook he is sure of a public. That public will enjoy 'Windyridge' and its friendly Yorkshire folk, and Miss Grace Holden, who goes to live among them and relates the happenings of the village. And in chapter vii we have 'The Cynic on Woman' and foresee the end. What more can anyone want?

The *Manchester Guardian* was proved to be wrong regarding one aspect of this review; *Windyridge* never sold well in America, and, after attempting to sell his first three books in America with little success, his American publisher (G.P. Putnam & Sons, New York) gave up.

In contrast, *The New Age* of twenty-fourth of October had nothing good to say of the book in its brief and dismissive review:

With a lengthy parade of utter and absolute modesty about ever on any account publishing at all, Mr. Riley, 'a new writer', permits the public to read the novel which in manuscript so entertained some of his friends. We are not entertained, however. The style is aggressively cheery, and really suggests no more aesthetic conscience than might satisfy a private audience. Further, the author has not feared to pretend to be a woman writing in the first person … A decidedly amateur and superfluous novel.

The *Daily Express* of thirty-first of October gave the book a short but approving review:

It is not always the practised novelist who produces the most readable story. Occasionally there happens along a new hand who has just the right touch, as has Mr. Riley …

The *Sunday Times* of tenth of November also liked the story:

> ... it is a really fine bit of work, full of moorland air, which will be appreciated by all who know good fiction when they come across it ... We trust Mr. Riley will give us more novels and that most of them will have similar charming backgrounds.

The Daily Telegraph of twentieth of November, like the *Manchester Guardian* before it, considered the book to be a natural for the American market, even suspecting that 'Miss Riley' was 'of a Transatlantic origin'.

Punch, also dated twentieth of November, dismissed the book in a brief review, spending much of the review in decrying what was written on the admittedly unusual dust cover, which other reviewers generally referred to more sympathetically:

> I have to confess to a perhaps churlish dislike and suspicion of the practice of puffs preliminary as printed by publishers upon the covers of books submitted to my critical notice. To be told that a novel was written to amuse a friend 'without thought of public or publisher,' or found in a cloak-room, or fished out of the Thames, is invariably, so far as I am concerned, to be prejudiced against its contents ... I admit willingly that Mr. W. Riley's pictures of the inhabitants of his Yorkshire village, and still more of its heather-clad landscape, are drawn with skill and sympathy ... To sum up, those who care for a tale of simple happenings, told in a manner that at best is tenderly sentimental, and at its worst not wholly free from sloppiness, will rejoice in *Windyridge*. The others can keep away.

The *Daily Citizen*, of thirteenth of December was impressed with Riley's ability to enter a woman's 'mental kingdom' and approved of both Riley and Jenkins:

> The immediate success of a first novel by a new writer is sufficiently rare to call for some remark, and Mr. W. Riley, the author of 'Windyridge', deserves all the bouquets that are being bestowed

upon him, while congratulations are also due to that recently-started publisher, Mr. Herbert Jenkins, for immediately scenting the possibilities of the story. It is an amusing fact that most reviewers spoke of the novel as the work of a woman. This is not surprising, since the book is written in the form of an autobiography, by the heroine, Grace Holden. Moreover, Mr. Riley has a very 'lady-like' style. I hesitate to say that he understands women, because it is a bold thing to say of any man ... in 'Windyridge' Mr. Riley seems to me to succeed very cleverly in entering the mental kingdom of woman, and depicting, too, a very charming specimen. Reviewers are not the only people who made a mistake as to the sex of the writer, for the publisher of the book, Mr. Herbert Jenkins, was so convinced that the work was feminine that he addressed the author as Miss Riley. And 'Miss Riley' he will be for me now and henceforth. While there are innumerable instances of women adopting men's pseudonyms in their work, there are very few instances of men posing as women ...

By December of 1912, *The Methodist Times,* which had already given the book an enthusiastic review on twenty-fourth of October, had sent a reporter to have 'an intimate chat across the tea-table with Mr. Riley on behalf of the readers of this journal'. In a long article the writer described the circumstances in which the book came to be written, and the debate over the author's gender. By this time *Windyridge* was already into its third print. The substantial item finishes:

> ... We are sure that Methodists everywhere will look forward with pleasant anticipations to Mr. Riley's next book; and, not only Methodists, but people everywhere who love pure and wholesome literature.

That was a perceptive remark. The hallmark of Riley's writing would always be its wholesome nature, for which he was to be renowned and acclaimed for the rest of his life.

The United Methodist reviewed the book on nineteenth of December, calling it 'A Charming Christmas Book'. It liked what it saw:

... A more delightful book we have not read for long and long ... It is a book of quite an exceptional variety of subjects with the pleasing charm of unity. In style it is simple, lucid, conversational, but never commonplace ... 'Windyridge' stands out as a first-rate piece of literary craftsmanship ... a book to read and re-read ... We are better for having read the book.

By this time Riley was becoming famous both in his native town and nationwide for his new and well-received novel. The *Bradford Daily Telegraph* sent a reporter to investigate the 'Bradfordian Literary Success'. It was now their turn to tell how this Bradford businessman and prominent Wesleyan had surprised the literary world and his own birthplace with his gentle but perceptive tale set in the nearby moors. Their edition of twenty-sixth of December carried a long article about the new author:

... He has written a book − a novel which has not only been accepted and published, but also warmly praised in review and widely circulated. Narrowly prejudiced and prophet-scorning though it may appear, one cannot help a certain shock of astonishment that a Bradfordian should have written a novel at all ... and its appearance has been followed by such a host of reviews, mainly appreciative, in every leading paper in the country that really, as much as one would like to snub a mere local author, it becomes necessary at length that 'his own country' should be told a little of him and his work. Our celebrities are not so numerous that we can afford to ignore such a new one as this.

In Mr. Riley I found a quiet humorist, who, unlike some humorists, was quite prepared to make fun at his own expense ...

The article then told the now well-known story of how it came to be written: that Jenkins published it as his first book from his new publishing house, and that many reviewers (as well as Jenkins) thought W. Riley was a woman. It concluded:

… The qualities I like best and the qualities whose praise has best pleased the author himself, are its essential simplicity, the charm of its authentic freshness and the directness of its style. In these days it seems almost dangerous to advocate a book as 'healthy', yet such is, I think, the best word for 'Windyridge'. It has been compared frequently and not inaptly with 'Cranford'. In his own person Mr. Riley reflects those attributes which make his book's most potent appeal. The Puritan element is strong in him, but it permeates without any petrifying effects. Many Bradfordians know him for a prominent Nonconformist, but it would, I think, be quite impossible to discover as much from his book.

That his Puritanism is of the kind which inspires a deep and reverent love of Nature finds a fragrant proof in his book. Reading 'Windyridge' one may feel afresh the moorland charm of that glorious country round Hawksworth. Through its descriptive pages there blows, not as a steady breeze, perhaps, but still in most grateful gusts, that keen and cleansing air.

Whatever else they may have said about the quality of his novel, the critics generally praised what they often called Riley's 'detailed pen-portraits' of both the scenery and people in *Windyridge*. This attention to descriptive detail, for both people and places, was to become a particularly strong feature in all of his books, endearing him to his very many fans, and was to become a hallmark of his output. Many reviewers from prestigious national publications, as well as the local press, referred warmly to the attractive and convincing way in which Riley described both people and places in his first novel. (This was even the case when a reviewer was less enthusiastic about the story content.) Here are some examples of reviewers appreciating Riley's pen portraits:

… It is not, however, for its dramatic action, or its interplay of character, that the new novel lives in the memory. It is the moor pictures, and the kindly Yorkshire village folk: the homely mother tongue, and the quaint characters that serve to mark the story from

the mediocre run … the whole village community live before
our eyes …

Windyridge review in
The Leeds Mercury, 25th September 1912.

… The sketches of village life and character are very good …

Windyridge review in
The Bookman, October 1912.

… The life at 'Windyridge' is depicted by a true artist of the pen,
and the reader will soon become enthralled in the simple narrative
… The characters are drawn from life … Such a book is as fresh as
a breeze from the moorland where the main scenes are placed, and
one lays the book down feeling that a real interpreter of human life
has made his debut to the reading public.

Windyridge review in
the *Dundee Advertiser*, 3rd October 1912.

… 'Windyridge' should be read by all who seek to find a perfect
expression of the charm of the moorland and a sympathetic picture
of the simple lives of the Yorkshire peasant folk … The descriptions
of nature, and, still more, of the Yorkshire folk, constitute the
attraction of 'Windyridge'. Mr. Riley … understands his fellow
country folk, and shows the deep sincerity and kindliness that lie
behind the rather brusque exterior of the Northern farmer or
labouring man.

Windyridge review in the
Sheffield Daily Telegraph, 10th October 1912.

Several years later in his lecture '*Windyridge* and its Story', Riley spoke
about the somewhat unnerving experience of having critics, who didn't
know him at all, making all sorts of claims and evaluations about him (or
as many said, her) and expressing highly personal remarks about the
author. He described his stance at that time:

One thing the author must avoid – indeed two things. He must not think that reviewers are infallible, and, (unless he wants to waver like a weather cock) he must not allow himself to be influenced by criticism … I don't think I was greatly disturbed by the vehemence and the variety of the criticisms, for I was prepared for violent contrasts in judgement …

In another lecture, 'Some Reflections of a Novelist', Riley talked more about the critics:

… when you become an object, and reviewers bring you into the arena to be tortured and slain … You discover that means have been devised with diabolical ingenuity whereby you learn punctually and periodically what the reviewers think about you and your work … You must pay a News Clipping Agency a couple of guineas or so to learn day by day what a sorry figure you cut in the literary world. Well now, whether this edifies you, or hurts you, or amuses you depends a good deal on your temperament. Poor George Borrow writhed under the treatment and wanted to go out and slay an editor. George Eliot refused to read anything that was unfavourable. Charlotte Brontë was hurt. Mrs. Gaskell was made nervous … your best course is to cultivate … a sense of humour, and then the News Clipping Agency becomes an Entertainment Agency. You have to remember that the reviewers … are a mixed crew … If you can laugh as you take your gruel the treatment may be wholesome enough.

At the end of this lecture he drew the conclusion that,

… as [the novelist] cannot hope to please everybody, he must do his best to please himself … an author should be more than content if he finds he has made a difference to a handful of people, or given innocent pleasure to even a small company.

The publicity that Jenkins supplied with *Windyridge* clearly stated that the author was a man; but, despite that clear statement, there was great disagreement among the critics as to the sex of the writer, helped by the fact that the author's Christian name was not declared in the book. Many reviewers insisted that it could only have been written by a woman. This controversy carried on for months. Some critics even asserted that the lady author was personally known to them! Jenkins wrote to Riley:

> You really must change your sex and become a woman! There is nothing else for it; otherwise you will have all the reviewers angry with you, because, without exception, they insist that you *are* a woman.[35]

Indeed, his first book revealed that Riley had a particular and unusual gift for a man; the rare ability to write convincingly from a woman's point of view. It is one of the more remarkable features of Riley's writings that over many years he would bring to life a relatively large number of females who would play major roles in his narratives. When he had started to write *Windyridge* for private amusement, he announced his intention to make the lead character a woman. His female audience laughed at him, declaring almost with derision that it was impossible for any mere man to take on the mantle of a woman. Despite – and maybe because of – the scepticism of his initial audience, he carried on regardless, doing all his research without any woman's assistance. In a later lecture called '*Windyridge* and its Story', he said:

> I did it deliberately, of malice aforethought, in order to interest – I might almost say to provoke – the limited audience of three ladies for whom the fare was prepared. The ruse succeeded ... The masquerading in woman's mental attire, and the knowledge that it would be searchingly criticised at the weekly readings, gave zest to my task.

---

35. *Sunset Reflections*, p. 103.

In the end, he did it so well that some critics, including women, remained reluctant to accept, and in some cases denied, that the author could possibly be a man, as the following extracts reveal:

… Although the publisher's note on the wrapper speaks of 'Mr.' Riley, one suspects from internal evidence that the author is of the other sex; the men in the book are a woman's men; the gentle sentiment of the story and its whole outlook upon humanity are essentially feminine …

Windyridge review in
The Bookman, October 1912.

… We shrewdly suspect that the author is an authoress, for the delicate touches in character, description and the intuitive insight into motives have all the hallmarks of female genius …

Windyridge review in
Church Family Newspaper, 11th October 1912.

This is Miss Riley's first book, and it is certainly a book of some promise …

Windyridge review in
The Standard, 18th October 1912.

… there is one thing disconcerting, that the author … should dare to be a man. With calm assurance he rummages about in woman's mind and pulls her heartstrings …

Windyridge review in
The Gentlewoman, October 12th 1912.

Because of this ongoing controversy, Riley eventually wrote a letter of clarification which went to the many reviewers who had queried the sex of this new author.:

I have a strong desire to conciliate my critics, a most natural one on the part of a new author – and I have been tempted to accept their decision as final and to claim their suffrages in that guise. But, alas! facts and the Registrar-General are against me. I hasten to assure you that I am really a man; and I hope the reviewers will not be angry when I inform them that my femininity has been merely spasmodic, and confined to those rare occasions when freedom from business duties allowed me to merge my personality in that of my heroine.[36]

Another reviewer, Winifrid Blatchford of *The Clarion*, enthusiastically reviewed the book on 18th October 1912 and also vigorously tackled the gender of the writer:

... Windyridge is a Yorkshire village, and to it comes the heroine, a real nice woman with no nonsense about her, and so real a woman that I was convinced none but a woman drew [Grace Holden]. In this I was wrong ... I was so sure that I had got on the right scent, and meant to unmask the villain who posed as a man and so robbed us women of some glory, when Mr. Herbert Jenkins ... sent unmistakable evidence in favour of the suspected, and almost accused ... The author ... is a man: a mere male man person; and the ranks of women are so far the poorer ... So jolly is his book ... that I am graciously inclined to forgive Mr. Riley for not being a woman, much as I regret the fact ...

However, that was not to be the end of that reviewer's suspicions and investigations. In Riley's '*Windyridge* and its Story' lecture, probably compiled some six years later, he said:

Only a little while ago Miss Blatchford who deals with literary matters in The Clarion wrote to ask me if I really was a male. My publisher, she said, assured her I was one; on the other hand a constant reader had taken her to task for always referring to me as one of the sterner sex. This correspondent assured her that I was a woman. He knew, for he had the privilege of acquaintanceship.

36. From the review of *Windyridge* in *The Methodist Recorder*
26th September 1912.

I had even offered to lend him my charming cottage on the Devonshire coast!

Riley was much amused about this assertion, and regretted he had no claim on this cottage.

Riley excelled himself by creating not just one, but two central female characters in *Windyridge*; Grace Holden and Mother Hubbard. The ongoing controversy about the gender of the author was cleverly used by Jenkins in promoting the book. From then on, in nearly half of Riley's novels the lead player would be a woman and in most of the rest of his output there were strong female characters. The many women who would feature in his later writing continued to be convincing, a rare ability for a male writer. The fact that he could create credible and attractive characters, both male and female alike, added to the general and popular appeal of his books. This ability of Riley to 'get into the skin' of his creations is a further indication of how well Riley observed, and, more importantly, understood, not only men but women as well. His always sympathetic and attentive attitude to all people was a great help to him when he was writing, as well as when he was socialising, and carrying out his many Wesleyan activities.

From the start Riley's writing appealed to a broad cross section of society. He received numerous letters over many years from important and famous people, as well as ordinary folk, telling him how much they appreciated his wholesome writings and his Christian message of hope and forgiveness. For example, a publican from Ireland wrote to say that the journal *John Bull* had given him *Windyridge* as a consolation prize, and he wished Riley to know that it had been a real consolation.[37]

Riley recalled that a man called at his house to ask him to autograph his copy of *Windyridge*:

It was to him a book of sacred memories. He had borrowed 'Windyridge' from the library and read it to his wife as she lay on what proved to be her death-bed. One of her last requests was that he should buy the book ... what he told me brought a lump to my throat.[38]

---

37. '*Windyridge* and its Story'.
38. '*Windyridge* and its Story'.

Many of his fans came to visit him. He greatly appreciated this feedback from the reading public, which confirmed to him both that he was writing what many people wanted to read, and that they were both discerning and appreciating the Christian message in his books that he had intended them to experience. He was always more comfortable with 'ordinary' people, who he clearly did not think of as at all ordinary. He valued them greatly, and they were very dear to him:

> My books, as some of you perhaps know, deal with men and women of the humbler classes, as we call them. A recent writer in 'World's Work' did me the honour to call me 'The Worker's Author' and I want no better title.[39]

The strong undercurrent of Christian thought and outlook that was present in Riley's books and other writing was nothing new to him, as he had already been producing (and reading) moral stories as scripts to accompany religious optical lantern slide sequences for many years, and his interests were focused on his active membership of the Methodist Church, including much preaching, teaching, and both religious and secular debating. When he turned from the slide-sequence short story to the long novel, he was able to express his Christian views more delicately than in the brief moral text accompanying a slide set. As a result, his Christian themes do not overpower his novels.

In 1946 a newspaper article summarised Riley's output almost at the end of his writing career, when he was eighty years old. It is a highly sympathetic and approving analysis of Riley's writing achievements, recognising both his qualities as a Christian, writer, and preacher, and his ability to use them appropriately, wisely, and well:

> ... he wrote without playing down to the baser elements in human nature. Not that his was a facile and shallow optimism; but his radiant Christian faith enabled him to see through the superficialities of what has been miscalled realism to the good that

---

39. 'The Yorkshirewoman at Home'.

so often lies deeper than wickedness in the human heart. He did not confuse the qualities of the preacher and the novelist: he kept his sermons for the pulpit – and few laymen preach more winsomely. Yet, while in no sense homilectical, his stories have always had a message, enshrined in the gold and the dross of character.[40]

Whilst Riley was a deeply committed Methodist, his expression of the Christian message was surprisingly non-denominational, and very modern for his day. Many of the characters in his novels were in fact staunch Church of England people. His interpretation and exposition of Christian principles stand up well when reread in the twenty-first century. His values were derived from the Bible and from his own insights, teaching skills, wisdom and experience, all gained through his long study of, and devotion to, scripture and church teaching. They are expressed in his unique style of refreshing clarity, and are both humane and uncomplicated. It was precisely *because* his Christianity was based on these fundamentals that his books were so widely appreciated *across* denominational boundaries, and even by those without strong faith or indeed any faith at all. The universal appeal of his books even surprised Riley:

How is it that 'Windyridge' should have made me friends in hard-hearted, cynical journalists, free-thinkers, socialists, Tories, Roman Catholics, Jews, men who read the Hibbert Journal and men who read the Pink 'Un? I have friends in all these, many called to see me.[41]

When he was interviewed by the *Yorkshire Evening News*, on the subject of 'My Faith', he clearly and unequivocally expressed the underlying purpose behind all his writings, but in his usual, modest way.

---

40. *Yorkshire Observer*, April 1946. (Exact date not known, but after 23rd.)
41. '*Windyridge* and its Story'.

... because I think God is misunderstood by vast masses of people who have seen Him only through distorted media, and who have heard Him misinterpreted, and who have failed to discover the splendour of His love and the largeness of His heart, it is my endeavour to make Him known in my books. My interpretation is honest though it may sometimes be mistaken; and I hope it won't be considered arrogant if I say that I try to let Him be seen in the commonplace men and women whose religion is evidenced by their lives. I give full consideration to the reviewers, and acknowledge the truth of much of their criticism; but in the end – to my own Master I stand or fall.[42]

THE MARKETING OF *WINDYRIDGE*:
THE IMPORTANCE OF HERBERT JENKINS

RILEY OWED A great deal to his enthusiastic and highly competent publisher, Herbert Jenkins. In 1911 Jenkins had written an extremely able *Life of George Borrow*, which was published by John Murray. Then, with backing from Sir George Chubb (later Lord Hayter), he started his own publishing house. It was just as he was about to launch his new enterprise that Riley's manuscript arrived. Jenkins quickly recognised the commercial potential of the novel and, remarkably, chose it to be the very first book to be published by this new company. Riley said of this decision later:

It was to me a great honour and for Mr. Jenkins a great risk. For a new publisher to appear on the market with the work of a new author was regarded as a daring and doubtful experiment.[43]

However, Jenkins' confidence was proved to be correct. *Windyridge* sold well right from the beginning. This was to be the start of an enduring and productive friendship between author and publisher. Riley later recalled, 'Jenkins always referred to "Windyridge" as "our first-born; yours and mine"'.[44]

---

42. *Yorkshire Evening News* item, the W. Riley Archive. The date is not known.
43. *Sunset Reflections*, p. 102.
44. *Sunset Reflections*, p. 103.

Riley was extraordinarily fortunate that he picked the slip of paper bearing the name 'Herbert Jenkins' when he was randomly selecting a publisher to whom he would submit his manuscript. He was even more fortunate that Jenkins then selected *Windyridge* to be his very first publication. Jenkins's strengths were his energy and organising genius, coupled with great marketing and advertising skills. The book was marketed very shrewdly from the outset, in a way that was – for 1912 – revealingly and surprisingly modern in strategy.[45]

The potential markets were identified, then unashamedly targeted and penetrated. They were 'Yorkshire', 'Methodism', and 'The Idyllic'. Each of these three markets was individually tackled. Every copy of *Windyridge* sent to Yorkshire booksellers had a special cover band stating 'The Great Yorkshire Novel'. Those sent to strongly Methodist towns had a different cover band stating 'The Great Methodist Novel'. Once a reviewer (*The Globe*) had declared *Windyridge* to be comparable to *Cranford* (by Elizabeth Gaskell), Jenkins pounced on this and the book was then marketed in literary circles as 'The New *Cranford*', thus giving it the idyllic association that Jenkins had been seeking. Coincidentally, Riley refers to *Cranford* in the third chapter of *Windyridge*. Grace Holden recounts:

> I believe I shall soon feel at home here, for the villagers do not appear to resent the presence of a stranger, and there is no sign of the Cranford spirit, perhaps because there is an entire lack of the Cranford society.[46]

Mrs Gaskell's *Cranford*, first published in 1853, was still very popular in 1912, as *The Globe* review of twenty-seventh of September 1912, already referred to above, indicated.

Additionally, Jenkins made a great issue of the unusual and sad circumstances in which *Windyridge* came to be written; the modesty of the author in thinking that his book would never find a publisher and the unlikely way in which the author chose his publisher-to-be. Remarkably – and rather to Riley's annoyance – all this was explained in detail all over the dust cover of *Windyridge*, as follows.

---

45. The information regarding the marketing approach by Jenkins is taken from *The Advertiser's Weekly*, 28th April 1915.
46. *Windyridge*, p. 19.

A new novel. A new writer. 'Windyridge' is one of those rare books written without thought either of public or of publisher. Some friends of his being in great trouble, the author conceived the idea of writing a story that would amuse them and divert their thoughts. Chapter by chapter as it was written 'Windyridge' was read aloud by its author, and when it had served its charitable purpose the manuscript was put aside. The friends clamoured for publication, but Mr. Riley refused. At length he decided to gratify at once his friends' insistence and his own inclination for a joke at their expense; for he never doubted that the manuscript would be declined. Only when he received a definite offer for, not only 'Windyridge,' but other books from his pen, was Mr. Riley convinced of his own refreshing mistake.

Memorable phrases from some early reviews quickly found their way into Jenkins's publicity for further promotion of the book.

Notwithstanding the reservations of some critics, the book was an instant and lasting success, and was soon reprinted. First published in September 1912, by December it was already in its third impression.[47] It did not only sell in Britain. By October it was reviewed in the *New York Herald* – but despite the favourable opinion expressed by the reviewer, the book fell flat in the USA. and only one edition was ever called for. In November it was reviewed in the *Transvaal Leader* and the *Bloemfontein Post*, and by February the following year it was being reviewed in the *Melbourne Life*. The book travelled round the world. A missionary from Tibet wrote to Riley to tell him she had had the book sent from Australia. A Parsee professor from Bombay sent his own book *Indian Problems and Perplexities* and asked for *Windyridge* in return.[48]

Jenkins now sought further penetration of the market by varying the presentation. With 10,000 books already sold, in October of the following year an illustrated edition came out,[49] with eight photographs taken by Riley himself. These photographs now revealed the real places behind the

47. As reported in *The Methodist Times* of December 1912.
48. *Sunset Reflections*, p. 111.
49. As reported in reviews of the first illustrated edition of *Windyridge* in the *Academy*, October 18th, and *The Bookman*, of November 1913.

fictitious names for those who had not deciphered them. Later, a de luxe maroon leather-bound edition came out, complete with the title and the author's signature in gold on the cover.

In 1915, with 23,000 copies now sold, the first cheap 'popular edition' was published.[50] This was slightly smaller in page size, printed on cheaper paper, and was without pictures. It again proved very popular and a bookseller in the heavy woollen district affirmed that, 'it was going through the mills like an epidemic'.[51]

Each published variant brought the possibility of new reviews, and kept the book in the public eye. Jenkins also fed the press with stories about the book; for example, houses being named 'Windyridge', pairs of pet animals being named 'Windy' and 'Ridge', and so on.[52] The publicity was masterly, but it was the likeable story itself that was the real and enduring source of the book's popularity.

Immediately after the Great War was over, Jenkins encouraged Riley to embark on a series of lecture tours to promote *Windyridge*. He saw the marketing benefit of this charismatic author and preacher taking to the road, and travelling widely through the land telling his story about how the book came to be written. Riley's lecture '*Windyridge* and its Story' was very popular and took him all over the country. Whilst many authors have undertaken promotional lecture tours, it was most unusual for a new novelist to tour, and especially with an uncontroversial publication, a gentle novel. It is a measure of the exceptional popularity of both the book and the author that Riley was persuaded to go on tour, and then was well received by audiences everywhere.

Riley's first book continued to sell well, and Jenkins eventually referred to it in his publicity as 'one of the most popular first-novels ever published'. By 1930 it had sold over 250,000 copies,[53] and the book would remain in print throughout Riley's long life, until after he died in 1961. By the end of the Second World War it had sold nearly 300,000 copies,[54]

50. As reported in the *Methodist Times* of May 27th, and the *Scarborough Post* of June 8th, 1915.
51. *Sunset Reflections*, p. 111.
52. *Sunset Reflections*, p. 104.
53. The 31st edition, 'completing 250,147 copies' of *Windyridge* was published in 1930.
54. The 36th printing of *Windyridge* in 1946 stated 'completing 284,407 copies'.

and has been said to have reached about 500,000 by his death.[55] Jenkins and Riley enjoyed a special personal relationship, and the firm of Herbert Jenkins would eventually, over a total of almost fifty years, publish thirty-six out of Riley's thirty-nine books. Jenkins himself died young, but fortunately for Riley, the Directors of the publishing firm and Riley continued to have cordial and supportive dealings with each other.

THE CONSEQUENCES FOR THE VILLAGE OF HAWKSWORTH

THE BOOK HAD an unfortunate and unexpected result for Riley. He later said:

> Today the village is spoiled for me. If you want to continue to enjoy a place take my advice and don't write a book about it that makes it famous. A gentleman who occupied Grace Holden's cottage for a month a little while ago told me that I was blessed by all the tea-house proprietors (and they are all tea-house proprietors now) and cursed by all the farmers, and I have to avoid the blessings by staying away. I don't mind the cursings.[56]

Not all of the residents of the village thanked Riley for their unexpected fame. Denying that anything in the story was true, one inhabitant said, 'It's nowt but friction! [sic]'.[57] And in Riley's lecture on '*Windyridge* and its Story', he recounted the conversation between a visitor to a Hawksworth tearoom and its proprietress. The visitor asked, 'Have you read *Windyridge* and how do you like it?' The answer came, 'Aw mak nowt on't. It's nowt but a pack o' lies!'.

The farmers were unhappy because visitors to Hawksworth came tramping all over their fields. It was also reported in the local press that the police in the area all had to know where the village called 'Windyridge' was, because:

---

55. Quoted in the *Yorkshire Evening Post*, 22nd April 1961.
   Riley died on 6th June 1961.
56. '*Windyridge* and its Story'.
57. 'Those Yorkshiremen!', a lecture by W. Riley.

… constables on point duty at the White Cross, near Guiseley, have been asked the way to Windyridge as often as the way to Hawksworth on many a Bank Holiday.[58]

About the places he described in the village, Riley later remarked:

If I had written the book with a view to publication, and especially if I had foreseen the demand for picture post-cards, I should have sketched the cottages from nature instead of from memory, and saved the villagers and photographers a certain amount of uncertainty. As it is, though Mother Hubbard's and Grace Holden's cottages are sketched with sufficient accuracy, Carrier Ted's is a composite production, and some of the other houses don't exist at all except in my imagination.[59]

Despite this slight uncertainty, because of the many tourists now coming to the village, several series of postcards of the village were made commercially available; some confidently giving the fictitious names of the places, others referring to the book that had made the place a tourist honeypot. One could also buy a postcard of the author. It is salutary to realise that literary tourism is not really a recent phenomenon; day trippers flocked to places made famous by fiction as long as a century ago.

In the *Yorkshire Observer* of 12th July 1932 Grace Holden's cottage in Hawksworth was referred to as:

… undoubtedly one of the most delightful literary shrines in the world, for it has remained in a very appreciative ownership. Mother Hubbard's garden, for instance, still displays a 'profusion of flowers' of the old-fashioned variety … In Grace Holden's portion of the cottage one may enjoy a typical Yorkshire tea, and thus take the opportunity of admiring the old-world solidity of the building and also the fireplace, which remains just as Grace described it …

---

58. *The Yorkshire Observer*, 19th March 1928, from an article entitled 'Noted Writers of Yorkshire XI W. Riley'.
59. '*Windyridge* and its Story'.

Even as late as in 1943, Hawksworth was still a popular place to visit, not the least because of its literary association, but also because the war hampered longer distance travel. An article in the *Yorkshire Observer* of twenty-first October stated:

> News that an applicant for a catering licence has had it granted – against opposition from existing tea-making interests in the village – will not be unwelcome to the many townsfolk who like to include 'Windyridge' (W. Riley's name which has brought wide fame to this attractive place) in a moorland outing …

Today the tearooms have long gone and the connection between the village and this once-famous novel is known to almost no one there.

Let Riley have the last word about his attraction to Hawksworth. In 1948, Riley himself wrote in *Reader News*, the publication of Aireborough Public Libraries, about his youthful attraction to the village:

> It may be because I was born in a home that stood not far from a moor that from the days of my boyhood I felt the 'pull' of the moors and hills. Bradford Moor was little better than a grassy common in those far-off days, and it boasted no glories of heather and bracken, so that it never really satisfied me, and when quite a young schoolboy I began to explore the country that lay not far beyond the town. The windswept moors beyond Baildon fascinated me, and for a time the localities that are now included in Aireborough formed my Ultima Thule. How vividly I recall my excursions and explorations in that region of fairyland – for after the smoke and grime of the big industrial town, and the confined spaces of the Grammar School classrooms, Hawksworth and the paths and lanes that led through Rawdon to Apperley Bridge took me into a new world that was almost too good to be true. Little wonder that when I sat down to write the first chapter of an unpremeditated story I should fix upon Hawksworth as my dream village.[60]

---

60. As reported in the *Yorkshire Post and Leeds Mercury*, 23rd October 1948.

RILEY'S EARLY HISTORY

IT IS APPROPRIATE now to take a brief look at the origins of the man who, in middle age, was to have such an unexpected impact as a novelist, not only in his native Yorkshire, but internationally.

Willie Riley was born on 23ʳᵈ April 1866, in Wellington Terrace, Laisterdyke, a suburb of Bradford. He was the second child of Joseph and Hannah Riley. His father, also Bradford-born in 1838, was at that time a Mill Manager working for his father-in-law Joseph Jowett. Tragedy soon struck the family. Hannah died of smallpox soon after giving birth prematurely to her third child, who also quickly died. Both were buried just after Willie's second birthday. Four years later his father remarried, in 1872. His second wife, Mary, not only took on two step-sons, but over the next thirteen years had seven children of her own. Riley later recorded what a good and loving mother she was to her two step-children.[61]

In 1882 Riley left Bradford Grammar School at the end of his fifth year, at the behest of his autocratic father. Initially he reluctantly joined his father's Stuff business, but to his relief, within two years, he was moved into the newly formed – and to Riley much more interesting – magic lantern operation. Joseph Riley was a Wesleyan local preacher, and Willie and his elder brother Herbert both also became local preachers by the time they were twenty-one years old. Moving in Bradford Wesleyan circles brought the Rileys into close contact with many influential people of the West Riding. Riley was also deeply interested in the nearby moors, dales, and the people who lived there, and would spend much time walking in remote parts of the area.

In 1892 Riley married Clara Hirst, the eldest daughter of Councillor Benjamin Hirst, a prominent businessman in Morley. Her health was delicate; and because of that her mother had been doubtful if she should marry. They set up home close to the Riley family residence. The marriage brought Riley into contact with even more influential people of the district.

---

61. *Sunset Reflections*, p. 26.

Clara encouraged Riley to write, convinced of his talent and ability. It would take twenty years of her encouraging him before he finally tried his hand at doing so in a serious way. Later, in a speech he gave at Mirfield Grammar School Prize Day on 16th January 1923, whilst encouraging the pupils to discover their powers and use them, he said:

> I am here today because of a certain success that has come to me as a writer of books. I was 46 when my first book was published and met with an astounding success. I had to be goaded into offering it to a publisher. I did not believe it had any chance of acceptance. Yet the first man who read it accepted it. For twenty years I had been urged to write for publication and had distrusted my powers.

However, in 1912, despite his unexpected triumph with *Windyridge*, Riley still had no inclination to take his writing abilities seriously. He had no need to, being fully extended running his successful lantern business. That and his extensive Wesleyan activities kept him fully occupied, along with attending cultural events in Bradford.

The contract between Riley and Jenkins gave Jenkins the rights to publish any future books initially for the next five years. As soon as the success of *Windyridge* became plain, Jenkins started pestering Riley for a second book. He declined, pointing out that his thriving business took up all his time – not to mention his many church commitments. However, circumstances were about to change drastically for Riley.

RILEY HAS TO CHANGE CAREER AND JOINS THE LITERARY WORLD

RILEY LATER COMMENTED that in 1912 his magic lantern business was in excellent shape:

> ... the prospect for the future was exhilarating and there was no cloud on the horizon. Even the bank manager was satisfied.[62]

---

62. *Sunset Reflections,* p. 107.

But by early 1914, things were far from well with the optical operation. Despite research, it is not yet clear what went wrong; but in March 1914 Riley Brothers Limited was wound up voluntarily.[63] Perhaps the overall international decline in the magic lantern business had at last caught up with Riley Brothers, which had until then had seemed to carry on unaffected by the new and rival cinematographic technology.

A new, much smaller operation, Riley Brothers (1914) Ltd emerged, with brothers Arnold and Bernard named as the two Directors of the new business.[64] They quickly moved to smaller premises, still in Bradford. Soon afterwards war was declared and Bernard, already a Sergeant in the 6th West Yorkshire Volunteers, joined up immediately. Arnold alone was left to run a much-reduced operation until he died in 1935. His widow Edith continued to run the business, which by then had become a small arts materials and crafts shop.

Riley had to endure the great disappointment of seeing his company go bankrupt, just as his father had experienced when his Stuff business collapsed in 1902. He now faced an uncertain future. As he later wrote, 'My shares in the company were now valueless. I was too old for military service, too old and inexperienced to start afresh in a new line of business'.[65]

Jenkins had been urging Riley to write a follow-up to *Windyridge*. Now he suddenly had all the time needed to complete the new novel that he had already started. *Netherleigh*, set in and around nearby Otley, came out in 1915. As a result of the enormous and continuing success of *Windyridge*, he already had a loyal readership, not only in the West Riding, but across Britain and beyond. *Windyridge* was already selling well in South Africa, Canada, Australia and New Zealand. He was receiving friendly, appreciative letters from his audience.

The publishing of Riley's first books brought him into the literary world. At that time distinguished authors such as Arthur Conan Doyle, Thomas Hardy, H. G. Wells, Joseph Conrad, Arnold Bennett, Somerset Maugham, John Masefield, John Buchan and G. K. Chesterton already

---

63. Report in *The London Gazette*, 24th March 1914.
64. Reported in *The Optician and Photographic Trade Journal*, 27th March 1914.
65. *Sunset Reflections*, p. 109.

occupied centre stage. Riley did not consider himself to be in their league, despite receiving some very favourable criticisms and reviews. In one of his lectures given in 1915 he declared, 'I do not deceive myself. I am neither a Victor Hugo nor a Thomas Hardy, but I am myself ...'.[66]

When speaking at Mirfield Grammar School in January 1923, he repeated: 'I know my place in literature today. I don't need to be told I am not a Hardy or a Conrad or a Wells, but that doesn't trouble me. I fill my own niche ...'. Nevertheless, he was recognised to be of national importance, and he moved in significant national circles. For example, he was a speaker at the Annual Dinner of the Associated Booksellers of Great Britain and Ireland in 1921, and attended a Royal Wedding Reception at Buckingham Palace in 1922. This invitation followed his gift to Princess Mary of a richly bound copy of Windyridge, on the occasion of her marriage to Viscount Lascelles of Harewood, West Yorkshire. It was noted in the press at the time how unusual it was for such a gift to be accepted, as the rule was that only gifts from donors personally known to the royal couple would be accepted. A news item drew attention to this fact:

> ... the exception that has been made in the case of Mr. Riley will be a matter of satisfaction to West Riding people, in view of the fact that 'Windyridge' is a book in which the atmosphere of the Yorkshire moors and the characteristics of Yorkshire folks are so faithfully delineated.[67]

At the 1932 *Daily Mail* Ideal Home Exhibition he was represented in the 'Gardens of our Novelists' alongside such nationally famous writers as Mrs Gaskell, Charles Dickens and J. B. Priestley. This indicated his stature at this time. As he continued to write, it is useful to note that he was joining such contemporary authors as D. H. Lawrence, Aldous Huxley, James Joyce, P. G. Wodehouse (many of whose books would also be published by Herbert Jenkins), and Agatha Christie.

---

66. 'The True Culture (Self-Culture)', a lecture by W. Riley.
67. Unidentified newspaper account, the W. Riley Archive.

With writing now his only source of income, Riley was not only writing books, but was turning his hand to short stories and newspaper articles; and, with more time on his hands, lectures and addresses, which were very popular. Although set in similar locations in the Yorkshire Dales, all disguised by his fictitious names, each of his novels was different in storyline. Apart from eventually writing a sequel to *Windyridge* many years later, with only one exception he never repeated any character, although in the course of time he would write several books set in the same parts of the Yorkshire Dales.

Another common theme that occurs in almost all of his books is an underlying sense of Christian outlook and values. His books were often referred to as wholesome and uplifting. He always declared that he preferred to expose the good in his characters where possible, and would avoid salacious writing, which he considered unnecessary, prurient and unhealthy. In his lecture, 'Some Reflections of a Novelist' (written in 1924) he asserted:

> There are quarters, I know, in which I should earn a warmer approval if I were to join the ranks of those who gild and glorify what is bestial in men and women, and exalt prostitution to an act of worship. It seems to me to require no great genius to prepare that sort of dish. Take one man and one woman; add a second woman; mix the ingredients and beat into a foam; season with strong spices and serve hot. I don't believe the dish warrants the praise which is bestowed upon it, and I don't believe the taste for it will last much longer. At any rate, I didn't leave the paths of commerce to build on the edge of such evil-smelling swamps.

At this time he would be referring to the output of such writers as D. H. Lawrence.

Not only were Riley's books valued for his astute pen-portraits of places and people, but they also gave a remarkable picture of life in this part of Yorkshire over very many years. His vivid descriptions of the way people behaved and the circumstances in which they lived were realistic, contemporary, and acknowledged to be true to life.

Marion Troughton, a journalist who had interviewed Riley several times, some years after his death wrote, '[Riley] had a great ability to give a feeling of what life must have been like for the ordinary people of the time ...'.[68]

In a similar vein author Derek Lister in a recent, mere page-long summary of Riley also remarked on his accurate descriptions of life in the dales:

> The charm of Riley's novels lay in their homely simplicity; there is a faithful reproduction of the Yorkshire scene and of the life that people lived in humble abodes.[69]

Riley was a lifelong student of people and places around him, as his notebooks show; and his descriptions were clearly taken from his own extensive and collected experiences over many years:

> With lords and ladies and powdered footmen I have hardly any acquaintance, but with mill operatives and mill-masters; with quarrymen and farmers' labourers; with roadmen and moormen, and with the wives and daughters of them all, I have.[70]

Given his strong Wesleyan background, it is not unexpected that he identified with the common people and felt less at ease with the landed gentry. This is a feature of his books; and whilst he did not hesitate to write about rich people, he was most convincing when he wrote of working folk, their characteristics, their strengths and their weaknesses, and their 'rebellious' nature. He identified himself with these people throughout his life. In a later lecture he said:

> I wonder if I have interested you in these rebels ... the men and women who make their home [in the moors] and catch the colour of their surroundings; who live hard lives and are in love with

---

68. Troughton, M., *Pens, Profiles and Places,* (Smith Settle, 1989), p. 86.
69. Lister, Derek A. J., *Bradford's Own,* (Sutton Publishing, 2004), p. 118.
70. 'The Yorkshirewoman at Home'.

hardship; whose passions are strong, whose natures are deep, whose love is hot and volcanic, whose devotion is incorruptible – they are worthy of your affection, rebels though they may be. Moors and moorland folk, I commend them to you.[71]

As a proud West Riding moor man himself, having been born in Bradford Moor, Riley identified with their attitudes, values and outlooks, which he saw as linked to the very characteristics of the land where they lived. As a writer he interpreted and represented them and their features, both men and women. He included himself in the group of moor-struck authors, and provided his own interpretation of the message of the moors.

> … the moorlands … have their voice and message too. They bid us to be strong to endure, independent, courageous; to look the facts of life in the face and march 'breast forward' to meet them; to be men and women of the 'baffled to fight better' type, with characters resolute, tenacious and yet beautiful, like the golden gorse and the purple heather.[72]

For Riley this 'message of the moors' epitomised the very same message of his own Christian belief, experience, and practice, and he expressed it in most of his books.

CLARA'S SERIOUS ILLNESS AND THE MOVE TO SILVERDALE

EARLY IN 1919, Clara fell victim to the great influenza pandemic. Always delicate of health, she nearly died. Very slowly, and against the odds, she recovered. Now their doctor warned them that they must leave the polluted Bradford air if Clara were to have any prospect of good health and a decent quality of life. They took this warning seriously, despite the close ties of family, church and friends that they both had in the Bradford area. When Clara was somewhat better, they went for a few convalescent

---

71. 'West Riding Moors and Moorland Folk', a lecture by W. Riley.
72. 'The Voice of the Moors', a lecture by W. Riley. The quotes are from a poem by Browning, 'Epilogue to Asoldo'.

weeks to Morecambe. Whilst here, Riley came across a vacant property in nearby Silverdale. Located on a slope above the village, it enjoyed commanding views of the surrounding district. The next day he returned with Clara. They both loved the house, and he bought it straight away. By September of the same year they had relocated. The sale was made even easier as the previous owner had admired Riley's books and was glad to think that her favourite author would live and write within its walls.

So it was that, at the age of fifty-three, and for the second time in five years, Riley's life changed profoundly again. From having been an urban dweller from earliest childhood to middle-aged businessman, he now found himself in a small and scattered village, with none of the resources and facilities of the city. He gave them all up for the sake of his wife. He now had only his pen to provide for them both.

The Rileys quickly became involved in village life. Already a well-known and popular author and lecturer, and Methodist local preacher, his reputation went before him. Now he had to get down to writing in earnest again. The immediate locality was much to his liking, and he was now actually living in closer proximity to much of his beloved dales country than when he had been in Bradford. He only had to climb to the top of the hill behind his house and he could see his favourite hill country in the east:

> The sight acted as a bugle-call to my spirit, and I set to work on my Yorkshire stories with a new zest.[73]

By 1920 his then nine titles together had already sold over 500,000 copies.[74] *Windyridge* at least was eventually translated into other languages; in 1922 Riley received royalties for the Danish and Norwegian rights.

---

73. *Sunset Reflections*, p. 139.
74. Quoted in an unpublished paper read before the Manchester Literary Club on 8th March 1920. The lecturer had recently visited and interviewed Riley.

WINDYRIDGE REVISITED: AT LAST – THE SEQUEL

FOR MANY YEARS Riley was pestered by his very many readers and his publisher to write more about the people who populated Windyridge. For a long time he resisted the call, fearing that he would be unable to recreate the magic of his first novel. But at last he overcame his hesitancy, and in 1928 he published his eighteenth book, *Windyridge Revisited*, in which he brought Grace Derwent (née Holden) back to Windyridge village twenty years later, while her husband Philip made a business trip to Melbourne. There she would meet old friends and enjoy more adventures, this time accompanied for part of her stay by her nineteen-year-old daughter Mary. (Notice that Riley introduced yet another female main character.) Once again the devil sees fit to joust among the village folk, and Grace does her best to withstand his influence and bring healing and solace to those in trouble. She meets new characters too. This time Grace sees her beloved farmer friend and one-time landlord Reuben Goodenough in his declining years. As Mother Hubbard died in *Windyridge*, so does Reuben, near the end of *Windyridge Revisited*.

The book ends with Grace and Philip reunited back in London again. Daughter Mary, who has had her own adventures throughout the story, has found her husband-to-be in the curate from nearby Romanton (Ilkley). He is the Rev. Charles Bertram Kirkland-Morris, usually known as Morris for short. He has been a thread through the whole narrative, arguing with the outspoken vicar's wife, chiefly about celibacy; but his negativity towards marriage is overcome once he gets to know and appreciate Mary.

In *The Bookman* of May 1928, the reviewer stated:

> … Mr. Riley is here at his best. He knows his simple Yorkshire folk with the knowledge that comes of true love and sympathy; he has a real passion for the moorland and the open air; and if he is a trifle sentimental at times, is that not a welcome fault in these days when the voice of the highbrow is too much heard in the land?

In publicity for the book Jenkins advertised it as follows:

Mr. Riley takes us back to Windyridge as it is today – A Windyridge of short skirts, and motors, and wireless aerials, but a Windyridge strangely unchanged in many ways.[75]

Windyridge Revisited was voted a hit by Riley's fans, who generally considered that this sequel equalled the original novel for atmosphere, characterisation, and fascination, and Hawksworth again became a literary Mecca. But it never matched the sales of the original *Windyridge*, although it became his ninth most popular book and received good reviews. It would eventually go out of print in 1949, leaving only fourteen of his titles still in print. By 1952 that number would be further reduced to just seven.[76]

RILEY'S LATTER YEARS

A YEAR AFTER the publication of *Windyridge Revisited*, Riley's wife Clara died at the age of sixty-five. He eventually remarried; his second wife Edith had been widowed at about the same time as he had, and they were already near neighbours and friends. Their shared experience of loss drew them closer together. He later wrote that their decision to marry 'met with the approval of relatives and friends'.[77] They would now grow old together, supporting each other. The Second World War brought three young evacuees into their house, but otherwise little occurred to disturb their relative tranquillity. Then in 1946 Riley published his penultimate novel, *A Stick for God*, based around the experience of having the evacuees, following which he became in his own words 'a back number', quietly living out his life with Edith. In these latter years he was nevertheless still

---

75. Jenkins' advertisement for *Windyridge Revisited* printed in *Squire Goodall*.
76. Information regarding popularity of *Windyridge Revisited* and the dates when Riley's books went out of print are derived from Riley's royalty payment records.
77. *Sunset Reflections*, p. 160.

a celebrity, and his activities continued to be reported in the northern press. Eventually, encouraged by family and friends, and his doctor, he wrote his autobiography, *Sunset Reflections*. It was published in 1957 and was so popular that it was into the third printing within six months. Now at the age of ninety-one, once again he was reviewed, very warmly, in the national, regional and religious press and his life story was greatly welcomed by his many supporters. Willie Riley died of a heart attack in June 1961, whilst on a short holiday in St Annes. His passing was mourned by many who had loved the man, his writings and his preaching. In the Bradford *Telegraph and Argus*, a reader wrote:

> All Yorkshire mourns the death of Willie Riley. He was among the greatest of our Yorkshire novelists, and by far the dearest to our hearts.[78]

Four ministers officiated at Willie's funeral service. The Rev. George Groves said:

> William Riley was a man of the people, having an essential humanity. He was a Yorkshireman of Yorkshiremen and that made him impatient of any pretence. It gave him a very generous heart … He had a clear insight, and was a man of logical thought, wise counsel and very sound judgement – always able to say the right word on every occasion … He was a delightful Christian gentleman to the end. [Of death] Mr. Riley said confidently, '… when God calls I am ready' … He, the mortal, by his life, makes the immortal more credible to me and to you.[79]

Willie was buried with his first wife, in Silverdale Cemetery. His writings live on.

---

78. Bradford *Telegraph and Argus*, 8th June 1961.
79. Taken from a typewritten report of the funeral service, the W. Riley Archive.

WINDYRIDGE

BY
W. RILEY

WHAT THIS STORY IS ABOUT

"WINDYRIDGE" IS ONE of the most popular first-novels ever published.

It is a story of the Yorkshire moors, and it has a history. Some friends being in great trouble, Mr. Riley conceived the idea of writing something that would amuse them, and divert their thoughts. Chapter by chapter, as it was written, "Windyridge" was read aloud by its author.

When it had served its charitable purpose, the manuscript was laid aside.

The friends clamoured for publication; Mr. Riley, being a modest man, shrugged his shoulders and smiled.

At length, determined to have a joke at the expense of his insistent friends, he sent it to Herbert Jenkins. It was accepted immediately. It was hailed by the reviewers as "a new Cranford," and proceeded to break all records.

TO

THE THREE KINDLY CRITICS

FOR WHOSE PLEASURE IT WAS COMMENCED, AND
WITHOUT WHOSE CONSTANT ENCOURAGEMENT IT
WOULD NOT HAVE BEEN COMPLETED, I DEDICATE
THIS BOOK WITH MUCH AFFECTION

THE BRIDGE NEAR WINDYRIDGE

CHAPTER ONE

THE CALL OF
THE HEATHER

I AM BEGINNING to-day a new volume in the book of my life. I wrote the Prologue to it yesterday when I chanced upon this hamlet, and my Inner Self peremptorily bade me take up my abode here. My Inner Self often insists upon a course which has neither rhyme nor reason to recommend it, but as I am a woman I can plead instinct as the explanation—or shall I say the excuse?—of my eccentric conduct. Yet I don't think I have ever been quite so mad before as I fully realise that I am now, and the delight of it all is that I don't care and I don't repent, although twenty-four hours have passed since I impulsively asked the price of my cottage, and found that I could have it, studio and all, for a yearly rental of ten pounds. I have never been a tenant "on my own" before, and the knowledge that I am not going back to the attic bedroom and the hard "easy" chairs of the Chelsea lodging-house which has been my home for the last three years fills me with a great joy. I feel as if I should suffocate if I were to go back, but it is my soul which would be smothered. Subconsciously I have been panting for Windyridge for months, and my soul recognised the place and leaped to the discovery instantaneously.

Yet how strange it all seems: how ridiculously fantastic! I cannot get away from that thought, and I am constantly asking myself whether Providence or Fate, or any other power with a capital letter at the beginning, is directing the move for my good, or whether it is just whimsicalness on my part, self-originated and self-explanatory—the explanation being that I am mad, as I said before.

When I look back on the events of the last three days and realise that I have crossed my Rubicon and burned my boats behind me, and that I had no conscious intention of doing anything of the kind when I set out, I just gasp. If I had stayed to reason with myself I should never have had the courage to pack a few things into a bag and take a third-class ticket for Airlee at King's Cross, with the avowed intention of hearing a Yorkshire choir sing in a summer festival. Yet it seems almost prophetic as I recall the incident that I declined to take a return ticket, though, to be sure, there was no advantage in doing so: no reduction, I mean. Whether there was an advantage remains to be seen; I verily believe I should have returned rather than have wasted that return half. I dislike waste.

That was on Tuesday; on Wednesday I went to the Town Hall and entered a new world. It cost me a good deal in coin of the realm—much more than I had dreamed of—but I got it all back in the currency of heaven before I came away. It may have been my excitable temperament—for my mother, I remember, used to condone my faults by explaining that I was "highly-strung," whatever that may mean—or it may have been the Yorkshire blood in my veins which turned to fever heat as the vast volume of sweet sound rose and fell; one thing is certain, I lost myself completely, and did not find myself again until I discovered that the room was almost bare of people, and realised by the good-humoured glances of the few who remained that I appeared to be more vacant than the room, and was making myself foolishly conspicuous by remaining seated with my head in my hands and that far-away look in my eyes which tells of "yonderliness."

To be quite candid, I am not quite sure that I *did* find myself; I suspect some tenant moved out and another moved in that afternoon, and I am disposed to think that Airlee explains Windyridge. If I were to attempt to put down in cold words what I heard or what I felt I should fail, and it would seem very ordinary and uninspiring, so I shall not make the attempt. But when I got outside, the noise of the busy city grated on my senses, and the atmosphere—which was really not bad, for the day was bright and sunny—seemed heavy and stifling. I longed for something which I had not previously cared about; I did not understand my yearnings—I do not yet—but I wanted to get away from the wooden pavements, and the granite banks, and the brick warehouses, and the huge hotels, and the smoke and bustle and din, and lay my head in the lap of Nature, and think.

I slept a little, I am sure, but I tossed about a good deal in the cosy little bed of the modest hotel where I took lodging, and when morning came I found my Inner Self still harping on the same string, and more vigorously than ever. Perhaps, if I had been sensible, I should have gone straight to the station, and by this time have been going through the old routine in Bloomsbury and Chelsea, instead of which I made my way into the street after breakfast, and asked a kind-faced clergyman which tramcar would take me farthest away from the turmoil. He was a fatherly man, but his answers were so vague, and he seemed in so much doubt of their reliability, that I disregarded them and accosted a bright young workman who crossed the square a moment later. "A good long ride?" he repeated; "right into the country, eh? Take this car and go to the far end." With this he led me to one which bore the fateful sign "Fawkshill."

It was a lovely day even in the city, warm but not muggy. When I had found an outside seat at the extreme front of the upper deck of the car, the greater part of which was covered, and redolent of tobacco fumes, I made up my mind to enjoy the breeze and the experience. So far as I knew it was just a parenthesis in a chapter of my life, not the beginning of a new volume. In the background of my thoughts there was always Chelsea, though I affected to forget it. Meantime, in the foreground, there was a good deal to make even Chelsea attractive by comparison.

We made our way slowly along the grimy road, with its rows of monotonously uninteresting warehouses, and its endless drays filled with the city's merchandise. When the warehouses ended the grime remained. We passed street after street of brick-built cottages, over which spread a canopy of smoke from a hundred factory chimneys. When the country was reached—if the bleak and sad-looking fields could be called country—the mill chimneys were just as evident. They were everywhere, even on the horizon, and my spirits sank. The villages through which we passed were just suburbs, with the thumb-print of the city on them all. Every cottage, every villa, spoke of the mill or the shop. As we neared the terminus I found to my dismay that so far from leaving these things behind we were entering a prosperous-looking little town which was just

Airlee on a smaller scale, with its full quota of smoke-producing factories.
How I blamed myself for following the advice of the young workman and
regretted that I had not trusted the parson!

I had an early lunch at a confectioner's and then wandered, aimlessly
enough, up a quiet road which led away from the town and the tram-lines.
It was not very promising at first, but when I had passed the last row of
houses and found myself hemmed in by green, moss-grown walls, my
spirits rose. By and by I reached cross-roads and a broad, white highway,
which was manifestly one of the great arteries of this thriving district. It
had no attractions for me and I crossed it, and continued my upward path.
A signpost told me that I was on my way to Windyridge.

I was now in a rather pleasant country road, but one which certainly
could boast few attractions. Yet I *was* attracted, perhaps because I could
see so little in front of me, perhaps because I could not see a single factory
chimney, look where I would.

Fifteen minutes after leaving Fawkshill I had reached the brow of the
hill, and my spirits rose with a bound. Just in front of me, on a rising knoll,
some fine sycamores and beeches clustered together, guarding the
approach to a grey, ivy-coated hall. The rooks cawed dismally in the
highest branches of the sycamores, the leaves of which were already
beginning to fall. Autumn, apparently, lays her hand in good time upon
the foliage in these northern regions, for some of the trees had already
grown ruddy at her touch.

When I came to the bend of the road I think my heart stood still for
a second or two. There in front of me and to my left—almost, as it seemed,
at my feet—were the heather-covered moors, gloriously purple, and the
tears came into my eyes. I could not help it; it was so unexpected, and it
unlocked too suddenly the chamber where a memory was preserved—a
hallowed, never-to-be-forgotten memory.

Years ago, and long before his sufferings ended, my father was leaning
back in his chair one day, his hand clasping its arms, as his custom was,
when there came into his eyes a look of inexpressible longing, almost of
pain. I went and knelt by his side, and passed my hand gently through his
hair, and asked, "What is it, dad dear?" He drew my face to his and
answered sadly—it was little more than a whisper, for he was very weak,—
"It was the heather calling me, lassie; I felt its sweet breath upon my cheek

for a moment, and longed to fall upon its comfortable breast. But it cannot be; it cannot be!"

That was ten years ago, and now the heather was to call me and I was to respond to the call. How long I stood there, with the tear-drops dimming my vision, I do not know, but presently I became conscious of a village street, if the few houses which straggled back from the roadway could with any propriety be termed a village. I walked along the path and drank in every sight and sound, and thirsted for more. I thought, in the intoxication of that hour, that peace and contentment must be the portion of every dweller in that quiet spot. I know it will not be so, of course. I suppose sorrow and heartache may inhabit that quaint one-storeyed cottage from which the wreath of blue smoke curls so lazily; that the seeds of greed and falsehood and discontent may thrive and grow here, and be just as hateful and hideous as the flowers which fill the gardens around me are bright and beautiful. But for the moment I did not realise this.

A woman was washing the flags at her cottage door, and she smiled upon me as I passed. It was my first human welcome to the moors. At the sound of my footsteps a whole regiment of hens flew from the hilly field which was their pasture, and perched in line upon the wall to give me greeting.

I saw no sign of church or inn; no shop save a blacksmith's, and that was closed. The cottage windows and the little white curtains behind them were spotlessly clean. Within, I caught a glimpse here and there of shining steel and polished brass which sparkled in the firelight; and the comfort and cosiness of it all appealed to me strongly.

I do not think there are more than a score houses in the village, but before I had come to the end of the street my soul had made the discovery I referred to just now. "Surely," I said to myself, "it is good to be here; this people shall be my people."

It was doubtless a mad thing to say, but I was prospered in my madness. At the extreme end of the village, just past the little Methodist chapel which by its newness struck a jarring note in the otherwise perfect harmony, I saw a long, low building, of one storey like most of its fellows, roofed with stone, and fronted by a large garden. It was separated by a field-length from its nearest neighbour, and the field was just the side of a hill, nothing more. Two doors gave access to the building, which was apparently unevenly divided into two cottages, for a couple of windows appertained to the one door and one only to the other. A board at the bottom of the garden and abutting upon the road conveyed the information that this "Desirable cottage" was "to let, furnished."

Then and there I gave hostages to fortune. If that cottage was to be had for a sum which came within the limits of my slender purse, it should be mine from that hour. For I saw at a glance that it faced the moors and the sunset; and I vowed that the windows should be always open, so that the breath of the heather might have free entrance.

I pushed aside the little green gate and walked up the tiny path amid a profusion of flowers whose names are as yet unknown to me. I promise myself to know them all ere long: to know their habits and their humours: to learn their secrets and the story of their lives; but that is for the future. Something almost as sweet and dainty as the flowers claimed my attention first.

At the sound of the creaking gate, a dear old lady appeared at the door of the doll's house which was joined to my cottage and advanced to meet me. She had the pleasantest of faces, and was pink and pretty in spite of her sixty odd years. She wore a cap with strings, in the style of long ago: it was a rather jaunty cap and not devoid of colour. A faded shawl hung loosely around her shoulders, and a white apron protected her neat black frock. I saw at once that she was a nervous little body, yet there was dignity as well as deference in the face which looked smilingly into mine. But the manner of her address took my heart by storm. I had never been accosted in this way before, and I nearly took the old lady in my arms and kissed her. I have done since!

"Yes, love!" she said. It was not an inquiry exactly, though there may have been the faintest note of interrogation in her voice. It was as though I had told her of my desire to rent the cottage, and she was expressing a gratified assent.

"I see this little house is to let," I began; "may I look at it, and will you tell me all about it?"

"To be sure, love," was the reply. "Now, just come inside my cottage and rest yourself, and I'll pour you out a cup of tea if you're in no hurry, for there's sure to be someone passing who will tell Reuben Goodenough to come hither."

GRACE HOLDEN'S COTTAGE

"How sweet of you!" I replied. "A cup of tea will be like the nectar of the gods. I will drink it thankfully."

The inside of that room was a revelation to me. It was, oh, so very, very small—the smallest living-room I am sure that I ever set eyes upon—but so marvellously clean, and so comfortably homelike that I uttered an exclamation of surprise and delight as I crossed the threshold.

The ceiling was of oak, with deep, broad, uneven beams of the same material, all dark and glossy with age. The stone floor was covered for the most part with druggeting, whilst a thick rug composed of small cuttings of black cloth with a design in scarlet was laid before the ample hearth. An old oak sideboard, or dresser, nearly filled the wall facing the window, and on its open shelves was an array of china which would make some people I know break the tenth commandment. A magnificent grandfather's clock, also in oak, with wonderful carving, ticked importantly in one corner, and a capacious cupboard filled another.

The wall decorations consisted of a bright but battered copper warming-pan, which hung perpendicularly from the ceiling, looking like the immense pendulum of some giant clock; and three "pictures" which aroused my interest. Two of them were framed examples of their owner's skill in needlework, as evidenced by the inscription, carefully worked in coloured wool—"Mary Jackson, her work, aged 13." The letters of the alphabet, and the numerals from 1 to 20, with certain enigmatical figures which I took to represent flowers, completed the one effort, whilst familiar texts of Scripture, after the style of "Thou God Seest Me," made up the other.

The third frame was of mahogany like the others, and contained a collection of deep, black-edged funeral cards of ancient date.

But the fireplace! My father's description of a real, old-fashioned Yorkshire range was understood now for the first time, as I saw the high mantelpiece, the deep oven and the wide-mouthed grate and chimney, in which the yellow flames were dancing merrily, covering the whole room with the amber glow which made it so warm and enticing. Through an open door I caught sight of a white counterpane, and found that there was, after all, a wee bedroom built out at the back.

Drawn quite close to the hearthrug was a round deal table covered with a snowy cloth. Two minutes later I was seated there, sipping tea and eating toast, deliciously crisp and hot, and taking my new friend into my confidence.

I confess it pleased me to find that my mad proposal was all as natural as the sunshine to her. The dear old soul never uttered one word of warning or suggestion. She was delighted with the scheme I rapidly evolved and ready to be my willing helper. I won her affection at once when I told her that I was a "Yorkshireman," and she took me to her heart and begged me to let her "mother" me. I lost my own mother before I had learned to value her, and I think I shall like to be "mothered," though I shall be thirty-five in April.

God bless Mother Hubbard! I must tell how I took the cottage to-morrow.

CHAPTER TWO

FARMER GOODENOUGH
STATES HIS TERMS

A FEE OF one penny, paid in advance, lent wings to the feet of the small boy who was pressed into my service, and before many minutes had passed Farmer Goodenough appeared upon the scene.

He shook hands with me, after Mother Hubbard had performed the ceremony of introduction, and I can feel the warmth of his greeting in my right hand yet. I shall be careful in future when I get to close grips with big, horny-handed Yorkshire farmers.

I almost regretted that I had felt it necessary to explain the situation to him when I heard his hearty and somewhat patronising laugh, but Mother Hubbard's previous treatment had emboldened me.

"Well, I do declare, Miss . . ." he hesitated and looked at me inquiringly, for my hostess had not mentioned my name.

"Grace Holden is my name, and I am unmarried," I said in reply.

"Oh!" he answered—only he pronounced it "Aw!"

"Well now, miss, you must excuse *me*, for I mostly speaks straight and no offence meant, and I hope none taken; but isn't this just a little bit daft-like? 'Marry in 'aste an' repent at leisure,' as t' Owd Book says. I'm thinkin' this'll be summat o' t' same sort. Hadn't you better sleep on it, think ye? It'll happen be a mucky day to-morrow, an' Windyridge 'll hev t' polish ta'en off it."

I have written this down with Mother Hubbard's assistance, and I required a little help from her at the time in the interpretation of it. But the farmer's candour pleased me.

"If the rent is more than I can afford to pay I shall return to London early to-morrow," I said; "but if it is within my means I shall certainly stay—at any rate for twelve months," I added guardedly.

"Now look you here, miss," returned the farmer; "I've got this cottage to let, an' if you take it for three months, *or* for six months, *or* for twelve months—for three months *or* for six months *or* for twelve months you'll hev it to pay for. Right's right, an' a bargain's a bargain all the world over. Frenchman, Scotchman *or* Yorkshireman, a bargain's a bargain. But nob'dy shall say 'at Reuben Goodenough took advantage of a woman. I won't let you this cottage, if you like it so as never, an' whether you can afford it or no, not until to-morrow I won't. An' I'll tell you why.

"You've just come an' seen Windyridge when all t' glory o' t' sunshine's on it, an' t' birds is singin' an' t' flowers is bloomin'; but it isn't allus like that. Not 'at I'm runnin' Windyridge down. *I'm* content here, but then I were born here, an' my work's here, an' t' missus an' t' youngsters were brought up here. But when you've slept on it you'll happen see different. Now you've no 'casion to speak"—as I was about to protest—"I've made up my mind, an' I'm as stupid as a mule when I set myself, an' there can be no harm done by waiting a toathree hours. Come, I'll show you what I can let you have for a ten-pun' note a year, if so be as you decide to take it at t' finish."

He unlocked the door and stepped aside to let us enter. The kitchen was almost a duplicate of Mother Hubbard's, but longer. There were the same oak rafters, the same oak sideboard, the same huge fireplace, the same cupboard. A horrible contrivance of cocoa-matting covered the floor, and a hearthrug, neatly folded, was conspicuous in one corner. A bed - room, of ample size for one woman of modest requirements, opened out of the kitchen, and I saw at a glance that I might have as cosy a home as Mother Hubbard herself. My mind was made up; but then so was Farmer Goodenough's, and as I looked at the square jaw and the thin lips I was convinced that this man with the good-natured face was not to be moved from his resolution.

"I shall take the cottage for twelve months," I said; "but I recognise the force of your objection, and I will not ask you to make out an agreement until to-morrow—to-morrow morning.

"But I claim to be a Yorkshirewoman, and so can be just a wee bit stupid myself, and you know the proverb says, 'When a woman says she will, she *will*, you may depend on 't.' Tell me, though, is not ten pounds per annum a very low rental, seeing that the cottage is furnished?"

"Low enough," he answered, "sadly too low; but it's as much as I can get. I charge fifteen shillin' a week in summer time, but then it never lets for more'n three months at t' outside, an' for t' rest o' t' year it 'ud go to rack an' ruin if I didn't put fires in it now an' then, an' get Mrs. 'Ubbard here to look after it. So I reckon it'll pay me as well to have someone in for a twelvemonth, even if I make no more money. But, miss"—he hesitated a moment, and thrust his hands deep into his trousers' pockets, whilst his eyes, as I thought, became tender and fatherly—"you must excuse *me*; I'm a deal older nor you, an' though I haven't knocked about t' world much, I've learned a thing or two i' my time, an' I have it on my mind to warn you. What t' Owd Book says is true: 'As you make your bed, so you must lie on 't,' an' it's uncommon hard an' lumpy at times. You know your own business best, an' I will say 'at I like t' look on you, an' it 'ud be a good thing for Mrs. 'Ubbard here to have you for a neighbour, but—think it well over, an' don't do nowt daft."

I suppose some people would not have liked it, but I did, and I told him so. And really it had the opposite effect from that he intended, for it showed me that I might have at least two friends in Windyridge, and that one of them would not be wanting in candour.

These preliminaries settled, the farmer handed the key to Mother Hubbard, so that it would be handy for me, as he explained, IF I should turn up again in the morning, and prepared to take his departure. Just as he reached the gate, however, he turned back.

"I should ha' said 'at you're welcome to t' use o' t' paddock. If so be as you care to keep a few hens there's pasture enough for 'em an' nob'dy hurt. An' if you want a greenhouse"—he laughed heartily—"why, here you are!"

He motioned that I should follow him, and I stepped through a gate in the wall into the hilly field which he called the paddock. There, firmly secured to the end of the house, was a structure of wood and glass which seemed out of all proportion to the size of the cottage.

"What in the world is this?" I exclaimed, but my landlord only laughed the louder.

"Now then, what d'ye think of that, eh? Kind o' Crystal Palace, that is. Strikes me I should ha' put this cottage in t' *Airlee Mercury*—'Desirable country residence with conserva*tory*. Apply, Goodenough, Windyridge.' Them 'at takes t' cottage gets t' conserva*tory* thrown in at t' same rent. It was put up by t' last tenant wi' my consent, an' he was as daft as——"

"As I am ?" I suggested.

"Well, he *proved* hisself daft. He kep' hens i' one part an' flowers in t' other, but he neither fed t' hens nor t' flowers, bein' one o' them menseless creatures 'at gets their heads buried i' books, an' forgets their own meals, let alone t' meals o' them 'at can't sing out for 'em. T' upshot of it all was he left t' cottage an' made me a present of all t' bag o' tricks."

Then and there the idea of my studio had its birth. With a very little alteration I saw that I could easily adapt it to photographic purposes; and I was more determined than before—if that were possible—to take possession of my Yorkshire home. I know people will laugh and call me madder than ever. It does seem rather ridiculous to fit up a studio in a village of perhaps a hundred inhabitants, but my Inner Self urges it, and I am going to live by faith and not by sight. I am irrational, I know, but I just don't care. I have got a theory of life—not a very definite one just now, though it is getting clearer—and I am sure I am taking a right step, though I could not explain it if I wished, and I don't wish.

Mother Hubbard was tearful when I wished her goodnight, and it was as an antidote to pessimism that I took the dear old soul into my arms and bade her stifle her tears and look confidently for my return. Farmer Goodenough's worldly wisdom had convinced her that the anticipations of a quarter-hour ago had been ill-founded. She had counted only too prematurely on my companionship, but the farmer's words had led her to see how unreasonable it was. She was stricken with remorse, too, at the selfishness of her conduct.

"You see, love," she explained, as we sought her cottage again and drew our chairs up to the fire—she had turned back her skirt lest the heat should scorch it—"I was just thinking about myself. I'm a lonely old woman, love, and it's only natural I should like the company of a nice, friendly young lady like yourself; but that's just selfishness. You must think over what Reuben has said, and don't do anything rash, but——"

"Mother Hubbard," I said, "you need not crumple your apron by turning it into a handkerchief, nor wet it by shedding useless tears. And I'm not a hair-brained young lady, fresh from school, but a sensible woman of thirty-five. Mark my word! At twelve o'clock to-morrow I shall be with you again, and I shall have lunch with you; and you'll oblige me by airing my bed for me, and getting things ship-shape, for to-morrow night I shall be your next-door neighbour."

I went back to Airlee by train from Fawkshill. I had noticed the railway as I came in the morning, and I felt that the tram would be too slow. As a matter of fact it took nearly as long and cost me more money. But my mind was full of Windyridge and I was oblivious to everything else. When I reached the coffee-room of the hotel I was calmer, for somehow the old familiar sights and sounds of the city threw my cottage into the background, and I was able to view the situation dispassionately.

Had I been a fool? Was not Farmer Goodenough right, after all; and had not his sound common sense saved me from committing myself to a rash and quixotic adventure?

"Grace Holden," I said, "you have got to face this question, and not make an ass of yourself. Weigh up the pros and cons. Get pencil and paper and make your calculations and strike your balance, and don't for goodness' sake be emotional."

Then my Inner Self said with great distinctness, "Grace Holden, the heather has called you! Listen to it!" And I went to bed and slept the sleep of the just.

My first sensation on awaking was one of exhilaration. Not a single cloud of doubt or apprehension appeared upon the sky of my hopes; on the contrary, it was rosy bright with the promise of success. I like to trust my intuitions, for it seems to me you treat them unfairly and do not give them a chance of developing upon really strong lines if you don't do so. Intuitions are bound to become weak and flabby if you are always coddling them and hesitating whether to let them feel their feet. An intuition that comes to you deprecatingly, and hints that it does not expect to be trusted, is a useless thing that is dying of starvation. *My* intuitions are healthy and reliable because I believe in them and treat them as advisers, and am becomingly deferential. It's nice to feel that your Inner Self likes you too well to lead you astray.

I wrote several letters and chuckled to myself when I thought of the effect they would produce in certain quarters. I am just a nonentity, of course, in the city of London, and nobody outside of it ever heard of me so far as I know, and I am my own mistress, without a relative of any kind to lay a restraining hand upon my actions; yet there are just two or three people who will be interested in this new phase of madness.

I can see Madam Rusty adjust her pince-nez and scan the postmark carefully before unfolding my note. And I dare bet anything that the glasses will fly the full length of the chain when she finds she has to pack up my belongings and despatch them to Windyridge. I always carry my cheque book with me in case of emergencies, so I have sent her a blank cheque "under five pounds" to cover her charges. I guess there won't be much change out of that when madam has filled it in.

And Rose! I wonder what Rose will say. I think she will be rather sorry, but she has many other friends and will soon console herself. And, after all, she *did* say I was "*swanky*"; but I daresay I shall ask her down some day, and I am sure she will attend to the little matters I have mentioned.

I paid my bill, and by ten o'clock was once more in the Fawkshill car; but I went inside this time, and closed my eyes and dreamed dreams. I got rid of the factory chimneys that way.

It was approaching twelve when I walked up the garden path to my new abode, and heard the joyful "Yes, love!" of my new mother. She could not forbear giving me one peep into my own cottage as we passed the door. A cheerful fire was blazing in the grate, the rug was in its place, the mattress and all its belongings were heaped around the hearth, and the clock upon the wall was ticking away in homeliest fashion and preparing to strike the noontide hour. There was not a speck of dust anywhere. Evidently Mother Hubbard had been up early and had worked with a will, and I was touched by this evidence of her faith, and glad that I had proved worthy of it.

"But what will Farmer Goodenough say?" I asked jocularly, as we discussed the appetising ham and eggs which she had prepared in her own kitchen.

"Reuben? Oh, I take no notice of him, love. He called out as he passed, whilst I was in the garden this morning, that I was to remember that he had not yet let you the house, and that we might never see your face again;

but I said, 'For shame! Reuben Goodenough,' though I will admit I was glad to see you, love. And now we'll just go in together and get everything made tidy. Bless you! I'm glad you've come. I think the Lord must have sent you to cheer a lonely old woman."

CHAPTER THREE

GRACE MEETS THE SQUIRE

I HAVE SPENT my first Sunday in Windyridge, and have made a new acquaintance. I believe I shall soon feel at home here, for the villagers do not appear to resent the presence of a stranger, and there is no sign of the Cranford spirit, perhaps because there is an entire lack of the Cranford society.

My adventure befell me as I walked back from church in the morning. It was too far for Mother Hubbard to accompany me to Fawkshill if she had wished to do so, but she has no leanings in the direction of the Establishment, being, as I have discovered, a staunch dissenter. She has asked me to go with her to the little Methodist chapel one day, but I put her off with a caress.

I was as full of the joy of life as a healthy woman can be, whose church-going garments are two hundred miles away, and I filled my lungs again and again with the sweet moorland air as I sauntered leisurely up the village street. A delightful breeze was blowing from the west, and I knew that my hair would be all about my ears before I reached the church; but that was a small matter, for who was there to care or criticise? The village rested in the calm of the Sabbath: no sound of human voice or human feet disturbed its quiet. But the cocks crowed proudly from their elevated perches by the roadside, and the rooks cawed noisily in the sycamores as they saw their lofty homes rocked to and fro in the swell of the wind. I stood for a moment or two to watch the behaviour of the trees when Boreas, rude as ever, flung himself upon them. How irritable and angry they became! How they shook their branches and shrieked their defiance, trembling all the time through every stem and leaf!

As I passed the entrance gate at the farther end of the Hall grounds a carriage was leaving it, and I caught sight of an old gentleman sitting alone within. I guessed him to be the owner of the place and dubbed him the Squire, and I was right, except as to the title, which I find he disavows.

I must have dawdled away more time than I realised, for they were well on with the prayers when I entered the church, but I will guard against that in future, for I pride myself on my methodical and punctual habits. But hurrying makes one hot, and churches are often chilly, as this one was! I was glad when the service was over and I could get out into the sunshine again.

The squire's carriage passed me on its homeward way soon after I had left the church, but when I reached the cross-roads I saw that its owner must have sent it forward and decided to continue the journey on foot, for he was standing at the bend of the lane in conversation with Farmer Goodenough.

The latter smiled as I approached and half raised his cap; and the squire turned and saluted me with grave politeness.

"Mornin', Miss 'Olden, mornin'," said my landlord. "So you've exchanged the 'eath for the 'assock, in a manner o' speakin'," and he laughed loudly at his alliterative success. "Well, well, some must pray an' some must work. 'There's a time for everything,' as t' Owd Book says; that's it, isn't it, sir, eh?" and without waiting for an answer Farmer Goodenough strode off. In a few seconds, however, he was back.

"Excuse me, miss, but I should ha' made you two known to each other. Miss 'Olden, this is Mr. Evans of the 'All, an' this is my new tenant, sir; a lady from London, Miss 'Olden, who's taken the cottage for twelve months for a sort of a whim, as far as I can make out." He touched his cap, and turned on his heel once more.

The situation was amusing and a little embarrassing, but I was left in no suspense. The old gentleman smiled and looked down into my eyes. He is a fine old man, something over seventy years of age, I should say, but very erect, with deep, rather cold eyes, surmounted by bushy eyebrows, and a head of thick, steely-grey hair. One glance at his face told me that he was a man of intellect and culture.

"We may as well be companions, Miss Holden, if you do not object," he said smilingly. "I should like to ascertain for myself whether the village report is true, for I may inform you that I have heard all that my butler can tell me, which means all that he can ascertain by shrewd and persistent inquiry."

"I am flattered by the attention of my neighbours," I replied, "and I can quite understand that in a little place like this the advent of a stranger will create a mild sensation, but I was not aware that there was anything so dreadful as a 'report' in circulation. The knowledge makes me uneasy; can you relieve my anxiety?"

He was walking along with his hands holding the lapels of his jacket, his light overcoat blowing about behind him, and he looked quizzically at me for a moment or two before he replied:

"I think you are able to take it in good part, for—if you will permit me to say so—I judge that you have too much common sense to be easily offended, and therefore I will admit that the villagers are prepared to look upon you as slightly 'daft,' to use their own expression. They cannot understand how, on any other supposition, you should act on a momentary impulse and leave the excitements of the metropolis for the simple life of a tiny village. I need hardly say that I realise that this is distinctly your own affair, and I am not asking you to give me your confidence, but you will not mind my telling you in what light the village regards this somewhat—unusual conduct."

I laughed. Goodness knows I am not touchy, and the opinion of my neighbours only amused me. But somehow I felt that I must justify my action to the squire, and my Inner Self put on her defensive armour in readiness for the battle. I seemed to know that this rather stern old man would regard my action as childish,—and indeed the scheme could not be regarded as reasonable; it was simply intuitive, and who can defend an intuition? I therefore replied:

"You have certainly relieved my disquietude. I thought the villagers might have conceived the notion that I was a fugitive from justice, and had a good reason for hiding myself in an out-of-the-way place. If they consider me inoffensive in my daftness I am quite content; for, after all, there are hundreds of people of much wider experience who would be not a whit more lenient in their judgment. In fact, I suspect that you yourself would endorse it emphatically, especially when I admit that the premise is correct from which the conclusion is drawn."

"You invite my interest," he returned, "but your silence will be a sufficient rebuke if my inquiries overstep the bounds of your indulgence. You tell me that the premise is correct. I understand, therefore, that you admit that you have acted on mere impulse; that, in fact, our friend Goodenough was speaking truly when he called it bluntly a 'whim.'"

"I am not skilled in dialectics," I said, feeling rather proud of the word all the same, and mightily astonished at my coolness; "but I should not call it a whim, but rather an intuition. I suppose there is a difference?"

He bent his brows together and paused in his walk; then he replied:

"Yes: there is a distinct difference. I cannot deny or disregard the power of the mind to discern truth without reasoning, but the two have so much in common that I think a whim may sometimes be mistaken for an intuition. Can you prove to me that this was an intuition?"

"No," I said, and I think it was a wise answer; at any rate it seemed to please him; "nobody could do that. Time alone can justify my action even to myself. I am going to be on the lookout for the proof daily."

He smiled again. "You know what would have been said if a man had done this?" he said deliberately; "it would be asked, Who is the woman?"

I blushed furiously, and hated myself for it, though he was nearly old enough to have been my grandfather. "I always feel glad that Eve did not blame the other sex," I replied, "and, in spite of the annoying colour in my face, I can say with a clear conscience that there is no man in the case at all."

"Do not be grieved with me," he said, just as calmly as ever. "I realised that I was taking a big risk, but I wished to clear the ground at the outset. I have done so, but I hesitate to venture further."

His tone was so very kindly that I, too, determined to take a big risk, though I half feared he would not understand, or understanding would be amused. So I told him something of my life in London, and how its problems had perplexed and depressed me, and I told him of the heather and how it had called me; and I think something of the passion of life shook my voice as I spoke, and I expressed more than I had realised myself until then.

He listened with grave and fixed attention, and did not reply at once. Then, halting again in his walk, though only for a second, he said:

"Miss Holden, subconscious influences have been at work upon you for some time past. You have experienced the loneliness which is never so hard to bear as when one is jostled by the crowd. I gather that the wickedness of London—its injustice and inequalities—have been weighing upon your spirits, and you feel for the moment like some escaped bird which has gained the freedom of the woods after beating its wings for many weary months against the bars of its city cage. You may have done well to escape, but beware of false ideals, and beware of the inevitable reaction when you discover the wickedness of the village, and learn that injustice and vice and slander, and a hundred other hateful things, are not peculiar to city life."

"But surely," I interposed, "the overcrowding, and the sweating and the awful, awful wretchedness of the poor are wanting here."

"My dear young lady," he said, "I suppose you think that the devil is a city gentleman whose attention is so much occupied with great concerns that he has had no time to discover so insignificant a place as Windyridge. You will find out your mistake. There are times when he is very active here, but he has wit enough to vary his methods as occasion requires.

"Sometimes, as Scripture and experience have shown you, he goes about as a roaring lion, and there is no mistaking his presence; but at other times he masquerades as an angel of light. You speak of the evils you know, and it may be admitted that most of these are absent from Windyridge, at any rate in their aggravated forms. But analyse these various evils which have caused you to chafe against your environment, and you will find that selfishness is at the root of them all, and selfishness flourishes even in the soil which breeds the moorland heather.

"Don't let this discourage you, however," he continued, as he held out his hand, for we had now reached the gateway of the Hall; "the devil has not undisputed possession here or elsewhere, and Windyridge may help you to strike the eternal balance.

"Come to see me sometimes; I am an unconventional old man, and you need not hesitate. I can at least lend you good books, and give you advice from an experience dearly bought."

He grasped the collar of his coat again and walked slowly up the drive.

Dinner had been waiting quite ten minutes when I reached home, and I found Mother Hubbard in a state of apprehension, partly lest some evil should have befallen me, and partly lest the Yorkshire pudding, whose acquaintance I was to make for the first time, should be so spoiled as to prejudice my appreciation of its excellences from the beginning.

But no such untoward event occurred, and my appetite enabled me to do full justice to Mother Hubbard's preparations. We have come to a convenient and economical arrangement by which we are to share supplies, Mother Hubbard being appointed cook, and I housemaid to the two establishments. In her delight at the prospect of my companionship the dear old lady was prepared to unite the two offices in her one person, but this was an impossible proposition, as I promptly pointed out. She might be prime minister, but not the entire Cabinet.

So we shall take our meals together in her cottage or in mine, as may be most convenient, and I think I shall be able to spare her some of the delightful drudgery which is harming her body whilst it leaves her spirit untouched. Not that I shall ever be able to maintain the spotless cleanliness which she guards as jealously as a reputation; and I cannot help thinking that her unwillingness to consent to this part of the bargain was due in some degree to doubts of my competency. But I am willing to be taught and corrected, and I will encourage her not to spare the rod.

CHAPTER FOUR

THE
STUDIO

I HAVE BEEN here a whole week, and as for being busy, I think the proverbial bee would have to give me points. Monday was occupied with a variety of odd jobs which were individually insignificant enough but meant a good deal in the aggregate. First of all I attended to household duties under the keen but kindly supervision of Mother Hubbard, and acquitted myself fairly well.

Then I turned my attention to the studio and drew up my plans for its equipment. A young girl from the village readily undertook the work of cleaning, and the muscle she put into it was a revelation to me after my experience of the leisurely ways of London charwomen! I soon discovered that she is a sworn enemy of every form of dirt—or "muck" as she prefers to call it—that she has a profound contempt for all modern cleansing substances and mechanical methods, and a supreme and unshakable belief in the virtues of soft soap, the scrubbing-brush, and "elbow-grease."

Four hours of "Sar'-Ann" brought joy to my heart and sweetness to my studio.

Then, with some difficulty, for he was at work in the fields, I found a sturdy and very diffident young man who has had some experience of carpentry, and who can also wield a paint-brush. To him I explained my requirements, and also handed over the plan I had prepared. He stood chewing the neb of his cap, and repeated in most irritating fashion: "Aw, yes 'm" whenever I paused to plumb the depths of his intelligence; but would only promise to do his best. As a matter of fact his "best" is not at all bad.

Sar'-Ann informed me in his presence, when he showed a little difficulty in understanding one of my requirements, that he was "gurt and gawmless," whereat he blushed furiously, and most unnecessarily so far as I was concerned, for the description was Greek to me. His awkwardness disappears, I find, when my back is turned; and he is really a very capable workman, and he and Sar'-Ann between them have made my studio most presentable.

But I am anticipating.

Tuesday morning brought me a small budget of letters and several parcels. I opened Madam Rusty's first, with some mischievous anticipation of its contents. I knew the sort of thing I might expect: the quasi-dignified remonstrance, the pained surprise, and the final submission to the will of an inscrutable providence which had seen fit to relieve me of my senses and her of a great responsibility.

I leaned back in my chair, put my feet upon the fender, and prepared for a good time. The precise, angular handwriting was as plain as the estimable lady herself, and no difficulty in decipherment impeded my progress.

"MY DEAR MISS HOLDEN," it ran,

"I have received your most extraordinary communication, which I have perused with mingled feelings of astonishment, sorrow and dismay. I am astonished that you should leave my house, where I am sure you have been surrounded by every home comfort, without a single expression of your intention to do so, or one word of explanation or farewell to myself or your fellow-boarders. Conduct of this kind I have never experienced before, and you must pardon me saying that next to an actual elopement it seems to me the most indelicate thing a young person in your position could do. And I am sorry because I feel sure there is more behind all this than you have been willing to inform me of, and I do think I have not deserved to be deceived, for I can honestly say that I have endea - voured to act a mother's part towards you; and as to any little differences we have had and complaints and so on, I did not think you had an unforgiving spirit. Not that one expects gratitude from one's boarders in the ordinary way, which being human is unlikely, but there are exceptions, of which I thought you were one. But if you believe me I am dismayed when I think of you going out into these wild parts which I have always understood are as bad as a foreign country, and without anyone to look after you, and no buses and policemen, and what you would do in case of fire I don't know. However, they do say that providence takes care of babies and drunken people and the insane, and we can only hope for the best. I know it's no use trying to persuade you different, for if there's one thing about you that is known to all the boarders it is that you are self-willed, and you must excuse me telling the plain truth, seeing that it is said for your good. So I have had your things packed up, and Carter Patersons have taken them away to-day. You will find it all in the bill enclosed, and I have filled in the cheque accordingly. Of course if you change your mind I shall try to accommodate you if I am not full up. I cannot help signing myself

"Yours sorrowfully,

"MARTHA RUSSEN.

"N.B.—I may say that the other boarders are very shocked."

Poor old Rusty! She is really not half a bad sort, and I am glad to have known her: almost as glad as I am to get away from her. It is my misfortune, I suppose, to be "nervy," and the sound and sight of Madam in these latter days was enough to bring on an attack.

I turned to the letter from Rose, which was short, sharp and sisterly—sisterly, I mean, in its shameless candour and freedom from reserve. Rose rather affects the rôle of the superior person, and has patronised me ever since I discovered her. This is what she wrote:

"MY DEAR GRACE,

"I am not sure that I ought not to write '*dis*grace.' I always have said that you are as mad as the March hare in 'Alice' and now I am sure of it. Your letter has not one line of sense in it from beginning to end except that in which you suggest that I may come to see you some time. So I may, if the funds ever run to it. It will be an education to do so. I would go to see you in your native haunts just as I would go to see any other natural freak in which I might be interested. But I won't pay ordinary railway fare, so that's flat. If the railway companies won't reduce their charges by running cheap excursions as they do for other exhibitions, I shall not come. For if you are not an exhibition (of crass folly) I don't know what an exhibition is. However, you have a bit of money and a trade (sorry! I mean a profession) at your finger-ends, so I can only hope you'll not starve whilst your native air is bringing you to your senses. I will see to your various commissions, and if I can be of further use to you up here,

"I am, as I have ever been,
Your humble, but not always obedient servant,
"ROSE."

This concluded what may be termed the social portion of my correspondence, and I took up the other letters with less zest. One, a mere formal acknowledgment of my changed address, was from the bankers who have the privilege of taking care of my money, and who have never manifested any sense of oppression under the responsibility. Nevertheless, two hundred and forty odd pounds is something to fall back upon, and it looms large when it represents savings; and in any case it is all I have except the interest which comes to me from a few small investments—all that was rescued from the wreck of my father's fortunes. Well, well! I am a good deal richer than some very wealthy people I have met.

Two others were business communications from firms which give me employment, and I may frankly admit that I was just a little relieved to find that distance was not going to affect our relationships. Not that I had been actually uneasy on that score, for I have discernment enough to know my own value. I am not a genius, but what I *can* do is *well* done; and I have lived long enough to discover that that counts for much in these days. The parcels which accompanied the letters contained sufficient work for a month at least.

Then came a letter from Shuter and Lenz with all sorts of suggestions for the furnishing of my studio. The consideration of this occupied a couple of hours, but my list was made out at last, and I expect I shall receive the bulk of the goods before the end of next week. Transit between

London and Windyridge is quick—much more so than I anticipated, for my boxes were delivered during the afternoon, and I spent the rest of the day and some part of the night in unpacking them. It was no easy matter to find storage for my small possessions, but I accomplished it in the end, and arranged all my household goods to the best possible advantage.

Since then I have been sewing for all I am worth. The joint establishments do not boast the possession of a sewing machine, so I have had to make my studio curtains by hand. Mother Hubbard was delighted to be able to help in this department, and between us we finished them yesterday, and with Ginty's assistance I have hung them to-day! "Ginty" is the carpenter. The "g" is hard and the name is unusual, but I am inclined to doubt whether it was ever bestowed upon him by his godparents in baptism. I suspect Sar'-Ann of having a hand in that nomenclature.

If my landlord could see my studio now he would hardly recognise his conserva*tory*. One end has been boarded off for a dark-room, and the whole has been neatly painted slate colour. When my few backgrounds and accessories arrive I shall have a very presentable studio indeed.

Ginty is now engaged painting the outside in white and buff, and he is then going to make me a board which will be placed at the bottom of the garden to inform all and sundry that "Grace Holden is prepared to do all kinds of photographic work at reasonable prices." I don't anticipate that barriers will be needed to keep back the crowd.

How tired I am, and yet how wonderfully fresh and buoyant! My limbs tremble and my head aches, but my soul just skips within me. I have had a week in which to repent, and I have never come within sight of repentance. And yet I have seen no more of Windyridge. I have not been near the heather. I have not even climbed to the top of the hill behind my cottage in order to look over the other side. I have wanted to, but I dare not; I am terrified lest there should be factory chimneys in close proximity.

Once or twice it has been warm enough for me to stretch myself full length upon the grass, and I have lain awhile in blissful contemplation of the work of the Great Architect in the high vault of His cathedral. That always rests me, always fills me with a sense of mystery, always gives me somehow or other a feeling of peace and of partnership. I rise up feeling that I must do my best to make the world beautiful, and use all my abilities—such as they are—to bring gladness into the lives of other people. I cannot make clouds and sunsets, but I can paint miniatures, and I can take portraits (or I think I can), and these things make some homes bright and some folk happy. But I must not moralise.

More often I bring out the deck-chair, which is one of my luxuries, and sit in front of the cottage with Mother Hubbard as a companion. She is splendid company. If I encourage her she will tell me interesting stories of her youth and married life, or repeat the gossip of the village; for none is better versed than she in all the doings of the countryside. If, however, I wish to be quiet she sits silently by my side, as only a real friend can. But whether she talks or is silent her knitting needles never stop their musical clatter. What she does with all the stockings is beyond my knowledge, but I believe Sar'-Ann could tell me if she would, and I am sure all this knitting contributes no little to Mother Hubbard's happiness.

So I lean back in my chair and feast upon the scene before me and am satisfied. I wonder if it would appeal to many as it does to me. Probably not, for, after all, I suppose there are many more beautiful places than Windyridge, but I have never travelled and so cannot compare them. Then again, this is Yorkshire and I am "Yorkshire," and that explains something. Still, I ought to try to write down what it is that impresses me, so I will paint as well as I can the picture that is spread before me as I sit.

First of all, as a fitting foreground, the garden—past its best, I can see, but still gay with all the wild profusion of Flora's providing; plants whose names are as yet unknown to me, but which are a constant delight to sight and smell. Then the road, with its border of cool, green grass, winding down into the valley between hedges of hawthorn and holly—ragged, untidy hedges, brown and green where the sun catches them, blue-grey and confused in the shadows. Beyond them a stretch of fields—meadow and pasture, and the brown and kindly face of Mother Earth dipping steeply down to meet the trees which fill the narrow valley, and are just beginning to catch the colours of the sunset. Footpaths cross the fields, and I see at times those who tread them and climb the stiles between the rough grey walls; and I promise myself many a good time there, but not yet.

On the other side, beyond the trees, the climb is stiffer, and the hills rise, as it sometimes seems, into the low-lying clouds. I can see a few houses under the shelter of a clump of chestnuts and sycamores, the farthest outposts of their comrades in the valley, but far above them rises the moor, the glorious moor, heather-clad, wild, and, but for the winding roads, as God made it. Far away to the west it stretches, and when the day is clear I catch the glow of the gorse and the daily decreasing hint of purple on the horizon miles away; but in these autumn days the distance is often wrapped in a diaphanous shawl of mist, which yet lends a charm to the glories it half conceals.

High up the hill to the left is the village of Marsland, with its squat, grey church, which I must visit one day; and farther away still—for I must be candid at all costs—there are a few factory chimneys, but they are too distant to be obtrusive.

Such is my picture: would that I could paint it better. Looking upon it my spirit bathes and is refreshed.

CHAPTER FIVE

FARMER BROWN IS PHOTOGRAPHED

MY STUDIO IS complete at last, and I have already had one customer, not counting Mother Hubbard, who had the privilege of performing the opening ceremony, and who was my first sitter. I insisted upon that, all the more because the dear old soul had never been photographed before in her life, and was disposed to regard the transaction in the light of an adventure.

She is altogether too gentle and pliant to oppose her will to mine on anything less important than a matter of principle, but I could see that she was grievously disappointed when I would not let her put on her very best garment, a remarkable black satin dress in the fashion of a past generation, which she keeps in lavender and tissue paper at the bottom of the special drawer which is full of memories and fading grandeur.

I wanted her just as she was, with the shawl loose upon her shoulders, and the knitting-needles in her hand, and that pleasant expression of countenance which makes all soulful people fall in love with her at first sight.

I succeeded in the end, and the delight of the old lady when I showed her a rough print a day or two later was good to see.

"But I wish you could have taken me in my satin, love, and with the lace collar. Matthew always thought I looked nice in them."

"You look nice in anything," I replied, "and I am sure your husband thought so; but *I* want the dear old Mother Hubbard of to-day; for, do you know, I am going to send you to a big News Agency, and if you are accepted you and I will make holiday, and do it right royally."

But my real customer arrived on the second Wednesday in October. My board had been in position for several days, and had attracted a good deal of curiosity but no clients, which was as much as one had a right to expect. I knew, of course, that sitters would be rare, but I had my own plans for turning the studio to profitable use, and I did not worry. "Everything comes to him who waits."

I was busy with my miniatures, and was just deciding to lay them aside for a time and do a little re-touching on Mother Hubbard's negatives, when I happened to glance out of the window, and saw an elderly man stop to read my board. He stood quite a long time looking at it, and then turned in at the gate.

I went to the door to meet him, and asked if he would like me to take his portrait, and he replied: "Ay, if it doesn't cost too much, I should."

I led the way into the studio and asked him to sit down, but he would not do so until we had discussed terms. I soon satisfied him on this point, for, of course, high charges in Windyridge would be ridiculous, and then I inquired how he would like to be "taken."

"I shan't make much of a picter, miss," he said, "but there's them 'at'll like to look at my face, such as it is. If you can make ought o' my head and shoulders it'll do nicely."

I looked at him as I made my preparations, and was puzzled. He was a tall man, somewhat bent and grey, his face tanned with exposure to the weather. It was clean shaven, and there was character in the set of his features—the firm mouth, the square jaw, and the brown eyes. They were dreamy eyes just now, and I wondered why, and was surprised that he should seem so natural and free from constraint. I judged him to be a farmer clad in his Sunday clothes, but why he should be so garbed on a bright afternoon in mid-week I could not guess. That he was no resident in the village was certain, for by this time I know them all; or rather I should say that I can recognise them all—to know them is another thing.

He gave me no trouble, except that I had some difficulty in driving the sad look away from his eyes. It went at last, however, though only momentarily, yet in that moment I got my negative. It was in this way.

"Cheer up!" I said, when I was ready for the exposure. "Your friends would think me a poor photographer if I should send them home such a sad-looking portrait."

"Ay, right enough," he agreed; "that 'ud never do. But I'm not much of a hand at looking lively."

"I want to do you justice for my own sake as well as yours," I said. "Now if *I* wanted to have a pleasing expression I should just think of the moors, radiant in gold, and the cloud-shadows playing leap-frog over them, and that would be sufficient."

"Ay, ay, I can follow that," he said; and before the glow left his eyes I had gained my point.

"Shall I post the proof to you?" I asked. He did not understand, and I explained.

"No, no," he replied; "if you're satisfied 'at they'll do it'll be right to me, miss. This is your line, not mine, and there's nobody at our end 'at knows ought much about photygraphs. And there's one thing more 'at I want to say, only I hardly know how to say it. But it comes to this: I don't want you to send any o' these photygraphs home until you hear from Dr. Trempest. When he lets you know, just send 'em on, and put a bit of a note in, like, to say 'at they're paid for. It'll none be so long—a matter o' five weeks, maybe."

He unbuttoned a capacious pocket and drew out a bag of money, from which he carefully counted out the amount of my bill, but when I offered him a receipt he declined to take it.

"Nay, nay," he said, "I want nowt o' that sort. I can trust you; but you'll have 'em ready when t' time comes, won't you?"

I assured him confidently, and as he turned to leave I expressed the hope that he would like the prints when he saw them. Then it all came out.

"I shall never see 'em. I shall be on t' moorside, with t' cloud-shadows you talk about playing loup-frog aboon *me* by then. That's why I wanted t' photygraphs. I only thought on 't when I passed t' board, but there's them at home 'at 'll be glad to have 'em when I'm gone."

Tears filled my eyes, for I am a woman as well as a photographer, and I felt that I was face to face with a tragedy.

"Cannot you tell me about it?" I asked. "Believe me, I am very sorry. Perhaps I could help. But please don't say anything if you would rather not."

"There's not much to tell," he responded, "but what there is 'll soon be all round t' moorside. You see, I've lived at yon farm, two miles off, all my life, and I'm well known, and folks talk a good deal in these country places, where there isn't much going on.

"I walked into Fawkshill to see Dr. Trempest this morning, and he's been with me to Airlee to see a big doctor there—one o' these consulting men—and he gives me a month or happen five weeks at t' outside. There's nought can be done. Summat growing i' t' inside 'at can't be fairly got at, and we shall have to make t' best on 't. But it'll be a sad tale for t' missus and t' lass, and telling 'em is a job I don't care for.

"You see, we none of us thought it was ought much 'at ailed me, for I've always been a worker, and I haven't missed many meals i' five and fifty year, and it comes a bit sudden-like at t' finish."

What could I say? I saw it all and felt the pity of it. God knows I would have helped him if I could. The old wave of emotion which used to sweep over me so often surged forward again; and again I was powerless in the presence of the enemy.

I said something of this, but my friend shook his head in protest.

"Nay, but I don't look at it i' that way. I'm no preacher, but there's One above 'at knows better than us, and I wouldn't like to think 'at t' Old Enemy 'ad ought to do wi' it. I've always been one to work wi' my hands, and book-learning hasn't been o' much account to me, but there's *one* Book, miss, 'at I have read in, and it says, 'O death, where is thy sting? O grave, where is thy victory? Thanks be to God which giveth *us* the victory through our Lord Jesus Christ.'"

I sat with my head in my hands for a long time after Farmer Brown had left, and when at length I raised my eyes the shadows had left the moor, and I saw that the sun would set in a clear sky.

CHAPTER SIX

OVER THE MOOR
TO ROMANTON

WE HAVE HAD our promised holiday, Mother Hubbard and I, and a right royal one. On those rare occasions when work may be laid aside and hard-earned coin expended upon the gratification of the senses, our younger neighbours turn their steps to Airlee or Broadbeck, and seek the excitements of the picture palace or the music-hall; their elders are seldom drawn from the village unless to the solemn festivities of a "burying."

We spent our day in the great alfresco palace of Nature, amid pictures of God's painting, and returned at night, tired in body, but with heart and soul and brain refreshed by unseen dews of heaven's own distilling.

Fortunately we have had a spell of fine, dry weather, with occasional strong winds—at least, they were strong to me, but the folk about here dismiss them contemptuously as "a bit of a blow." Had the weather been wet Mother Hubbard's cherished desire to "take me across the moor" to Romanton would have had to be postponed indefinitely.

We were to drive as far as "Uncle Ned's" in Mr. Higgins' market cart, Mr. Higgins having volunteered to "give us a lift," as it was "nowt out of his way."

We started early, before the morning mists had forsaken the valleys, and whilst night's kindly tears still sparkled on the face of the meadows. It was good to lean back, my hand in Mother Hubbard's and my feet resting on the baskets in the bottom of the cart, and drink in sight and sound and crisp morning air.

What a peaceful world it was! I thought for a moment of the mad rush of petrol-driven buses along Holborn, and the surging tide of sombre humanity which filled the footpaths there. This had been the familiar moving picture of my morning experience for more years than I care to remember, and now—this.

Beyond, the meadows and the shawl of mist in the valley, a long stretch of gold and golden-brown where gorse and bracken company together, the one in its vigorous and glowing prime, the other in the ruddy evening of its days, but not a whit less resplendent.

Overhead, a grey-blue sky, with the grey just now predominating, but a sky of promise, according to Mr. Higgins, with never a hint of breakdown. By and by the blue was to conquer, and the sportive winds were to let loose and drive before them the whitest and fleeciest of clouds, but always far up in high heaven.

In the distance, just that delightful haze which the members of our Photographic Society so often referred to as "atmosphere"—a mighty word, full of mystic meaning.

Here and there we pass a clump of trees, heavily hung with bright scarlet berries, whose abundance, our conductor informs us, foretells a winter of unusual severity. "That's t' way Providence provides for t' birds," he says. It may be so, though I daresay naturalists would offer another explanation. All the same, it is pleasing to see how the blackbirds and thrushes enjoy the feast, though they have already stripped some of the trees bare, and to that extent have spoiled the picture.

Mr. Higgins was not disposed to leave us to the uninterrupted enjoyment of the landscape. He is a thick-set little man, on the wrong side of sixty, I should judge, with a clean top lip and a rather heavy beard; and I suspect that the hair upon his head is growing scanty, but that is a suspicion founded upon the flimsiest of evidence, as I have never yet seen him without the old brown hat which does service Sundays and weekdays alike.

He jogged along by the side of the steady mare, who never varied her four-miles-an-hour pace, and who, I am sure, treated her master's reiterated injunction to "come up" with cool contempt; but he fell back occasionally to jerk a few disjointed remarks towards the occupants of the cart.

"Fox," he said, inclining his head vaguely in the direction of a lonely farm away on the hillside to the right. "Caught him yesterda'... been playin' Old 'Arry wi' t' fowls ... shot him ... good riddance."

We made no comment beyond a polite and inquiring "Oh?" and he continued to be communicative.

"Just swore, did Jake ... swore an' stamped about ... but t' missus ... now there's a woman for you ... she played Old 'Arry wi' him ... set a trap herself... caught him."

Mother Hubbard ventured to surmise that it was the fox which had been captured and not the husband, and Mr. Higgins acquiesced.

"Nought like women for... settin' traps," he continued, with a chuckle, shaking his head slowly for emphasis; "they're all alike ... barrin' they don't catch foxes.... Man-traps mostly ... aye, mantraps."

"That is just like Barjona, love," Mother Hubbard whispered; "he has never a good word for the women."

"You have managed to evade them so far, Mr. Higgins?" I suggested meekly.

"Nay ... bad job ... bad job ... been as big a fool as most ... dead this many a year... dead an' buried twenty year... wide awake now ... old fox now ... no traps ... no, no, no!"

He strode forward to the mare's side again, but I saw him wagging his head for many a minute as he chewed the cud of his reflections. Meanwhile Mother Hubbard, with some hesitation and many an apprehensive look ahead, told me something of his story.

"His mother was a very religious woman, love, but she was no scholar, though she knew her Bible well. And you know, love, the best of people have generally their little fads and failings, and she would call all her boys after the twelve Apostles. At least, love, you understand, she had four sons—not twelve—but she called the first John because he was the beloved disciple, and the next James because he was John's brother. Then came Andrew and afterwards Simon Barjona. They do say—but you know, love, how people talk—that she would have liked eleven boys, missing out Judas because he was a thief and betrayed his Master, but she had only nine children, and five of them were girls.

"I have heard my husband say, love, that when they came to christen the youngest boy the minister was quite angry, and would not have the

'Barjona,' but the mother was much bent on it, and would not substitute Peter, which was what the parson suggested. Anyhow, she registered him in his full name."

"Which name was he called by?" I inquired.

"Oh, Barjona, love, always. And behind his back he is Barjona yet, though he likes to be called Mr. Higgins. But you may give a man a good name when you cannot give him a good nature, and he might as well have been christened Buonaparte for all it has done for him. Oh yes, love, he is close-fisted, is Barjona, and it *is* said that his wife was so tired of his nagging ways that she was quite pleased to go. I'm sure I thank the Lord that I am not Mrs. Higgins, though they do say in the village that Widow Robertshaw would have had him this many a year back."

"But he is an old fox now," I remarked, "and avoids the trap."

It lacked still a couple of hours of noon when Mr. Higgins deposited us at Uncle Ned's lonely hostelry, and drove off in the company of the tired mare and his own complacent thoughts. Ten minutes later I had completely forgotten his existence in the joy of a new experience.

I was there at last! The moors of which I had dreamed so long were a conscious reality. Before me, and on either hand, they stretched until they touched the grey of the sky. The glory of the heather was gone, though sufficient colour lingered in the faded little bells to give a warm glow to the landscape, and to hint of former splendour. My heart ached a wee bit to think that I had come so late, but why should I grudge Nature's silent children their hour of rest? The morning will come when they will again fling aside the garb of night and deck themselves in purple. Besides, there was the gorse, regal amid the sombre browns and olives and neutral tints of the vegetation; and there were green little pools and treacherous-looking bogs, and the uneven, stony pathway which made a thin, grey dividing line as far as the eye could see. What more could the heart of man desire?

How sweet the breath of the air was as it covered my cheeks with its caresses! I *tasted* the fragrance of it, and it gave buoyancy to my body, and the wings of a dove to my soul. I flew back down the years to the dingy sitting-room which held my sacred memories, and saw dear old dad painting his moorland pictures in the glowing embers on the hearth; and I flew upwards to the realms which eye hath not seen, and was glad to

THE MOORS NEAR WINDYRIDGE

remember that the moors are not included amongst the things that are not to be.

Then, characteristically, my mood changed. The sense of desolation got hold of me. I looked for sound of throbbing life and found none: only tokens of a great, an irresistible Power. It may seem strange, but in the silence of that vast wilderness I felt, as I had never felt before, that there must be a God, and that He must be all-powerful. I have not tried to analyse the emotion, but I know my heart began to beat as though I were in the presence of Majesty, and a great awe brooded over my spirit.

Suddenly there was a fluttering of wings in the tangled undergrowth a few yards away, and as my soul came back to earth I saw a hawk swoop down and seize its prey, and then I choked. "If I take the wings of the morning and fly to the uttermost parts of the earth," I said to myself, "I cannot escape the tragedy of life and death—the mystery of suffering."

Mother Hubbard put an arm around my waist and looked questioningly into my eyes, her own being bright with tears. I put my hands upon her cheeks and kissed her.

"Grace Holden is a goose," I said. "How many hours have I been standing still or floating about in vacancy? I believe my dear old Mother Hubbard thought her companion had flown away and left only her chrysalis behind!"

We moved on, and my spirits came out with the sun and the blue sky. After all, I fear I am an emotional creature, for I am my father's daughter, but I think my mother must have been a very practical woman, and bequeathed to me somewhat of the counterpoise, because on the whole I am sure I have more common sense than dreaminess.

We had the moor pretty much to ourselves except for the game, which we rarely saw, and the snipe which frequented the swamps. The one outstanding recollection of the remainder of our two hours' tramp is of a young couple (of human beings, not snipe) who came sauntering along, sucking oranges and throwing the peel on the heath. It seemed like sacrilege, and I went hot with indignation.

"I feel as if I could swear and stamp around, like the ineffective Jake," I exclaimed.

"Yes, love," said Mother Hubbard, but I doubt if she understood.

Mother Hubbard was in excellent trim, and I am beginning to think that there must be a good deal of reserve force in her delicate-looking little body. She led me to the brow of the hill whence one gets an unexpected view of the enchanting beauty of the Romanton valley, and said "There!" with such an air of proud proprietorship, as if she had ordered the show for my special gratification, that I laughed outright.

I negotiated the steep downward path with difficulty, but she went steadily on with the assurance of familiarity, pausing at intervals to point out the more notable landmarks.

We had lunch at one of the large hotels, and if Rose had seen the spread I ordered she would have had good cause to charge me with "swankiness," but I was having a "day out," and such occurrences at Windyridge are destined to be uncommon. Besides, no fewer than three magazines are going to print my old lady's picture, so the agents have sent me thirty shillings—quite a decent sum, and one which you simply *cannot* spend on a day's frolicking in these regions.

When it was over Mother Hubbard showed me all the lions of the place; and after we had drunk a refreshing cup of tea at a café that would do no discredit to Buckingham Palace Road we set out on the return journey.

I was tired already, but I soon forgot the flesh in the spirit sensations that flooded me. We were now traversing the miniature high road which skirts the edge of the moor, and reveals a scene of quiet pastoral beauty along its entire length which is simply charming. I cannot adequately describe it, but I know that viewed in the opalescent light of the early setting sun it was just a fairy wonderland.

The valley is beautifully wooded, and Solomon and the Queen of Sheba together were not so gorgeously arrayed as were the trees on the farther side. A white thread of river gleamed for a while through the meadows, but was soon lost in the haze of evening.

Comfortable grey farms and red-tiled villas lent a homely look to the landscape, and at intervals we passed pretty cottages with old-fashioned gardens, where the men smoked pipes and stood about in their shirt-sleeves, whilst the women lounged in the gateways with an eye to the children whose bed-time was come all too soon for the unwilling spirit.

And, best of all, my journey ended with a great discovery. We had climbed a steep hill, and after a last long look back over my fairy valley I set my face to the dull and level fields. Two hundred yards farther and my astonished eyes saw down below—the back of my own cottage!

That night no vision of factory chimneys disturbed the serenity of my sleep, for a haunting fear had been dispelled.

CHAPTER SEVEN

THE CYNIC DISCOURSES
ON WOMAN

"WOMAN," SAID THE Cynic sententiously, "may be divided into five parts: the Domestic woman, the Social woman, the Woman with a Mission, the New Woman, and the Widow."

"Nonsense!" snapped the vicar's wife, "the widow may be any one of the rest. The mere accident of widowhood cannot affect her special characteristics. The worst of you smart men is that you entirely divorce verity from vivacity. The domestic woman is still a domestic woman, though she become a widow."

"No," returned the Cynic, "the widow is a thing apart, if I may so designate any of your captivating sex. Domestic she may still be in a certain or uncertain subordinate sense, just as the social woman or the woman with a mission may have a strain of domesticity in her make-up; but when all has been said she is still in a separate class; she is, in fact—a widow."

"I remember reading somewhere," I remarked, "that a little widow is a dangerous thing. Manifestly the author of that brilliant epigram was of your way of thinking. He would probably have classed her as an explosive."

He turned to me and smiled mockingly.

"I think all men who have seriously studied the subject, as I have, must have formed a similar opinion. The widow is dangerous because she is a widow. She has tasted of the tree of knowledge of good and evil. She knows the weak places in man's defensive armour. She has acquired skill in generalship which enables her to win her battles. Added to all this is the pathos of her position, which is an asset of no inconsiderable value. She knows to a tick of time when to allure by smiles and melt by tears, and woe to the man who thinketh he standeth when she proposes his downfall."

"My dear Derwent," interposed the squire from the other side the hearth; "you speak, no doubt, from a ripe experience, if an outside one, and no one here will question your authority; but surely the new woman and the woman with a mission may be bracketed together."

The squire was leaning back in a comfortable saddlebag, one leg thrown easily over the other and his hands clasped behind his head. A tolerant half-smile hung about the corners of his lips and lurked in the shadows of his eyes. He has a grand face, and it shows to perfection on an occasion like this.

The vicar sat near him. He is a spare, rather cadaverous man, who lives among Egyptian mummies and Assyrian tablets and palimpsests and first editions, and knows nothing of any statesman later than Cardinal Wolsey. An open book of antiquities lay upon his knee, and his finger-tips were pressed together upon it, but the eyes which blinked over the top of his gold-rimmed spectacles were fixed upon space, and the Cynic's vapourings were as unheeded as yesterday.

The vicar's wife is the very antithesis of her husband. She is a plump, round-faced little body, and was tidily dressed in a black silk of quite modern style with just a trace of elegance, and a berthe of fine old lace which made me break the tenth commandment every time I looked at her. She was evidently on the best of terms with herself, and stood in no awe of anybody, and least of all of the Cynic, whom she regarded with a half-affectionate, half-contemptuous air. She had a way of tossing her head and pursing her lips when he was more than usually aggressive that obviously amused him. I had soon found out that they were old antagonists.

The Cynic himself puzzled me. I scarcely dared to look at him very closely, for I had the feeling that none of my movements escaped his notice, and I had not been able to decide whether his age was thirty or fifty. He is of average height and build, and was somewhat carelessly dressed, I thought. His dinner jacket seemed rather loose, and his starched shirt was decidedly crumpled. I wondered who looked after his ménage.

His hands are clean and shapely, and he knows where to put them, which is generally an indication of good breeding and always of a lack of self-consciousness, and from their condition I judged that he earned his bread in the sweat of his brain rather than of his brow.

As to his face—well, I liked it. It is dark, but frank and open, and he has a good mouth, which can be seen, because he is clean shaven, and his teeth are also good. But then in these degenerate days anyone who has attained middle life may have good teeth: it is all a matter of money.

I think it is the eyes that make the face, however. They are deep grey and remarkably luminous, and on this occasion they simply bubbled over with mischievousness. His smile was never very pronounced, and always more or less satirical, but his eyes flashed and sparkled when he was roused, though they had looked kindly and even plaintive when he arrived, and before he was warmed. He is the sort of man who can do all his talking with his eyes.

A high forehead is surmounted by a mass of hair—once black, but rapidly turning grey—which he evidently treats as of no importance, for it lies, as the children say, "anyhow." But how old he is—I give it up.

He passed his hand through his hair now, with a quick involuntary movement, as he turned to the squire.

"You may bracket the new woman and the woman with a mission together, but you can never make them one. That they have some things in common is nothing to the point. The new woman, as I understand her, has no mission, not even a commission. The new woman is Protest, embodied and at present skirted, but with a protest against the skirt. Her most longed-for goal is the Unattainable, and if by some chance she should reach it she would be dismayed and annoyed. Meantime, with the vision before her eyes of the table of the gods, she cries aloud that she is forced to feed on husks, and as she must hug something, hugs a grievance."

"Philip Derwent," interposed the vicar's wife, "you are in danger of becoming vulgar."

"Vulgarity, madam," he rejoined, "is in these days the brand of refinement. It is only your truly refined man who has the courage to be vulgar in polite society. No other dares to call a spade a spade or a lie a lie. Those who wish to be considered refined speak of the one as an 'agricultural implement' and of the other as a 'terminological inexactitude.'

But to return to our sheep who are clamouring for wolves' clothing——"

"Really, Philip!" protested the vicar's wife, pursing her lips more emphatically than ever.

"The latest incarnation of Protest, if I may so speak, takes the form of a demand for the suffrage, and is accompanied by much beating of drums and——"

"Smashing of windows," I ventured.

He bowed. "And smashing of windows. By and by they will get their desire."

"And so have fulfilled their mission," the squire smiled.

"By no means; they have no mission; they have simply a hunger, or rather a pain which goes away when their appetite is stayed, and comes on again before the meal has been well digested. Then they go forth once more seeking whom or what they may devour."

"Tell us of the woman with a mission," I pleaded.

"Miss Holden is anxious to discover in what category she is to be classed," laughed the squire. "You are treading on dangerous ground, Derwent. Let me advise you to proceed warily."

"Mr. Evans, when a boy at school I learned the Latin maxim—'Truth is often attended with danger,' but I am sure Miss Holden will be merciful towards its humble votary."

I smiled and he continued: "The woman with a mission, Miss Holden, is an altogether superior creature. She may be adorable; on the other hand she may be a nuisance and a bore. Everything depends on the mission—and the woman."

"A safe answer, Philip," sneered the vicar's wife, and the squire smiled.

"There is no other safe way, madam, than the way of Truth, and I am treading it now. Even if the woman be a nuisance, even if the mission be unworthy, she who makes it hers may be ennobled. Let us assume that she believes with all her heart that she has been sent into the world for one definite purpose—shall we say to work for the abatement of the smoke nuisance? That involves, amongst other things——"

"Depriving poor weak man of his chief solace—tobacco," snapped the vicar's wife.

"Exactly. Now see how this strengthens her character and calls out qualities of endurance and self-sacrifice. The poor weak man, her husband, deprived of his chief solace, tobacco, turns to peppermints, moroseness and bad language. His courtesy is changed to boorishness, his placidity to snappishness. All this is trying to his wife, but being a woman with a mission she regards these things philosophically as incidental to a transition period, and she bears her cross with ever-increasing gentleness and——"

"Drives her husband to the devil and herself into the widows' compartment," interrupted the vicar's wife, with disgust in her voice. "Miss Holden, do you sing?"

"I have no music," I replied, "but may I 'say a piece' instead, as the village children put it?" I turned to the Cynic and made him a mock curtsey:

> "Small blame is ours
> For this unsexing of ourselves, and worse
> Effeminising of the male. We were
> Content, sir, till you starved us, heart and brain.
> All we have done, or wise or otherwise
> Traced to the root was done for love of you.
> Let us taboo all vain comparisons,
> And go forth as God meant us, hand in hand,
> Companions, mates and comrades evermore;
> Two parts of one divinely ordained whole."

"Bravo!" said the squire, and the vicar murmured, "Thank you," very politely. The Cynic laughed and rose from his chair.

"I will take it lying down," he said. "Mr. Evans, may I look in the cabinet and see if there is anything Miss Holden can sing?"

I had to do it, because the cabinet contained all the Scotch songs I love so well. I was my own accompanist, *faute de mieux*, but the Cynic turned the leaves, and contributed a couple of songs himself. He talks better than he sings. The squire wanted us to try a duet, and the vicar's wife was also very pressing, but one has to draw the line somewhere. The only pieces we both knew were so sentimental that my sense of humour would have tripped me up, I know, and I should have come a cropper.

Just as coffee was brought in the squire asked me if I would sing for him, "Oh wert thou in the cauld blast." I saw he really wanted it, so I found the music, though I had to choke back the lump in my throat. I had never sung it since that memorable evening when we sat together—dad and I—on the eve of his death, and he had begged for it with his eyes. "I know, dad, dear," I said; "I must close with your favourite," and he whispered, "For the last time, lassie." And so it had been.

The tears fell as I sang, and the Hall and its inmates faded from my view. The Cynic must have left my side, for when at length I ventured to look round he was across the room examining a curio. But the squire rose and thanked me in a very low voice, and his own eyes were bright with tears that did not fall.

Soon after, the vicar's carriage came, and the Cynic accepted the offer of a lift to the cross-roads. I left at the same time, but the squire insisted on accompanying me. Under cover of the darkness he remarked:

"That was my wife's song. It gave me much pleasure and some pain to hear it again; but it hurt you?"

I told him why, and he said quite simply, "Then we have another bond in common."

"Another?" I inquired, but he did not explain; instead he asked:

"How fares your ideal? Have you met him of the cloven foot in Windyridge yet?"

"I fear I brought him with me," I replied, "and I fancy I have seen his footprints in the village. All the same, I do not yet regret my decision. I am very happy here and have forgotten some of my London nightmares, and am no longer 'tossed by storm and flood.' My Inner Self and I are on the best of terms."

He sighed. "Far be it from me to discourage you; and indeed I am glad that the moors have brought you peace. To brood over wrongs we cannot put right is morbid and unhealthy; it saps our vitality and makes us unfit for the conflicts we have to wage. And yet how easy it is for us to let this consideration lead us to the bypath meadows of indifference and self-indulgence. You remember Tennyson:

"'Is it well that while we range with Science, glorying in the Time,
City children soak and blacken soul and sense in city slime?'

"I have led a strenuous life, and taken some part in the battle, but now
I have degenerated into a Lotus-eater, with no heart for the fray, 'Lame
and old and past my time, and passing now into the night.'"
"Nay," I said, "let me quote Clough in answer to your Tennyson:

"'Say not the struggle nought availeth,
    The labour and the wounds are vain,
The enemy faints not nor faileth,
    And as things have been they remain.

For while the tired waves, vainly breaking,
    Seem here no painful inch to gain,
Far back, through creeks and inlets making,
    Comes silent, flooding in, the main.'

"You are no Lotus-eater: no shirker. You are just resting in the garden
in the evening of a well-spent day, and that is right."
"For me there is no rest," he replied. "To-morrow I go to Biarritz, and
thence wherever my fancy or my doctor's instructions send me; but I shall
carry with me the burdens of the village. It is selfish of me to tell you this,
for I would not make you sad, but I am a lonely man, and I am going away
alone, and somewhat against my will, but Trempest insists.

"I think it has done me good to unburden myself to you, and I will say
only this one word more. Always, when I return, there has been some
tragedy, great or small, which I think I might have hindered."
"Surely not," I murmured, "in so small a place."
He rested his arm upon my garden gate and smiled. "A week ago
I witnessed a terrible encounter between two redbreasts in the lane yonder.
They are very tenacious of their rights, and one of them, I imagine, was a
trespasser from the other side the hedge. They are country birds, yet very
pugnacious, and the little breasts of these two throbbed with passion. But
when I came near them they flew away, and I hope forgot their differences.

I never even raised a stick—my mere presence was sufficient. And therein is a parable. Good-night, Miss Holden, and au revoir!"

He opened the gate, raised his hat, and was gone.

CHAPTER EIGHT

CHRISTMAS DAY AT WINDYRIDGE

CHRISTMAS HAS COME and gone, and so far not a flake of snow has fallen. Rain there has been in abundance, and in the distance dense banks of fog, but no frost to speak of, and none of the atmospheric conditions I have always associated with a northern Yuletide.

Christmas Day itself, however, proved enjoyable if not wildly exciting. The air was "soft," as the natives say, and the sun was shining mistily when I stepped into the garden, now bare of attractions save for the Christmas roses, whose pure white petals bowed their heads in kindly greeting to the wrinkled face of Earth, their mother. The starlings were whistling as cheerily as if spring was come, and a solitary missel-thrush was diligently practising a Christmas ditty on the bare branches of the hawthorn.

"A merry Christmas, Mother Hubbard!" I called through the open window, with such unwonted vigour that the old lady, whose toilet was not completed, flung a shawl hastily around her shoulders, only to be reassured by my hearty laugh.

Over the breakfast table we drew up the day's programme. It was no difficult task. Mother Hubbard would occupy the morning in preparing the great dinner, and from these preparations I was to be rigorously excluded. To my old friend this was a holy-day, but one to be marked by a sacrificial offering of exceptional magnitude, she being the High Priestess who alone might enter into the mysteries; but I did not mind, seeing that I was to be allowed to do my part in consuming the sacrifice.

The afternoon was to be devoted to rest, and in the evening we were to go to Farmer Goodenough's, where the youngsters were already wild in anticipation of the glories of a Christmas-tree.

So I was dismissed to "make the beds" and dust my own room, and having done this I went to church in the temple which is not made with hands. I had intended going to Fawkshill, but the angels of God met me on the way, and turned me aside into the fields which lead to Marsland. When I reached the wood I knelt on the soft, thick carpet of fallen leaves and said my prayers amid the solitude, with the running brook for music and all Nature for priest.

What a loud voice Nature has to those who have ears to hear, yet withal how sweet and forceful. They tell us that if our faculties were less dull we should hear in every stem and twig and blade of grass the throbbing of the engines and the whir and clatter of the looms which go on day and night unceasingly. It is well for us that we are not so highly tuned, but it is also well if our spiritual perceptions are keen enough to find tongues in trees and sermons in stones, and to interpret their language. I am but a dunce as yet, but I have learned one thing since I came to this northern school—I have learned to listen, and I am beginning to understand something of what God has to teach us by the mouth of his dumb prophets. Anyhow, I went home with peace in my heart and goodwill to all men; also with a mighty hunger.

The menu was roast turkey and plum pudding, to be followed by cheese and dessert, but on this occasion there was no "following." Imagine two domesticated women, and one of them—the little one—with the appetite and capacity of a pet canary, seated opposite a bird like that the squire had sent us, which had meat enough upon it to serve a Polytechnic party; and imagine the same couple, having done their duty womanfully upon the bird, confronted with a plum pudding of the dimensions Mother Hubbard's sense of proportion had judged necessary, and one of the twain compelled either to eat to repletion or to wound the feelings of the pudding's author—and then say whether in your opinion cheese and dessert were not works of supererogation!

After we had cleared the things away and drawn our rocking chairs up to the fire, the old clock ticked us off to sleep in five minutes; and then that part of me which it is not polite to mention took its revenge for having been made to work overtime on a holiday. I dreamed!

I was running away from Chelsea in the dead of night, clothed in my night-dress and holding my bedroom slippers in my hand. A great fear was upon me that I should be discovered and frustrated in my purpose; and as I strove to turn the heavy key in the lock my heart thumped against my chest and the perspiration poured down my face. At first the bolt resisted my efforts, but at length it shot back with a great noise, which awakened Madam Rusty, who opened her bedroom window as I rushed out on to the pavement and cried "Murder!" at the same time emptying the contents of the water jug upon me.

Fear gave wings to my feet and I fled, followed by a howling crowd which grew bigger every moment and gained on me rapidly. By this time I realised that I was carrying madam's best silver tea-pot under my arm, and I wanted to drop it but dared not.

Then I found myself in the lane at Windyridge, with the squire dressed as a policeman keeping back the crowd, whilst Mother Hubbard, without her bodice, as I had seen her in the morning, took my hand—and the tea-pot—and hurried me towards the cottage. It was just in sight when Madam Rusty jumped out of a doorway in her night-cap and dressing-gown and shouted 'Bo!' waving her arms about wildly, and as I hesitated which way to turn she flung herself upon me and seized my hair in both her hands. As I screamed wildly, I saw the Cynic leap the wall in his golf suit, and woke just in time to save myself considerable embarrassment.

"What was it, love?" inquired Mother Hubbard, who had been aroused by my screams and was genuinely alarmed.

"I don't quite know," I replied; "but I think the turkey was quarrelsome and could not quite hit it with the plum pudding."

Mother Hubbard composed herself to sleep again; and in order to prevent a repetition of my unhappy experience I got my books and proceeded to do my accounts.

I have not been idle by any means during these months, and my balance is quite satisfactory. I have painted quite a number of miniatures, and have prepared and sold several floral designs for book covers and decorative purposes. I see plainly that I am not likely to starve if health is vouchsafed to me, and I was never more contented in my life. I wonder, though, what it really is that makes me so. It cannot be sufficiency of work merely, for that was never lacking in the London days; and as for friends, I have, besides Mother Hubbard, only Farmer Goodenough and the squire, and he is away and likely to be for months. I think it is the sense of "aliveness" that makes me happy. Some folk would call my life mere existence, but I feel as if I never really lived until now; and I hanker after neither theatres, nor whist-drives, nor picture-shows, nor parties.

Parties! Why, we have parties in Windyridge, and the motherkin and I went to one that evening. We put on our best bibs and tuckers—not our *very* best, but I wore my blue voile with the oriental trimmings which even Rose used to admit set off my figure to advantage, and Mother Hubbard donned the famous black satin, and added to its glories the soft Shetland shawl which I had given her that morning.

Tea was prepared in the spacious kitchen, which had room enough and to spare for the fifteen people of all ages who were assembled there. It is a kitchen lifted bodily out of a story book, without one single alteration. The room is low, so that Farmer Goodenough touches the beams quite easily when he raises his hand, and his head only just clears the hams which are suspended from them; and it is panelled all the way round in oak. There are oak doors, oak cupboards, oak settles and tables, and an oak dresser, all with the polish of old age upon them and with much quaint carving; all of which is calculated to drive a connoisseur to covetousness and mental arithmetic. An immense fire roared up the great chimney, and its flames were reflected in the polished case of the mahogany grand-father's clock, which seemed to me rather out of place amongst so much oak, but which, with slow dignity, ticked off the time in one corner.

On the far side of the room, near the deeply recessed window, was the Christmas-tree—a huge tree for that low room, and gay with glittering glass ornaments in many grotesque shapes, brightly coloured toys, and wax candles, as yet unlighted.

The younger members of the party were gathered near it in a little group, whispering excitedly, and pointing out objects of delight with every one of which each individual had made himself familiar hours before.

Grandpa Goodenough, a hale old man of eighty, and to be distinguished from Grand*father* Goodenough, his son, smoked a long clay pipe from his place on the settle near the hearth, and smiled on everybody.

His daughter-in-law, who looked much too young to be a grandmother, bustled about in the scullery, being assisted in her activities by her eldest daughter, Ruth, and her son Ben's wife, Susie, and obstructed by her husband who, with a sincere desire to be useful, contrived to be always in the most inconvenient place at the most awkward time.

Mother Hubbard and I had been invited to step into the parlour, but preferred the more homely atmosphere of the kitchen, so we took our seats on the settle, opposite to that occupied by Grandpa.

By and by tea was ready and we were instructed to "pull our chairs up" and "reach to." What a time we had! If tables ever do groan that one ought to have done so, for it had a heavy load which we were all expected to lighten, but nobody seemed to think it might be necessary to press anybody to eat.

"Now you know you're all welcome," said Farmer Goodenough heartily, when the youngest grandchild had asked what I took to be a blessing. "We're not allus botherin' folks to have some more when there's plenty before 'em, an' all they've got to do is to reach out for 't; but if you don't all have a good tea it's your own fault, an' don't blame *me*. 'Let us eat, drink, an' be merry,' as t' Owd Book bids us."

The way the ham disappeared was a revelation to me. Farmer Goodenough stood to carve, and after a while took off his coat, apparently in order that he might be able to mop his face with his shirt sleeves and so not seriously interrupt his operations. Plates followed each other in unbroken succession, until at last the good man threw down the knife and fork and pushed back his chair.

"Well, this beats all!" he said. "Amos, lad, thee take hold. Thou's had a fair innings: give thy dad a chance."

Where the little Goodenoughs put the ham and the sponge cake, the tarts and the trifle, the red jelly and the yellow jelly and the jelly with the pine-apple in it I do not pretend to know. They expanded visibly, and when the youngest grandchild, a cherubic infant of three, leaned back and sighed, and whispered with tears in his voice, "Reggie can't eat no more, muvver," I felt relieved.

It was over at last and the table cleared in a twinkling. Ben whisked away the remnants of the ham into the larder. The women folk carried the crockery into the scullery, and whilst they were engaged in washing it up the boys disappeared into remote places with the fragments of the feast, and Mother Hubbard swept the crumbs away and folded the cloth.

"Now," said Reggie, with another little sigh, but with just a suspicion of sunshine in his eyes, "now we'se goin' to p'ay, an 'ave ze pwesents off ze Kwismastwee."

And so we did. Amos, as the eldest son at home, lit the candles, and Grandpa distributed the gifts, which were insignificant enough from the monetary point of view, but weighted in every case with the affection and goodwill of the burly farmer and his wife. There was even a box of chocolates for me, and with its aid I succeeded in winning the heart of the melancholy Reggie.

Then came the games. I wish Rose and the boarders at No. 8 could have seen the demure Miss Holden of former days walking round and round a big circle, one hand in Reggie's and the other clasped by a red-cheeked farmer, whilst a dozen voices sang, and hers as loudly as any:

"The farmer's dog was in the yard
And Bingo was his name-O!"

Then came the mad scramble of "Shy Widow" and the embarrassments of the "Postman's Knock," though nobody had letters for me, except Reggie, who had one—very sticky and perfumed with chocolate—and Susie's little daughter, Maud, who gave me three, very shyly, but accompanied by an affectionate hug, which I returned. After this, crackers, with all their accompaniments of paper caps and aprons, and by the time these had been worn and exchanged and torn the youngsters were clamouring for supper. Supper! Ye gods!

When this repast was ended and the younger members of the party had been packed off to bed—for only Mother Hubbard and I were to leave the farmer's hospitable home that night—some of the grown-ups proposed a dance.

Grandpa shook his head in protest. "Nay, nay," he said in his thin, piping voice; "I don't hold wi' dancin'. Never did. You were never browt up to dance, Reuben, you weren't."

"Reyt enough, father," responded his son, "but you know things has changed sin' I were a lad. You remember what t' Owd Book says; I don't just rightly call t' words to mind, but summat about t' owd order changin'. We mun let t' young uns have a bit of a fling."

"They danced in t' Bible, grandpa," said Rebecca saucily.

"Well, they may ha' done," rejoined the old man, retiring to the settle; "but I weren't browt up i' that way, an' your father weren't neither. I were allus taught 'at it were a sort of a devil's game, were dancing."

However, dance they did, and I played for them, doing my best with the crazy old box-o'-music in the parlour; and as I glanced through the open door I saw that Grandpa was following it all with great interest, beating time the while, in uncertain fashion, with head and hand.

CHAPTER NINE

MRS. BROWN
EXPLAINS

THERE WAS A funeral in the village on the Wednesday of last week. On the previous Sunday Mother Hubbard had assured me with great solemnity that something of the sort was going to happen, for had not a solitary magpie perched upon our garden wall and waved his handsome tail in full view of the window for at least a minute? What connection there was between his visit and the calamity which it foretold was not clear to me, but it appears that the magpie is a bird of omen, and there is an old rhyme which in these parts is considered oracular:

"One for sorrow,
      And two for mirth;
Three for a wedding
      And four for a birth."

However that may be, it is a fact that in the late afternoon Dr. Trempest called to inform me that Farmer Brown was dead.

"He has lasted twice as long as anyone could have foreseen," he said. "Poor chap, it's a mercy it's all over."

The whole countryside was inches deep in snow when they buried him in the little God's acre that clings to the side of the hill at the point where the roads diverge. The grave-digger had a hard task, for we had had a fortnight of severe frost; but he bent to his work with the grim persistence of the man who knows that the last enemy is a hard master, and that there must be no tarrying in his service.

All the village turned out to the funeral, and there was a great crowd of invited mourners. It struck me as strange that so many coaches should be provided and that the last sad rites should partake of the nature of a public spectacle, for surely when we have given our loved ones into God's keeping it is most seemly to lay all that is human of them in the lap of earth reverently and with simplicity; but the Yorkshire folk make it an occasion of display, fearing, perhaps, to dishonour their dead, and dreading even more the criticism and displeasure of their neighbours.

When the grave had been filled in and the upturned earth was covered with the evergreens and wreaths which loving hands had brought and left there, I went and stood beside the grave and thought of Farmer Brown's parting words. I suppose it is heretical to pray for the dead, but I did it.

Yesterday I went to see Mrs. Brown, taking the photographs and a framed enlargement with me. It was a hard tramp, and my arms ached before the journey's end was reached, but I am wonderfully "fit" just now, and I thoroughly enjoyed the walk. Well—perhaps I must modify that. There was always present with me the anticipation of a depressing scene, and that marred the enjoyment somewhat, though it could not destroy it.

Yet to feel the sting of a north-easterly wind on one's cheek, and the sensation of crunching snow beneath one's feet, with a bright blue sky overhead and the far-away smell of spring in one's nostrils, was to experience something of the joy of life.

Here and there great drifts of snow were piled up against the banks and walls, and I knew that sheep and even men were sometimes lost in them, but I was safe enough, for the road was fairly well trodden, and when I left it and climbed the stile into the fields leading to the farm the track was quite discernible.

It is a mistake to anticipate, and to dread what lies behind the veil is folly. Mrs. Brown taught me that in a very few moments. There was no gloom about the kitchen where she and her daughter Jane were busily engaged in household duties, though somehow one felt that sorrow dwelt there as a guest.

I explained the purpose of my visit, and the mother's eyes grew dim with tears.

"He never breathed a word," she said; "but that was just Greenwood to nowt. He was allus tryin' to do someb'dy a good turn, but so as they shouldn't know it, and it was just like the dear lad to think o' them he was goin' to leave, an' try to pleasure 'em."

"Perhaps you would rather open the parcels yourselves when I am gone," I suggested, but the widow shook her head.

"Nay, I'd like to see them whilst you're here, miss, if you don't mind. Jane, love, put the kettle on an' make a cup of tea for the young lady. I will confess 'at I had fret just a bit 'cos we haven't any picture of father, except one 'at was took soon after we were wed, and that's over thirty year sin'; and I can't tell you how glad I shall be to 'ave 'em."

I had done my best, and I will admit that the enlargement pleased *me*, but I was ill prepared for the effect it produced upon the widow and the daughter. The girl was in her twenties, and looked matter-of-fact enough, but the moment she saw it she took the frame in her hands, pressed her lips to the glass, and cried with a dry sob, "Oh, dad, dear, I cannot bear it!" and then knelt down on the broad fender and prepared some toast.

But her mother placed the picture against the big Bible on the high drawers and gazed steadily at it for a moment or two, after which she came up to me where I was standing, and throwing her arms around my neck drew my head on to her shoulder, for she is a tall woman, and kissed me again and again. But only one or two big tears fell upon my cheek, and she wiped them away hastily with her apron.

"I can't help it, miss," she said, "you'll not take offence, I'm sure. But I can't do anything but love you for what you've done for me an' Jane. You've brought more comfort to this house than I ever thought the Lord 'ud send us, an' I hope He'll pay you back a hundredfold, for I cannot."

I wonder why one should feel so warm and virtuous for having done one's duty. I had put my heart into the work, as I always do—for who would be a mere mechanic whom God meant for a craftsman?—but the farmer had paid me the price I asked, and the whole transaction had been conducted on strict business lines. What right had I to be pleased with the super-payment of love? But I was.

Over the teacups Mrs. Brown opened her heart to me. Jane had gone away to the dairy, and I think her mother spoke more freely in her absence, or perhaps the feeling of strangeness had by that time been dispelled.

I saw it did her good to talk and I rarely interrupted her. She sat with her cup on her knee, and her eyes fixed, for the most part, upon the hearth.

"He seemed to suffer terrible towards the end," she said, "but he allus put a good face on it an' tried to keep it from us. But choose how he suffered you never 'eard one word of complaint, an' he wouldn't let us say ought hard against Him above. And yet, you know, he was never what you might call a church member, an' he wasn't one 'at went regular to either church or chapel. You see, it's a matter o' two mile to t' chapel at Windyridge, an' t' nearest church 'll be gettin' on for four mile away.

"An' he wasn't one 'at spoke a deal about religion, neither, nobbut he wouldn't hear anybody speak a word agen it. There isn't a labourer or a farmer or t' doctor himself 'at 'ud use a bad word i' front o' Greenwood, an' he never did himself. He used to sit i' that high-backed chair where you're sittin' now, every night of his life, wi' that big Bible on his knee, an' read in it, but he never read it out loud, an' what Scripture we got we'd to read for ourselves. Nobbut he'd quote it now an' then, like, when there were any 'casion.

"I've thought often sin' he came home that day an' told us what were goin' to happen, an' especially sin' he were laid up, 'at it 'ud maybe have been better if he'd read it up for us all to hear, an' talked about it a bit, but it wasn't his way, wasn't that. He was same as he couldn't, but I wonder sometimes if it 'ud have saved us this trouble."

"But could anything really have saved it?" I inquired. "He told me it was something internal which could not be accounted for."

"Ah, miss," she replied, "there's a kind of illness 'at you can't get any doctor to cure, but Greenwood's illness could be accounted for when you know all. It's true enough 'at there wasn't a stronger nor likelier man i' t' West Ridin' than my 'usband, nor a steadier. And he never ailed owt, never. Day in an' day out he did his work wi' t' best on 'em, an' took all his meals hearty. But he lived wi' a great big wound in his inside this last ten year for all that, an' they can say what they like, but I know if he hadn't had that sore in his soul he'd never have had that bad place in his body.

"You can't go by appearances, miss. My husband was right enough in his body, but he was sick at heart. It's not easy tellin', but I can tell you, though I'm sure I don't know why. We never had but two children, Jane an' her brother Joseph. My husband was called after his mother—her name was Greenwood afore she was married—so we called our lad Joseph after his grandfather. He came within a year of our gettin' wed, and a brighter little lad never breathed. Eh! he was that bonny an' sweet . . .

"How is it, miss, 'at some grows up so crook'd an' others i' t' same family never gives you a minute's trouble? Our Jane has been a comfort to us both all her life, but Joe has broke our rest many a hundred nights. He was same as he took t' wrong road from bein' a little lad o' twelve. He would go his own road, an' it was allus t' wrong road. He'd work if it pleased him, an' he wouldn't if it didn't, an' you could neither coax him nor thrash him into it. His father tried both ways, an' I'm sure I did all I could. An' the way he sauced his father you wouldn't believe for a young lad.

"He had his good points, too, for he wouldn't lie to save his own skin or anybody else's, an' he was as honest as they make 'em. But he was self-willed and 'eadstrong past all tellin'. He used to laugh about the devil, an' say it was all bosh an' old wives' tales, but if ever a man was possessed wi' one our Joseph was when he were nineteen.

"There isn't a church for four mile; no, but there are two drink shops easy enough to get at. Oh, miss, why do they let the devil set traps to catch the souls o' men? They can't keep him out of us, God knows, but they've no need to build places for him to live in, and license him to do his devil's work. O Lord, why didn't You save our Joe?

"He came home drunk the day he was nineteen, an' his father was just full up wi' grief an' vexation. An' men don't bear wi' it same as women do. He put the Bible down on the table, Greenwood did, an' he went up to t' lad, an' he said:

"'I won't have it, Joe. I've told you afore an' I tell you again, if you're goin' to come home drunk ye'll sleep in t' barn, for I won't have you in t' house.'

"Oh, I can't bide to think of it, but Joe swore a great oath, an' clenched his fist an' hit his father in t' body; an' then Greenwood seized him by t' coat collar an' flung him in t' yard, an' locked t' door agen him. I shall never forget it. I cried an' begged him to go out to t' lad, but he wouldn't. He said he could sleep in t' barn, but until he were sober he shouldn't come into t' house.

"Well, I said no more, but crept upstairs to bed an' sobbed for an hour, an' then I heard Greenwood shouting 'at t' barn was afire. We all rushed out, an' there was soon plenty of 'elp, but we lost two cows an' a lot o' hay that night; but worse than that, we lost our Joe. Not 'at he were burned or ought o' that sort. He fired t' barn an' made off, an' his father never tried to follow him. But from that day to this we've never heard one word of our lad.

"I can hear them beasts roaring with pain in the night yet, but you know, miss, that was soon over, an' they got their release. But it's different wi' us. We aren't beasts. Greenwood could bear pain. He made nought o' the blow, though it was a savage 'un, but it was the thought of it 'at hurt him, an' the thought of him 'at did it, an' wondering what had come of him. Pain's nought; any woman can bide pain—an' God knows 'at we have to do, oft enough—but when your soul gets hurt there's no putting any ointment on *it*, an' there's no doctor in t' world can do you any good.

"God? Oh yes, miss, I know, but I don't understand. I believe Greenwood did, an' he went home peaceful, if not happy; an' I'm not murmuring. I believe the Lord 'll work it all out i' time, but it's a puzzle. I should ha' lost heart an' hope but for Greenwood; but I'm goin' to hold on for his sake an' Jane's—an' for our Joe's."

As I walked home the lingering sun cast long, black shadows athwart the snow, but the shadows were only on the surface, and did not soil the purity of the mantle which God had thrown over the earth.

CHAPTER TEN

INTRODUCES WIDOW ROBERTSHAW

I HAVE BEEN having quite an exciting time lately. If you have never lived in a small hamlet of a hundred souls or thereabouts, with smaller tributary hamlets dropped down in the funniest and most unlikely places within easy walking distance, you do not know how very full of excitement life can be.

Why, when I was living at No. 8 nobody displayed very much emotion when the jeweller at the end of the street suffered "the slings and arrows of outrageous fortune" as the result of the undesired patronage of connoisseurs in diamonds; and even when we learned that the poor man had been found gagged and bound to his office chair and more dead than alive, the languid interest of the company was sufficiently expressed in the "Hard luck!" of the gentlemen, and the "What a shame!" of the ladies.

"That's the fire-engine," someone would remark, as the horses dashed past to the clang of the warning bell; but we sent up our plates for a second helping of boiled mutton with never a thought as to the destination and fate of the brave fellows who might be about to risk their lives in a grim struggle with flame and smoke.

Murders and assassinations and suicides were discussed, if they had been conducted respectably, with the same air of commiseration as was employed when a fellow-boarder complained of headache; if they were not respectable we did not discuss them at all. It took a first-class society scandal to really stir us, and then we gathered in groups and became thoroughly interested—the women, I mean, of course. The men were just as interested but not so ready to admit it, and professed to be debating politics. I sometimes wonder if what the Psalmist said in his haste might not have been affirmed more leisurely. However, that is nothing to the point; ordinarily, there is no denying the fact that we were bored, or perhaps I ought to adopt the modern expression and say "blasé."

Here in Windyridge that word and its significance are unknown.

When old Mrs. Smithies' sow had a litter of seventeen pigs we all threw down our work and went across to congratulate her, and stopped each other in the street to discuss the momentous event, and to speculate on the difference it would make in that worthy lady's fortunes.

On the other hand, when old Woodman's dog, Cæsar, was reported to have gone mad, we were wildly excited for the space of one whole day, and spent our time in telling each other what dreadful things *might* have happened if he had not been securely chained up from the moment the symptoms became ominous; and recalling lurid and highly-imaginative stories of men who, as the result of dog-bites, had foamed at the mouth, and had to be roped down to their beds. Which reminded someone else of the bull that old Green used to have, away yonder past Uncle Ned's, which went mad one Whitsuntide, and tore along the road three good miles to Windyridge, roaring furiously, and scattering the school children, who were assembled for the treat, in all directions; and badly goring this very dog Cæsar, who had pluckily charged him.

This week's excitements began on Monday, when young Smiddles, who had been "gas-acting," according to his mother, ran his fist through the window-pane, and cut his arm very badly and even dangerously. Smiddles' roaring must have rivalled that of old Green's bull, and, supplemented by his mother's screams, it served to rouse the whole village.

Smiddles' sister, a buxom young woman of plain appearance but sound sense, threatened to box the sufferer's ears if he did not "stop that din," and though much alarmed at the flow of blood, made some efforts to staunch it with her apron.

I had already gained an ill-deserved reputation for surgery, principally on account of the possession of a medicine chest and an "Ambulance" certificate, and my services were speedily requisitioned by the fleet-footed son of the next door neighbour, who bade me come at once, as "Smiddles' lad" was "bleeding to death on t' hearthstone."

After I had prevented the realisation of this fatality by means of a tight bandage, and made the patient as comfortable as a sling permits, I despatched the mercuric youth to summon Dr. Trempest, as I was afraid some stitches would be necessary, and went out to find the street buzzing with excitement, and my humble self regarded as only slightly less than superhuman.

No sooner had this sensation died down than the village thermometer rose, two days later, to fever heat on the report that little Willie Jones had ventured to test the ice upon the huge water-butt which occupied a slightly elevated position at the end of his father's house and was "drownded dead for sure."

Not a soul in the village knew what course to pursue under the circumstances, and every eager helper might have avowed with truth and sincerity that he had done the things he ought not to have done, and left undone the things he ought to have done; and it was fortunate for poor little Willie that my First Aid lessons had qualified me for dealing with an emergency of this kind.

Farmer Goodenough and I worked hard for an hour, and my arms ached with the effort, but at length the reluctant engine began to move, throbbing fitfully but with increasing strength; and hot flannels and heated bricks, with judicious but energetic rubbing, completed the treatment and brought life and colour back again, so that when the doctor arrived there was little left to be done.

I believe I was excited myself when it was all over, and if my head had not been fixed very solidly upon my shoulders it would certainly have been turned that day by the ridiculous and extravagant eulogies of my neighbours.

Then followed the great blizzard. I suppose our cousins across the water would have small respect for such an unpretentious specimen as we experienced, but to me it was a revelation of what old Mother Nature can do when she clenches her teeth and puts her hand to it.

A bright but grey sky overhung the earth when I set out soon after dinner for a brisk constitutional, and I never for a moment anticipated any change in the conditions. For some weeks past we had had alternations of frost and snow and thaw, and for several days the bare, brown earth had been frozen hard, and the roadway was furrowed as a field, with ice filling every rut and wrinkle.

It was an ideal day for a sharp walk, provided one's organs were sound and one's limbs supple, and though a thousand needles pricked my cheeks and hands, and my ears smarted with the pinching they got, my whole body was soon aglow and I revelled in the encounter.

I took the downward road which winds slowly round to Marsland, and tried to discover the heralds of spring. On such a day everybody should be an optimist. I think I generally am as regards myself, whatever the weather may be like, but I must admit that so far I have had little cause for being anything else. It is only when I begin to dwell on the miseries of other people, and the wrongs which it seems impossible to put right, that the black mood settles upon me.

But on this particular day I felt on good terms with the world, and thought of the sunny days which lay ahead, and of the coming morning, when the heather bells would feel the warm breath of summer upon their face, and open their eyes in loving response to her kiss.

And here and there in the shelter of the hedges, and by the banks of the ice-bound stream where the bridge crosses it, I found the heralds I sought—tiny shoots of green pushing their way through the hard soil or the warm coverlet of faded leaves. By and by the icy fingers will have to relax their grasp, and the woods and hedgerows will be gay with the little fairy creatures, who dress so daintily in colours of a hundred hues for our enjoyment, and who smile, perhaps, to think what a limited monarchy King Frost maintains after all.

I am well known by now, and every farmer's boy who passes me exchanges greetings, sometimes with a half-hearted movement of the hand in the direction of the cap, but oftener with the smile of recognition which betokens comradeship. For our relations are on the most cordial footing of strict equality; we are all workmen, each after his kind, servants of one Master; and if God gives us grace to use our opportunities as we ought we may all enter, even now, into the joy of the Lord. There is a vast difference, as I have learned, between servility and respectfulness, and I believe I am as much respected as the squire, though with less reason: and nobody is unduly deferential even to him.

THE ROAD TO MARSLAND

The good women in the cluster of cottages down the lane waved their hands as I passed, and a couple of maidens of tender years, one fair, the other with raven locks, ran out and seized each an arm, and escorted me a hundred yards along my way.

I sat on the bridge for a while at the foot of the hill, and it may have been the network of trees in the little wood which hid from my eyes the approaching storm. For with the suddenness of a panther it sprang upon me. There had been a fairly stiff breeze at my back, which had helped me along famously, taking toll of my ears for its fee, but now, as if its playful humour had been changed to madness, it lashed me mercilessly with knotted whips of frozen rain.

Expecting every minute to reach the shelter of a farm I hurried forward, whilst the storm howled and raged behind and about me. It was well for me that the storm was at my back, for my face was entirely unprotected and the sleet was driven past me in straight, almost horizontal lines, which obliterated the landscape in a moment, and stung my neck so that I could have cried with pain. When I had rounded the bend and climbed the stiff ascent my plight was worse. There was no protection of any kind, and my face suffered so terribly that I began to be alarmed. To add to my difficulties every landmark had been blotted out, and the road itself was becoming indistinguishable from the low-lying edge of moor over which it wound.

Like ten thousand shrouded demons let loose to work destruction the wind hissed and shrieked and roared, and tore across my path with a force I could scarcely resist. Ten minutes after its commencement I was treading ankle-deep in snow, and I could see that drifts were beginning to form where the road had been brought below the level of the rising and lumpy moor. I would have given much to have been sitting by Mother Hubbard's side, listening to the click of the needles, but I was indeed thankful that she had not accompanied me.

After the first sensation of alarm and dismay the novelty of the situation began to appeal to me. One can get accustomed even to being thrashed by the genii of the air, and I became conscious of a certain exhilaration which was almost pleasant, even whilst I was ardently longing for the sight of a friendly roof.

I know now that I missed the broad road, and took a narrower one which sloped down at an acute angle, but I was unconscious of this at the time, and was only grateful to find some protection from the high wall upon my left. I know also that I had passed two or three farms where I might have been hospitably received, but no fog could have proved a thicker curtain than that impenetrable veil of driven snow, and I never even guessed at their existence.

The moor now began to rise steeply upon my right, and as I stumbled forward, holding my hat upon my head with both hands, I suddenly found myself upon hard ground again, with scarcely a trace of snow to be seen, and with a whole row of cottages on one side of the road, in which blazing fires offered me a warm welcome. I could hardly realise that I had found refuge.

The roadway was only wide enough to accommodate a good-sized dray, and was separated from the houses by the narrowest of footpaths, and flanked on the right by the bare side of the hill, which rose precipitously from the ground, to be soon concealed in the mantle of the storm. Seen indistinctly as I saw it then it appeared more like a railway cutting than anything else, and I could only marvel at the eccentricity of man in erecting houses in such an unpromising locality. However, for the mariner in danger of shipwreck to criticise the harbour of refuge in which he finds himself is mean ingratitude.

"Nay, to be sure!" The ejaculation came from the mouth of a comely woman of considerable proportions who filled up the doorway of the cottage opposite to which I was standing. She wore a brown skirt protected by a holland apron, and surmounted by a paisley blouse bearing a fawn design on a ground of crudest green. The sleeves of the blouse buttoned and were turned back to the elbow, and as two hooks were loose at the neck I felt justified in assuming that my new acquaintance was an enemy of constraint. Her feet were encased in carpet slippers of shameless masculinity, and a black belt encircled her ample waist, which at this moment was partly hidden by the outstretched fingers of her hands, as she stood, arms akimbo, in the doorway.

Her face, plump, pleasant and rosy, had for its principal feature two merry, twinkling eyes, which sparkled with humour as she gazed upon me; and her hair, which was beginning to turn grey, was drawn tightly back and coiled in one large plait upon the crown. Altogether she was a very homely, approachable woman, who had seen, as I judged, some fifty summers, and I hailed her appearance with joy.

"Nay, to be sure!" she repeated; "are ye Lot's wife? or has t' lads, young monkeys, planted a snow man at my door? Here, bide a bit while I brush ye down, an' then come inside wi' ye."

I laughed, and submitted to the operation, vigorously performed in the street, and then followed my rescuer indoors.

All my explanations were greeted with the same expressive utterance. "To be sures" came as thickly as currants in a Yorkshire tea-cake. We were unknown to each other by sight—for I was now, I found, in Marsland Gap, with the valley between me and Windyridge—but my fame had preceded me.

"Well, to be sure! So you're t' young lady what takes fotygraphs up at Windyridge. Why, bless ye, I can show ye t' very house ye live in, an' t' glass place where I reckon ye take yer fotygraphs from this window in t' scullery. Nay, to be sure! it's that wild ye cannot see an arm's length. Well, well, let's hev yer wet things off, for ye're fair steamin' afore that fire."

I protested in vain. My hat and coat had already been removed, and now my hostess insisted that my dress skirt should be hung upon the clothes-horse to dry. Oh, Rose, Rose! what would you not have given to see me ten minutes later clad in a garment which was reasonable enough as to length, but which had to be pinned in a great overlapping fold half round my body? I looked at myself and roared, whilst the owner of the dress shook her sides with merriment. All the same, I had found the inn of the Good Samaritan, and my stay there did not even cost me the two pence of the story.

What do you think we had for tea? Muffins, toasted cheese, home-made jam and "spice cake"! I helped to "wash-up," and as the storm continued with unabated fury I resigned myself cheerfully to the snug rocking-chair and the glowing hearth. Thoughts of Mother Hubbard's anxiety worried me a little, but I hoped she would realise that I had found shelter.

"You have not told me your name yet," I began, when we were comfortably settled, I with my hands idle upon my lap, and she with a heap of "mending" upon her knee.

MARSLAND GAP

"Well, to be sure! so I haven't," she replied. "Maria Robertsha''s my name, an' it's a name I'm noan ashamed on. Not but what I'd change it if someb'dy 'ud give me a better. It's all right livin' by yerself if ye can't 'elp it; an' to be sure, when ye live by yerself ye know what comp'ny ye keep; but them can 'ave it 'at likes for me."

"Then do you live here quite alone?" I inquired.

"Barring the cat, I do. I did 'ave a parrot one time, 'cos its nasty temper seemed to make it more 'omelike; but t' lads, young imps, taught it all sorts o' indecent stuff, which made it as I 'ad to part wi' it, an' it was nearly like losing a 'usband a second time. It used to be that gruff an' masterful you wouldn't think! No, I reckon nowt o' livin' by mysen."

"It is not good that man should be alone," I quoted.

"It's worse for woman," she said, "an' yet, to be sure, I don't know, for a woman 'at *is* a woman can allus make shift somehow, an' doesn't stand pullin' a long face an' cussin' providence. But men are poor menseless creatures when they're left to theirsens; an' it allus caps me to think 'at they call theirsens 'lords o' creation,' an' yet 'as to fetch a woman to sew a gallus button on, an' 'ud let t' 'ouse get lost i' muck afore they'd clean it. Suppose a man lived 'ere by hissen, do you think this kitchen 'ud look like this?"

"I am very sure it would not," I replied, "and it wouldn't if some women lived here."

"Well, anyway, it just goes to prove 'at men need women to look after 'em, but for all that it's bad enough for a woman to be alone. To be sure, she's a poor sort 'at hasn't more about 'er nor a man, an' it isn't 'at she's flayed o' bein' by hersen or can't manage for hersen, or owt o' that. No, no. But there's summat short, for all that. Ye can take it from me, miss, 'at Eve 'ud sooner have been driven out o' Eden wi' her 'usband, nor have left there to fend for hersen. Women doesn't want to be t' boss: they want to be bossed, or anyway they like t' man to think 'at he's bossin' 'em. An' they like 'im to come in wi' his great dirty boots spreadin' t' muck all ovver t' floor, an' puttin' 'em on t' scoured 'earthstone, so as they can 'call' 'im an' clear up after 'im.

"Oh, aye, to be sure, an' they like to see 'im light his pipe an' then fratch wi' 'im for fillin' t' 'ouse wi' smoke; an' even if he knocks ye about a bit now an' then, he sidles up to ye at after, an' 'appen puts 'is arms round ye, an'—

an' makes a fool of hissen; but ye feel t' want on it when ye've been used to 't."

"But we cannot all have husbands," I objected; "there are not enough of the other sex to go round."

"To be sure, that's so," she consented; "but that doesn't alter t' fact 'at we want 'em, does it? But I'd tax all t' men 'at isn't married, the selfish beggars. The Almighty meant 'em to pair off. Two an' two they went into t' ark, an' two an' two they should go yet if I'd my way. It's nature. An' I never could see yet why t' wimmen should 'ave to sit quiet an' wait for t' men to come an' ask for 'em. A woman knows better by 'alf what man 'ud suit 'er, an' 'er 'im, than t' man knows. She knows without knowing how she knows; whereas t' man just sees a pretty face, an' some dainty little feet i' 'igh-heeled boots, an' some frizzy 'air, 'at she's bought as like as not at a barber's, an' there ye are! But where are ye in toathree years' time? Aye, to be sure, where are ye then?"

"Perhaps if conventionality had permitted, your state might have been changed again by now," I suggested slyly.

"Well, now, to be sure, Miss Holden," she replied, drawing her chair a little nearer to mine, and laying one hand upon my lap for emphasis, "I thought after Robertsha' died 'at it were a case of 'once bitten, twice shy,' for there were odd times when he filled up the cup, so to speak. But, ye know, I missed 'im; an' though it's twelve year sin' come Shrove-tide, I miss 'im yet; an' if I had the askin' I've known for a long time who it 'ud be 'at 'ud take his place; but ye see I 'aven't, so I bide as I am."

I thought of the old fox, Simon Barjona, and laughed inwardly as well as outwardly. Widow Robertshaw little realised that I knew her secret.

Outside the storm raged furiously. The snow lay thick upon the ground, moist as it fell, but frozen in a moment, and to venture out seemed in my case impossible. We held a council of ways and means which resulted in the production of a young man of strong build from a cottage a few doors away, who smiled at the storm and readily undertook, in exchange for a shilling, coin of the realm—to convey a note to Mother Hubbard, describing my predicament.

I enjoyed Widow Robertshaw's hospitality, perforce, for two days, and when I returned home it was in Mr. Higgins' market cart, he having called in the Gap "casual-like" to see how Mrs. Robertshaw was "going on."

CHAPTER ELEVEN

GINTY
RUNS AWAY

WHAT A CURIOUS medley life is! How crowded with dramatic situations and sudden anticlimaxes! Even in Windyridge the programme of existence is as varied and full of interest as that of any picture palace. We have all the combinations of tragedy and pathos and humour, and he who has eyes to see and ears to hear and a heart to feel need not complain of the monotony of the village, nor pine for the manufactured excitements of the metropolis.

A letter with a foreign postmark and an Egyptian stamp was handed to me on Monday morning, and I have been excited and troubled ever since, though it brought me a great joy. The handwriting was unfamiliar, but when I turned to the signature I found it was from the squire, and I began to read it eagerly. I was astonished to find how small and particularly neat his handwriting is.

The letter ran thus, omitting certain descriptive and unimportant paragraphs:

> "Assouan, Upper Nile,
> "*March* 12*th*, 19—.

"DEAR MISS HOLDEN,

"I wonder if I might claim an old man's privilege and call you 'Grace'? I should like to do so, for do you know there is not one of your sex in the wide world whom I have a right to address by the christian name, and, what is perhaps more noteworthy, there is no other whose permission I have the least desire to ask. But somehow or other I am longing for kinsfolk to-day, and the sensation is almost inexpressibly acute, so much so that I actually feel the pain of loneliness, and that 'Inner Self' in which, I remember, you trust so completely, cries out for sympathy and companionship. If I mistake not we have common ideals and aspirations—you and I—which make us kin, and I am disposed to 'stretch out lame hands of faith' in your direction if haply I may find you and draw your soul to mine. So if it be your will, let us be friends, and do you send across the seas and deserts those mysterious waves of kindly feeling which will vibrate upon the heart of the solitary old man, to whom earth's messages of love come but seldom—now.

"Have I ever told you that I have not a relative on earth, and that I have outlived all my own friends? I sometimes feel to be like these old monuments on the banks of Nile, which stand calm and impassive whilst the children of this age picnic around their ruins; yet I am no patriarch, for I have not much overstepped the natural span of man's existence. I hope you may never experience the sensation, but the fact that you are yourself amongst earth's lone ones is not the least of the links that connect you to me.

"I stayed some weeks in Biarritz . . . but the weather turned cold and wet, and the doctors bade me journey to Egypt. It is an unknown land to my material senses, but not to my spiritual. Every stone preaches to me of the familiar past. I have always revelled in ancient history and have kept abreast of modern discovery and research. For a while I enjoyed the company of my imagination, and we trod together the courts and temple corridors of the mighty kings of ancient days, and reconstructed their history. Sometimes, for brief periods, I have interesting conversations with men who are learned in all this lore; but imagination and learning are but cold companions, and I am longing for a hand-grasp and the look of love—longing, like the modern woman of whom Derwent speaks—for the unattainable.

"I am half ashamed of myself for writing in this strain, and half afraid of bringing a shadow over the spirit of the gentle soul whose sympathy I seek; but you must not worry on my account, for I am neither morbid nor unhappy, though sadness usually walks by my side. Indeed, life is strangely and even unaccountably dear to me just now, though I am perfectly sure that the 'call' is not far away, and when it comes I shall pass behind the curtain and face the unknown without fear and without regret.

"Of late I have caught myself wondering whether I shall ever return home and see the brown and purple moors again, and the homely people whom I love; and when the thought that I may not do so grips me I have just one overwhelming desire—a curious desire for the 'archaeological old fossil' I am generally taken to be. Perhaps I am becoming weak and sentimental, but when the time comes and I have to go, I want someone who cares for me to 'see me off.' I should like my eyes to close to the sound of a woman's voice, I should like to feel the touch of a woman's hand, and maybe the kiss of a woman's lips; and I should like a few verses of Scripture and a simple hymn.

"I am an old fool, but the thought brings sweetness and peace with it; and it is as a father to a daughter that I ask this boon of you: When I hear the summons, will you come to me? Whether I am at home or abroad will you do me this service for love's sake? I have no claim upon anyone, and certainly none upon you, but my heart calls for you, and I believe yours will answer the call.

"For the present, letters addressed to the British Post Office, Cairo, will be forwarded to me, for I have no fixed address, but I shall look eagerly for your reply. Let me say in one word that I shall make provision for the expense of your journey if I should send for you, and I shall not send unless the call is clear.

"And now tell me of Windyridge. . . . Write to me when you can: give me all the news; tell me how the great quest for peace progresses, and believe that I am ever,

"Your very sincere friend,
"GEORGE EVANS."

Womanlike, I watered this missive with my tears, but they were April showers, after all, with great patches of blue sky in between, and plenty of warm sunshine; for it was sweet to know that I was cared for and that someone wanted me.

I hope none would mistake me. I am an emotional goose at times, I know, but thank goodness! I am no sentimentalist. I am not possessed with the idea that the squire wants to marry me and leave me his fortune, for I am perfectly sure that he does not. I heard his voice the night before he went away, and it told me the secret of his fidelity. Besides, I wouldn't marry him if he did want it, for though my heart tells me that I have loved him instinctively from the first day of our acquaintance, and I love him now more than ever, it also tells me that the affection is filial and nothing more. What more should it be? It is all the more likely to be unselfish and sincere on both sides that it has nothing of passion in it. You see, unlike Widow Robertshaw, I am not eager to change my state.

As to my decision, I did not hesitate for one moment. When he needs me I will go to him and, God helping me, I will act a daughter's part. Act? Nay, rather, I will do a daughter's loving duty.

I wrote him yesterday, telling him all the news of the little world of Windyridge, but painting the shadows lightly. In truth, they are heavy and full of gloom just now.

I had just commenced work in my studio after reading the squire's letter when Sar'-Ann burst in upon me, and throwing herself into one of my ornamental chairs commenced to cry and sob hysterically, holding her apron to her eyes and rocking her body to and fro in a frenzy of abandonment. I saw there was trouble of some sort, but recognised at the same time the need of firmness.

"Sar'-Ann," I said, "you will break that chair if you carry on in that fashion. Restrain yourself, and tell me what is the matter."

Restraint and Sar'-Ann, however, were strangers to each other, and her only response was to redouble her groans, until I lost patience.

"If you don't stop this noise, Sar'-Ann," I threatened, "I will get you a strong dose of sal-volatile and make you drink it. Do you hear?"

She did hear. Sal-volatile, as a remedy, had been unknown in Windyridge before my advent, but the few who had experienced it had not remained silent witnesses to its power, so that the very dread of the strange drug had been known to perform miraculously sudden cures in certain cases; and "that sally-stuff o' Miss Holden's" had become a word to charm with.

Sar'-Ann's groans subsided, but her breast heaved heavily, and her apron still concealed her face.

"Cannot you speak, child?" I asked. "What is the matter? If you want me to help you, you must do more than sob and cry. Now come!"

"It's Ginty!" she stammered; "he's run away an' robbed his mother of every penny, an' brokken her heart an' mine. Oh, Ginty! Ginty! Whatever shall I do?" and the rocking and sobbing began again.

I got the sal-volatile this time and forced her to swallow it, taking no heed of her protests. Mother Hubbard came in, too, and added her entreaties to my commands; and after a while she became calmer, and then the whole story came out.

Ginty had been mixing in bad company for some months past. Somewhere in the hollow of the moors a couple of miles away he had stumbled one Sunday upon a gambling school, conducted, I imagine, by city rogues who come out here to avoid the police, and had been threatened with violence for his unwelcome intrusion. He had purchased immunity by joining the school, and, unknown to everybody except Sar'-Ann, he had visited it, Sunday by Sunday, with unfailing regularity, for the greed of gain soon got hold of him. Sometimes he had won small sums, but more often he had lost all his wages and even pledged his credit, until he had not known where to turn for money.

"I gave 'im all I had," said Sar'-Ann, "an' I begged him to drop it, but he said he couldn't, an' he'd only to go on long enough to be sure to get it all back an' more to it. An' now, oh dear! oh dear! he's robbed his poor mother an' made off; an' whatever I'm goin' to do I don't know. O God! I wish I was dead!"

I left Mother Hubbard to console the stricken girl, fearing in my heart that she had not revealed the extent of her trouble, and went straight to Ginty's cottage, where a half-dozen women were doing their best to comfort the poor mother, bereaved of her only support by what was worse than death. Children were there, too, their fingers in their mouths and their eyes wide with wonder, staring vacantly at the object of universal commiseration, and silent in the presence of a sorrow they could feel but not understand.

The little garden was gay from end to end with multi-coloured crocuses, and two or three men stood looking at them, not daring to venture within the house, but ready to offer help if required. One of them muttered: "Bad job, this, miss!" as I passed; and the rest moved their heads in affirmation.

Ginty's mother was seated at the little round table, her head in her hands, and her eyes fixed upon an old cash box in front of her. The lid was thrown back and the box was empty. The picture told its own story; and to complete it a framed photograph of Ginty, which I had given him only a few weeks previously, hung upon the wall opposite, so that the author and his work were closely associated.

The women turned as I entered, and began to explain and discuss the situation before the poor woman who was its victim, in that seemingly callous manner with which the poor cloak and yet express their sympathy.

"Them's best off as has no bairns," said the blacksmith's wife; "ye moil an' toil for 'em, an' bring 'em up through their teethin' an' all make o' ailments, an' lay down yer varry life for 'em, an' this is how they pay you back in t' end."

"Ay," said Sar'-Ann's mother, "shoo'll hev to be thankful 'at it's no worse. So far as I know he's ta'en nob'dy's money but 'er's, so I don't suppose t' police 'll be after 'im. Eh! but it's a sad job an' all, an' he were bahn to wed our Sar'-Ann in a toathree week. Well, it's a rare good job for 'er 'at it's happened afore they were wed, rayther than at after."

"But whativver is shoo goin' to do now 'at Ginty's gone?" inquired the next door neighbour, Susannah; "Ginty kept 'er, an' *shoo* can't do nowt, not wi' them rheumatics in her legs, an' all that pile o' money gone. Nay, 'Lizabeth, lass, I nivver thowt ye'd scraped so mich together. It 'ud ha' served ye nicely for yer old age, but ye sud ha' put it in a bank. Whativver ye're bahn to do now, God only knows."

"We must see what can be done," I interposed. "We must all be her friends now that this trouble has come upon her, and do not let us add to her distress by our discussion. You will let us help you, won't you?" I asked.

She did not speak or move, but just stared stonily into the empty box; one would have said that she had not even heard.

I withdrew my hand as Susannah came forward. Susannah is a good woman, with a kind heart, and had known 'Lizabeth all her life. She knelt down on the stone floor and put an arm around her neighbour's waist.

"'Lizabeth, lass! Ye munnot tak' on like this. 'E'll be comin' back i' now. It's 'appen nowt but a bit of a marlackin', an' ye shall come an' live wi' us while 'e turns up. Now what say ye?"

The mother's mouth set hard and her brow contracted.

"I shall go into t' work'us, Susannah; where else should I go?"

There was a murmur of dissent, broken by Susannah's:

"No, no, lass, nowt o' t' sort. Ye'll come an' live wi' us; one mouth more 'll none mak' that difference, an' Mr. Evans 'll be back i' now an' put things straight for ye."

"Do ye think, Susannah, 'at your lasses 'll want to live wi' a thief's mother, an' do ye think 'at I'll let 'em? Ginty's a thief, an' all t' worse thief because he's robbed his own mother, an' left 'er to starve. But I won't be beholden to none of ye; I never 'ave been, an' I never will be. I've worked hard while I could work, an' I've saved what I could an' lived careful, so as I wouldn't need to be beholden to nob'dy; an' if Ginty has robbed me of my all 'e shall 'ave a pauper for his mother, an' 'e shall 'ear tell of 'er in a pauper's grave. I thank ye kindly, neighbours, but ye must all go an' leave me, for I amn't wantin' any comp'ny just now."

I saw that I could not be of service just then, so I came away with some of the other women, intending to go again on the morrow. But though I went immediately after breakfast I found that she had gone.

"She was off afore I'd well got t' fire lit," said Mrs. Smithies, who was my informant; "I looked across an' chanced to see 'er open t' door and pull it to behind 'er. She didn't lock it nor nowt, just like snecked it. She had a bundle in a red handkercher in 'er 'and, an' such a 'ard look on her face, an' she never once glanced be'ind nor at all them grand flowers, but just kept 'er eyes straight afore 'er.

"But I runs out an' I says: 'Nay 'Lizabeth, wherever are ye off, like?' An' she says, 'I'm off to t' workus, so good-bye, 'Becca; an' if there's ought in t' 'ouse after t' landlord's paid, you neighbours are all welcome to 't.' Not 'at I'd touch ought there is, miss, unless it were that chiney ornament on t' mantelpiece, which I could like if it were goin' a-beggin'.

"Well, I couldn't 'elp cryin' a bit, an' I axed 'er if she wouldn't change 'er mind, but she were same as if she were turned to stone. So I went up t' road wi' her a bit, just a piece beyond t' 'All gates, an' there she turned me back. 'Good-bye, 'Becca,' she says, 'an' thank God on yer knees 'at ye've no son to rob his mother! An' if my lad ever comes back, tell 'im he'll find *his* mother in a pauper's grave.'"

I walked down the fields into the sanctuary of the wood, where understanding is sometimes to be found and freedom from painful thoughts. It was bitterly cold, but the sky was blue, so that in the clear atmosphere every twig stood out with microscopic sharpness, and it was impossible to miss the note of hope in the song of new-born spring.

The trees were for the most part bare of colour—oak and elm and beech were alike in the grey garb of winter—but the sycamores had burst their buds and were clad in living green that delighted the eye and quickened the pulse, whilst great blotches of yellow celandine blazed in the sunshine of the open spaces like cloth of gold.

But the wood was voiceless at first to the question of my heart, and I told myself that the "Why?" of life is unanswerable. Then suddenly there came into my mind the familiar words of Tennyson:

"Behold, we know not anything;
   I can but trust that good shall fall
    At last—far off—at last, to all,
And every winter change to spring,"

and at a bound my Inner Self found firm ground again.

"Grace," I said, "have you forgotten the closing verse of a preceding stanza?" and I repeated aloud:

"So fret not, like an idle girl,
   That life is dash'd with flecks of sin.
    Abide: thy wealth is gathered in
When time hath sundered shell from pearl."

and I determined to conquer my morbid tendencies and take a broader outlook on life. "An idle girl!" That stuck. "Ineffective depression is a kind of idleness," I said to myself, "and I will kill it with industry."

In obedience to this impulse I rose to my feet, and saw Farmer Goodenough crossing the brook just below. He smiled a greeting as he came up, and we walked homewards together.

"Now I durst bet a new bonnet to a new hat, Miss 'Olden," he began, "that I can guess at twice why you've come down 'ere, an' I'll throw one guess away. You're on what I should call in a manner o' speakin' a 'mopin' expedition;' now isn't that so?"

"But I don't wear bonnets, my dear sir," I rejoined; "and if you should win a new hat you wouldn't wear it, being of such conservative leanings. Nevertheless, I am going to plead guilty to your indictment, and I hope I shall be let off with nothing worse than a lecture."

"Nay, it's none for me to lecture anybody, for I know as little about the rights o' things as I know about bonnets, but I've lived long enough to know 'at 'man's born to trouble as the sparks fly upwards,' as t' Owd Book puts it; an' if you're goin' to fret your heart out every time it comes your way you'll spend your life in a mournin' coach.

"'Cordin' to my way o' thinkin', Miss 'Olden, so long as human natur's what it is you'll never get rid o' sufferin' an' trouble, an' what good does it do to worrit yourself to death over what you can't mend? If you could mend it ever so little it 'ud be another matter. Now look at it i' this way. We can all choose our own road when it comes to a question o' right an' wrong, an' we should be in a poor way if we couldn't. My plough goes where t' horse pulls it, an' t' horse goes where I guide it. Now, neither t' plough nor t' horse has any responsibility, so to speak; but I'd rather be a man an' have t' power to choose where I go, even if I go wrong, nor be a beast or a machine.

"Now yon lad has gone wrong, an' I'm sorry for 'im, but accordin' to t' Owd Book it's no use cryin' over spilt milk, an' both 'im an' us 'll have to make t' best on 't. So will Sar'-Ann; so will Ginty's mother. Ginty knows he's done wrong, an' he's known t' difference between right an' wrong all along t' road. He's chosen, an' chosen badly, poor lad, an' he's sufferin' for it, wherever he is, an' 'e'll have to sup more sorrow still, there's no doubt about it, an' a bitter cup it'll be.

"But don't you see, this same bitter cup is med'cine for t' lad at same time. He's gone into t' far country now, but like t' other prodigal he'll come to himself, as t' Owd Book says, one o' these days, an' we shall have to leave him there till that time comes.

"But now, take t' lad's mother. She's chosen her own way an' all. Ginty's sin were greediness an' love o' money, an' his mother's sin is pride. We haven't all t' same nature, an' I'm not settin' up for a preacher, for Reuben Goodenough doesn't live up to his name by a long chalk, so I'm not judgin' t' woman, like a Pharisee.

"But I know this, if she'd just ha' let t' neighbours 'elp her a bit, her 'eart wouldn't have been so sore, and t' blow 'ud have been lightened for her. We're a roughish lot i' Windyridge, but there isn't many 'at wouldn't have made shift to help t' owd woman as well as they could, but she couldn't stomach bein' helped.

"An' there's a taste o' revenge in it too, unless I'm sadly mista'en. She thinks she'll pay t' lad out better wi' goin' to t' workus nor ought else she could do; an' she likes to believe 'at he'll be 'eart-brokken if she's put in a pauper's grave.

"That's how I size things up. All this trouble needn't have been, but it *is* there, an' you an' me has no 'casion to mope over it. Mopin' won't help neither of 'em, but I daresay we can both 'elp 'em a bit if we try. I'm goin' to see if I can hear ought o' t' lad, an' if I do I shall follow 'im up; an' I shall do my best to bring a bit o' sense to his mother. An' if you'll excuse me, miss—well, you're a woman. Try what a word o' prayer now an' again 'll do for 'em, i'stead o' frettin' over 'em; an' 'be strong an' of a good courage.' That's in t' Owd Book, an' it's good advice."

CHAPTER TWELVE

THE CYNIC EXAGGERATES

EASTER IS PAST and spring has burst upon us in all her glory. The landscape is painted in the freshest and daintiest tints: the beeches are a sight to make glad the heart of man; the chestnuts with their cones of cream and pink look in the distance like huge, newly-replenished candelabra; the slender birches, decked in silvery white and vivid green, stand gracefully erect, veritable "ladies of the woods," as Coleridge called them. Here and there a blackthorn bends beneath its burden of snowy blossom, and calls a challenge to the hedgerows which have wakened late, and are slow in their dressing.

Occasionally primroses may be seen, though they are not common in these parts; but on the banks of the lower lane modest violets peep out shyly from the shadows, and the dull purple flowers of a species of nettle offer their bashful welcome to spring. The gardens are gorgeous with daffodils, and the woods with celandine and wild hyacinth; whilst our humble friends, the buttercups, daisies, and dandelions, have sprung up in abundance, the merry children of field and wayside charming us all with their simple beauty.

I spend almost all my leisure time in watching the birds, an occupation which is in itself a never-failing delight, and I puzzle myself with questions which no man can answer, but which are imperatively asked all the same.

Who guides these flocks of tiny travellers, who have journeyed by trackless routes from distant lands hundreds of miles away, depending only on the strength of their own wings, and the mysterious vital power with which God has endowed them? How do they recognise the familiar haunts of a year ago? How do they know that the woods in these northern regions are ready for habitation?

I give it up; but I love to see them approach from the distance like a swiftly-moving cloud, and disappear into the haze again after circling over the trees which surround the Hall; and I love to walk through the meadows and see how my feathered brothers and sisters are making the most of the sunshine and the softened soil.

The blackbird is in full song now, and it darts past me with its chirpy "tuck-tuck-tuck"; whilst the lark soars upwards into the azure with quivering song, full-throated, inimitable.

The sagacious rooks have been busy for days past with household cares, and have gone about thieving (with a clear conscience, I trust) for strictly domestic purposes; and the thrushes are just as industrious in their search for dainties hidden in Mother Earth.

East winds prevail, and rheumatism holds some of my neighbours in prison and in torment, but to me they bring exhilaration, a voracious appetite, and the joy of life. Mother Hubbard looks upon me with loving envy and sighs for the days that are beyond recall.

Poor Mother Hubbard! The hard winter has tried her severely, but she never complains and is always sweet and cheerful, and promises herself and me that she will be all right when summer comes. I hope so, for she has grown inexpressibly dear to her adopted daughter whom she does her level best to spoil, and if we were parted now we should miss each other sorely.

I have discovered that she is an excellent chaperon, and enjoys the rôle beyond my power of description. What a remarkable little woman she is! She knows that I keep a record of my experiences, and has got it into her head that I am writing a book, and she is therefore always on the look-out for the appearance of the hero. She has given me to understand that if she can only be in at the *dénouement*, when the hero leads the blushing bride to the altar amid the ill-restrained murmur of admiration from the crowd, she will be then ready to depart in peace. Needless to say, it is *I* who am to be the blushing bride! It is no doubt a very pleasing fancy, but

I am afraid the dear old lady will have to find contentment in an abstraction.

What amuses me most is her well-founded misgiving as to my ability to deal adequately with such a situation in my "book."

"You are not very romantic, love," she said to me one evening, when she had been making unusually large demands upon her imagination, to my considerable amusement, "and I don't think you will ever be equal to the greatest writers unless you cultivate that side of your nature. You know, love, you are rather practical and common-sense and all that sort of thing, and the men might not know how very nice you are." She came across and kissed me, hoping I did not mind her candour.

"You see, love, I was always rather romantic myself, and I think I could help you a bit; though, of course, I am not clever like you. But I could just tell you what I think ought to be put in, and you could find suitable language for it. . . . Now you're laughing at me!"

I believe she thought the hero had arrived when the Cynic turned up on Easter Monday.

It was a truly beautiful day, typically April, except that the showers were wanting, and the much-abused clerk who controls the Weather Department must have been unusually complaisant when he crowded so many pleasing features into his holiday programme. Until the long shadows began to creep across the fields it was warm enough to sit out in the sunshine, whilst there was just sufficient "bite" in the air to make exercise agreeable.

Every cottage garden had on its gala clothing and smiled a friendly welcome to the passer-by, and a sky that was almost really blue bent over a landscape of meadow, moor, and wood that was a perfect fantasy in every delicate shade of green. And the beasts of the field and the fowls of the air lifted up their voices in their several degrees of melody.

It had been a glorious Easter Day, and perhaps on that account I had risen early on the Monday and gone out bareheaded to catch the Spirit of the Morning. Farmer Goodenough passed as I stood at the gate, and threw one of his hearty greetings over his shoulder without pausing in his walk.

"Look out for customers to-day, Miss 'Olden! There'll be scores in t' village this afternoon from Broadbeck way."

"But suppose I don't want them, Mr. Goodenough," I replied; "it's holiday to-day."

"That 'ud be a sin," he shouted; "'make hay while t' sun shines,' as t' Owd Book says, holiday or no holiday."

There was sense in this. Customers had so far been scarce enough, for I had been favoured with the patronage of only three paying sitters, although I had been established in business for eight months. My total takings from the portraiture branch had not totalled thirty shillings; and if my neighbours had not grown accustomed to it, the sign at the bottom of the garden must have appeared very ridiculous indeed. I therefore anticipated the arrival of excursionists with no little eager interest.

Half a dozen houses in the village had got out brand new boards indicating that Teas were provided within, and I knew that from this date forward until the autumn a very brisk trade would be done on sunny Saturday afternoons and holidays.

Soon after half-past twelve I caught sight of the advance guard approaching. The footpaths between Windyridge and Marsland Moor became dotted with microscopic moving figures which materialised usually into male and female, walking two and two, even as they went into the ark, as Widow Robertshaw might have observed.

When they reached the village street the sight of my studio seemed to astonish them and tickle their fancy. "In the spring a young man's fancy lightly turns to thoughts of love"—and portraiture. Quite a group of young people gathered about my sign before two o'clock, and from that time until five I never sat down for one minute. As fast as I bowed out one couple another entered, amid a fusillade of good-humoured chaff and curtly-expressed injunctions to "be quick about it." I took so much money, comparatively speaking, in three short hours that I began to see visions and dream dreams—but the Cynic dispelled them.

He was standing in the garden, talking to Mother Hubbard, when I locked up the studio, and although he was in shorts I recognised him at once, for thus had I seen him in my dream. I involuntarily glanced at myself to make sure that I was correctly garbed and that it was really the key, and not Madam Rusty's teapot, that I held in my hand.

He came forward smilingly and held out his hand. "How do you do, Miss Holden? I had intended asking you to take my photograph, but competition for your favour was so keen that the modesty which has always been my curse forced me to the background."

"If it had forced you to the background you would have entered my studio, Mr. Derwent," I replied; "all those who have competed successfully for my favour were not deterred by dread of the background. I fear, however, it is now too late to endeavour to encourage you to overcome your bashfulness."

"Indeed, yes:

"'The shadows of departing day
   Creep on once more,'

as the poet hath it, and when one has walked eight or nine miles across the moors the man within cries out for food and drink even more than for art. And therefore I have ventured to introduce myself to Mrs. Hubbard and to inquire if she would make me a cup of tea, and she has very kindly consented to do so."

I looked at Mother Hubbard, who had sufficient sense of the appropriate to blush very becomingly.

"You old sinner!" I said, "how dare you impose upon my good nature! Are there so few neighbours of ours who cater professionally for the requirements of these 'men within' that we must needs enter into competition with them?"

Mother Hubbard's nods and winks became so alarmingly expressive, however, during the course of my speech, that I was in real danger of becoming confused, so I turned to our guest and extricated myself.

"Be pleased to enter our humble abode, to which we make you heartily welcome. And in return for such poor hospitality as we can offer you, you shall regulate the clock, which has lately developed certain eccentricities, and nail up the creeper on the gable end. Then if time permits you shall rest your limbs on the wicker chair in the garden and enlighten us as to what is going on in the world of men."

"With all my heart," he agreed, "and I promise to make so good a tea that the debt will not be easily repaid."

He did pretty well, I must admit, and when it was over Mother Hubbard, with a self-conscious cough, and a look that was eloquence itself, expressed her fixed determination to clear away without my help.

"It's just a little fancy I have, love," she protested, as I tied on my apron; "I really would like to do it all myself. I am tired of sitting, and knitting seems to try my eyes to-day."

"Mother Hubbard," I replied, "you are a hypocritical old humbug, and you are wanting to persuade Mr. Derwent that I am not domesticated, which is too bad of you. And you *know* that I take my share of the work."

"Really, love," said Mother Hubbard, who was almost in tears at the denseness of my intelligence, "I'm sure Mr. Derwent will understand my meaning."

I am only too much afraid that he did, for he looked at me out of the corners of his eyes and said, with a merry twinkle which was provoking:

"I shall certainly need some information about the clock, and a little assistance with the creeper. Miss Holden, you had better yield to Mrs. Hubbard's wishes."

"If you cannot regulate a clock without a woman standing over you, or hold a bit of jasmine in one hand and a hammer in the other without a woman's assistance, you deserve to remain in your ridiculous background. You will find the tools in the top drawer of the dresser. If you will be good enough to get them and go on with your work, Mother Hubbard and I will soon finish ours."

He grinned, and Mother Hubbard groaned; but before long we were sitting together in the garden, with the knitting needles making music as usual.

The Cynic leaned back in his chair and watched the blue smoke curl lazily from his cigarette. The laughter of the visitors had ceased in the streets, but the voice of song was wafted occasionally to our ears from the fields below. How is it that homeward-bound excursionists always sing?

"I take it, Miss Holden, that you are a Prototype, which I spell in capitals. But I venture to predict that you will not have a large following. The modern craze is for kudos, and in this particular the success of an enterprise like yours is not likely to be remarkable."

"What, exactly, is my enterprise?" I inquired. "Please interpret me to myself."

"The surface reading is easy," he replied, "but the significance is hieroglyphic. Who can read the riddle of woman's motives? They are past finding out, and man can only grope for the meaning with half-blind observation, having eyes indeed, but seeing not; hearing, but not understanding."

"As, for instance?" I again inquired.

"I will come to your case shortly," he continued, "and meantime I will speak in parables. I went into a fashionable draper's shop the other day, as I had business with one of the principals. He was engaged, and I elected to wait and was accommodated with a seat near the glove counter. My experiences were distinctly interesting, but I cannot yet read the riddle they offered me. Before I was summoned to the office three customers had approached the counter at separate times, and the procedure was in all three cases on approximately similar lines.

"The lady sailed up to the counter, deposited her parcels upon it, seated herself upon the waiting chair, adjusted her skirt, and then, turning to the deferential young gentleman whose head was inclined artistically to one side in the way that is characteristic of the most genteel establishments, murmured languidly: 'Gloves, please.'

"The deferential young gentleman brought his head to the perpendicular and replied: 'Gloves! Yes, madam,' and proceeded to reach down a half-dozen boxes from the shelves at his back.

"'This, madam,' he said, bringing forth a pair of grey suedes, 'is a beautiful glove. One of Flint's very best make, and they are produced specially for our firm. Every pair is guaranteed. We can very strongly recommend them.'

"The lady took the gloves in her hand, stretched them, and examined them slowly and critically, whilst the D.Y.G.'s head dropped to the artistic angle again.

"After having eyed them in silence for a minute or more, and half conveyed the impression that they were the very gloves she was seeking, the lady placed them without a word on the counter, and the D.Y.G. with perfect understanding replaced them in the box.

"He opened another box containing suede gloves in tan.

"'This also is an excellent glove, madam,' he repeated, with all the precision of a gramophone; 'it is one of our best selling lines, and its wearing qualities are unsurpassed. You may buy more expensive gloves, but none of better value.'

"This pair is subjected to the same slow and critical examination, after which the lady inquires:

"'What is the price?'

"'The price of these gloves, madam, is seven-and-six.' Professing to confirm his statement by minutely examining the ticket, though, of course, he is perfectly well aware that there is no mistake, he repeats: 'Yes, madam, seven-and-six.'

"Again the gloves are laid upon the counter, and again the D.Y.G. replaces the lid and attacks another box! Meanwhile the lady's gaze is wandering abstractedly around the shop; picking out an acquaintance here and there she smiles a recognition; and she seems a little vexed when a third pair of gloves is placed before her. The same performance follows, with the same serenity on both sides, but the price has dropped to five shillings.

"Then the kids are produced, in all shades and at all prices, and are in turn deposited upon the counter without comment.

"At last the D.Y.G. has exhausted his stock and his familiar recitations, but fortunately not his urbanity, and he looks at his customer with deprecation in his eyes.

"'You had some white kid gloves in the window a week or two ago,' she murmurs, smiling sweetly; 'ten buttons; they were a special price, I think.'

"'Two-and-eleven, madam?' he asks, hopefully.

"'I believe they were. Yes, two-and-eleven,' she responds, as though consideration had confirmed her recollection; and in two minutes more her wants are satisfied, and she departs to another counter to the performance of Scene 2 in the same act."

"And this is typical of woman's methods?" I ask.

"It serves to show," he replies, "how unfathomable her methods are to mere man. When *we* unimaginative mortals enter a shop for a similar purpose we say:

"'I want a pair of tan kids, seven and three-quarters, about three-and-six,' and before the current of cold air which came in with us has circulated round the shop, we are going out with the little parcel in our pocket. Now why does not woman do the same? *You* don't know—nobody knows; nobody really wants to know, or to see her act otherwise."

"It is a very silly exaggeration," I said, "and if it is characteristic of *your* methods they are certainly not past finding out."

The Cynic is really a very irritating person. He has a way of ignoring your rejoinders which is most annoying, and makes you want to rise up and shake him. Besides, it isn't courteous.

"Now to return to your own case, Miss Holden. It is not typical and therefore I call it prototypical. *Why* you have forsaken London society (which in this case I spell with a small 's,' to guard against possible repudiation) is possibly known to yourself, though personally I doubt it. Why, having found the hermitage and the simple life, you have adopted photography as a profession in a village where you will be fortunate if you make an annual profit of ten pounds is another enigma. But kudos is not everything, and I see in you the archetype of a race of women philosophers of whom the world stands sorely in need."

"You talk like a book," I said, "and use mighty big words which in my case need the interpretation of a dictionary, but I'm afraid they cover a good deal of rubbish, which is typical, if I may say so, of the ordinary conversation of the modern smart man."

"Nay," said he, "but I am in downright earnest. For every effect there must be an adequate cause. You may not understand yourself. The why and wherefore of your action may be hard to discover, but I was wrong when I said that it was unfathomable. Given skill and perseverance, the most subtle compound must yield its analysis, but it is not given to every man to submit a woman's actions to the test, and I beg you to believe that I was not impertinent enough to make any such suggestion."

"Nevertheless," I said, "I may some day allow you to put my actions into the crucible, and see if you can find my real motives. I confess I do not understand myself, and I have nothing to conceal. I think I should rather like to be analysed."

"Then I may come again?" he asked.

"You may come to be photographed, of course," I replied.

I wonder how old he is, and what he does!

CHAPTER THIRTEEN

WHITSUNTIDE EXPERIENCES

NEW SENSATIONS HAVE elbowed and jostled each other to secure my special attention this Whitsuntide, until I have been positively alarmed for my mental equilibrium. The good people here seem so sedate on ordinary occasions that one fails to realise that after all there is a good deal of the peacock and the kitten in the make-up of many of them; but Whitsuntide reveals this.

The peacock in them manifests itself as they strut up and down in new clothing of brilliant dye, affecting an unconsciousness and unconcern which deceives nobody. The shocks I received during that memorable Sunday, when the village turned out in its new finery, I still experience, like the after-tremors of an earthquake.

Pray do not imagine that Windyridge knows nothing of the rule of fashion. Every mother's daughter, though not every daughter's mother, owns her sway and is her devoted subject. If the imperious Dame bids her votaries hobble, the Windyridge belle limps awkwardly to and fro—on Sundays and feast days—in proud and painful obedience, heedless of the unconcealed sneers and contempt of her elders. If headgear after the form of the beehive or the castle of the termite ant is decreed, she counts it a joy, like any fashionable lady of fortune, to suffer the eclipse of her good looks under the vilest monstrosity the milliner's ingenuity can devise. Ah, me! How fine a line, after all, divides Windyridge from Mayfair!

The kitten in them gambols and makes fun wholeheartedly for several hours at a stretch on the afternoon of Whit Monday, and with such kindliness and good humour that one cannot help feeling that the world is very young and one's self not so *very* old either.

I thought the rain was going to spoil everything. Day by day for a week it had come down with a steady determination that seemed to mean the ruin of holiday prospects. The foliage certainly looked all the fresher for it, and the ash took heart to burst its black buds and help to swell the harmony of the woods. But these are æsthetic considerations which do not appeal to people who are looking forward to a good time—a time of fun and frolic for some, and harvesting of shekels for others.

When I woke on the Sunday, however, old Father Sol had shaken off his lethargy, bundled the surly clouds into the store-room, locked the door and put the key into his pocket, and strolled forth to enjoy the sight of his welcome. Meadow, pasture and moor, green hedgerow and brown road were silvered over with sunshine, and the flowers looked up and laughed the tears away from their faces, and told themselves that everything had been for the best; and the cocks crowed lustily from the walls where they had flown to greet the sun, and all the birds came out from eave and tree and lowly nest, and sang their doxology in happy and tuneful notes which told how brimful they were of joy.

Long before church-time it was so hot that the fields were steaming like drying clothes before the fire, and as I walked back from Fawkshill after the morning service I felt sure that there need be no misgiving about the dryness of the grass for the children's treat on the morrow. Everybody was concerned for the children! Young women of eighteen and young men of the same age had no real concern or interest in the weather except in so far as it involved disappointment to the children! Well, well! How easily we deceive ourselves, and how unwilling we are to acknowledge the child within the man!

In the afternoon I went to chapel with Mother Hubbard, and saw and heard that which made me want to laugh and cry at the same time, and I really do not know why I should have done either. My emotions seem to take holiday sometimes and enjoy themselves in their own peculiar way without restraint. Let me set down my experiences.

Do you know what a "sitting-up" is? If you live in Yorkshire or Lancashire no doubt you do, but if you are a southerner or a more northern northerner the probability is that you do not. When Mother

Hubbard told me that the children were to "sit up" at the chapel on Whit Sunday I stared at her without understanding. "Do they usually stand up or lie down?" I inquired.

Then it occurred to me that this was, perhaps, a metaphorical way of speaking, and that there was, so to speak, a "rod in pickle" for the bairns on this special occasion, but why I could not imagine. Yet I knew that when an irate Windyridge father undertook to make his lad "sit up," it usually betokened some little difficulty in sitting at all until the soreness wore off.

This, however, foreboded nothing of so unpleasant a nature. When I entered the light and airy little sanctuary I found thirty or forty children ranged in rows one above the other, in front of the little pulpit. Not many boys were there, and there was nothing specially attractive about those who were, beyond the attractiveness that lurks within the face of every cleanly-washed child. But the girls were a picture; they were all in white, but most of them had coloured sashes round their waists, and coloured ribbons in their hair, and one or two were distinguished by black adornments, betokening the recent visit of that guest who is so seldom regarded as a friend.

Some of the frocks were new, but most of them were old; and it is safe to assume that the younger children were wearing what had served the turn of a past generation of "sitters-up." In some cases they were so inadequate to the requirements of the long-limbed, growing maidens who wore them, that it cannot be denied that the dresses "sat up" even more than their owners, so that the white cotton stockings were taxed to the utmost to maintain conventional decency.

To listen to the children's performances, rather than to the address of the preacher, the chapel was uncomfortably crowded by what the handbills called "parents, relatives and friends."

The door was wide open, and my eyes often strayed to it before the service began, for it framed a picture of yellow meadows and waving trees, of brown moorland and ultramarine sky, with drowsy cattle in the pastures a hundred feet below, which seemed strangely unfamiliar, and rather reminiscent of something I had once seen or dreamed of, than of what I looked upon every day of my life. The explanation is simple enough, of course. I saw just a *panel* of the landscape, and with limited vision the eye observed more clearly and found the beauty of the scene intensified.

But when the prayer was ended—a rather long and wearisome one, to my thinking, on such a fine day, when all nature was offering praise so cheerily—the children's part began.

They sang children's hymns, the simple hymns I had sung myself as a child, which I hope all English-speaking Christian children sing: the hymns which belong to the English language and to no one church, but are broad enough to embrace all creeds, and tender enough to move all hearts, and which must find an echo in the Higher Temple, where thousands of children stand around the throne of God.

A wee lassie of five stood up to sing alone. As the thin, childish voice rose and fell my heart began to beat fast, and I looked at the fair little head through a veil of tears. They made an aureole which transformed Roger Treffit's firstborn into a heavenly cherub, and I was carried into that exalted state when imperfect speech and neglected aspirates are forgotten:

"Jesus, tender Shep'erd 'ear me:
    Bless Thy little lamb to-night;
Through the darkness be Thou near me;
    Keep me safe till mornin' light."

Was there one present who did not at that moment feel very near to the sheep-fold of the Good Shepherd? I am a Churchwoman, and by training and association inclined to look distrustfully upon Dissent, but that child's lispingly tuneful prayer taught me that I was in the House of God; for surely I know at the heart of me that neither in the Catholic mountain nor the Anglican Jerusalem is God solely to be worshipped, but wherever men seek Him in spirit and in truth; and this afternoon a little child was leading us.

"All this day Thy 'and has led me,
    And I thank Thee for Thy care;
Thou 'ast clothed me, warmed an' fed me;
    Listen to my evenin' prayer."

It was not evening, for the sun was still high in the heavens and the shadows short upon the earth; but He with whom the night and the morning are one day heard and understood, I do not doubt.

Without a pause the sweet voice went on:

"Let my sins be all forgiven;
    Bless the friends I love so well;
Take me, when I die, to 'eaven,
    'Appy there with Thee to dwell."

Amen and amen, dear little Lucy! Surely no stain of sin as yet has darkened your soul, but the thought of the good Lord who "forgiveth iniquity, transgression and sin" cannot come to us too soon. Let it sink into the plastic wax of your memory and your heart, and harden into certainty, and then when the time comes for you to die—whether the day be near or distant—it will be well with you, "happy there with Thee to dwell!"

There were other solos, but none which moved me like this of little Lucy's, and there were recitations by two of the boys which affected an entirely different compartment of my emotions.

They were highly moral pieces, I know, and they exhorted us to a course of conduct which must have been beneficial if followed; the trouble was that the eye had so much employment that the ear was neglected and so missed its opportunities.

Each boy licked his lips vigorously to start with, and then glued his eyes upon one fixed spot, as if he saw the words in bold type there. If he did, an invisible compositor had set them up in the west window for the one lad, and on a corner of the ceiling for the other. The swiftness with which the words came out reminded me of a brakeless gramophone running at top speed; and it made the performers gasp for breath, which they dared hardly stop to renew lest memory should take wings and fly away. I am sure I was relieved when the final bob to the congregation was reached and the contortions ended.

The address was tedious, like the prayer, but fortunately it was not long; then the preacher came in to tea, it being Mother Hubbard's turn to entertain him.

The chapel people take the preachers according to an arranged plan with which they are all familiar. My old lady regards the privilege as in the nature of a heavenly endowment, and she has more than once reminded me that those who show hospitality to God's ministers sometimes entertain angels unawares. No doubt that is so, but the wings were very, very inconspicuous in the one who ate our buttered toast that Sunday.

All the same he is, I am sure, a very good man, and a man of large and cheerful self-sacrifice which calls for admiration and respect, and I do sincerely honour him; and it is no fault of his that his great big hands are deeply seamed over their entire surface, and that the crevices are filled with black. He works, I discovered, at an iron-foundry, and I believe his hands were really as clean as soap and water could make them. But when all has been said, he need not have spread them over all the plate whenever he helped himself to another slice of bread, and he might just as well have taken the first piece he touched. I suppose I am squeamish, but I cannot help it. I found some amusement in pressing him to eat all he had touched, however, and seeing that he did it.

His conversation was chiefly remarkable for the use he made of the phrase "as it were." Mother Hubbard regards him as a genius, but I doubt if he is anything more than an intelligent eccentric. It must have been his flow of language which got him "on the plan"—that is to say, into the ranks of the local preachers of the Wesleyan Church—for, like the brook, he could "go on for ever."

He is a tall, heavy man, perhaps fifty years of age, with a mass of hair upon his head but none upon his face, except where thick eyebrows hang like brushwood over the twin caverns of his eyes. As he speaks he raises his right hand and holds the palm towards you, moving it slowly to and fro for emphasis, and he measures his words as he goes along.

He was describing his experiences in a new chapel where he had recently preached, a gothic building, "more like a church, as it were, than a chapel."

"Ah yes, Mrs. Hubbard," he said (he never addressed me direct, perhaps because he suspected that I was not one of the confraternity), "I always mistrust a chapel with a spire to it; and the spirit of Methodism, as it were, cannot dwell in transepts or chancels. There is not the heartiness, not the freedom, which we associate with our chapels. The air is heavy, as it were, with the spirit of sacerdotalism. Why, ma'am, at this particular chapel—church, they call it—they had choir stalls, filled with men and boys, and a liturgical service, as it were. Ah yes! No sound of 'Hallelujah!' or 'Praise the Lord!' escaped the lips of the devout worshipper. They were stifled stillborn, as it were. It was cold, ma'am, cold and formal; John Wesley would never have found his heart strangely warmed in such an atmosphere. No!

"And yet, ma'am, there was something in the arrangements that stirred my feelings, as it were. Here, on my right hand, were grouped the scholars; children in the springtime of life, as it were. Yes! it was a moving sight, ma'am, to a man of feeling." (I wickedly thought of his hands.) "Life was before them—spread out like a map, as it were, with nothing but the outline; or like a copy-book which would be soiled and disfigured with many blots, as it were, before the end was reached. Yes!

"And on my left were the elders of the flock, gathered there, I was told, because the acoustic properties, as it were, are excellent in the transepts: the greyheaded sires, who had almost fought through the battle and were now awaiting the recall, as it were. Men and women in the late evening of life, as it were, who would soon pass behind the sunset.

"And in front of me were the middle-aged, those who were bearing the burden and heat of the day, as it were. Yes! labourers in life's vineyard; earning their bread in the sweat of their brow, going forth to their work until the evening, as it were.

"Yes! And as I looked upon them, young and middle-aged and old, I said to myself in the language of the preacher: 'All go unto one place; all are of the dust, and all turn to dust again.'—Ecclesiastes iii. 20, ma'am."

I got up and went into the garden, and filled my nostrils with the fragrance which earth was sending to heaven—as it were—and felt better.

Whit Monday was a hard day for me. After dinner my Easter experiences were repeated, and sitters came thick and fast. I really believe my work is giving satisfaction, for some of my last holiday customers had sent their friends to be "taken"; and some called themselves to say "How d'ye do?"

Nothing eventful transpired, however, and no Cynic turned up to disturb the serenity of my temper with sarcastic observations upon women, so I climbed the hill at the back of the house and joined the merry

throng of school-children who were having a jolly time with their elders
in a field at the top. And there I forgot my tiredness, and romped for a
couple of hours with the wildest of them, having as much of the kitten in
me as most folk.

When the red had finally died out of the western sky the dustman
came round, and the eyes of the little ones grew heavy. But the grown-
ups were enjoying themselves far too much to think of leaving so soon, so
I gathered the infants around me and told them all the wonderful stories
which had been locked away in the dusty cabinets of my memory. Not
the ordinary nursery tales, which are as well known in Windyridge as in
Westminster, but some of the simpler records of Greek mythology, and
extracts from the lives of the saints.

Little Lucy came and laid her head upon my shoulder and asked if it
was all true. I tried to show her the truth that was hidden in the make-
believe, but I fear with small success. Her eyelids were held open with
difficulty as she continued to question me.

"Is comets true?"

"Comets?" I inquired; "what do you know of comets?" (One is about
due now, and the children are on the tip-toe of excitement.)

"Dada says they has long tails, an' runs up an' down the sky when I'se
asleep, like little mouseys."

"You are not afraid of them, are you?" I asked.

"Dunno. I think I is afraid of them, but I always asks God."

"What do you say?" I ventured.

The little head was growing heavier, and it was a very sleepy voice
that murmured:

"God bless ev'ybody . . . an' don't let them be 'ungry, so they won't die
. . . until You makes 'em . . . 'cept it be comets an' things."

Now what could anybody make of that? I carried the child home, and
she did not wake when I undressed her and put her to bed.

CHAPTER FOURTEEN

BARJONA FALLS INTO THE TRAP

"ARTERNOON, MISS!"

It certainly was afternoon, for only a few minutes earlier the little clock in my studio had chimed three, and I was not in the least expecting visitors, particularly of the paying kind, and was hard at work upon the accumulated negatives of Whitweek, when the blunt ejaculation caused me to turn with a start. My astonished eyes fell upon a transformed Barjona!

Barjona in a frock coat of modern cut, with a white waistcoat, and slate-coloured trousers, correctly creased! Barjona, with a starched shirt and a satin tie, vividly blue! Above all, Barjona in a silk hat, which he was at that moment carefully removing from his head, as though anxious to prevent the escape of some bird imprisoned within!

It was not a bird, however, that he captured and produced, but an elaborate "button-hole," properly wired, as one could see at a glance, and with its stems wrapped in silvered paper; and Barjona chuckled as he stepped to the mirror and adjusted it in the lapel of his coat.

"Took that out quick, I can tell you.... Gives the show away, that does ... thought once over I'd throw it in t' gutter ... but I says, 'Nay, it cost fourpence'... sixpence she asked for it ... sixpence ... mustn't waste it ... smarten up my photygraph, too.... No, no, mustn't waste fourpence!"

"Why, Mr. Higgins," I exclaimed, "you must surely have been to a wedding! But none of our friends in Windyridge have been getting married to-day, have they?"

"No, no . . . Marsland Gap . . . widow-woman . . . name o' Robertsha'
. . . now Mrs. Higgins . . . Mrs. S. B. Higgins . . . she's in the trap now,"
jerking his head towards the roadway.

This was too much for my gravity. I had just enough presence of mind
to shake hands with him and offer my congratulations, and then gave way
to uncontrollable laughter.

"It's your own fault, Mr. Higgins," I blurted out at length. "Last
October you told me that you were too old a fox to be caught again; there
were to be no traps for you, and when you said Mrs. Higgins was in the
trap it amused me vastly."

"Meanin' the cart, of course," he interrupted, looking somewhat
sheepish, but still sufficiently pleased with himself.

"I know," I replied, "but I was just wondering how you come to be
caught in the other trap, the trap of wedlock—you, a man of years and
experience, and pre-eminently a man of caution."

He hung his hat on the support of my reflecting-screen, and passed
his hand thoughtfully over his smooth crown—I had always felt sure
that his head was bald—and I imagined I saw an uneasy look creep into
his eyes.

"It be very cur'ous, Miss Holden," he said, in a confidential tone, "very
cur'ous. . . . Said to myself many a time . . . hunderds of times. . . . 'Don't
'ee be a fool, Simon . . . women be kittle cattle,' I says . . . some weepin'
sort . . . some blusterin' . . . but all masterful . . . an' costs a lot o' money . . .
awful lot o' money to keep up. . . . Went into 't wi' my eyes open . . . oh yes;
very cur'ous. . . . Come to think on 't . . . dunno why I done it."

"Don't worry, Mr. Higgins," I said soothingly; "many animals flourish
splendidly in captivity, and if they miss their freedom they never say
anything about it, but look quite sleek and contented. And I am sure you
have secured a very capable and good-natured wife, and are to be heartily
congratulated. Now fetch her in and I will be getting the camera ready."

"Fetch her in?" he inquired.

"Yes, I shall be ready by the time you return, and it will be the work of
only a moment or two to arrange you suitably."

"But she isn't goin' to have 'er photygraph taken," he said, with an
emphatic shake of the head; "only me."

"Do you mean to tell me," I remarked severely, "that you will not be photographed together on your wedding day? Mr. Higgins, it is quite the customary thing, and I certainly never heard of such a procedure as you are suggesting. Besides, it costs no more."

"Costs the same? . . . for two as for one?"

"Certainly," I replied.

"Taken separate, like?" he continued.

"No, if taken separately the cost would be doubled, but on wedding occasions the bride and bridegroom are almost invariably photographed together, and that involves no extra cost."

He thought this over for half a minute and then made up his mind definitely.

"I'll be taken by myself," he said, ". . . to match this 'ere."—He drew from his breast-pocket a rather faded photograph, cabinet size, which displayed a younger Mrs. Robertshaw in the fashion of a dozen years before.—"Maria got these . . . just afore Robertsha' died . . . has best part of a dozen on 'em . . . . gave Robertsha''s away . . . pity to waste these . . . 'll do nicely."

"But Mr. Higgins," I protested, "these photographs are faded, and they are not the Mrs. Higgins of to-day. Nobody wears that style of dress now, and she has actually a fringe! Throw them away, and do as I propose."

"I see nowt wrong wi''t," he replied, examining it critically. "She's fatter now, an' isn't as good lookin' . . . more wrinkles, like. . . . Makes a nicer pictur, this does . . . plenty good enough for 'er."

"Mr. Higgins!" I exclaimed indignantly.

"If—you—please—miss," he said emphatically, "it's me as gives the order . . . one dozen, miss . . . to match this 'ere."

There was nothing more to be said, and I took two negatives of the wretched little man, in the first of which he is shown standing as erect as nature permits, with the silk hat fixed firmly upon his head, and one hand in his trousers' pocket, so that the white waistcoat might not be concealed; and in the second, sitting with one leg thrown over the other, and the silk hat upon his knee. It was in vain that I pointed out that neither pose would correspond with that of his wife, which was a mere vignetted head and shoulders; Barjona had made up his mind, and was not to be moved, and I felt thankful, with Mother Hubbard, that I was not Mrs. Higgins.

I went out to speak to her when the operation had been completed, and at our approach the neighbours who had been keeping her company smiled and drew back a little.

"Good-afternoon, Mrs. Higgins," I said. "I have already congratulated your husband; let me now wish you much happiness."

"Well, now, to be sure, Miss Holden," she replied, and accompanying the words with a most decided wink, "that remains to be seen. But if he doesn't give me much, he'll 'ave less, I can tell you. I think we shall get on when we've settled down a bit; an' anyway, time won't hang as 'eavy on my 'ands, so to speak."

"Come, lass, we must be going," interrupted Barjona, who had climbed up beside her.

"As soon as ever I've finished," replied Mrs. Higgins, smiling upon him sweetly. Nevertheless, she tightened the reins and prepared to move.

"I'll drive, lass," said Barjona, holding out his hand.

"I'll keep 'em mysen, lad," replied his wife; "I've 'eld 'em all this time while t' mare was still: I'll 'old 'em now when she's on t' move. Come up, lass!"

She threw me another portentous wink, and the mare moved slowly down the lane.

"Poor Barjona!" murmured Mother Hubbard, as we sauntered back to the cottage.

"I wonder if you are right," I remarked rather viciously. "I certainly hope you are. At present my sympathies lie in the other direction, and I am disposed to say 'Poor Maria!'"

"Yes, love," said Mother Hubbard, "perhaps she has the worse of the bargain; but I think the old fox has got into a trap that is going to hold him very tight this time, and it will nip hard."

"I hope it nips until he squeals," I said impenitently.

This was on the Monday following Whitweek. The next day brought me a long, chatty letter from the squire, who feels wonderfully better and talks of coming home again soon. He cannot understand why the doctors always say "not just yet." He is at Sorrento now, and chaffingly condoles with me on the remote prospects of a continental trip, at any rate on his account. I wonder if he guesses how relieved I am, and how eagerly I anticipate his home-coming.

In him I seem to have a friend who understands, and I am beginning to think that is the only *real* kind of friend. I have said all along that I do not understand myself. I am always coming across odd little tracts of territory in my nature which surprise me and make me feel something of an explorer, whereas I cannot help feeling, somehow or other, that the squire knows all about me, and could make a map of my character if he chose, with all my moods and whims and angularities accurately indicated, like so many rivers and mountains. And so far from resenting this I am glad of it, because he is so kind and fatherly with it all, and not a bit superior. Now the Cynic, although he is no doubt a mighty clever man, makes you so frightfully conscious of his cleverness.

By the way, I have made a discovery about him. He is a barrister, and quite an eminent one in his way. I suppose I might have found this out long ago by asking any of the Windyridge men, but for some occult reason I have never cared to inquire. The discovery came about in this way.

When I had finished reading the squire's letter, and before proceeding to my work, I took up the *Airlee Despatch* which Farmer Goodenough had left with us, solely because it contained a short paragraph on the "Wedding of a well-known Windyridge character"—no other, in fact, than our friend Barjona.

As my eyes travelled cursorily over the columns they were arrested by the following:

"Mr. Philip Derwent, whose brilliant advocacy admittedly secured a verdict for the plaintiff in the recently concluded case of Lessingham v. Mainwaring, which has occupied so much space in all the newspapers recently, is, as most of our readers will know, a native of Broadbeck. His father, Mr. Stephen Derwent, was engaged in the staple trade of that town, but was better known for the interest he took in many religious and philanthropic movements, and in those circles his death five years ago occasioned a considerable gap. If report may be relied upon Mr. Philip Derwent's decision to read for the bar was a disappointment to his father, but the striking success which has attended him all through his legal career has sufficiently justified his choice. It was a matter of general comment in legal circles during the recent proceedings that Mr. Derwent more than held his own against such eminent luminaries as Sir George Ritson and Mr. Montgomery Friend, who were the King's Counsel opposed to him. He showed remarkable versatility in the conduct of his case, and his cross-examinations and repartees were brilliant in the extreme. Whether his law is as reliable as his rhetoric may be open to question, but one looks forward to his future career with special interest, as he is still on the sunny side of forty, and is therefore young enough to win many laurels. His mother died when he was quite young, and he is himself unmarried."

Why I should have felt low-spirited when I put the paper down I do not know. It is just these unexplained "moodinesses" which make me feel so cross with myself. The squire's letter had been bright, and the paragraph about Barjona amusing, and certainly the reference to Mr. Derwent was ordinary enough. Still I stared at nothing quite intently for a few minutes after reading it. Then I shook myself.

"Grace Holden!" I said, "plunge your face into cold water, and go straight to your work in the studio. You have negatives to retouch, and prints to tone and develop, and nearly a dozen miniatures to paint, all of which are shamefully overdue; and no amount of wool-gathering will bring you in the thirty shillings which you have fixed as your weekly minimum. Now be a sensible woman, and 'frame,' as your neighbours say."

So I "framed," thinking the while how contemptuously the Cynic would smile at my thirty shillings.

CHAPTER FIFTEEN

ROSE ARRIVES

THE SURPRISES OF life are sometimes to be counted amongst its blessings. I daresay Reuben Goodenough, who is one of the most religious men I have met—though I am puzzled to know where his religion comes from, seeing that he rarely visits church or chapel—would affirm that *all* life's incidents are to be regarded as blessings. "All things work together for good," as "t' Owd Book" says.

He argued this point with me at considerable length one day, and though he did not convince my head he secured the approval of my heart. He is distinctly a philosopher after his kind, with the important advantage that his philosophy is not too ethereal and transcendent, but designed for everyday use. He professes to believe that there are no such things as "misfortunes," and so takes each day's events calmly. For the life of me I cannot see it, but I rather cling to the thought when the untoward happens.

Be that as it may, the surprise which "struck me all of a heap," to use a common expression of my neighbours, in the last week of June was a blessing that one could count at the time.

It was evening, and I was standing in the garden among the roses and pinks, engaged in removing the few weeds which had escaped Mother Hubbard's observant eye, and pausing occasionally to wonder which I admired the more—the stately irises in their magnificent and varied robes, or the great crimson peonies which made a glorious show in one corner— when the gate was pushed open, and an elegant young lady, in a smart, tailor-made costume and a becoming toque, glided towards me. I took another look and gasped for breath.

"Well, Grace," said the apparition, holding out a neatly gloved hand, "one would say that you were astonished to see me."

"Rose, you darling!" I ejaculated, "come and kiss me this minute, and show me which particular cloud has dropped you at my feet! My dear girl, you have stunned me, and I feel that I must pinch you to see if you are really flesh and blood."

"If there is to be any pinching, my dear Grace, *I* prefer to do it. It will prove my corporeal existence just as conclusively, and be less painful—to me. So this is Windyridge?"

"Rose!" I exclaimed, "for goodness' sake don't be so absurdly practical and commonplace, but tell me why you have come, and where you are staying, and how everybody is at old Rusty's, and how long you are going to be in the north, and all about yourself, and—and—everything."

"All that will take time," replied Rose calmly, as she removed her gloves; "but I will answer the more important parts of your questions. I am staying here, with you. If you are very nice and kind to me you will press me to remain ten days with you, and I shall yield to pressure, after the customary formal and insincere protests. Then you will put on your hat and walk with me down to Fawkshill station, and as there are no cabs to be had there we will bring up my bag between us."

"*That* we need not do," I said. "There are half a dozen strong boys in the village, any one of whom would fetch your belongings for love of me and threepence of your money."

"Happy Grace!" she sighed; "'love rules the court, the camp, the grove,' as saith the poet. Be it even so. Summon the favoured swain, discharge his debt, and I will be in thine."

"Rose! Rose! you are the same incorrigible, pert, saucy girl as of yore, but you have filled my heart with joy. I am treading on air and giddy with delight. We will have ten days of undiluted rapture. Come inside and look round my home. Mother Hubbard is 'meeting for tickets' to-night, and will not be back for a good half-hour."

"Meeting for what?" inquired Rose blankly.

"Meeting for tickets," I repeated. "My dear old lady is a Methodist class leader, and to 'meet for tickets' is a shibboleth beyond your untutored comprehension. But the occasion is one of vast importance to her, and you are not to make fun of her."

She was pleased with everything and expressed her pleasure readily. In spite of her composed manner she is a very dear girl indeed, and though she is years younger than I am she and I always hit it exactly. When she saw the tiny bed and realised that we should have to share it she laughed merrily.

"*I* will sleep next to the wall to-night," she said, "because I am very tired, and it would be annoying to be always falling out. I shall sleep so soundly that your bumping the floor will not disturb me, so you will have nothing to worry about. Then to-morrow night I will take the post of danger, and so alternately."

"We might rope ourselves together," I suggested, "and fasten the ends to a stake outside the window. I don't think the bumping idea appeals to me."

But Mother Hubbard planned a better way on her return, and contrived a simple and ingenious addition to the width of the bed by means of chairs and pillows, which served our purpose admirably.

Over the supper table Rose told us all about her visit. "You see, I have not been quite the thing lately: nervy and irritable and that sort of nonsense, which the chief charitably construed into an indication of ill-health. He was awfully decent about it and suggested that I should see a doctor. I told him I was all right, but he insisted, so I saw Dr. Needham, and he told me I was run down and required bracing air. 'Mountain air would be better than the seaside,' he said. 'You haven't friends in Scotland or Yorkshire, I suppose?' Then I thought of you. 'I have a friend who went wrong in her head about twelve months ago,' I said (or words to that effect), 'and she ran away to the Yorkshire moors. She might take me in if I could get off.' 'The very thing,' he said. 'Will you have any difficulty with your employer?'

"'I don't think so,' I replied; 'not if it is really necessary. The chief is a discriminating man, and I believe realises that my services are invaluable, and he will put up with a little temporary inconvenience in order to retain them permanently, I imagine.' You are accustomed to my modesty, Grace, and will not be surprised that I spoke with humility.

"Well, he smiled and said he would give me a certificate, so I took the certificate and my departure and interviewed the chief in his den! It was as I had anticipated. I was to get away at once. Ten days on the moors would put the wine of life into my blood. That was theory. The practical assumed the form of a five-pound note, which enables me to play the part of the grand lady—a rôle for which I was designed by nature, but which providence spitefully denied me. I stated my intentions to the Rusty one, who coldly sent you her regards, but I determined to take *you* by surprise, hoping to catch you unprepared and unadorned, whereas you are neither the one nor the other. Then I boarded the two o'clock Scotch express at St. Pancras, changed trains at Airlee, and *me voilà!* By the way, what about my bag?"

The bag came all right in due course, and in the days that followed Rose and I gave ourselves up to enjoyment. It was like living one's life twice over to share the delight she showed in her surroundings.

Fortunately I had got abreast of my work, and we ordinarily devoted our afternoons to business and spent the mornings and evenings in Nature's wonderland.

During those ten glorious days the sun worked overtime for our special benefit, and put in seventeen hours with unfailing regularity. He smiled so fiercely on Rose's cheeks that she would have justified her godmother's choice if she had not preferred the hue of the berry, and turned a rich chestnut.

Mowing was in full swing in the meadows, and we took our forks and tossed the hay about and drank barley-water with the rest. We followed the men whose heads were lost in the loads of hay which they carried on their backs, and saw how they dropped their burden in the haymow. We stood like children, open-mouthed, admiring the skill and industry of the man who there gathered it up and scattered it evenly round and round the mow.

We went into Reuben Goodenough's farmyard, and I showed her the barn owls which have taken up their abode in his pigeon loft, and which live amicably with their hosts and feed on mice. We descended the fields to the woods, which the recent felling has thinned considerably, but which have all the rank luxuriance of summer, and revelled amid the bracken and trailing roses. We stood by the streamlet where the green dragon-flies flitted in the sunshine, and where millions of midges hovered in the air to become the prey of the swallows which rushed through with widely open mouths and took their fill without effort.

We spent hours on the moor, where the heather, alas! had not yet appeared, but which was a perfect storehouse of novelties and marvels. Who would have thought, for instance, that the little golden bundles which cling to the furze, and which we thought were moss, were just so many colonies of baby spiders? We watched the merlins, the fierce cannibals of the moors, which dash upon the smaller birds and are even bold enough to attack the young grouse at times. What did we not do! Where did we not go! And neither of us suffered from surfeit.

"Grace," said Rose, as we lay on our backs in my paddock, and gazed upon the white cumulus clouds which floated above, "I withdraw all I have said about your madness, and I now declare you to be particularly sane. If ever I go back to town, which is doubtful, I will describe your sanity in terms which will relieve the fears of all at No. 8. My personal appearance will give colour to my statements, and I shall probably observe, with the originality which is a mark of genius, that God made the country and man made the town. But I have not yet decided to return, although I took a ten days' ticket. Your studio seems to have served its purpose: is there any opening in Windyridge for a talented stenographer and typist?"

"The prospects would not appear to be exactly dazzling," I replied, "but I'm willing to keep you here on the off-chance that something may turn up."

"Some*body*'s turning up," said Rose, hurriedly assuming a sitting posture, "and *we* had better *get* up."

I imitated her example, and saw that the Cynic had leaped the wall and was coming towards us.

I did the necessary introductions and we sat down again. "I called," said the Cynic, "in the hope that there might be a clock to regulate or a creeper to nail up, in which case I might earn a cup of tea. Also, to make arrangements for my photograph."

"I couldn't expect you to do any work in those clothes." I replied. "Is this a visit of ceremony, or have you come in your Sunday best in order to have your portrait taken? All my local sitters insist upon putting on the clothes in which they feel and look the least comfortable."

"No," he said, with a glance at his black trousers—the rest of him was hidden by a light dust-coat—"the fact is, I am dining with the vicar and spending the night at the vicarage. I must go to town on Saturday, but to-day and to-morrow are free. I propose, with your gracious permission, to spend an hour here, walk on to Fawkshill, and return to-morrow for the dread operation to which I have referred."

"I am afraid it will not be convenient to-morrow," I said; "really I am very sorry to upset your plans, but Miss Fleming returns to town on Saturday, and we have promised ourselves a full day on the moors. Of course, if you could come very early——"

Rose interrupted. "Don't let me hinder business, my dear Grace, or I shall have you on my conscience, and that will be no light burden. We can modify our arrangements, of course."

"What about my conscience, in that case?" said the Cynic. "I am not really very particular about the photograph, especially in my 'Sunday best,' and I can easily come up some other day. But—who is going to carry the luncheon basket?"

"There is no basket," I returned; "our arrangements are much more primitive, and the burden grows lighter as the day proceeds. Moreover, I don't think it is very nice of you to suggest that the photograph is of slight importance. Don't you realise that it is my living?"

"I realise the truth of the poet's assertion that woman is 'uncertain, coy, and hard to please.' A moment ago you were declining business—declining it with an air of polite regret, it is true, but quite emphatically. *Now*, when I not only refuse to disturb your arrangements, but actually hint an offer of assistance, you scent a grievance."

Rose was looking very hard at me, and I felt vexed with the man for placing me in such an awkward position. And to make matters worse the consciousness of Rose's stare upset my self-possession, and it was she who spoke first.

"If Mr. Derwent would join us I think it would be very nice," she said, so demurely that I stared at her in my turn, "and it would be an—education for him. And he certainly could carry the sandwiches and our wraps, which are a bit of a nuisance."

What could I say? I was annoyed, but I could only mutter something incoherent which my companions construed into an assent, and Rose instructed the Cynic to be at the cottage at ten o'clock in the morning.

To add to my confusion, Mother Hubbard was manifestly excited when we went in to tea, and she telegraphed all sorts of meaning messages to Rose when the Cynic's back was turned. I was cross with myself for becoming embarrassed, but I hate to be placed in a false position. What on earth is the Cynic to me?

I thought he was rather subdued and not quite as satirical as usual, but he was obviously very much taken with Rose, who was quite brilliant in her cuts and thrusts. She soon took the Cynic's measure, and I saw how keenly he enjoyed the encounter. I left them to it very largely, much to the disappointment of Mother Hubbard, who developed a series of short, admonitory coughs, and pressed my foot beneath the table a score of times in a vain effort to induce me to shine. It was not my "night out," and her laudable endeavours simply resulted in a sore foot—the injured member being mine.

We accompanied him a little way along the road, and when we left him Rose turned upon me:

"Now 'fess!" she said.

"Rose, don't be a goose!" I replied, whilst the stupid colour flooded my face; "there is nothing to confess. I have seen Mr. Derwent only twice before in my life. He is little more than a stranger to me."

"A remarkable circumstance, however, my dear Grace, is that you have never mentioned his name in your rather voluminous correspondence, and yet you seem to be on familiar and even friendly terms; and our good friend Mother Hubbard——"

"Mother Hubbard, Rose, is romantic. The moment the man turned up at Easter she designated him as my lover. Let me be quite candid with you. If I was not so constituted that blushing comes as naturally to me as to a ripe cherry you would have had no reason to suspect anything. It is the innocent, I would remind you, who blush and look guilty. Mr. Derwent is a barrister—a friend of the vicar and of the squire—and he amuses himself by calling here when he is in the village—that is all. And if you are going to be as silly as Mother Hubbard it is too bad of you."

I felt this was frightfully weak and unconvincing, as the truth so often is.

"U-m!" said Rose, spreading the ejaculation over ten seconds; "I see. Then there's nothing more to be said about it. He isn't a bad sort, is he? Why in the world you never mentioned him in your letters I cannot conceive."

It was too bad of Rose.

CHAPTER SIXTEEN

THE CYNIC SPEAKS
IN PARABLES

"WHAT MAKES YOU call me the Cynic?" he inquired.

It was Rose's fault; she is really incorrigible, and absolutely heedless of consequences! If I had dreamed that she would have done such a thing I would never have told her, but that is the worst of blanket confidences. I call them "blanket" confidences because it was after we had gone to bed, when it was quite dark and Rose was inclined to be reasonable, that I had explained to her calmly and quite seriously that I had not mentioned the Cynic in my letters because there had been no reason to do so; and Rose had accepted the explanation, like a good girl, and kissed me to show her penitence. Then I told her of the nickname I had given him, which she thought very appropriate. But I would have held my tongue between my teeth if I had contemplated the possibility of her revealing the secret; and here she had blurted it out with a laugh, to my utter and dire confusion.

We had had a glorious day, and I must admit that the Cynic had added not a little to our enjoyment. He said he would have felt like a fool to be walking out in black West of Englands, so he had called at the Hall and got the butler to find up an old shooting jacket of the squire's, which was much too large for him, but in which he appeared quite unconcernedly a full ten minutes before the time appointed.

"It isn't a good fit," he remarked with a laugh, "but the other toggery was impossible for the moors."

Under his guidance we had gone farther than we should otherwise have ventured, and he had pointed out a hundred beauties and wonders

our untrained eyes would never have seen. He had interpreted the varying
cries of the curlew, and shown us how intently the gamekeeper listened
to them, so that he might know whether man or beast or bird was
attracting the watcher's notice. He had pointed out the trustful little twite,
which I should have mistaken for a linnet, and followed it to its abode,
where he told us we should find a single feather stuck conspicuously in
the edge of the nest; and it had been even so. Our botanical knowledge
would have been greatly increased if we had remembered all he told us,
but though we did not do so we were deeply interested, for he had none
of the air of the schoolmaster, and he did not expect us to take our lessons
very seriously.

And now the day was spent, and our energy, though not our spirits,
had flagged considerably. We were sitting on the edge of the moor, a mile
or so away from home, and the flush of evening spread over the valley and
the distant hills, turning the landscape into mystery. The lamp of the
setting sun was flickering out in the west, but the handmaidens of the
night had lit their tiny torches here and there, and they shone faintly
behind the veil of twilight, giving promise of greater radiance when the
time should come for them to go forth to meet the crescent bride who
tarried in her coming.

I was gazing on it dreamily, and breathing out peace and goodwill
towards men when Rose dropped her bomb, and shattered my complacency.

"What makes you call me the Cynic?" He turned his eyes upon me
and awaited my answer with evident curiosity.

I looked at him in my turn. He had been bareheaded all day, for he
had left his hat at the Hall, and he was now leaning back against a rock,
his hands clasped behind his head, and the mischievous look I have so
often noticed sparkling in his eyes. He really is rather a fine man, and he
has certainly a good strong face. I replied, calmly enough to outward
seeming:

"Because it has seemed to me an apt description."

"I hope not," he replied. "Cynicism is the small change of shallow
minds. All the same, it is interesting to be criticised. I did not know
when I offered to analyse your character that I was being subjected to the
same test."

"Indeed you were not," I protested; "it was an appellation that came to me spontaneously whilst you were discoursing so luminously on woman a few months ago, and it is not to be taken seriously. It was wicked of Rose to tell you."

Rose laughed and put an arm around me. "Never mind, old girl," she said, "I'm going back to-morrow, so you must forgive me."

"I'm afraid you have not distinguished with sufficient care, Miss Holden, between satire and cynicism. I daresay there is a strain of satire in my composition, but I do not plead guilty to cynicism. A cynic is a surly, misanthropical man, with a disordered liver and a contempt for the good things of life."

"Oh, Grace!" murmured Rose in pathetic tones, "how could you!"

"Nonsense!" I said, "I am not going to allow you to pretend to take me seriously. Do you think I subjected the word to subtle analysis before I adopted it? I tell you it came to me as an inspiration, heaven-born, doubtless, but if you don't like it pray forget it; and for your comfort I will add that I have never attached to the word the meaning you read into it. I know you have no contempt for art and poetry and the good things of life. Now tell us what you see before you?"

I wished to change the subject, and referred simply to the view, as anyone might have known. Night was dropping her blue curtain as gently, as silently, as the nurse spreads the coverlet over the sleeping babe; but the stupid man professed to misunderstand me.

"I see before me," he replied, "two interesting specimens of the sex which ruins the peace and creates the paradise of the bulk of mankind. I would call them charming but for the fear that my candour might be mistaken for cajolery, which my soul abhorreth."

"Oh, please stop this!" I pleaded, but Rose said: "Let him ramble on," and he continued:

"The one whom I judge to be the elder is tall and well proportioned. She has a fairly deep brow which indicates some intellectual power, but whether this is modified or intensified by cranial depressions and pro-tuberances, a mass of dark hair, arranged in a fashion that beggars my feeble powers of description, hides from my eyes.

"Her mouth is firm, and set above a determined chin, which would lead me to conclude that she has a will of her own and is accustomed to exercise it; but her eyes are tender and pleading, and so near the reservoir of her emotions that the waters readily overflow, and this in some measure counteracts the qualities of the chin. She has a pretty wit and a ready tongue—usually—and has lived long enough to be convinced of her own powers; rather masterful with the world at large, but not mistress of herself."

"Thank you!" I interrupted. He bowed.

"She dresses with taste and has tidy and methodical habits; is ever ready with sympathy, but would never care deeply for anybody who did not show her a heap of affection."

"Do I cross your hand with silver?" I inquired.

He ignored my interruption and turned his whimsical gaze upon Rose.

"Her companion, whom I have had fewer opportunities of observing, is slight, fair, and small of stature. I should say she might be scheduled as 'dangerous,' for she flashes most unexpectedly. She is rather proud of her self-possession, and delights in appearing cool and unemotional, but in reality she is neither. She has simply cultivated repression for the sake of effect. She is intense in her likes and dislikes and quite capable of hating those whom she regards with aversion, whilst she would apotheosise anyone for whom she really cared. Her wit is more brilliant but also more superficial than that of her friend, and her mental outlook is clearer and consequently more optimistic. She prides herself on unconventionality, and is at heart the slave of conventionalism. In a word she is a paradox, but a very agreeable and fascinating one."

"I had much rather be a paradox than a paragon," said Rose; "but after your very inadequate delineation of my character I am trying to determine in which pigeon-hole of my carefully concealed emotions I am to docket you."

"Is that quite true, Miss Fleming?" inquired the Cynic, looking at her keenly. "I should have said you made up your mind on that point last evening."

The tan upon her cheeks and the cloak of twilight covered Rose's blushes to a large extent, but I am sure the colour deepened, and I am convinced the Cynic saw it.

He rose and gathered up the wraps. "It is getting chilly," he observed; "shall we be moving?"

I turned the conversation into another channel. "You are going to town this week-end. Is most of your time spent there?"

"Yes," he replied, "my work lies in London, though Broadbeck is my home, and I run down very often, merely, I believe, to breathe the murky air and refresh my soul with the Yorkshire burr. I go back refreshed without knowing why. I have no relatives here now, and few friends, but the few I have, though they do not guess it, are my greatest comfort."

"Comfort!" ejaculated Rose; "what can you know of the need of comfort? You, at any rate, are self-centred and self-possessed. You have evidently a sufficient income and lots of the good things of life; you are entirely your own master, and on the highroad to fame; what more can you want?"

"Much," he replied simply; "and chiefly the sympathy which understands without explanations, and I get that only amongst my own folk. Do you know what that means? I have all the things you speak of: an increasing practice, an adequate income, good health, work that brings its own pleasure, an appreciation of life, consequent, no doubt, upon all these things, and an ardent longing for the relief which only real sympathy affords."

"I don't understand," said Rose, "notwithstanding my clear outlook on life."

"Do you?" The Cynic turned to me.

"Partially," I replied. "I can understand that none of these things satisfies in itself, and that you may have 'all things and abound,' and yet crave something you cannot work for and earn. But I should have thought your profession would have left you little time for sentiment, even if it afforded scope for it."

"You know, then, what my profession is?"

"You are a barrister, and, as Rose says, on the highroad to fame."

"Well," he replied, "I suppose that is true. I have as much work as I can undertake and I am well paid for it. Success, in that sense, has come, though slowly, and I am considered by many a lucky fellow. My future is said to be full of promise. I have, in the sense in which you spoke, 'all things and abound,' and when I step into the arena of conflict I am conscious of this, and of this only. In the heat of the fray the joy of battle comes upon me, and I am oblivious to all else.

"Then comes the after-thought, when the fray is ended and the arena has been swept clean for the next encounter. 'What lack I yet?' In the process of gaining the whole world am I going to lose myself? And the throng presses upon me and slaps my back and shakes my hand and shouts, 'Lucky dog!' into my ear, and I smile and look pleased—am pleased—until my Good Spirit drives me north, where the air is not soft, but biting, and men speak their minds without circumlocution and talk to you without deference, and give you a rough but kindly thrust if they think you need it. And there I find vision and comfort."

"You are utterly beyond me," said Rose. "You are soaring in the clouds miles above my head, and I cannot yet understand why you need comfort."

"Do you remember the young ruler who went away sorrowful?" he replied. He was looking straight ahead, with a sad, fixed look in his eyes such as I had not seen there before. "I wonder if he went north and found a friend who understood, and from him gained comfort. You see, he *knew* that something was lacking, but could not make up his mind to pay the price of the remedy, and even the Great Physician, whilst He gave the unwelcome prescription, pitied and loved him. The world called him a lucky dog, and he called himself one—with a reservation. And he wanted comfort; not the comfort which simply says, 'Buck-up, old man!' but that which says, 'Brace-up, old man! If to sell all is the summum bonum, go, see the broker now and have done with it.' I wonder if he went eventually."

This was a new mood, and I glanced at the Cynic curiously. What had become of his cynicism? He was speaking quietly, contemplatively, and I felt sure there was meaning behind his words.

I said nothing, but Rose shook her head and muttered: "You speak in parables."

"Let me give you a parable," he continued. "Once upon a time a certain boy on leaving school left also a large number of marbles. These were claimed by two of his companions, and one of the two took possession of them. Then arose a great outcry on the part of him who would have taken them if he could, and he dragged his fellow before a council of their peers. The monitor was judge, and two sharp young fellows who were good in debate and of ready tongue acted as counsel for the claimant and his foe respectively.

"In the end judgment was given for the claimant, who carried off triumphantly the spoils of battle. And this judgment was given, not because the defendant had no right to the marbles, but because the lad who championed his cause was not so glib of speech nor so ready in argument as the fellow on the other side. Now it came to pass that the lad who won the case for his friend discovered soon after, what he had suspected all along—that the latter had no real claim to the marbles at all, and that they had been taken unjustly from the lad to whom they rightfully belonged. Yet the judgment of the court could not be upset. What was he to do?"

"Nothing," replied Rose promptly.

"Why?" inquired the Cynic.

"It was the fortune of war," she answered; "the case was properly tried by an impartial court, and the defendant should have taken care to secure the services of the smarter advocate. It would be a lesson to him for the future. The world would never get on if everyone worried about things of that sort."

"And you?" he said, turning to me.

"Was there no chance of reversing the judgment?" I inquired.

"None: it was irrevocable."

"Had the plaintiff's counsel reason to suspect, did you say, that his client's cause was unjust before the verdict was given?"

"He became practically convinced of it as the case proceeded, but not absolutely certain. Yet he fought for his client with might and main."

"Had the plaintiff's counsel any marbles of his own?" I continued.

"He had. Quite a fair store."

"Sufficient to pay back the lad who had suffered the unjust judgment?" About sufficient; no more."

My heart thumped painfully, but I did not hesitate to answer: "I think he ought to have parted with his own marbles, and so redressed the wrong and saved his soul."

There was silence for a moment before the Cynic spoke: "I think so, too." Then, irrelevantly: "There is something about this northern air that is very bracing."

CHAPTER SEVENTEEN

GRACE BECOMES DEJECTED

I HAD NO time to feel depressed after Rose left on Saturday, for the afternoon brought me more customers than I could well accommodate.

My reputation must have travelled as far as Broadbeck, for the greater number of my patrons are from that town. They consist for the most part of engaged couples, or couples that obviously intend to become engaged; and whether it is the excellence of my productions, or the low charges, or just the fun of being photographed by a woman in a hamlet like Windyridge that attracts them, I have not been able to determine, and it does not very much matter. Mother Hubbard, on the other hand, finds the explanation simple. I am the most talented of artists, with all the indifference of the genuine genius to adequate remuneration.

I was thoroughly tired when tea-time came and my day's labours ended, and was quite ready to be petted and made a fuss of by my dear old lady. By the way, the summer has unfortunately not brought back her old vigour, and I cannot help worrying a little about her, though she is as bright and optimistic as ever.

I got a long letter from Rose on Monday morning. It had been written, of course, on the Sunday, whilst the scent of the moors was still in her nostrils; but though she feels the change pretty badly I am sure she is not so depressed as I am. It must have taken her a heap of time to fill so many sheets of notepaper with her small, business-like handwriting. There were a good many sparkling sentences in the letter, but I cannot say that I felt particularly cheerful when I had finished it.

It appears that the Cynic was travelling by the Midland express, and they were companions all the way from Airlee. He was already in the train, which starts from Broadbeck, and he caught sight of her on the platform. It seems strange that he should have gone round that way, for I remember he told us once that he always travelled by Great Northern, as it is the shorter route.

I fancy he was rather taken with Rose, and I know she liked him very much, for she said so quite openly. It would do the Cynic good to be married, especially as he seems to need comforting, and Rose is one of the dearest girls in existence, and would make him a good wife—at least, I hope she would. And although she has to earn her own living, she is really very well connected, and had a quite superior education. It was simply her father's recklessness that threw her on her own resources, and I should say that her origin is as good as the Cynic's.

And yet I should hardly have thought that she was just his sort. He is a man who will make large demands upon his wife if she is to be a real helpmeet, and he needs to be understood. I am sure Rose did not understand him. But perhaps, after all, she would be very suitable in one way. She is ambitious, and would see that he did not hide his light under a bushel in social circles; though, to be sure, society might turn up its nose at *her*. It would worry me terribly if anything should come of this chance encounter under my chaperonage, and either party should be unhappy. It may be undue sensitiveness on my part, but I feel rather oppressed with a sense of responsibility.

Of course, looking at the matter quite calmly, it seems ridiculous to be building air-castles like this, but I am *very fond* of Rose and I would not for worlds have her marry unsuitably; and I cannot help respecting the Cynic after what he said the other night. It would be just terrible if they were to make a mess of their lives. Marriage is such a very serious undertaking, and lots of really sensible people appear to lose their heads altogether when they come to make the important choice. However, it is none of my business, and I won't refer to it again.

Rose says he was very attentive to her during the journey, and handed her quite a number of illustrated papers, including some ladies' journals. If I were a barrister I should never dream of buying papers which make their appeal to the other sex; but perhaps he finds it necessary to the study of human nature. A man in his profession must have to be as many-sided as a poet.

I conclude that she did not read the magazines, for she says so much about their conversation that it is evident there was little opportunity, and besides, they lunched together in the diner, and that must have taken up a lot of time. She admits that she teased him, and that he seemed to like it, but she does not say what about. He said the other day that she was dangerous. I wonder if he really thought so, and is on his guard against the danger, for Rose has always been somewhat of a flirt, and it would hurt a man like him deeply if he really cared and found she was only playing with him. He is the sort that—— But I said I would not refer to it, and here I am doing so.

He told her he hoped to see something of her occasionally, and she was unconventional enough to hope the same. They are sure to make opportunities easily enough when they are both in London. I feel glad for Rose, for he is the kind of man who will steady her a bit, but I hope she—— Oh, bother it!

Madam Rusty received my kind messages, it appears, with apparent indifference, so Rose waxed eloquent over the Sunday dinner table, and painted a picture of my surroundings in the most brilliant colours from the palette of her imagination. She stimulated the curiosity of the boarders, who showed a great interest in me and my adventures, and were eager to know what kind of fare was provided in the wilderness, and what was the character of the heathen in whose midst I dwelt; to all of which she replied in a strain of subdued enthusiasm which she assured me carried conviction. I was regarded, she informed them, with the same respect as was naturally accorded to the squire of the place, with whom I was on terms of extreme intimacy. Good air and really good food (Rose emphasised this for madam's benefit) had brought to my cheeks the glow of health; and my abilities had secured for me a *clientèle* which would make a West End photographer think sad thoughts. This, goodness knows, was true enough.

She went into ecstasies over Mother Hubbard's cooking, and caused the company to believe that the fatted calf, and all other makes of fatted beasts and birds of the primest and tenderest quality, appeared upon my table regularly during her visit. When I remember the "pot-luck" we had so often laughed over at dinner-time, my admiration for Rose's imaginative faculties assumed huge proportions.

The heathen amongst whom I dwelt were, it appears, Nature's gentlefolk, hating unreality and humbug as they hated the devil. I think this was really rather clever of Rose, for it hits off some of my neighbours exactly, though the devil with whom they are on speaking terms might possibly seem a mild and blunt-horned personage to some of my London acquaintances.

There was a good deal more to the same effect, and having driven the Rusty one to the verge of apoplexy, Rose retired to her own room and penned her epistle. Seclusion evidently induced reaction, and she confessed to the depression I have hinted at. I don't wonder, poor girl. I should hate to be going to work in the crowded city after having tasted the freedom of the moors. All the same, there are compensations if you look for them. If you have friends who are congenial you have more opportunities of seeing them in a place like London. Everybody goes to London. Perhaps the Cynic will take her to see the new play at the St. James's Theatre. I shall be very glad, I am sure, if they become firm friends. My only doubt is of Rose. She is so thoughtless and flighty, and might do harm without meaning it. . . .

Oh, bother it again! I'm going to bed.

CHAPTER EIGHTEEN

CARRIER TED RECEIVES
NOTICE TO QUIT

I HAVE NOT been sleeping very well lately, and my dreams have given me the creeps and left me so irritable that if I had only a considerate and philanthropic employer like the one Rose patronises I am sure I should have been sent away somewhere for a change. Being my own employer, I stay on and make Mother Hubbard look worried. And the worst of it is she does not discuss my state of health as a sensible woman should, but just pets me and tells me it "will all come right in the end." When I ask her what it is that is to come right she smiles and relapses into silence. If she were not so gentle and loving and altogether sweet I should feel inclined to shake her.

Did I not say that the devil had his intimates in Windyridge? I nod to him myself just now, but Simon Barjona Higgins has gone into business with him on quite a large scale, and my friend Maria must surely be casting longing backward glances in the direction of widowhood. It makes one feel that matrimony is a snare which women are fools to enter with their eyes open; though I suppose all men are not given up to Satan.

Fancy Rose saying there were no humbugs about here, when such a man as Barjona flourishes unabashed! But when I come to think of it, she didn't quite say that: she simply said that my neighbours hated humbug as they hate the devil, and Barjona loves them both. The thought of him makes me sick, and when I found out what an old Shylock the man is I went into the studio with a hammer and smashed his negatives into a hundred pieces, with as much zest as if I had been a militant suffragette breaking windows in Regent Street under the eyes of a scandalised policeman.

If nature had been clothed in drab on Wednesday afternoon when the report of unusual occurrences in the village drew me to the little group of excited people who were discussing them it would have been appropriate to the occasion. But she wasn't—she was dressed in her gayest and most captivating summer clothing.

I think that in itself is vexing. Why should nature look so pleased and happy when people are miserable, and so emphasise the contrast? If I am grumpy to begin with it makes me feel ever so much worse to know that nature is laughing at me, and is just as bright and optimistic as I am wretched. And, contrariwise, if I do wake up one morning determined to "bid dull care begone"—who was it used that expression recently?—and be merry and cheerful, the skies are sure to be like lead, and the rain is certain to drip, drip, in that sullen, persistent fashion that would drive Mark Tapley himself to pessimism. There is a law of cussedness, I am convinced, and I believe I have discovered it. Mother Hubbard says it is my liver, and prescribes pills!

When I joined the group there were so many eager to tell me the story that it was some time before I could make out its purport. By the way, I ought to point out that I am *not* becoming a gossip, but I *am* interested in the news of the village. We have no *Daily Mail* to chronicle our doings, and our methods are therefore necessarily primitive. Besides, to hold aloof from one's neighbours is a sign of what Rose calls "snorkiness."

One of the dearest little cottages in the village is inhabited by a man called Carrier Ted. I had never been inside it, but its picturesqueness appeals to me every time I pass it, and you may often see visitors leaning over the low wall of the garden and enthusing about it. It is just a little one-storeyed, two-roomed cot, not nearly so big as some gentlemen's motor garages, but large enough for one occupant, or even for two if their tastes are simple.

The ground rises steeply behind it, and tall trees cover the hill from base to summit, so that the little white house is quite overshadowed by them. I call it a white house, but the walls are almost concealed by green and yellow and crimson, where the canary creeper and climbing roses stretch forth their slender arms to embrace the brown, thatched roof.

WINDYRIDGE VILLAGE

The garden is evenly divided into two parts by the flagged footpath which leads straight to the door, and it is always ablaze with colour in the summer time; but the arrangement is more orderly than in some of our Windyridge gardens, for Carrier Ted, albeit old-fashioned in his tastes, is an epicure in horticulture. Only a few days ago Rose and I had stopped to admire his bloom, and especially the wonderful moss roses which were his especial pride, and to have a word with the old man whose skill and industry had aroused my friend's enthusiasm.

When I first came to the village I took him to be of weak intellect, principally, I believe, because he always wore a tall silk hat of antiquated pattern. It was a very rough silk of uncertain colour, and gave one the impression that it was constantly brushed the wrong way; but whether working in the garden or walking along the road, Carrier Ted might always be recognised by his peculiar headgear.

But there is no daftness about him really. He is just a quiet, even taciturn old man, who is alone in the world and has saved sufficient money to enable him to spend the evening of life in comfort, and who finds in his home and garden both business, recreation and religion.

He is a little, bent man, round-faced and ruddy in spite of his eighty odd years, with thick grey eyebrows, and a half-circle of beard stretching from ear to ear beneath his chin. When you praise his flowers he pauses for a moment, draws his sleeve across his brow in a confused sort of way, as if to remove perspiration, and smiles. The smile and the action always remind me of a bashful child who would like to be friendly but dare not all at once. The smile lights up his face and reveals the angel within him; but he answers only in monosyllables, and seems relieved when you pass on your way. It was this man and his cottage who were the subject of excited conversation.

"It's a burnin' shame, Miss 'Olden, that's what it is!" exclaimed Widow Smithies, "an' if I'd my way I'd wring that old heathen of a Barjona his neck for 'im, that I would; the good-for-nowt, graspin' old money-lender 'at he is."

"He wants hoss-whippin'," said Sar'-Ann's mother, "an' if I were a man I'd do it! But our men fowk are no more use nor two penn'orth o' cowd gin, an' I'll be bound ther' isn't one on 'em 'at'll lift a little finger agen 'im."

"An' I'm sure anyone 'at can find it in their 'eart to do ought wrong to poor old Ted isn't fit to bide in t' village," said Martha Treffit; "an' one 'ud ha' thought wi' 'avin' been in t' same trade, like, Barjona 'ud never ha' tried to 'urt Ted."

"They may have been in t' same trade, Martha," interposed Susannah, "but Ted comes off a better pastur' nor ivver Barjona wa' raised on. 'E's as keen as mustard, is Barjona, an' 'ud mor'gage his soul for owt he took a fancy tul."

"He's as 'ard as iron in his 'eart," snapped Mrs. Smithies, "but as soft as a boiled turnup in his 'ead. I'd like to put 'im through t' wringin' machine, an' squeeze 'im for once, as is so ready to squeeze other fowk. 'Ere comes Reuben. What'll Reuben 'ave to say about it, I wonder?"

Reuben shook his head. "It's a sad job, neighbours, but law's law, an' we shall have to make t' best on 't."

"Hark to him!" said Sar'-Ann's mother; "didn't I tell you there isn't a man in t' village wi' as mich sperrit as a kitlin'? If Reuben won't do nowt ye can go bail 'at t' rest 'll noan stir."

"Right's right, an' law's law, all the world over," said Reuben, shaking his head; "an' it'll be no manner o' use tryin' to persuade Barjona ought different. I could easy throw him on t' midden, but that wouldn't mend matters. 'Ye can take t' horse to t' water, but ye can't make 'im drink,' as t' Owd Book says. It'll be a trial to t' owd man, but Ted 'll have to make up 'is mind to flit."

Reuben walked home with me and gave me a connected account of what had happened. "You see, Ted's lived i' yon cottage ever sin' I can remember, Miss 'Olden. I mind him bringin' his wife to it, maybe forty year sin', though I were just a lad at t' time, an' it'll be 'appen five year sin' she died. They were neither on 'em chickens when they were wed, an' they never 'ad any childer; but they allus seemed to get on right enough, an' I don't know 'at I ever 'eard tell of 'em 'aving a wrong word wi' one another, or wi' anyone else, for that matter. They lived peaceable wi' all men, as t' Owd Book puts it, an' kept theirselves *to* theirselves. But they never really made any friends, as you may say. If you looked in you were welcome, but you were never asked to stop, an' they never called in to see t' neighbours. His missis wasn't one o' t' gossipin' sort, an' 'e were away a good deal wi' his cart; an' so we got into t' 'abit o' leavin' 'em alone.

"She must have been seventy—ay, more than seventy—when she died (I believe it tells on t' stone, but I never took that much notice), an' one or two o' t' neighbours did look in during t' time 'at she were ill, an' did what they could for 'em both, and he were very grateful. But he made no fuss, an' when they put her away 'e just wiped 'is sleeve across 'is face, an' walked back an' started diggin' a trench in t' garden.

"Well, it come out this mornin' 'at Barjona's bought t' cottage, an' it appears he gave Ted notice to quit last week-end, an' his time's up on Saturda'. They say he's goin' to live there himself, an' I daresay it's likely enough. It belonged to a young chap down i' Fawkshill, an' Barjona has a 'old on him somehow, an' he's forced 'im to sell. I've been to see t' chap just now, but Barjona has got it right enough, deeds an' everything, an' law's law all the world over. Ted's fair rooted in t' soil o' that land, but he'll 'ave to shift, an' quick too. 'E's as hard as nails, is Barjona, an' Ted 'll have to clear out on Saturda'."

"But what a shame!" I remarked; "could not someone be induced to buy it from Barjona? Perhaps he would sell at a profit."

"I'm goin' to see him in t' mornin'," replied Reuben, "but I durst bet a five-pun note to a toothpick 'at he won't sell at any figure. I know Barjona. There's good wheat i' all men, but it's so lost among t' chaff i' Barjona's case 'at only t' Day o' Judgment 'll find it."

Reuben called the next day to report the fruitlessness of his mission.

"It's no use," he said, and for once the cheerful farmer had become gloomy; "I haven't got a right hang o' t' words, but t' Owd Book says summat, if I'm not mista'en, about ye can crush a man's 'ead up in a mortar wi' a pestle, an' if he's a fool at t' start, he'll be a fool at t' finish. Barjona says he's stalled o' livin' down yonder i' Maria's house in t' Gap, an' he's set 'is 'eart on yon cottage o' Ted's ever sin' he thought o' gettin' wed again. He's shut his teeth, an' ye couldn't prize 'em open wi' a chisel an' hammer."

"Could the squire do anything if I wrote him?" I asked.

"Mr. Evans? What can 'e do? T' cottage isn't his. Law's law, an' Barjona has t' law on his side. Ye can't fight agen law. Ted 'll have to shift. It's a pity, but it's no killin' matter, an' 'e'll get over it i' time."

"Not if he's rooted to the soil," I said; "old plants often die when transplanted."

"Now look 'ere, Miss 'Olden," he replied kindly; "don't you take on over this job. You're too fond o' suppin' sorrow. We all 'ave our own crosses to carry, an' it's right 'at we should 'elp to carry other folkses. But it's no use carryin' theirs unless you can lighten t' load for 'em. Frettin' for owd Ted 'll none make it any easier for 'im. You want to learn 'ow to be sorry i' reason, without frettin' yourself to death. Why aren't ye sorry for Barjona?"

"The miserable old fox!" I exclaimed.

"I dunno but what he's more to be pitied nor Ted," replied Reuben thoughtfully. "Now you just study a minute. Don't ye think the Lord 'll be more sorry to see Barjona's 'eart shrivelled up like a dried pig-skin, so as it can't beat like other people's, nor what 'E will for Ted, what's as 'armless as a baby? If I read t' Owd Book right 'E allus seemed t' sorriest for them 'at were t' worst. 'E wept over Lazarus, I know, but 'E didn't fret about him an' his sisters in t' same way as 'E fret over t' city when 'E wept over it. You see, Lazarus 'adn't gone wrong, an' t' city had. Lazarus an' t' girls had suffered i' their bodies an' their minds, same as we all 'ave to do, an' same as Ted is doin', but t' city 'at rejected 'Im was sufferin' in its soul.

"No, I pity Ted, but I pity Barjona more. It's t' sick 'at need t' physician, as t' Owd Book says, an' Barjona's got t' fatal disease o' greed an' selfishness an' covetousness an' 'ard-'eartedness, wi' all sorts o' complications, an' it doesn't make me pity 'im any less 'at 'e doesn't know 'at 'e ails ought. You never found the Lord ought but kind to them 'at 'E drave t' devils out of. Now you think it over, an' keep your sperrits up."

I have thought it over. Just now, perhaps, I am not in the mood to view the case philosophically. My own feelings reflect the mood of the village generally. I don't doubt Barjona's sickness, but my prescription would be a drastic one, and whipping with scorpions would be too good for him. There are some people whom kindness does not cure, and I imagine Barjona to be one of them.

I would go over to see Maria, but Farmer Goodenough is emphatic that I ought not to interfere. "It's ill comin' between married fowk," he says. He is sure I should make trouble, and he is very likely right. I was astonished when I heard that Barjona had left his lodgings and gone to live in the Gap, for it certainly seems out of the way for his business; but he has no right to disturb poor old Ted for his own convenience. I hope judgment will overtake him speedily.

Did I not say I had a nodding acquaintance with the devil?

CHAPTER NINETEEN

BARJONA'S DOWNFALL

SOON AFTER BREAKFAST on Saturday a furniture cart stopped at Carrier Ted's gate, and the village turned out *en masse*. There had been a heavy downpour of rain during the night, but the sun struggled through the clouds at breakfast time, and by nine o'clock had gained the mastery. It was dirty on the roadway, so the half-dozen neighbourly men who were piling the household effects on to the cart had to be careful not to rest them in the mud.

Not that Carrier Ted cared anything about it. He stood in the garden with the old silk hat pushed deep down over his brow, and looked abstractedly at his peonies. He seemed oblivious to the busy scene that was being enacted about him: of all the spectators he was the least moved: he, the most interested of all, was less interested than any.

By and by Barjona drove up and was greeted with scowls and muttered imprecations. Two or three of the women went a step beyond muttering, and expressed their views in terms that lacked nothing of directness.

"You ought to be ashamed o' yerself, Barjona Higgins!" said one; "yes, you ought! To turn the old man out of his 'ome at his time o' life. You'd turn a corpse out of its coffin, you would!"

Barjona's cold eyes contracted. "What's wrong now, eh?" he jerked; "house is mine, isn't it? . . . . Paid good money for it. . . . Can do as I like wi' my own, can't I? . . . You mind your business; I'll mind mine."

He walked up the path to the house, merely nodding to Ted as he passed; but Ted did not see him.

After a while he returned and went up to the old man, and shouted in his ear as though he were deaf, so that we all could hear:

"There'll be a bit o' plasterin' to do . . . your expense . . . an' there's a cracked winda-pane . . . ye'll pay for that, Ted?"

The old man looked up and passed his sleeve across his brow, then rubbed his knuckles in his eyes as though awaking from sleep.

"Owt 'at's right, Barjona; owt 'at's right, lad."

Reuben Goodenough's eldest son was passing at the time, with a heavy fender over his shoulder. Hearing these words he stopped, and I thought for a moment that he was going to bring it down on Barjona's head, but with an angry gesture he moved on and deposited his burden on the cart. Then he went up to the new owner and laid a heavy hand on his shoulder. How I admired the strong, well-set man, and the man within him.

"Mr. Higgins," he said, "you can see for yourself 'at Ted isn't fit for business. If you've ought to say, say it to me. I'm actin' for 'im."

There had been no such arrangement, of course, but this provisional government met with the approval of the crowd.

"That's right, Ben lad, you tak' both t' reins an' t' whip!" shouted Sar'-Ann's mother; "I'm fain to see there's one man in t' village."

"Now, you look here, Mr. Higgins," continued Ben, thus encouraged, "ought 'at it's right for Ted to pay shall be paid, but you send your list an' bill in to me, an' if my father an' me passes it ye'll be paid, an' if we don't ye won't; so you can put that in your pipe an' smoke it."

"Keep cool, Ben, keep cool!" said Barjona, who himself was not in the least ruffled; "only want what's right, you know . . . only what's right. . . . You or Ted, Ted or you . . . all the same to me."

"I feel dead beat, lad," said Ted, who still seemed dazed; "I'll go inside an' lie down a bit."

Ben motioned to me, and I stepped through the gate and joined them.

"Ted's tired," he said, "and wants to lie down. Would you mind taking him across to Susannah's and askin' her to let 'im rest on t' sofa a bit?" Then turning to the old man he said: "Go with this lady, Ted: go with Miss Holden. We've nearly finished packing all your stuff on t' cart, you know. But Susannah 'll get you a sup o' something warm, an' you can lie down on her sofa, an' Miss Holden 'll talk to you a bit." He spoke soothingly, as to a child, and the old man turned his eyes upon me.

"Shoo's a stranger, Ben?"

"Nay, she's lived here a twelvemonth, Ted. Now come, you go with 'er. She'll look after you nicely."

He suffered himself to be led away, but when we reached the group about the gate he would go no farther, but suddenly found tongue, and began to speak in a ruminating way, looking first at one and then another, but keeping fast hold of my arm.

"Ye'll none o' ye mind my mother? No, no, ye're ower young, all o' ye. It'll be seventy year an' more sin' she died, an' I wor only a lad at t' time. That wor her rockin'-chair 'at they're puttin' on t' cart, an' when I browt my missis 'ome, shoo hed it. First my mother, neighbours, an' then t' missis; an' t' owd chair lasts 'em both out, an' 'll last me out. I nivver thowt but it 'ud stand there aside o' t' chimley till they carried me out o' t' door, feet for'most. T' old chair 'll feel kind o' lonesome, neighbours, kind o' lonesome, in a strange kitchin."

"Nivver 'eed, lad," said one of the older women; "ye'll be varry comfortable down i' t' Clough."

"Aye, happen so," he replied, "but lonesome, neighbours, lonesome. There isn't a crack i' t' beams but what looked friendly-like, for we've grown old together; an' all t' furnitur' spake to me abaht old times, for I nivver shifted 'em out o' their places. An' them two chaney orniments o' t' chimley-piece, they wor allus comp'ny, too—Duke o' Wellington an' Lord Nelson, they are. My mother wor varry proud on 'em i' her time, an' t' missis wor just t' same; an' sin' shoo went they've allus felt to be comp'ny like. I doubt they'll nivver look t' same on another chimley-piece."

"It's a shame 'at 'e's turned ye out, Ted," said Susannah, "an' I 'ope 'e'll 'ave to suffer for it, I do."

"Aye, lass," he replied, "I could ha' liked well to ha' drawn my last breath i' t' old cottage, I could, for sure. I think Barjona mud ha' let me live on i' t' old 'ome. I shouldn't ha' troubled 'im so long—not so long."

"Come inside, Ted," said Susannah, whose eyes were filling with tears, "an' lie down while I get you a sup o' tea."

He appeared not to hear her, however, but stared fixedly at the flagged footpath and muttered, as he slowly shook his head:

"I shouldn't ha' troubled 'im so long—not so long."

Somebody fetched him a stool, and he sat down outside the gate with his back against the wall, whilst the women sympathised volubly, arms akimbo.

It was very pathetic, but no words of comfort came to my lips, though my heart ached for the silent old man who was leaving behind everything that counted in life, and who was sure to feel keenly the loss of familiar faces and friendly looks, even though he had not shown himself neighbourly. I said something of the sort to Mother Hubbard, who had now joined us, but she was doubtful.

"Well, love, I don't know. Ted has never shown much feeling. I have known him nearly all his life, and I don't think he has very deep feelings, love. He always seemed friendly with his wife, but not what you would call affectionate, you know, love. Of course, one doesn't know what he really felt when she died, but it didn't seem to trouble him very much."

"That proves nothing," I replied, with the emphasis born of observation; "the proverb says that 'still waters run deep,' and it is never more true than in this connection. The wailing widower is usually easily consoled."

"Yes, love, but I have discovered that you are very imaginative, though at one time I didn't think so, and you may read your own feelings into Ted's, you know. I really do think, love, that he has not very deep feelings."

Soon everything was piled upon the cart, and Ben Goodenough came up to the old man to inform him that they were ready to leave.

"Now, Ted!" he said, with an assumption of cheerfulness; "we've got everything on nicely, an' we'll step down with you to t' Clough an' get 'em into their places at t' other end. You'll want to have a look round, 'appen, before we leave."

"Aye, Ben lad, I tak' it varry kindly 'at ye're givin' yerself all this trouble. It's friendly, lad, friendly. Aye, I sud like to hev a look round for t' last time afore we start."

He rose wearily and accompanied Ben up the path. Barjona was standing at the door, and all three went in. They came out before long, and there were no traces of emotion on Ted's ruddy face. But as he looked up and down the garden his lips quivered, though he mastered himself with an effort. The gladioli and hollyhocks made a brave show amid the humbler sweet-williams and marigolds, but they would have to be left. He stopped opposite the rose-bush.

"Ben, lad," he said, "ye'll do me one more favour, willn't ye? Get me a spade off o' t' cart, will ye? I've left it till t' last minute, for I can 'ardly bide to root it up, but I munnut leave that tree be'ind."

One of the men had darted off at the mention of the word "spade," and the beloved implement—the old man's faithful friend—was placed in his hand.

"Thee an' me's hed monny a grand time together, lad," he said, apostrophising the spade, "but nivver such a sad job as this afore. A sad job, aye, a sad job. But we've got to do it, lad, ye an' me."

He put his foot upon it and prepared to dig up the tree, when Barjona interposed. Every word was clearly heard by the group in the roadway.

"Steady there! . . . what ye goin' to do?"

"Nobbut just dig t' tree up, Barjona."

"Leave t' tree alone . . . that tree's mine."

Ted looked at him and his hands began to tremble. "Ye don't meean, Barjona, 'at ye won't let me tak' t' rose-tree away wi' me?"

"Ye tak' nowt out of t' garden . . . all what's rooted in t' soil belongs to me . . . paid good money for it. . . . Put yer spade away."

"Look 'ere, Mr. Higgins," interrupted Ben, "do you mean to tell me 'at you're going to prevent Ted takin' a bit of a rose-tree with him? If you do, you're a harder-'earted old wretch than I took you for."

Angry murmurs arose from the crowd, but Barjona's jaw stiffened and there was no hint of yielding in his tone.

"Right's right," he said . . . "that rose-tree's mine . . . took a partic'lar fancy to it . . . won't part with it for nob'dy."

Ted fumbled in his pocket and produced a wash-leather bag, the neck of which was tied round with string. With shaking fingers he felt for a coin and drew out a half-sovereign.

"I'll pay ye for't, Barjona. Sitha, I'll give ye ten shillin' for t' plant."

"Put yer brass back, Ted . . . brass willn't buy it . . . took my fancy, that tree has . . . you mun buy another."

Sar'-Ann's mother pushed her way through and strode up to the stubborn, grasping man, and shook her fist in his face.

"You miserable old devil!" she cried. "Oh, if I were only a man I'd thrash ye while ever I could stand over ye. Yes, I would, if they sent me to gaol for 't. I wish the earth 'ud open an' swalla' ye up. But t' varry worms 'ud turn at ye."

Barjona thrust his hands deep into his trousers' pockets and assumed an air of weariness.

"Isn't there a man among ye?" continued the infuriated woman. "Ben, haven't ye spunk enough to fell 'im to t' ground? Eh, these men! God forgive me 'at I call 'em men!"

She fell back, and burst into hysterical tears, and Ben made another attempt.

"What the hangment do ye mean by it, Mr. Higgins? Have ye no 'eart at all? Ye'll never miss t' tree. I'll give you two just as good out of our own garden, hanged if I won't. Let him take t' tree, an' we'll be going."

"He—leaves—that—tree—where—it—is," replied Barjona with emphasis; "an' ye can all clear out o' this garden. . . . That tree's mine."

Ben took Ted's arm, but the old man refused to move. A tear forced its way out of the corner of his eye, and he drew a red cotton handkerchief from his trousers' pocket and wiped it away.

"Barjona, lad," he pleaded tremulously, "only just this one tree—nowt else; just this one tree, there's a good lad."

"I've said my say," replied Barjona.

"Take no notice of him, Ted," said Ben. "I'll give you one o' t' grandest rose-trees i' Yorkshire. Let t' old skinflint have his tree."

"Nay, but I mun hev it, I mun hev it," moaned the old man. "I mun hev it, lad; I mun hev it."

I wondered if I could influence Barjona, and I stepped up to him.

"Mr. Higgins, you see how distressed Ted is. Surely you will not make the parting more bitter for him. Think how unpleasant it will be for you to live among us if you make us all your enemies."

"Much obliged, Miss 'Olden. . . . If you mind your business . . . I'll mind mine."

"But why are you so set upon it, Mr. Higgins?"

"'Cos I am . . . that's enough . . . that plant's mine, an' mine it's goin' to be."

I turned to Ted. "Cannot you make up your mind to do without it?" I asked. "Do you want it so very much?"

He nodded, and the tears now followed each other fast down his cheeks. "I mun hev it; I mun hev it," he moaned.

We were all gathered round now; not a soul was left in the roadway, and the flower-beds were suffering.

"But why?" I persisted. "What makes you so very anxious to have it? You shall have another just as fine. Why do you want this particular one so badly?"

He shook his head, and raised his sleeve to his brow with the old nervous, familiar action.

"Cannot you tell me?" I asked.

Then the answer came, low but clearly heard by everybody: "*Shoo* liked it!"

The shame of the confession made him shake from head to foot, but the revelation of unsuspected deeps thrilled us, every one, and set us on fire with indignation and contempt.

"You heard him!" I said, turning to Barjona. "Now listen! I will give you five pounds for that rose-bush."

"That—tree—will—bide—where—it—is," replied Barjona doggedly.

There was a movement in the crowd as a raging woman forced her way through. She was hatless, like the rest of us, but her arms were bare to the elbows. Until I noticed the tightly-coiled hair I did not recognise Barjona's wife, for the usually pleasant face was clouded in storm.

She strode up to her husband and seized him by the collar of his coat with both hands.

"You heartless rascal!" she hissed in his ears; "so this is your blessed secret 'at you've kept for a surprise, is it? I'll surprise ye, ye good-for-nowt old Jew. What do ye mean by it, eh?" She shook him as if he had been a lad of ten, and he was helpless in her grip.

"You leave me alone!" he threatened, but all the brag was gone from him.

"Leave—you—alone!" she hissed between her clenched teeth; "I wish to God I had; but I took ye for better or worse, an' it isn't goin' to be all worse, I can tell ye! I hearkened to ye while I could 'earken no longer. The Lord gi' me grace to keep my 'ands off o' ye!"

It was a remarkably futile prayer, seeing that she was holding him as in a vice, and shaking him at intervals.

"D'ye think I'd ever live 'ere, an' let a poor old man like Ted fend for hisself anywhere? What do ye take me for? Ye knew better than to tell me while ye'd gotten yer dirty work done, but thank the Lord I was just in time. 'Ere, get away! I'm stalled o' talkin' to ye!"

She pushed him away roughly, but he made one more sulky struggle for mastery.

"Are ye t' boss 'ere, or am I?" he growled; "I've bought it . . . an' I'll live in it."

"Will ye?" she said with scorn, "then ye'll live by yersen. But I'll show ye who's t' boss. You may thank the Lord 'at ye've got a wife wi' a bit o' gumption. Ye shall be t' master when ye can master yersen. I'm fair shamed o' ye! We'll 'appen live 'ere when owt 'appens Ted, but never as long as 'e wants it; so that's flat!"

The crowd cheered, and Maria brightened visibly. "Nay, to be sure, Miss 'Olden, an' friends," she said, "to think 'at any 'usband o' mine should disgrace hisself an' me i' this fashion! I never knew a word, believe me, while 'alf an hour sin' when I chanced across young Smiddles, an' he let into me right an' left. I can tell you I didn't let t' grass grow under my feet afore I set off 'ere. Don't you fret, Ted, lad! Turn ye out? Not we! Sitha, Barjona's fair shamed of hisself, an' well he might be. Nay, to be sure, I stood at back on ye all an' hearkened while my blood boiled. He must ha' been wrong i' his 'ead, Barjona must. Come, friends, get out o' t' gate, an' we'll carry t' furnitur' in agen, an' soon hev t' place to rights. Now you can stop that mutterin', Barjona, an' just get into t' trap out o' t' road!"

Many willing hands made the task a light one, and in an hour's time the cottage had assumed its old aspect, and the women had swept and dusted and given the finishing touches to everything. Mrs. Higgins was critical, but expressed herself satisfied at last. Then she climbed into the trap and seated herself beside her husband.

"Good-bye, friends," she shouted, as they drove off. "Don't ye worry. He can drive t' owd mare, but 'e can't drive me. I'll bring 'im to 'is sops!"

"Gosh!" snapped Sar'-Ann's mother, "now that's some bit like! Gi' me a woman for mettle an' sperrit! Lord 'elp us, but I reckon nowt o' such a white-livered lot o' men as we hev i' Windyridge. She'll mak' a man o' yon old rascal yet, will Maria!"

As I looked back on my way home I saw that Ted had fetched his rake, and was busy getting the garden into order again.

CHAPTER TWENTY

THE CYNIC'S RENUNCIATION

EXCITEMENTS TREAD UPON each other's heels. After Barjona, the Cynic. He appeared unexpectedly on Monday morning, and I took the long-promised photographs, which have turned out very badly; why, I don't know. He was not in his Sunday best, so the fault did not lie there; and his expression was all right, but I could not catch it on the plate, try as I might. He was very much amused, and accused me of looking haggard over the business, which was absurd. Every photographer is anxious to secure a satisfactory result, or if he is not he does not deserve to succeed. I think really I was afraid of his waxing sarcastic over my attempts at portraying his features. He is not a handsome man, as I may have remarked before, but he is not the sort that passes unnoticed, and I wanted to secure on the plate the something that makes people look twice at him; and I failed. I took several negatives, but none of them was half as nice as the original; and yet we are told that photography flatters!

He professed an indifference which I am afraid he felt, and Mother Hubbard assured him over the dinner-table that there was not the slightest ground for anxiety. It will be a long time, I fear, before he gets the proofs.

He stayed to dinner on his own invitation, and Mother Hubbard prepared one of her extra special Yorkshire puddings in his honour. Fortunately, we had not cooked the beef on the Sunday, or he would have had to be content with the remains of the cold joint; and though I should not have minded, I know Mother Hubbard would have been greatly distressed.

He spoke quite naturally about Rose, and appeared to have enjoyed her company immensely, but he had not seen her again up to then.

When the meal was over we went out into the garden and sat down, and somehow or other the sense of quiet and the beauty of the view soothed me, and I felt less irritable than for days past. I never get tired of the dip of green fields and the stretch of moor on the far side of the wood.

"Can you spare me a full hour, Miss Holden?" he asked. "I have come down specially to see you, principally because I have had a letter from Mr. Evans which in some measure concerns you, and also because I want to continue the discussion of the parable of the marbles which we were considering the other evening."

How pretty the landscape looked from our garden! Cloud shadows were racing each other across the pastures as I lay back and watched them, and I thought the view had never been bonnier.

"I am not overworked," I replied, "and I can give up a whole afternoon, if necessary. What is the news from the squire? Nothing serious, I hope; and yet it must be important to bring you down here specially."

"I hardly know what to say. Something in his letter conveys the impression that he is far from well again, though he does not definitely say so. But it appears that he has asked you to go out to him if he becomes seriously ill. That is so, isn't it?"

"Yes," I answered, "and I have promised to go. It touches me deeply that he should want me."

"I don't wonder," he said; but whether at my emotion or the squire's proposal did not transpire.

"If and when he sends for you," he continued, "he wishes you to communicate with me, and he asks me to make all the business arrangements for you. I need hardly say that it will afford me much pleasure to do whatever I can. I will give you my Broadbeck and town addresses, and if you will wire me whenever you need my services I will reply at once. Please don't feel obliged to look anything up for yourself, as I will see to every detail, and provide all that is necessary for the journey in accordance with my old friend's instructions."

"It is extremely good of you," I said, "and very thoughtful on the squire's part. I accept your offer gratefully. But do you think there is much likelihood of my being sent for?"

"Candidly, I think there is; equally candidly, I hope the necessity may not arise. If the end comes whilst he is abroad, a man ought by all means to be present, for there will be no end of difficulties, and it will be absolutely necessary for someone to go out. But that takes time, and meanwhile the position would not be a pleasant one for you. I would go to him myself now but for two insuperable difficulties, one being that certain important duties keep me in London at present, and the other that Mr. Evans most distinctly does not want me."

"I quite see what you mean," I said; "but if the worst happens, and I am there at the time, I shall do my best and not mind the unpleasantness."

"I am sure of that," he returned, "but you don't at all realise what is involved. However, we won't discuss this further. On his account I should be heartily glad for you to go, and I am relieved that he has had the good sense to suggest it."

"I regard him very highly," I said.

"You do more: you love him," he remarked, with a sharp, keen glance at my face.

"Yes, I think I love him," I replied without confusion. "I could easily be his daughter; we have much in common."

He said nothing for quite a long time, during which he threw his cigarette away and lit a pipe. Then he turned to me:

"Now for my parable."

"Yes," I said; "tell me about it."

"You guessed, of course, that it is a matter that affects me deeply and seriously?"

"I was afraid so. I could not be certain, of course, but I felt that it was much more than an ethical conundrum."

"God knows it was, and He knows, too, that I am grateful to you for the clear lead you gave, suspecting, as you must have done, that it meant much to me."

Had I suspected? I suppose I did, for my heart, I remember, beat painfully; yet I had not thought much more of it since. I looked at him, and saw that his face was white but resolute, and I said hesitatingly:

"I am sorry if you are in trouble, but Farmer Goodenough thinks that troubles are blessings in disguise. I wish I could give you more than second-hand comfort."

"I am going to tell you exactly where I stand," he said, "and you must not allow your woman's instinct of comfort to cloud or bias your judgment. Goodenough may be right, but if I take the step I contemplate it will not be because I expect good to result to myself—though there may be, no doubt, a certain spiritual gain—but because it is the only course possible to me if I am to retain my self-respect.

"You will hardly have heard of a rather prominent case in which I figured recently as counsel for the plaintiff."

"Lessingham *versus* Mainwaring?" I queried.

"You have heard of it then? Do you know the details?"

"Not at all. I simply read in the paper that you had won the case for your client."

"I see. Well, it would take too long, and would be too uninteresting to you to explain everything, but put briefly the case was this. Mainwaring had got hold of a considerable sum of money—over £7,000, as a matter of fact—which Lessingham claimed belonged to him. There were a great many points which were interesting to lawyers, and when the plaintiffs brief was offered to me I jumped at it. A barrister has often to wait a long time before any plums fall to his share, but this was a big one, for the other side had engaged two of the most eminent counsel in the land; and I had a big figure marked on my brief.

"We had a tremendous fight, and in the heat of the forensic duel I lost sight of everything except the one goal of triumphant and overwhelming victory. I have no desire to speak of my accomplishment in terms that may sound egotistical, but I may say without affectation that I found all the weak places in the defence and used every talent I could command to crush my opponents, and I succeeded, and became for a week one of the most talked-of men in London. Outwardly collected, I was inwardly exalted above measure, for I knew what the winning of the case meant for me.

"I say I knew. I should have said I thought I knew. All I realised was that briefs would now be showered upon me, as they have been—as they are being. What I failed to realise was that I should have to stand at the bar of my own conscience, and be tried by the inexorable judge whose sentences are without mercy. That came to pass quickly, and I was condemned, and on appeal you confirmed the judgment."

"I? Oh, Mr. Derwent!"

"During the course of the trial I became convinced, or at any rate I had grave reasons for suspecting that my client was a scoundrel, and had no right to a penny of the money. The conviction came in part from what was revealed to me in conversation with him, and in part from what came out in evidence, but at the moment I did not care. I was paid to win my case, not to secure justice. That was for the judge and jury. There was more than that, however. It was not the lust of gain, but the lust of glory that obsessed me. I, Philip Derwent, was going to defeat Ritson and Friend at whatever cost.

"But, Miss Holden, I have inherited certain qualities which are likely to put awkward obstacles in the path of ambition. My father was a good man. He was scrupulously, fastidiously honest. He believed that the principles of the Sermon on the Mount could and should be practised in everyday life. Consequently he never made much money, and was terribly disappointed when his only son adopted the law as a profession. Some— not all, but some—of his qualities are in my blood; and the voice of conscience is always telling me that the father was a better man than the son, and that, unless I am careful, I shall sell my life for power and possessions; and I have made up my mind to be careful.

"Well, I have made inquiries—carefully and without hurry—and I now know for a fact that Mainwaring had every right to that money, and that Lessingham is a fraud, so that my course is clear. I have seen Lessingham, and he laughs in my face. 'You knew it at the time, old man!' he said; 'and a jolly good thing you've made out of it.' There was no chance of putting things right from that quarter."

"But, Mr. Derwent," I interrupted, "surely in your profession this is an everyday occurrence. Both sides cannot be right, and both need legal assistance."

"True," he replied, "and you must quite understand my attitude. I am not judging any of my brethren: to their own master they stand or fall. But for myself, I am not going to support any case, in the future, which I am not convinced is a just one. If, after accepting a brief, I have reason to believe that I am espousing an unjust cause I will throw it up at whatever sacrifice."

"I am afraid it will mean *great* sacrifice," I murmured.

"Would you recommend me not to do it?" he asked.

"You must obey your Inner Self, or suffer torment," I replied.

"I must, and I will," he said firmly. "Now listen to me. My father was not, as I have said, a wealthy man, and on his death I inherited little beyond good principles and good books. The waiting period for financial success was long, but latterly I have made money. I have £7,000 in the bank, and a good income. And my judgment agrees with yours: I must part with my marbles."

"Oh, Mr. Derwent," I exclaimed; "think well before you take so serious a step! What is my hasty decision worth? It was given on the spur of the moment: it was the immature judgment of an inexperienced woman!"

"It was the spontaneous expression of pure, instinctive truth," he replied. "Yet do not feel any sense of responsibility. I had already reached the same conclusion: you merely confirmed it, and in doing so helped and strengthened me—though the decision set back a hope that had arisen within me."

"But, Mr. Derwent"—I was groping around vainly for a loophole of escape—"this Mr. Mainwaring, is he poor? does he need the money? will he use it well?"

"What does that matter?" he replied. "His wealth or poverty cannot affect the question of right or wrong. The money is his by right. *I* robbed him of it by forensic cunning and rhetoric, and I will repay him. As a matter of fact he is fabulously wealthy, and £7,000 is to him a mere drop in an ocean. And he spends his money on horses and dissipation. He is a bigger scoundrel than Lessingham, and that is saying much."

"But what a shame, Mr. Derwent! It does not seem right."

"It can never be wrong to do right. Besides, I misled you at the outset of our conversation—misled you purposely. I could not change my mind now if I wished to do so, for I posted Mainwaring a cheque for the full amount this morning."

I felt ready to cry, but there was as much joy as sorrow in my breast. I believe I smiled, and I held out my hand, which he grasped and retained a moment.

At that instant a telegraph boy pushed open the gate and advanced towards me.

"Miss Holden?" he inquired.

I took the envelope and tore it open. It contained only a brief message:

"Zermatt. *July 22nd,*

"Please come soon as possible. See Derwent.

"EVANS. Hotel Victoria."

I burst into tears, and went into the house.

CHAPTER TWENTY-ONE

AT
ZERMATT

I CANNOT TRUTHFULLY say that sad thoughts were uppermost during the hours that followed. After all, it was my first trip to the Continent, and although I am thirty-six years old, and might be expected to have got over mere juvenile excitements, I confess to a feeling of cheerful anticipation. Of course the squire was always in the background of my thoughts, but I had no sense of apprehension such as sometimes oppresses one before an approaching calamity.

And it was so nice to have everything arranged for me, and to find myself in possession of time-tables and railway-coupons and a clear itinerary of the journey without the slightest effort or inconvenience on my part. Undoubtedly man has his uses, if he is a clear-headed, kind-hearted fellow like the Cynic.

When the whistle sounded and the boat express glided out of Charing Cross I waved my handkerchief from the window as long as I could see him, and then settled down into the luxurious cushions and gave myself up to reflection. How nice and brotherly he had been all the way to town, and since! I do not wonder that Rose enjoyed the journey. Rose! I might have let her know that I was leaving by the morning train, but then she would have had to ask for an hour off; and when she has just been away for ten days her chief might not have liked it. Besides, the Cynic had such a lot of minute instructions and emphatic warnings to which I was forced to listen attentively.

Then there was Mother Hubbard, who had been set upon accompanying me on the ground that I ought not to travel alone and unchaperoned; but the Cynic agreed with me that at my age chaperonage is unnecessary. I am not the sort that needs protection; and the little motherkin would merely have added to my anxieties.

No, though there was a sick and perhaps dying man at the other end, and though sorrow might soon compass me about, I determined to enjoy the present moment, and I did. I enjoyed the breeze upon the Channel, the glimpses of peasant life in France as the train rushed through the flat and rather tame country, the dinner in the Northern railway station at Paris, and the novel experience of the tiny bed which was reserved for my use on the night journey. I was travelling in luxury, of course, and am never likely to repeat the experience.

But my chief enjoyment was one which could be shared by any who had eyes to see, though they were sitting upright on the bare and narrow boards of the miserable third-class compartments which I caught sight of occasionally in the stations when morning came.

The glory of the dawn! of the sun rising behind the mountains, when a pink flush spread over the sky, dissolving quickly into rose and amber and azure, delicately pencilled in diverging rays which spread like a great fan to the zenith! The crags of a great hill caught the glow, and the mountain burned with fire. Below, the grass was gold and emerald; there were fruit-laden trees in the foreground, and in the distance, away beyond the belt of low-lying mist and the vague neutral tints which concealed their bases, were the snow mountains! I pushed down the window and gorged myself with the heavenly vision.

There was no time to see Geneva, but the ride along the banks of the lake and through the fertile Rhone valley was one long, delightful dream. Luncheon was provided at Visp, and then began the journey on the mountain railway which I can never forget.

As the train snorted and grunted up the steep incline I rejoiced to realise that it could not travel more quickly. Stream, mountain and forest; fertile valley, rushing waterfall and lofty precipice—all contributed to the charm of the experience. But the rush of the Visp, as it poured down the narrow gorge, and boiled and fretted in turbulent cascades which hurled their spray through the windows of the passing train is the one outstanding remembrance. It was glorious! Then the Matterhorn came in sight for a moment, and just afterwards the toy train drew up at the toy platform in Zermatt.

The concierge of the Hotel Victoria took my bag and pointed me out to a diminutive young lady who was standing near. She at once came forward and held out her hand, whilst a winning smile spread over her pleasant face.

"You are Miss Holden, are you not? I have stepped across to meet you, so that you might not feel so strange on your arrival. My husband is a doctor—Dr. Grey—and he has taken an interest in Mr. Evans, and continues to do so even though I have fallen in love with the old gentleman."

I liked the girl straight away. She is quite young—only just twenty-three, as she told me frankly, and ever such a little creature, though she carries herself with the dignity of a duchess—in fact, with much more dignity than some duchesses I have seen.

"Now that is 'real good' of you, as the Americans whose company I have just left would say," I replied; "and I think it was very nice of you to think of it. Tell me first, please, if Mr. Evans is worse."

"I really cannot say with certainty," she replied; "the Zermatt doctor thinks he is not going to recover, and my husband says that he will live for months. Now my husband, dear, is a *very clever man indeed*, though he is only young; and although the other man looks very formidable and wears spectacles I don't believe he is as clever as Ralph."

I smiled. "You have known the one doctor longer than the other," I said.

"Not much, as a doctor," she confided. "To let you into a secret which nobody here has discovered, Ralph and I are on our honeymoon, so that my experience of his medical abilities is limited, but I am sure he is very clever. But come! the hotel is only just across the way."

She accompanied me to my room and chatted incessantly whilst I was endeavouring to remove the grime and grit which the continental engines deposit so generously upon the traveller behind them.

"There!" she said, as I emptied the water for the third time, and sponged my face and neck preparatory to a brisk towelling; "you have emerged at last. But you will never be quite yourself until you have washed your hair. Do it to-night, dear. I know a splendid way of tying your head up in a towel so that you can sleep quite comfy."

The squire's face brightened when he saw me. He was sitting near the window in a great easy-chair which was almost a couch, and his hair was whiter than when he left England, and his face was—oh! so thin and grey; but what a gentleman he looked! He held out both hands, but I bent over and kissed him. If it was a bold thing to do I don't mind. My Inner Self bade me do it and I obeyed.

He held my face against his for a moment, and neither of us spoke. Then he said:

"Look at my view, Grace, and tell me if you like it."

I sat on the arm of his chair and looked through the open window. I saw before me a scene of peaceful loveliness—a valley, richly green, with here and there oblong patches of yellow framed in olive hedges: a narrow valley, girded with mountains whose sides rise steeply to tremendous heights, jagged, scarped, and streaked with snow: a wooded valley, too, where sombre trees of fir and pine climb the heights and spread out into thickets which end only with the rock. Quaint, brown-timbered structures, built on piles and with overhanging roofs, sometimes isolated, sometimes in little groups, were dotted about the landscape. A white road wound down the valley, and the yellow waters of the Visp rushed, torrent-like, along the bottom, to be lost to view where the land dipped abruptly to the left.

In the far distance mountains of snow lifted up their hoary heads into the luminous haze; and light clouds, rivalling their whiteness, gave the illusion of loftier heights still, and led the eye to the brilliant blue of high heaven.

The sun was behind us, and banks of clouds must have intercepted his rays from time to time, for the play of light and shade varied like a kaleidoscope, and the bare, stony flanks of the mountains in the middle distance shone green or grey or red as the sun caught them. A rude bridge crossed the stream away below, and I could just make out some tourists in Tyrolese caps and with knapsacks on their backs, leaning over the white rails.

The squire put his arm on mine. "I will tell you the names of these giants later. Meanwhile, tell me, have I chosen well?"

"It is heavenly," I replied. "I should be content to sit here for days."

"I *am* content," he said; "there is grander scenery than this around Zermatt—grander by far. At the other end of the valley you will see and you will glory in the towering masses of crag and snow which the Matterhorn and Breithorn present. You will see miles of glaciers and sparkling waterfalls and a thousand wonders of God's providing; but it was too cold and massive and hard to suit the mood of a dying man. I wanted Nature in a kindlier temper, so I sit by the window and commune with her, and she is always friendly."

There was a stool in the room, and I drew it up and sat at his feet with one arm upon his knee, as I used to sit for hours in the days of old, before my father's death left me solitary; and when the squire placed a caressing hand upon my shoulder I could have thought that a chapter had been re-opened in the sealed pages of my life.

"Who is this Dr. Grey," I inquired, "whose charming little wife met me at the station, and told me you are not going to die for a long time?—for which I love her."

He smiled. "Grey is an optimist, my dear, and a downright good fellow, and he has picked up a prize in his wife. They are on their wedding-tour, as anyone quite unversed in that lore can see at a glance; and they ought to have left Zermatt a week ago or more, but they have cheerfully stayed on to minister to the physical and mental necessities of an old man and a stranger. Not many would have done it, for they are sacrificing one of the most attractive programmes that Switzerland offers, for my sake."

"What a lot of good people there are in the world," I said. "I am going to like Dr. Grey as much as I like his wife. He is a big, strong, well-developed man, of course?"

"Why 'of course?'?" he asked.

"Husbands of tiny wives invariably are; the infinitely small seems to have a remarkable affinity for the infinitely great."

"Well, he is certainly a strapping fellow, and he is devoted to the wee woman he has made his wife. I believe, too, he will get on in his profession."

"His wife says he is a very clever man indeed," I remarked.

"Does she? An unbiassed opinion of that kind is valuable. All the same, he has done me good, not so much with physic—for I take the Zermatt man's concoctions—as with his cheery outlook. I believe he thinks I am a trickster."

"Do you know what I believe, sir?" I asked.

"No; tell me," he said.

"I believe you are going to get better, and I shall take you back to Windyridge and the moors."

He sighed then, and laid a hand fondly upon mine. "Grace, my child, I will say now what it may be more difficult to say later. You have caught me in a good hour, and my weary spirits have been refreshed by the sight of your face and the sound of your voice; but you must be prepared for darker experiences. Sometimes I suffer; often I am terribly weak and depressed. Gottlieb, I know, does not expect me to recover, and my Inner Self (that is your expression, child, and I often think of it) tells me he is right. You are too sensible to be unduly distressed before the time comes, and I want to tell you what I have planned, and to tell you quite calmly and without emotion. Death to me is only a curtain between one room and the next, so that it does not disturb me to explain to you what I wish to be done when it is raised for me to pass through.

"Midway in the village you will find some gardens opposite the Mont Cervin Hotel. Pass through them and you will reach a little English church, surrounded by a tiny graveyard. There lie the bones of men who have been killed on the mountains, and of others who have found death instead of life in these health-giving heights. There is one sunny spot where I want my body to rest, and the chaplain knows it. You can bear to hear me speak of these things, can you?"

Yes, I could bear it. He spoke so naturally and with such ease that I hardly realised what it meant: it was unreal, far-off, fallacious.

"At first," he continued, "the idea was repugnant. I longed to be laid side by side with my wife in the homeland, but that feeling passed. It was nothing more than sentiment, though it was a sentiment that nearly took me home, in spite of the doctors. But the more I have thought of it the more childish it has seemed. I am conscious of her presence *here*, always.

Metaphysicians would explain that easily enough, no doubt, but to me it is an experience, and what can one want more? Why, then, should I run away to Windyridge and Fawkshill in order to find her, or be carried there for that purpose after death? No, no. Heaven is about me here, and our spirits will meet at once when the silver thread is loosed which binds me to earth. Am I right, Grace?"

I was crying a little now, but I could not contradict him.

"Gottlieb shakes his head, but Grey says I may last for months. Perhaps he is right, but I have no desire to live. Why should I? And where could I end my days more pleasantly than amidst these masterpieces of the great Architect?"

Mrs. Grey came for me when the dinner bell sounded, and we went down together. It has been arranged that I am to lunch with the squire in his own room, but to have dinner with the rest at a little table which I share with the Greys.

The doctor is just a great bouncing boy, with merry eyes and thick brown hair. He is on good terms with everybody—guests of high degree and low, waiters, porters, chambermaids—all the cosmopolitan crowd. He adores his little wife, and it is funny to see so big a man worshipping at so small a shrine.

I expressed my gratitude to them both as we sat at dinner, and he laughed—such a hearty, boisterous laugh.

"It's my wife. Dot wouldn't hear of leaving, and you cannot get a separation order in these wilds. She has spent so much time with the old gentleman that I have been madly jealous for hours at a stretch."

"Don't be untruthful, Ralph," said Mrs. Grey. "You know perfectly well that you have spoiled our honeymoon with the simple and sordid motive of gaining professional experience. Besides, you are nicest when you are jealous."

"Am I, by Jove!" he laughed. "Then 'niceness' will become habitual with me, for the way all the men look at you fans the flame of my jealousy. But this is poor stuff for Miss Holden, and I want to talk seriously to her."

"What is your candid opinion of Mr. Evans?" I asked.

"He is marked to fall, Miss Holden, but if he can be persuaded to make the effort to live he need not fall for months, perhaps even for years. The fact is, he has become indifferent to life, and that is against him."

"What is really the matter with him?"

"Now, there you corner me," he replied. "He has a weak heart, bronchial trouble, some diabetic tendencies and disordered nerves; but what is really the matter with him I have not discovered. Can you tell me?"

"I should have thought all these things were matter enough," I answered; "but what really ails him, I believe, is what is commonly termed a 'broken heart.' He is always mourning the loss of his wife and always dwelling upon reunion."

"He never told me that," replied the doctor thoughtfully; "I am glad to know it."

"Why should he remain abroad all this time?" I asked.

"Because he shouldn't!" he replied. "In my judgment he has been ill advised; but it is largely his own fault, too. I think he did well to leave England for the winter, but he ought to have gone home when the warm weather came. His medical advisers have always prescribed change of scene: told him to go anywhere he liked, and 'buck up' a bit, and he has gone. France, Spain, Egypt, Italy, and now Zermatt. And the old chap is dying of loneliness. Gottlieb shakes his mournful old head, and goes out to arrange with the English chaplain where to bury him. I'd bury them both! If you take my advice you'll pet him and make him think the world is a nice place to live in, and then we'll take him home, and let old Gottlieb find another tenant for his grave. If you will second me we'll have him out of this hole in a week's time."

I felt so cheered, and I will certainly follow his lead. I wrote a long, explanatory letter to the Cynic, an apologetic one to Rose, and a picture postcard, promising a longer communication, to Mother Hubbard, and then turned in and slept like a top.

CHAPTER TWENTY-TWO

THE HEATHER
PULLS

THE SENSATION OF dazzling light and the sound of tinkling silvery bells woke me early, and I jumped up and looked out of the window. The bells belonged to a herd of goats which were being driven slowly to pasture. Stalwart guides, with stout alpenstocks in their hands, and apparently heavy cloth bags upon their backs, were standing near the hotel and on the station platform. Tourists of both sexes were getting ready to accompany the guides, and there was much loud questioning and emphatic gesticulation on both sides. A few mules stood near, presumably for the use of the ladies. It was all too provocative, and I flung myself into my clothes and went out.

If I were writing a guide book I could wax eloquent, I believe, in my descriptions of Zermatt; but I am not, and I therefore refrain.

The squire was delighted with my enthusiasm, and insisted upon my "doing" the place thoroughly. He did not rise until noon, so that my mornings were always free, and the Greys took me all the shorter excursions. One day we had quite a long trip to the top of the Gorner Grat, whence one gets an unrivalled view of snow peaks and glaciers; and from thence we walked to the Schwarz See, where the Matterhorn towers in front of you like an absolute monarch in loneliness and grandeur.

Oh, those ravines, where the glacier-fed streams rage furiously in their rapid descent! Oh, those gorges, in whose depths the pent-up waters leap onward between high walls of rock to which the precarious gangway clings where you stand in momentary fear of disaster! Oh, those woods, with the steep and stony footpaths, and the sudden revelation of unsuspected objects: of kine munching the green herbage; of the women who tend them, working industriously with wool and needle; of wooden *châlets* with stone-protected roofs; of trickling cascades and roaring waterfalls!

Oh, those pastures, green as emerald, soft as velvet, where one might lie as on a couch of down and feast the eye on mountain and vale and sky, and never tire! Oh, those sunsets, and particularly the one which struck my imagination most, when the sky was not crimson, but topaz-tinted, and the huge cloud which hung suspended from the neck of the Matterhorn was changed in a second into beaten gold, as though touched by the rod of the alchemist; when the Breithorn flushed deep for a moment at the sun's caress, and the land lay flooded in a translucent yellow haze that spread like a vapour over the works of God and man, and turned mere stones and mortar into the fairy palaces of Eastern fable!

It seems now like a wonderful dream, but, thank God! it is something much less transient. For a memory is infinitely better than a dream: the memory of an experience such as this is a continual feast, whereas a dream too often excites hopes that may never be realised, and presents visions of delight which are as elusive as the grapes of Tantalus.

I stored up every detail for the squire's benefit. I cultivated my powers of observation more for his sake than my own, and reaped a double reward. All I saw is impressed still upon my brain with photographic sharpness, and it will be a long, long time before the image becomes faded or blurred. But what was better still, I saw the squire's eyes brighten and the "yonderly" look depart, as he came back to earth evening by evening and followed the story of my adventures.

I believe he would have been content to stay on indefinitely and give me as good a time as my heart could have desired, but that would not have been right. I had not gone out to enjoy a frolic, and at times I felt almost ashamed of myself for enjoying life so much. "Grace Holden," I said, "you are a very considerable fraud. Your special rôle just now is supposed to be that of the ministering angel, whereas you are flinging away your own time and somebody else's money like an irresponsible tripper."

Dr. Grey laughed when I told him that I had qualms of conscience on this score.

"Don't worry," he said; "Providence has her own notions of how angels can best minister, and I fancy you are carrying out her scheme pretty successfully. It's three days since the old gentleman spoke a word about dying, and I'm certain he is not nearly as anxious to be gone as he was before you came. But cannot you tempt him back to England by any means? My wife and I cannot remain here much longer, and I would like to help you to take him home."

I did my best, but I made little headway. The squire seemed to have lost all desire for home, and had quite made up his mind that his body would soon be laid to rest amid the eternal snows. He was constantly anticipating some further attack which would cut him down without warning, and Gottlieb seemed to find a mournful satisfaction in encouraging these forebodings, less perhaps by what he said than by what he left unsaid.

A tinge of annoyance began to mix with Dr. Grey's laugh, and he spoke to the squire with a touch of asperity. He had subjected him again to a thorough examination, and on its conclusion he broke out:

"Look here, Mr. Evans, I stake my professional reputation upon my verdict that you are not a dying man physically. If you die it's your own fault. There is no reason why we should not start for home to-morrow."

The squire took his hand and held it. "Grey," he said, "has science taught you that man has an inward voice that sometimes speaks more authoritatively and convincingly than doctor or parson, and that insists upon its dicta? Miss Holden knows it and calls it her 'Inner Self.'"

"No, sir," he replied, "science has taught me nothing of the kind. I am no psychologist, for my business is with the body rather than the soul. But science has taught me what the body is and is not able to accomplish, and whatever your 'Inner Self' may say I am convinced that your body is quite competent to take that perverse autocrat home if he will let it. But it cannot otherwise."

"Intuition is sometimes more powerful than logic," said the squire. "Grey, you are a good fellow and I owe you a debt of gratitude, but don't inconvenience yourself on my account. Go home, if you must, and believe me, I am sincerely thankful for all your goodness and attention."

The doctor tackled me again at dinner. "I'm not going home," he said, "and I'm not going to let him die without a struggle. But you'll have to make that Inner Self of his listen to reason. Now put your thinking cap on, and good luck to you."

"I cannot understand him," I replied; "he was always inclined to melancholy, but he was not morbid and listless as he now shows himself. He seems sometimes pitiably weak and childish, whereas ordinarily he is full of shrewd common sense."

"Of course he is," said the doctor, "and will be again. His Inner Self is sick just now, consequent upon his long seclusion from friends and home associations. It needs to be roused. If you can once make him *want* to go home, his body will take him there hard enough. I can't do that: you must. Can't you tell him you have got to go back?"

I had thought of that. I had left my work at the busiest season of the year, and, after all, it was my living. And there was Mother Hubbard, who had learned to lean upon me, and had yielded me so willingly to the more pressing duty. I owed something to her. As I thought upon these things a feeling of homesickness stole over me, and I went in and sat at the squire's feet.

It was falling dusk, and the cool breath of evening fanned our cheeks as we sat by the open window and watched the lights twinkling in the celestial dome, and the mountains growing more black and mysterious with the advancing night.

"It is very lovely," murmured the squire.

"Yes," I said, "it is. But close your eyes and I will paint you a more attractive picture than this. You will not interrupt me, will you? and I will try to tell you what I saw not long ago, and what I am aching to see again."

"No, my child," he replied, pressing my hand fondly. "I will be quite still and you shall paint your picture on my brain."

I hesitated a moment, and I think a wordless, formless prayer for help ascended to heaven. I endeavoured to visualise the scene in its fairest colours, and trembled lest my effort should be in vain. I closed my own eyes, too, for I feared distraction. Then I began:

"I am standing in a country lane, with ragged hedges on either hand. The hedges are brightly green, for they have been newly washed with the warm rain of summer, and they sparkle like gems in the bright sunshine of a glorious morning. There is a bank of grass, rank, luxurious grass, on one side of the roadway, and I clamber up to secure a wider view of the bounties nature has provided.

"There is a merry, frolicsome breeze—a rude one, in truth, for it winds my skirt about my limbs and blows my hair over my ears and eyes; and yet I love it, for it means no harm, and its crisp touch braces my body and gives me the taste of life.

"From my elevated standpoint I see the distant horizon, miles and miles away. Far off upon my right the clouds lie in long grey strata, like closely-piled packs of wool, but on my left the remoter sky is washed in silver, with here and there a rent revealing wonderfully delicate tints of blue.

"Overhead the wool-packs have been burst open by the wind which is tearing them apart and scattering their contents over the deep blue zenith. They are dazzlingly white, whether heaped together in massive bulk, or drawn out—as so many of them are—into transparent fluff which drifts in the rapid air current like down of thistles.

"The morning is cold and the air is keen, so that the sky-line is sharply defined and hints a threat of rain. But who cares about the evil of the hour after next when there are so many glories to delight the present sense? See, the sky-line of which I speak is dusky purple and reddish-brown, but broad, flat washes of verdigris stretch up to it, with here and there a yellow patch betokening fields of grain, and in the foreground meadows and pastures of brighter hue.

"In front of me is a clump of trees—fine, tall trees they are, with shining grey boles—standing erect and strong in spite of the fury of the gales. Sycamore and beech and elm, majestic, beautiful. I hear the cawing of the rooks from out the dark shadows.

"I climb over the wall a little farther on and walk fifty paces forward. I now see a grey Hall, a dear old place, stone-roofed and low, with tiny old-world window-panes around which the dark-hued ivy clings tenaciously. There are brightly coloured flower-beds in front, and a green lawn to one side, and a cluster of beeches stands sentinel before the closed door. For the door, alas! is closed, and as I look a thick thundercloud hangs over the house, and I turn away depressed and seek the sunshine on the other side.

"And now it is waste land upon which my delighted eyes rest, and the west wind brings to my nostrils the scent of the moors. Waste land! Who shall dare to call that russet-coloured hillside with the streaks of green upon it, waste? That stretch of country, bracken-covered, ending in the long expanse of heath which is now violet-purple in tint, but will soon be glowing and aflame when the heather bursts its bonds—can that be *waste?* Surely not!

"I see tiny cottages from whose chimneys the blue smoke is being twisted into fantastic forms by the wind's vagaries, and gardens gay with bloom, and a green-bordered street, and through an open door the dancing flame on a homely hearth. It is all very lovely and peaceful, and when I turn for a last look at the old Hall where the door is closed, lo! the thundercloud has gone, and the sky is blue over the smokeless stacks, and hope arises within my breast, and I go on my way with joy and peace in my heart. That is my picture!"

I stopped and opened my eyes. A tear was stealing down the squire's face, and the grasp on my hand had tightened.

"Have you finished, Grace?"

"Yes," I whispered.

"I think I should like to go home," he said. "I believe I could manage it, after all."

WINDYRIDGE HALL

CHAPTER TWENTY-THREE

THE PARABLE
OF THE HEATHER

WE LEFT ZERMATT on the following day. I must say that I entered the squire's room with some trepidation, but it was quite unnecessary. He smiled as I bent over to kiss him, and relieved my apprehension at once.

"It's all right, Grace," he said; "the heather pulls. You know, don't you?"

Dr. Grey was splendid. Motor cars are of no use in Zermatt, except to bring you there or take you away, so the smell of petrol does not often draw the tourist's attention from the sublime to the—nauseous; but it was characteristic of the almost impudent audacity of the man that he commandeered the only one there was at the Victoria.

"How have you managed it?" I asked, when I learned that we were all to travel as far as Lausanne in the Marquis d'Olsini's luxurious automobile.

"Oh, easily enough," he replied in his hearty way; "the marquis is no end of a decent sort, and when I explained matters, and pointed out that the car was rusting for want of use, he placed it at my disposal with the grace and courtliness that distinguish your true Italian nobleman."

It was a veritable little palace on tyres, and we reached Lausanne quickly and without inconvenience. The squire was not a bit worse for the effort, but the sight of old Gottlieb turning away from the door when he had bidden us good-bye, with a shrug of the shoulders that said as plainly as any words could have done that he washed his hands of all responsibility and was disgusted at the capriciousness of the mad English, afforded me much delight and remains with me still.

It took us four days to reach Folkestone, and we stayed there a couple of nights before we went on to London. Dr. and Mrs. Grey remained with us until we reached the St. Pancras hotel, where the Cynic was waiting to receive us. The squire will see a good deal of the Greys, as the doctor is a Manchester man and can easily run over. The Cynic took to them at once, and Mrs. Grey, or "Dot" as I have learned to call her, confided to me that my friend was a very nice fellow of whom she would be desperately afraid. Fancy any woman being afraid of the Cynic!

Mr. Derwent is, in his way, quite as good an organiser as the doctor, though he goes about his work so quietly that you hardly realise it. Instead of our having to change at Airlee he had arranged for a saloon to be attached to the Scotch express, so that we travelled with the utmost possible comfort. The squire was by this time so accustomed to travelling, and had borne the fatigue of the journey so well, that I should not have hesitated to accompany him alone, but it was very pleasant to have the Cynic's company and to feel that he shared the responsibility. He seemed pleased to see me, I thought, and congratulated me warmly on the success of my mission.

"You must thank Dr. Grey for all this," I said; "it was his persistence that brought Mr. Evans home."

"Nay, child," said the squire, "you and your word pictures sent me home."

Webster met us at Fawkshill with the pair of bays, and his eyes shone as he greeted the squire. It was good to observe the sympathy that exists between the two as they grasped hands at the station gate. One was master and the other servant, but they were just old friends reunited, and neither of them was ashamed of his emotion.

When we entered the lane the squire closed his eyes. "I will play at being a boy again, Grace. Tell me when we reach the brow of the hill, so that I may see it all at once."

I knew what he meant, and none of the three spoke a word until Webster pulled up his horses at my request. It was nearly five o'clock in the afternoon, and the warm August sun was well on his way to the west. A thin haze hung over the distant hills, but the moors were glorious in brown and purple, and there was here and there the glint of gorse.

"Now, sir," I said, "look and rejoice!"

He stood up in the carriage and looked around; and as he looked he filled his lungs with the sweet moorland air. Then he said, with deep emotion:

"Thank God for this!—Drive on, Webster, please."

I was anxious to see the motherkin, and leaving the squire to the companionship of Mr. Derwent I hastened to the cottage. It would be more correct to say that I did my best to hasten, but so many of the villagers stopped me to offer their greetings and inquire the news that my progress was considerably retarded.

When I was nearing the cottage I met Farmer Goodenough, whose hearty hand-grasp I accepted cautiously. After the usual preliminary questions had been asked and answered his voice became rather grave as he said:

"Miss 'Olden, I don't want to worry ye, knowing 'at you're an extra speshul hand at findin' trouble, but I don't altogether like the looks o' Mrs. Hubbard. She's gone a bit thin an' worn, in a manner o' speakin'. Ye'll excuse me saying ought, I know, but 'a stitch in time saves nine,' as t' Owd Book puts it."

I thanked him, and hurried home, feeling very troubled and uneasy, but when the dear old lady came tripping down to meet me my fears retired into the background. She was so bright and sweet and altogether dainty, and she looked so happy and so well, with the pink flush of pleasure on her cheeks, that I concluded the worthy farmer had for once deceived himself.

"Yes, love!" she exclaimed, flinging her arms around my neck as I stooped to kiss her; "but you are so brown, love, and you are really handsome. Do come in and have some tea."

She hovered about me all the time I was removing my hat and coat, anxious to render me service, and seizing every opportunity of stroking my hands and cheeks.

"You foolish old pussy-cat!" I said at length, as I forced her into her easy-chair and placed the hot toast before her. "Give over petting and spoiling me, and tell me all about yourself—the truth, the whole truth, and nothing but the truth."

She evaded all my questions, however, and insisted that I should describe for her every incident of my journey.

When we had cleared away the things and drawn our chairs up to the fire I returned to the attack. Perhaps she was a little thin, after all, and there was a tired look about the eyes that I did not like.

"What have you been doing in my absence?" I asked; "not working yourself to death in the vain attempt to impart a brighter surface to everything polishable, eh?"

"No, love, I have taken things very easily, and have just kept the cottages and your studio tidy. I have spent a good deal of time at Reuben's, where they have been very kind to me; but I have missed you very much, love."

"Well, I am back now, and not likely to leave you again for a long time. We must have another full day's jaunt on the moors and see the heather in all its royal magnificence."

Her eyes brightened, but I noticed they fell again, and there was doubt in her voice as she replied:

"Yes, love. That will be nice. I think the heat has been very trying, and you may find it so, too. You must take care not to overtire yourself."

Then I knew that there was something wrong, and was glad that I had not consented to live at the Hall. It had been a disappointment to the squire, but he had not pressed the point when he saw that I was unwilling, and I had, of course, readily agreed to spend a good deal of time with him. I know he would have welcomed my old lady as a permanent guest for my sake, but she would never have consented to abandon her own little Hall of Memories, though she would have sought by every cunning artifice which love could devise to induce me to leave her, and would have suffered smilingly. I registered a mental vow that she should never know, if I could keep the secret from her, and that I would do all in my power to make her declining days happy.

"Why are you so weary, dear?" I asked.

"Oh, it is nothing, love," she replied. "It is just the heat. I shall be better when the days are cooler. Indeed, love, I am feeling better already."

I slept soundly enough, in spite of my new anxiety, but the morrow brought me no alleviation. The old lady's vigour was gone, and she moved about the house without energy. But her cheerfulness never failed her, and her patience was something to marvel at.

Dr. Trempest pulled up his horse at the gate and stopped to have a chat one day, and I took the opportunity of mentioning my uneasiness.

"I'll pop in and look at her," he said. "Why don't you give her the same magic physic you've poured down the throat of my old friend Evans? He's taken on a new lease of life. I tell you it's a miracle, and he says you did it, but he won't divulge the secret. Dear! dear! we old fogeys are no use at all in competition with the women! But come, let's have a look at the old girl."

He walked brusquely in and sat astride a chair, leaning his chin on the high back, and talked with her for ten minutes. Then he came out to me again.

"Can't say much without an examination, but appears to me the machinery's getting done. We can none of us last for ever, you know. Keep her still, if you can, and tell her she needn't be up every two minutes to flick the dust off the fireirons. Drive her out, now and then, and let her have exercise without exertion; and don't you pull a long face before her or get excited or boisterous."

I pulled a face at *him*, and he grinned as he mounted his horse. "I'll send her up a bottle," he said; "works wonders, does a bottle, if it's mixed with faith in them that take it;" and the caustic old man moved slowly away.

The bottle came, but so far it has wrought no miracle, and there has crept into my heart the unwelcome suggestion of loss. I have tried not to admit it, not to recognise it when admitted, but the attempt is vain. Dr. Trempest shakes his head and repeats his sagacious remark that we can't live for ever, and the squire presses my hand in sympathy, being too honest to attempt to comfort me with hollow hopes.

Only Mother Hubbard herself is cheerful, and as her physical strength decreases she appears to gain self-possession and mental vigour. When the squire suggested that she should be asked to accompany us on the drives which he so much enjoys I anticipated considerable opposition, and felt certain that she would yield most reluctantly, but to my surprise she consented without demur.

"This is very kind of Mr. Evans, love," she said, "and if you do not mind having an old woman with you I shall be glad to go."

She did not say much on these excursions, but when she was directly spoken to she answered without confusion, and was quite unconscious that she occasionally addressed the squire as "love." He never betrayed any consciousness of it, but I once noticed a repressed smile steal over Webster's face as he sat upon the box.

Now it was that I saw the full beauty of the moorland which had made so strong an appeal to my father's heart. I felt my own strangely stirred, and my two companions were also full of emotion. I believe it spoke to each of us with a different voice, and had not quite the same message for any two of us. I have hardly analysed my own feelings, but I think the rich and yet subdued colouring got hold of my imagination, and the wildness of the scene impressed me powerfully.

I had always known these moors—known them from my childhood; but only as one knows many things—the moon or the Mauritius, for instance—from the description of others. The picture painted for me had been true to life, but not living; yet it had been sufficiently lifelike to make the reality strangely familiar. And now I looked at it with double vision— through my own eyes and my father's; and the thought of what he would have felt quickened my perceptions and attuned them to the spirit of my ancestors. The moors were sheeted in purple, brightened by clumps of golden gorse, and I could easily have followed the example of Linnæus, who, when he first saw the yellow blossom, is said to have fallen on his knees and praised God for its beauty.

The squire had known the moors always. To him the scene speaks of home. I do not think the actual beauty of it impresses him greatly, perhaps because of its extreme familiarity, and it does not arouse in him the same sensation of pleasure or appeal to his artistic sense in the same degree as the grander scenery he has so lately left behind.

But this *contents* him as nothing else does or could! It is as when one exchanges the gilded chairs of state for the old, familiar arm-chair which would appear shabby to some people, or the dress shoes of ceremony for the homely slippers on the hearth. He admits now that he is happier than he had ever been abroad, and that he is glad to spend the late evening of his days amid the friendly scenes of his youth and manhood.

As for Mother Hubbard, she is quite unconsciously a mixture of poet and prophet. Everything speaks to her of God.

"Yes, love," she said quite recently, "'He maketh everything beautiful in its season;'" and to her the country is always beautiful, because it is always as God made it. That is why she loves it so much, I am sure; and whether it glows and sparkles beneath the hot sun of August or lies dun and grey under the clouded skies of February it is always full of charm. To her, all God's paintings show the hand of the Master, whether done in monochrome or in the colours of the rainbow, and none of them fails to satisfy her.

And Nature preaches to her, but the sermons are always comforting to her soul, for her inward ear has never been trained to catch the gloomy messages which some of us hear so readily. But where she finds consolation I discover disquietude.

The horse had been pulled up at a point where the wide panorama stretched limitlessly before us, and for a time we had all been speechless. I had gathered a tiny bunch of heather and fastened it in my belt, and now stood, shading my eyes with my hand, as I looked across the billowy expanse. The squire had closed his eyes, but his face showed no trace of weariness, and I knew that he was happy.

Mother Hubbard broke the silence, as she sank back into her seat with a little sigh, and when I sat down Webster drove slowly on.

"It is nice to think, love, that though you have gathered and taken away a sprig of heather the landscape is still beautiful. And yet, you know, the little flowers you have plucked gave their share of beauty to the whole, and helped God to do His work. I think, love, that thought encourages me when I know that the Lord may soon stretch out His hand for me. Your little flowers have not lived in vain. Only their neighbours will miss them, but their little world would not have been quite as beautiful without them."

I think the squire was astonished, but he remained quite still, and I replied:

"That is very true, dear, but the heather has never thwarted its Maker's purpose, but has lived the life He designed, and so has perfectly fulfilled its mission. With man, alas! it is not so. He too often makes a sad bungle of life, and is so full of imperfections that he cannot add much to the beauty of the landscape."

Mother Hubbard shook her head and pointed to the moors. "Yet *that* is very beautiful, love, isn't it?"

"It is perfect," I replied.

"Perfect, is it? Look at the little flowers at your waist. See, one little bell has been blighted in some way, and there are several which seem to have been eaten away in parts, and here and there some have fallen off. I wonder if you could find a sprig, love, where every bell and tiny leaf is perfect. Not many, I think. Yet you say the view is perfect, though the parts are full of imperfections."

The squire opened his eyes and bent them gravely upon her, but he did not speak, and she did not observe him.

"Ah, but, dear Mother Hubbard," I said, "the heather bells cannot help their imperfections. The blight and the insect, the claw of bird, the foot of beast, the hand and heel of man—how can they resist these things? But again I say, with man it is not so. He is the master of his destiny. He has freedom of will, and when he fails and falls and spoils his life it is his own fault."

"Not always, love," the gentle voice replied; "perhaps not often entirely his own fault. I used to think like that, but God has given me clearer vision now. Here is poor Sar'-Ann, not daring to show her face outside the door; covered with shame for her own sin and Ginty's. Oh yes, love, she has spoiled her life. But think of how she has been brought up: in a little cottage where there was a big family and only two rooms; where the father was coarse and the boys—poor little fellows—imitated him; and the mother, though she has a kind heart, is vulgar and often thoughtless; where decency has been impossible and woman's frailty has been made a jest. It has not been Sar'-Ann's fault, love, that she has been placed there.

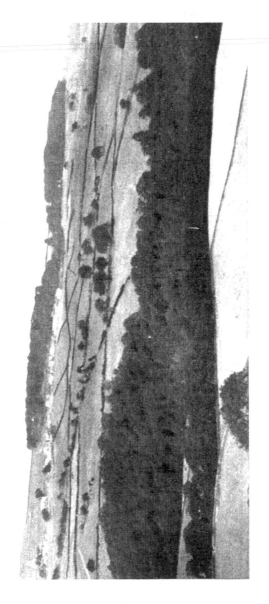

WINDYRIDGE FROM MARSLAND MOOR

She had no voice in the selection of her lot. She might have been in your home and you in hers. That little bunch of heather would have been safe yet if it had not been growing by the roadside where you stood."

"Then God is responsible for Sar'-Ann?" I asked.

"God is her Father, and He loves her very dearly," she replied simply. "There are lots of questions I cannot answer, love, but I am sure He will not throw Sar'-Ann away because she has been blighted and stained."

The squire broke in now, and there was just a little tremor in his voice as he spoke:

"'And when the vessel that he made of the clay was marred in the hands of the potter he made it again another vessel, as seemed good to the potter to make it.'"

Mother Hubbard's eyes lit up. "Yes, sir," she said, "and I do not think he grieved too much because the first design went wrong. He just made it again another vessel. Perhaps he meant at first to make a very beautiful and graceful vessel, but there were imperfections and flaws in the material, so he made it into a homely jug; and yet it was useful."

"Oh, Mother Hubbard!" I said, "there are all sorts of imperfections and flaws in your logic, and I know people who would shake it to pieces in a moment."

"Well, love, perhaps so; but they would not shake my faith:

"'To one fixed ground my spirit clings,
    I know that God is good.'"

"Stick to that, Mrs. Hubbard," said the squire earnestly; "never let go that belief. Faith is greater far than logic. I would sooner doubt God's existence than His goodness. Problems of sin and suffering have oppressed my brain and heart all my life, but like you I have got clearer vision during these later days. The clouds often disperse towards the sunset, and my mental horizon is undimmed now. You and I cannot explain life's mysteries, but God can, and meanwhile I hold

"'That nothing walks with aimless feet;
    That not one life shall be destroyed,

Or cast as rubbish to the void,
When God hath made the pile complete.'"

"Tennyson was not Paul," I remarked.

"Why should he have been?" he asked. "He was a Christian seer, none the less, and he had the heavenly vision."

"But you cannot call his theology orthodox," I persisted; "is it in any sense Biblical?"

"Whence came his vision and inspiration if not from God?" he replied. Then he turned to Mother Hubbard: "Thank you, thank you much," he said; "I shall not forget your parable of the heather."

CHAPTER TWENTY-FOUR

ROGER TREFFIT INTRODUCES "MISS TERRY"

I HAD A letter from Rose this morning. The lucky girl has got another holiday and is apparently having a fine time at Eastbourne. She says the chief insisted that her trip north was not a holiday, but a tonic. If so, it was a very palatable one, I am sure, from the way she took it. Whilst, therefore, I am exposing plates and developing negatives, she is enjoying refreshing sea-breezes, and listening to good music. It appears her chief recommended Eastbourne, and I gather from her letter that he is there himself with his family.

So is the Cynic! The courts are closed for the most part, but he told me a while ago that there were one or two Old Bailey cases in which he was interested which would prevent him from going very far away, and he is taking week-ends on the south coast. It is curious that he should have hit upon Eastbourne—quite by accident, Rose assures me—and that they should have met so early. I am not surprised that they should have been together for a long ramble over the downs, though I imagine they would have liked it better without the presence of a third party. Rose is not very clear about it, but apparently there were three of them. What a nuisance for them both!

The Cynic does not expect to be in Windyridge again before the end of this month. I always think September seems a particularly long month, and yet it has only thirty days.

Meantime the village is affording me further opportunities of studying Mother Hubbard's theories of human nature and discovering the germ of goodness in things evil. It is a difficult hunt!

Little Lucy Treffit's father has come home, and the fact has a good deal of significance for Lucy and her mother. I cannot bear the sight of the silly man. He struts about the village as though he were doing us a favour to grace it with his presence. He puts a thumb in each arm-hole of his waistcoat, wears a constant smile on his flabby face when in public, and nods at everybody as he passes, in the most condescending way imaginable.

He is quite an under-sized man, but broad all the way down; it looks as though at some time in his life, when he may have been very soft and putty-like, a heavy hand had been placed on his head, and he had been compressed into a foot less height. What gives reality to the impression is the extreme length of his trousers, which hang over his boots in folds.

The delight of his eyes and the joy of his heart is neither wife nor child, but a smooth-haired terrier which brings in the living, such as it is.

During the summer months Roger and his dog frequent the popular seaside resorts and give beach entertainments of "an 'igh-class character" to quote Roger himself. In the winter months they secure engagements at music-halls, bazaars, school-entertainments and the like, when the income is more precarious.

Ordinarily the man is not home until October, but unfortunately the dog's health broke down in the latter part of August, and Roger came home to save the cost of lodgings, and to get drink on credit. For, almost alone among the villagers, this man gets drunk day by day with marked consistency; and if he is irritating when sober he is nothing less than contemptible when intoxicated. He then becomes more suave than ever, and his mouth curves into a smile which reaches his ears, but he is more stupid and obstinate than the proverbial mule. And the worst of it is he drinks at home, for the nearest inn is above a mile away, so his unhappy wife has a rough time of it. Yet he is not actively unkind to her; he does not beat her body—he merely starves and wounds her soul.

She is a thin, wasted woman, about thirty years old, I suppose, of more than average intelligence, and one of the best needlewomen I have ever seen. She does beautiful work for which she is wretchedly paid, but it serves to keep the home together. I cannot help thinking that she is suffering from some serious disease, but she herself refuses to harbour any such thought. I am very much interested in her and little Lucy, and during the summer have paid them many a visit and been cheered by the little girl's delightful prattle.

They live in a very poor house, and a most peculiar one. It is two-storeyed, but unusually narrow, and the only window in the upper room is a fixture in the roof. It really is remarkable that in a place like Windyridge so many of the windows cannot be opened, either because they were so constructed at first, or because their owners have painted and varnished them until they are glued fast.

The stones in the walls are loose in many places and the stone slabs on the roof lie about at various angles, and seem to invite the thin, tall chimney-stack—and why it should be so tall I have never been able to surmise—to fall down and send them flying. It is a mean, rickety house, not worth the cost of repair.

Inside, however, it is as clean and comfortable as any other in the village. The floor is spotless, the deal tables are white as soap and water can make them, the steel fender and fire-irons shine like mirrors, and the short curtains at the window might always have come straight from the laundry.

I did not know Roger had come home when I raised the latch and entered the house, after the usual perfunctory knock, the other day, and I apologised for my unceremonious entrance with some confusion.

Roger waved his hand loftily. "Quite all right, ma'am; quite all right. Miss Terry, oblige me by getting the lady a chair."

The dog rose to its feet and with its nose and forepaws pushed a chair from the wall in the direction of the fireplace.

"Thank you, Miss Terry," remarked the man, "I am much obliged to you. Pray be seated, ma'am."

I was interested, in spite of myself. "Yours is a very remarkable dog, Mr. Treffit," I said.

"Yes'm; very much so indeed. Miss Terry is the name I gave 'er, because she is a 'mystery.' See? Ha! ha! Very good that, eh? Mystery—Miss Terry.

Miss Terry and me, ma'am, has appeared before the nobility, clergy and gentry of a dozen counties."

I expressed polite astonishment and inquired for Mrs. Treffit.

"My wife, ma'am, is upstairs in the chamber. If you want her I will send for her. Miss Terry, will you convey my respects to the missis, and ask her to step this way?" The request was accompanied by a significant gesture in the direction of the narrow staircase, and the dog, with an inclination of the head which might have been intended for a bow, bounded up the steps and returned with its mistress. Its mistress? No, I withdraw the word—with its master's wife.

She coughed a good deal as she came down, and I suggested that a short walk in the sunshine would do her good, but she shook her head.

"I'm sorry, Miss 'Olden, but I'm that busy I couldn't leave just now. I was wonderin' if you'd mind comin' upstairs while I get on with my work."

"Sit down a bit, can't you?" said the man; "I want Miss Terry to show this lady some of her tricks. You're always in such a desperate hurry, you are."

"Someb'dy has to be in a 'urry," she replied, "when there's naught comin' in, an' three mouths to feed, to say nothin' of the dog, which costs nearly as much as all t' rest put together."

"You leave the dog alone," he growled; "Miss Terry brings in as much as all t' rest put together, doesn't she?"

"I say nought against her," she answered wearily; "t' dog's right enough, but she's bringin' nought in now."

She sat down, however, at my side, and Miss Terry proceeded to justify her name. She dressed herself in a queer little hobble-skirt costume, put on a hat and veil, raised a sunshade, and moved about the room in the most amusing way. She fetched a miniature bedstead, undressed and put herself to bed in a manner calculated to bring down the house every time. She removed the handkerchief (a very dirty one, by the way) from her master's pocket, sneezed, wiped her nose, and then replaced it without apparently arousing its owner's attention. She drank out of his glass, simulated intoxication, and fell into a seemingly drunken sleep, with much exaggerated snoring.

And all the time Roger Treffit stood or sat, as circumstances required, addressing the dog in the politest and most deferential terms, with the smug smile of satisfaction threatening to cut the chin entirely from his face.

"Now, Miss Terry," he said in conclusion, "you must not overtire yourself. We are very grateful for the hentertainment you have pervided. Have the goodness to step up to the lady and say good-bye."

The dog extended a paw, and Martha and I were permitted to withdraw.

"It really is a very clever dog," I remarked, when we were alone in the prison-like bedroom.

"It's a very good dog, too," she replied; "it 'ud look after me more nor he would if he'd let it. It 'asn't a bit o' vice about it, an' I only wish I could say as much for its master."

"Why are you sitting up here in this wretched loft, where the light is so poor for such fine work?"

"To be out of his way, an' that's the truth," she replied bitterly. "I shall go down when Lucy comes in from t' school, and not afore. I've never no peace nor pleasure when he's at 'ome."

"He doesn't ill-treat you, does he?"

"No, but I cannot bear to see him all t' day through, soakin', soakin'. He can always walk straight, however much he takes, but 'e gets that nasty by tea-time there's no bidin' in t' 'ouse with 'im. And he natters so when I cough, an' I can't help coughin'. It's nought much, an' I've got used to it, but it vexes 'im, an' he says it worries t' dog."

"He's a brute!" I said; "anybody can see that he thinks more of his dog than of you."

"Well, you see, his dog's his business. I don't know 'at he's worse nor lots more 'at makes their business into their god, but it isn't always easy to bide. An' when I get to t' far end I answer back, an' that makes fireworks. I wish he wor at Blackpool yet."

At that moment a loud report rang through the house, and I sprang from my seat in alarm.

"It's nothin'," said Martha; "there's nought to be frightened of. He's teachin' t' dog some new fool's trick with a pistol, but I don't believe there's a bullet in it. He nearly frightened me an' our Lucy out of our wits t' first time he did it."

I sat down again, but my heart was still beating violently. "I fear I couldn't live with such a companion," I said.

"You'd 'ave to, if you were i' my shoes," she replied. "I'm tied up to 'im, ain't I? Tell me what *you'd* do. You couldn't get a divorce even if you'd plenty o' money, for he never bothers wi' other women. An' t' court wouldn't give me an order, 'cos he doesn't thrash me; an' t' vicar's wife says 'at it was for better or worse 'at I took 'im, an' I must kill him wi' kindness. But kindness doesn't kill 'im; nought does. Oh God, if it wasn't for our Lucy I'd be glad to go where he couldn't follow."

"You won't think I am preaching, will you, dear," I said, "if I ask you if you have tried really hard to make him love you? I don't quite know what you could do, but there must be some way of reaching his heart. And think how happy you would all be if you could change his heart and win his love."

"Miss 'Olden, there comes a time when you give up tryin', becos you fair 'aven't strength an' 'eart to go on. I've done all I could for that man. He's asked nought of me I 'aven't let 'im 'ave. I'm the mother of his child, an' I've tried to learn t' little lass to be as good as she's bonny, bless her! an' I keep her as neat as I know how; an' he thinks more o' t' dog. I've worked early an' late to keep t' 'ome together, an' he's never once found it ought but tidy, for I get up afore he wakes to scrub and polish. I've gone without food to give 'im luxuries, an' he never says so much as 'Thank ye'; but he thanks t' dog for every trick he's trained it to. I've smiled on 'im when my heart's been like lead, an' talked cheerful when it 'ud 'a done me good to cry—an' all for what? Not for curses: not for kicks. I could stand curses an' kicks when he wor i' drink, if he'd love me an' be sorry when he wor sober. No, after all I've done for 'im he just takes no notice of me. I'm his woman, not his wife, an' I'm too broken-hearted now to try any more."

One solitary tear stole down her cheek—a tiny tear, as though the fountain from which it had escaped were nearly dry; and she did not stop to wipe it away.

I bent over and kissed her. "The darkest night ends in day," I said. "Don't lose heart or hope. I cannot preach to you, and I fear if I were in your place I should not do so well as you. I should lose my temper as well as my spirits. But don't let love die if you can help it. I suppose you loved him once?"

"Yes, I loved him once," she said.

"And you still love him?" I ventured.

"No, I don't. I neither love 'im nor 'ate 'im. But I love his child. That's our Lucy's voice. I must be goin' down now."

CHAPTER TWENTY-FIVE

THE RETURN OF THE PRODIGAL

I HAVE BEEN one whole year in Windyridge, and like a good business woman I have taken stock and endeavoured to get out a balance sheet in regular "Profit and Loss" fashion. I am afraid a professional accountant would heap scorn upon it, as my methods are not those taught in the arithmetics; but that consideration does not concern me.

My nett profits from the portraiture branch amount to the huge sum of nine pounds, eighteen shillings and sevenpence. If these figures were to be published I do not think they would attract competitors to Windyridge, and I can see plainly that I shall not recoup my initial outlay on the studio for several years. But that matters little, as my London firms have kept me well supplied with work, and would give me a great deal more if I were willing to take it.

But I am *not* willing. Man does not live by bread alone, nor by painting miniatures and designing book illustrations, and I am determined to live and not just exist, and I *have* lived during these twelve months. And even from the monetary point of view I am better off than I was when I came, because if I have lost in the way of income I have gained by a saving in expenditure. You simply cannot spend money in Windyridge, and, what is more, the things best worth having cannot be bought with money.

These "more excellent" things appear upon another page in my balance sheet—a page which would make the professional auditor gasp for breath.

My experiences have made me a richer woman, though not a more important personage to my bankers. I am healthier and happier than I was a year ago. I have a living interest in an entire community, and an entire community has a living interest in me. And I have a few real friends in various stations of life, each of whom would do a great deal for me, and each of whom has taught me several valuable lessons without fee or reward. The moors and the glens, too, have had me to school and opened to me their secret stores of knowledge, and who shall compute the worth of that education? As a result, I have a saner outlook and a truer judgment, and that counts for much in my case. Undoubtedly the balance is on the right side, and I have no regrets as I turn and look back along the track of the year.

The anniversary day itself was marked by an incident of uncommon interest. The weather was atrocious, and in marked contrast to that of the previous year on the corresponding date. Had such conditions prevailed when I first saw Windyridge the village would not have known me as one of its householders.

It rained as though the floodgates of heaven had been opened and got rusted fast. For three days there had been one endless downpour, but on the fateful Wednesday it degenerated into a miserable, depressing drizzle which gave me the blues. The distance disappeared behind an impenetrable wall of mist, and the horizon was the hedge of the field fifty yards away. The drip, drip, drip from a leak in the glazing of my studio so got on my nerves that in the afternoon I put on my strong boots and a waterproof and set out for a walk.

But though the rain could not conquer me the sticky mud did. After covering a mile in half an hour I was so tired with the exertion that I turned back, and was relieved when the distance had been almost covered and only a few hundred yards separated me from the cottage.

I had had the road to myself so far, but as I came down the hill which skirts the graveyard I saw a stranger in the act of opening the gate and entering. At the same moment, apparently, he caught sight of me, and we scrutinised each other with interest as the distance between us lessened.

He was a well-dressed young fellow of about thirty, with a stern expression on an otherwise rather pleasing face. His mouth was hidden by a heavy moustache, but I liked his eyes, which had a frank look in them. His rather long raincoat was dripping wet, and he had no other protection from the rain, for he carried in his hand a stout stick of peculiar shape. His hands and face were brown from exposure, and I took him to be a prosperous, intelligent farmer.

He raised his hat at my approach. "I am sorry to detain you, even for a moment, in this rain," he said, "but I wondered if you could tell me whether anyone of the name of Brown—Greenwood Brown—is buried here."

Oh! thought I, you have come back, have you? But I merely replied:

"Yes, Mr. Brown's grave is near the top of the hill. I will show you which it is."

"Please do not put yourself to that trouble," he protested; "if you will be good enough to direct me I shall be able to find it."

"You could not identify it," I said, "for there is no stone, but just a grassy mound, like many of the rest. Let me point it out to you, and then I will go on my way."

He made no further objection, but held the gate open for me to enter. There are no paths, and he protested again when he saw me plunge into the long, wet grass, but I laughed at his fears and led the way to the spot where all that was mortal of poor Farmer Brown lay beneath the sod.

"This is his grave," I said, and he thanked me with another courteous inclination of the head. As I turned to leave he asked a further question.

"Can you tell me if any of his people still live in this neighbourhood? I—I have a message for them."

"If you will call at my cottage," I replied, indicating the little house a stone's-throw away, "I will tell you all I know. Pray do not stay too long in the rain. You have no umbrella."

"Thank you," he said, "I shall take no harm, and I will call at your house shortly, as you are so very kind."

I left him, but I could not forbear looking from the window in Mother Hubbard's bedroom, and I could distinctly see him standing with head bent and uncovered in an attitude of deep dejection over his father's grave. I had no misgiving on that point. In spite of the thick moustache the likeness was too strong to admit of doubt.

I went into the studio and brought out the copy of Farmer Brown's portrait which I had retained, and placed it on the chest of drawers where he could hardly fail to see it; but I said nothing to Mother Hubbard, who was laying the cloth for tea. The kettle was boiling when he came in, and I fetched a third cup and saucer and invited him to the table.

I could see that reluctance struggled with desire, but Mother Hubbard's added entreaties turned the scale, and he removed his soaking overcoat with many apologies for the trouble he was causing.

He drank his tea, but appeared to have little appetite for the crisp buttered toast which Mother Hubbard pressed upon him, and he took a rather absent part in the desultory conversation which accompanied the meal. I did not think it right to reveal the curiosity I felt, but after a while he made an opening.

"I only heard of Farmer Brown's death as I entered the village," he said. "I met a boy, of whom I inquired, and he told me the farmer was buried here in the beginning of the year."

Mother Hubbard put on her glasses and looked at him with a new interest, and removed them again in a minute or two as if satisfied.

"He died early in January," I said; "did you know him?"

"Yes," he said, and there was no sign of emotion in his voice or face; "but I have not seen him for several years. He had a wife and daughter; are they living, and still at the old place? I forgot to ask the boy."

I thought it curious that he should have overlooked so natural a question, if, as seemed likely, he had come to the neighbourhood with the intention of finding them; but after all, the explanation lay upon the surface—he manifestly did not wish to arouse too much curiosity.

"Yes, they are still at the farm, and both are well," I replied; "I often see them. If you knew the farmer you will perhaps recognise his photograph. It was taken only a little while before he died."

I got up and handed it to him, and I saw his mouth twitch at the corners as he took the card in his hand. All the same he examined it critically, and his voice was still firm as he replied:

"He had evidently aged a good deal since I knew him, but I am sure it was a good likeness."

"It was trouble that aged him, Joe," broke in Mother Hubbard's gentle voice; "the good Lord overrules all things for good, but it was you who brought his grey hairs with sorrow to the grave."

There was a mild severity of tone which astonished me and revealed Mother Hubbard in a new light, but I was too interested in the change which came over the startled man's face to think much of it at the time.

"So you recognise me," he said. "I thought your face was familiar, though the young lady's is not so. Well, everybody will know of my return soon, so I need not complain that you have anticipated the news by a few hours. Yes, the prodigal has come home, but too late to receive his father's blessing."

"Not too late to receive *a* Father's blessing, Joe," replied Mother Hubbard; "not too late to find forgiveness and reconciliation if you have come in the right spirit; but too late to bring the joy-light into your earthly father's eyes: too late to hear the welcome he would have offered you."

"I do not ask nor deserve to be spared," he said, with some dignity, "and my first explanations shall be offered to those who have most right to them. But this I will say, for I can see that you speak with sincerity. I came back to seek forgiveness and to find peace, but I am justly punished for my sin in that I forfeit both. You have not said much, but you have said enough to let me realise that the curse of Cain is upon me."

"It is not," said Mother Hubbard calmly and with firmness; "your father would have told you so. Go home to your mother, and you will find in her forgiveness and love a dim reflection of the forgiveness and love of God, and peace will follow."

He rested one elbow upon the table and leaned his head upon his hand, whilst his fingers tapped a mechanical tune upon his forehead, but he did not speak for several minutes—nor did we. Then he rose and took the still damp overcoat from the clothes-horse before the fire, and said as he put it on:

"Since I left home I have had many hard tasks to perform. But the hardest of them all now lies before me, and though I have made some little money I would give every penny I possess if the past could be undone and that grey-haired man brought back to life. I am accounted a bold man, but I would sooner face a lion in the Rhodesian jungle than my mother and sister on yonder farm."

"Go in peace!" said the little mother. "God stands by the side of every man who does his duty, and your mother, remember, is about to experience a great joy. Let them see that you love them both, and that you loved your father too, and that will heal the wound more quickly than anything else."

He shook Mother Hubbard's hand, bowed to me, and stepped out into the rain; and I watched him walk briskly forward until the mist swallowed him up.

Two days afterwards I heard the sequel. The rain had cleared away and the roads were fairly dry when I set off with the intention of walking as far as Uncle Ned's. Before I had gone very far I overtook Farmer Goodenough, who was journeying in the same direction, and almost immediately afterwards we met Jane Brown.

"I was just comin' to see you, Miss Holden," she said, "but as you're going my way I'll walk back with you if you'll let me. Mother wants to know if you can take our photographs—hers and Joe's and mine—on Monday."

I told her it would be quite convenient, and Farmer Goodenough began to question her about her brother's home-coming. I hardly expected much response, for Jane is not usually very communicative, but on this occasion she was full of talk.

"I came o' purpose to say my say," she explained, "for I must either talk or burst."

We encouraged the former alternative, and she began: "If you want to be made a fuss of, and have people lay down their lives for you, you mustn't stop at 'ome and do your duty; you must go wrong. Only you mustn't go wrong just a little bit: you must go the whole hog an' be a rank wrong 'un—kill your father or summat o' that sort—and then when you come back you'll be hugged an' kissed an' petted till it's fair sickenin'."

"Gently, lass, gently!" said Farmer Goodenough; "that sounds just a trifle bitter."

"I may well be bitter; you'd be bitter if you saw what I see," she replied.

I endeavoured to turn the conversation and to satisfy my curiosity. "Where has your brother been, and what has he been doing all these years?" I inquired.

"Oh, he tells a tale like a story-book," she replied impatiently. "I'm bound to believe him, I suppose, because whatever else he was he wasn't a liar, but it's more like a fairy tale than ought else. After he hit father an'

ran away he got to Liverpool, an' worked his passage on a boat to Cape
Town, an' for a long time he got more kicks than ha'pence—and serve
him right, too, *I* say. He tried first one thing an' then another, and landed
up in Rhodesia at last, an' sought work from a man who employed a lot o'
labour. He says he wouldn't have been taken on if the gentleman hadn't
spotted him for a Yorkshireman. 'Thou'rt Yorkshir', lad?' he said; an' our
Joe said: 'Aye! bred an' born.' 'Let's hear ta talk a bit o' t' owd tongue, lad,'
he said; 'aw've heeard nowt on 't for twelve yeear, an' t' missis willn't hev it
spokken i' t' haase.'

"Well, of course, Joe entered into t' spirit of it, an' the old gentleman
was delighted, an' gave him a job, an' he always had to speak broad
Yorkshire unless the missis was there. It wasn't exactly a farm, but they
grew fruit an' vegetables and kept poultry an' pigs an' bees an' such like,
and it was just to our Joe's taste. I won't deny but what he's clever, and he
was always steady an' honest. He says the old gentleman took to him an'
gave him every chance, an' t' missis liked him too, because he always spoke
so polite an' proper. An' then he fell in love wi' one o' t' daughters, an' they
were married last year, an' by what I can make out he's a sort of a partner
in t' business now. Anyway, he says it's his wife 'at brought him to see what
a wrong 'un he'd been, and when he'd told 'em all t' tale nothing 'ud do
but he was to come to England and make it up with his father. So he's
come, an' mother blubbers over him, an' holds his 'and, an' strokes his 'air
till I'm out of all patience."

Farmer Goodenough looked grave, but he did not speak, so I said:
"Isn't this rather unworthy of you, Jane? Your mother is naturally glad to
see her boy back again, and if she had not been here you would have
welcomed him just as cordially."

"Would I?" she replied. "No fear! He gave father ten years of sorrow
an' brought him to 'is grave. I loved my dad too well to forgive his
murderer that easy. He's taken no notice of us all this time, an' while he's
been makin' money an' courtin' a rich girl we might all have been in t'
workhouse for ought he knew or cared. And then he's to come home, an'
it's to be all right straight off, an' we must have t' best counterpane on t'
bed, an' t' china tea-service out 'at were my grandmother's, an' we must go
slobberin' round his neck the minute he puts his head in at t' door. Bah! it

makes me sick. You've only got to be a prodigal, as I say, an' then you can have t' fatted calf killed for you."

"Now look you here, lass," said Farmer Goodenough kindly, "I've said nought so far, 'cos it does you good to talk. It's poor policy to bung t' kettle up when t' water's boilin', but I think ye've let off enough steam now to keep from burstin', so we'll just look into this matter, an' see what we can make on 't."

"Oh, I know you of old, Reuben Goodenough," replied the girl; "you'd be every bit as bad as my mother."

"You'll be every bit as bad yerself, lass, when ye've as much sense; but now just let me ask you a question or two. T' Owd Book says, if I remember right, when t' father came out to talk to t' sulky brother: 'It was meet to make merry an' be glad,' an' I take that to mean 'at it was t' right an' proper thing to do. Now why were they glad, think ye?"

"Just because he'd come home," replied Jane bitterly, "an' his brother, like me, had never gone away. I don't wonder 'at he was sulky. But *that* prodigal hadn't killed his father."

"Well, now, Jane," replied the farmer, "'cordin' to my way o' sizin' that tale up, you've got hold of a wrong notion altogether. I don't know what t' parsons 'ud make of it, but it seems to me 'at t' owd man was glad, not so much because t' lad had come back, but because he'd come to hisself, an' that's a very deal different thing."

"I don't see no difference," said Jane.

"You will do if you think a minute, lass. Suppose a lad loses his senses an' runs away from 'ome, an' comes back one fine day as mad as ever. There'll be as much sorrow as joy, won't there, think ye, in that 'ome? But suppose while he's away his reason comes back to 'im, an' he gets cured, an' as soon as he's cured he says: 'I must go 'ome to t' owd folks,' an' he goes, an' they see 'at he's in his right mind, don't you think they'll make merry an' be glad? Wouldn't you?"

"Our Joe didn't lose his senses," the girl replied sullenly; "he was as clear-headed then as he is now. It's a different thing when they're mad."

"Nay, lass," he replied, "but unless I'm sadly mista'en all sin is a sort o' madness. You said just now 'at Joe went wrong. Now where did he go wrong—I mean what part of 'im?"

Jane made no reply.

"You'd say he was wrong in his 'ead to have treated his father as he did, but if 'is 'ead wasn't wrong 'is 'eart was, an' that's a worse kind o' madness. Doesn't t' Owd Book talk about 'em bein' possessed wi' devils? They mightn't be t' sort 'at has 'orns on, but they were t' sort 'at tormented 'em into wrong-doin', an' surely it was summat o' that sort 'at got hold o' your Joe. Now, if his wife has brought him to hisself, an' he's come 'ome to say he's sorry, 'it was meet to make merry an' be glad.'"

"It's hard on them that don't go wrong," said Jane.

"Well, now, how is it 'ard on them?" asked the farmer. "Talkin' quite straight, where does t' 'ardship come in?"

"Well, mother doesn't cry round *my* neck, an' stroke *my* hands, an' make a big fuss," replied the girl, "an' it's hard to see her thinkin' a deal more o' one 'at's done her so much wrong."

"Now you know better, Jane. Your mother thinks no more o' your Joe than she does o' you, only, as you say, she makes more fuss of him 'cos he's come round. It 'ud 'a been just t' same supposin' he'd been ill for ten year an' then got better. You'd ha' made a fuss over 'im then as well as your mother, an' you wouldn't ha' thought 'at your mother loved 'im more than you, if she did fuss over 'im a bit. Now you just look at it i' this way: Joe's been mad—clean daft—but he's come to hisself, an' it's 'meet to make merry an' be glad.'"

Jane is not at all a bad sort. She gave a little laugh as she said:

"Eh, Reuben! I never heard such a man for talkin'. However, I daresay you're right, an' my bark's worse than my bite, anyway. I was just feelin' full up when I came out, but I'm better now. I'll see if I can manage not to be jealous, for we shan't have 'im long. He's in a hurry to be back to his precious wife, an' he wants mother an' me to go with him, but mother says she'll have her bones laid aside father's, so he'll have to go by himself."

I took the photographs this morning, and was pleased to find that the reconciliation between brother and sister was complete. In the afternoon I went into the graveyard and found some beautiful flowers on Farmer Brown's grave, and a man was taking measurements for a stone. He told me that there was to be a curious inscription following the usual particulars, and fumbling in his pocket he drew forth a piece of paper on which I read these words:

"A foolish son is a grief to his father."

"A good man leaveth an inheritance to his children's children."

CHAPTER TWENTY-SIX

THE CYNIC BRINGS
NEWS OF GINTY

IT IS THE middle of October, and autumn is manifested on every side. It makes me rather sad, for bound up with these marvellous sunset tints which ravish the eye there is decay and death. The woods are carpeted in russet and gold; the green of the fields is dull and faded; every breath of wind helps to strip the trees a little barer; and as though Nature could not, unaided, work destruction fast enough, the hand of man is stretched forth to strip the glowing bracken from the moors, and great gaps on the hillsides tell of his handiwork.

I know, of course, that Nature is kindly and beneficent, and that death in this connection is a misnomer. I know that after the falling leaf and the bare branch and twig there will come the glory of spring, the glory of bursting bud and fragrant flower; but though that mitigates the feeling of sadness it does not entirely dispel it. The flowers and the foliage, the heather and the bracken have been my companions during these sunny days of summer, and it is hard to lose them, though only for a while.

And when I look on dear old Mother Hubbard, as she sits quietly by the fire, with her needles clicking ever more slowly, and the calm of a peaceful eventide deepening upon her face, my heart sinks within me, and I dare not look forward to the wintry months that lie ahead. What Windyridge will be to me when her sun sinks behind the hill I will not try to realise. I attempt to be cheerful, but my words mock me and my laugh rings hollow, and she, good soul, reads me through and through. I know I do not deceive her, and my Inner Self warns me that one of these days the motherkin will have it out with me and make me face realities, and I stand in dread of that hour.

The squire, on the other hand, looks far better than when he came home. He is still feeble, and he has his bad days, but the light in his eyes is not the light of sunset. Dr. Trempest means to be convincing, though he is merely vague when he assures the squire that he will "outlive some of us yet." I am glad he is better, for I cannot be with him as much as I should if Mother Hubbard did not claim my devotion.

I had tea with him and the Cynic on Sunday afternoon when some of her chapel friends were keeping Mother Hubbard company.

The Cynic was in the garden when I reached the Hall, and he told me that the squire was asleep in the library, so we drew two deck-chairs into the sunshine and sat down for an hour on the lawn.

He lit a cigarette, clasped his hands behind his head, and began:

"Well, I suppose you will want to know what is being done in the City of Destruction from which you fled so precipitately. I have not noticed any tendency on your part to stop your ears to its sounds, though you may not hanker after its fleshpots."

"Do not be horrid," I replied; "and if you are going to be cynical I will go in and chat with the housekeeper. I am not particularly anxious to know what is happening in your City of Destruction."

He elevated his eyebrows. "Miss Fleming, for instance?" he queried.

"Of course I shall be glad to hear of Rose. I always am. And that reminds me that her letters are few and unsatisfactory. Have you seen anything of her since the holidays?"

"Yes," he replied, "we have met several times; once at the house of a mutual friend, once at Olympia, and I believe twice at the theatre."

"Do people 'meet' at the theatre?" I inquired.

"They do if they arrange to do so, and keep their appointments," he replied provokingly. "I am fortunate in being acquainted with some of Miss Fleming's friends. I am sorry her letters leave something to be desired, but you need not be uneasy; she herself is as lively and fascinating as ever."

I should have liked to ask him who the friends were, for Rose has never mentioned them, and she had none who could possibly have been in the

Cynic's set in the old days; but friends can generally be found when the occasion demands them. I said nothing, of course, and he looked at me quizzically.

"Your comments," he remarked, "if I may quote, are 'few and unsatisfactory.'"

It was true, but he need not have noticed it. The fact is, I had nothing to say at the moment. That being the case there was plainly nothing for it but to abuse *him*.

"You are the Cynic to-day," I said, "and I foresee that you are going to sharpen your wit upon poor me. But I am not in the mood. You see, it is Sunday, and in Windyridge we are subdued and not brilliant on Sundays."

Perhaps his ear caught the weariness in my voice, for I was feeling tired and depressed; at any rate his tone changed immediately.

"I saw at once you were off colour," he said, "and I was making a clumsy attempt to buck you up; but, seriously, have you no questions you wish to ask me about the old place?"

"I should like to know how matters are progressing with you," I said. "I often wonder what the world thinks of your renunciation."

"The world knows nothing of it. I have never mentioned what I have done to anyone but you, and I do not propose to do so. As for myself— but what makes you wonder? Are you afraid I may have repented?"

"No," I replied, "you will never repent, you are not that sort. Not for one moment have I doubted your steadfastness."

"Thank you," he said simply; and then, after a moment's pause:

"I don't think it is anything to my credit. If I had been differently constituted the sacrifice would have entailed suffering, even if it had not proved too great for me. It was a lot of money, and if money is in any sense a man's god it must hurt him to lose so much. My god may be equally base, but it is not golden. In that respect I am like those ancient Athenians of whom Plato speaks, who 'bare lightly the burden of gold and of possessions,' though I fear I am not like them in despising all things except virtue. Besides, even now I am not exactly poor, for I have a good income."

"I have thirty shillings a week on the average," I interposed, "and I consider myself quite well to do."

"Exactly," he replied; "you and I take pleasure in our work for its own sake, and we are each paid, I suppose, fair value for what we do. Having food and clothing and a roof to shelter us we have all that is necessary, but we have luxuries thrown in—true friendships, for instance, which money cannot purchase. In my own case I am hoping to be quite wealthy if things turn out as I am beginning to dare to expect."

"I am glad to hear it," I said; "I am sure you deserve to succeed, and I trust you will be very happy in the possession of wealth when your expectation is realised."

He laughed, but with some constraint, I thought, and then said:

"We shall have to go in presently, Miss Holden, and before we do so, and whilst we are not likely to be interrupted, I have something to say to you which I find it difficult to mention."

I believe the colour left my face, and I know my stupid heart lost control of its beats again. His voice was so grave that I felt sure he had some communication to make which I should not relish, though I could not guess at its nature. I controlled myself with an effort, and encouraged him to proceed with an inquiring "Oh?"

He looked down at his boots for a moment and then continued:

"If it had not been for this I should not have come here this week-end, but I wanted to tell you what I have done, and to give you a message from one in whom you are interested. I have hesitated because I fear it may give you pain, though in one way it does not concern you in the slightest degree."

Why anything should give me pain which did not concern me was puzzling, and I wished the man would get to the story and skip the introduction. I never could bear to have news "broken gently" to me, it always seems like a mere prolongation of the agony; but I did not dare to interrupt.

"I had to be in attendance at the Central Criminal Court last Tuesday," he continued; "and the case in which I was interested was delayed by one in which the prisoner on trial was a young fellow whom you know."

It was very silly of me, but the revulsion of feeling was so great that I nearly cried, though goodness only knows what I had been expecting. The Cynic saw my emotion and mistook it for sympathy.

"I was afraid it would trouble you," he said kindly, "but you must not worry about it.

"The charge was quite an ordinary one and I had scarcely listened to the case at all, for my mind was occupied with what was to follow, but I heard sufficient to know that the man was one of a gang of sharpers, and that he had been caught red-handed whilst his companions had escaped. He had no one to defend him, but the judge nominated a junior who was present to be his counsel, and the lad did his best for him. But the youth had been in trouble before, and it was likely to go hard with him. All at once my neighbour nudged me: 'He's meaning you, Derwent,' he said.

"'What's that?' I asked.

"'I have just asked the prisoner if he has anyone who can speak to his character, and he says you know him slightly,' said the recorder with a smile.

"'To the best of my knowledge I never saw the man in my life before,' I replied.

"'Yes, you have, Mr. Derwent,' the prisoner said in a low voice—and you will understand what silence there was in the court—'you have seen me working at Windyridge 'All, sir, afore I sank to this. You remember, sir, I was allus known as Ginty.'"

I started, and the Cynic continued: "I looked at him closely then, and saw that it was indeed he, Ginty, ten years older than he was a year ago: haggard, seamed with lines of care, unkempt, but, unless I am mistaken, not altogether hardened.

"I turned to the recorder. 'I do know the prisoner, sir,' I said, 'but I did not recognise him, and therefore I have not paid attention to the case;' and as briefly as I could I told the court how he had been led astray. It was you, Miss Holden, who described it all so graphically, you may remember, and I repeated the story as you told it, and I pleaded hard for the young chap. He got off with three months, which was less than might have been expected."

"Poor Ginty!" I interrupted. "I wonder if his mother will hear of it. I suppose news of that kind rarely filters through the walls of a workhouse?"

"No walls are impervious to bad news," he replied, "but Ginty's concern was less for his mother than for his sweetheart, Sarah Ann. At bottom I believe Ginty is penitent, and would like to break with the rogues who have led him on; but the poor beggar is weak-willed, and the easy prey of his blustering companions. I managed to get an interview with him, and he wished me to ask you to tell the girl everything, and to beg her to pity and forgive him; and he promises to turn over a new leaf, and will marry her eventually if she is willing."

"Sarah Ann must not be told at present," I replied; "she is far from well, and the shock might be too much for her. She is a highly emotional girl, who would go into violent hysterics incontinently."

"Well," he said, "I can leave the matter to your discretion. I have fulfilled my promise, and I am sure you will do what is best. Would it be possible to tell the girl's mother?—if she has a mother."

"She has a mother," I answered, "but she is a woman entirely destitute of tact. To tell her would be to publish the news to the whole village, and to have it conveyed to Sarah Ann in the crudest manner conceivable. I think it will be best to hold back the message until I have a fitting opportunity of delivering it to the girl herself. But believe me, the present time is most inopportune."

"I do believe you," he said, "and I suppose it is hardly likely that information will reach the village in any other way. 'Ill news flies fast,' but the case was too insignificant to be reported in the provincial papers. Anyhow, we must take the risk, and you can deliver your soul of the message when you think fit. I am sorry to have laid this burden upon you."

"I accept it willingly," I said, "and am glad that I can be of service to these poor young folk."

I had a pleasant evening with the squire and the Cynic, both of whom were at their best in discussing disendowments, in regard to which they held opposite views. The squire showed the possession of a wealth of knowledge which aroused my admiration, and he was so courteous in argument, so magnanimous and altogether gentlemanly, that I could have hugged him for very pride; but I am bound to say that I think the Cynic had the best of it. He is just as generous and courtly as the squire, and he is absolutely sure of his facts and figures; but when he does corner his opponent he does not gloat over him. In my judgment—and I am sure I am impartial, for I like them both so much—he was more convincing than the squire; but then I don't think I ever met a more convincing speaker. Of course I have met very few good speakers, but I doubt if there are many to surpass Mr. Derwent.

He took me home about ten o'clock, and I saw that the village had got some new excitement, but the Cynic's presence barred me from participating in it. At the cottage, however, I learned everything, for a gossip had, as usual, hastened to tell Mother Hubbard the news, and she was still discussing it on my arrival, though my invalid ought to have been in bed.

Nobody in Windyridge takes a Sunday newspaper, but a visitor from Airlee had left a *News of the World* at Smiddles's, and after his departure Smiddles had glanced down its columns and found a report of Ginty's trial and sentence. Mrs. Smiddles, bursting with importance, hurried off to impart the information to Sar'-Ann's mother. Sar'-Ann's mother, as might have been anticipated, had expressed her opinion of Ginty's moral character in loud and emphatic language which echoed round the village and awakened a like response.

I closed the door wearily on the woman and went to bed, for it was too late to see Sar'-Ann that night. I wish I had made the endeavour now, for with the morning there came news that distressed me terribly. Sar'-Ann's baby had been born at midnight, and poor Sar'-Ann was dead!

CHAPTER TWENTY-SEVEN

MOTHER HUBBARD
HEARS THE CALL

THE WORLD IS very drab to-day, as I look out of my bedroom window at the Hall and once more open the book in which I set down the experiences of my pilgrimage. I am living in luxury again, a luxury which has, alas! more of permanency in it than before. The little room in which I am writing is charming in the daintiness of its colouring and the simplicity of its furnishings. There is just a suspicion of pink in the creamy wallpaper, and the deeper cream of the woodwork. The bed, like the dressing-table and the chairs, is in satinwood, beautifully inlaid, and the wardrobe is an enormous cavern in the wall, with mirrored doors behind which my few belongings hang suspended like ghostly stalactites. The floor is nearly covered with a Wilton rug, and the rest of it is polished until it looks like glass. A few choice etchings and engravings hang upon the walls—Elaine dreaming of Lancelot, Dante bending over the dead body of Beatrice, Helen of Troy, and similar subjects, with two of Leader's landscapes. The counterpane gleams, snowy white, beneath the lovely satin eider-down, which gives a splash of colour to the room; and the room is *mine!*

Mine! Yes, but the world is very drab all the same. The sky is grey to its farthest limits—an unrelieved greyness which presses upon one's spirits. The landscape is grey, with no solitary touch of brightness in it until you come to the lawn in front of my window, where there is a gorgeous display of chrysanthemums. The cawing of the rooks is a shade more mournful than usual, and the grey smoke from the stacks above my head floats languidly on the heavy air.

And for the moment I would have it so, for it harmonises with my mood and gives me the inspiration I need in order to write down the occurrences of these later days. It is not that I am morbid or downcast; I am sad, but not depressed; the outlook is not black—it is just drab.

I suppose if anyone were to read what I have written thus far they would guess the truth—that my dear old Mother Hubbard has been taken from me. We laid her to rest a week ago in the little plot of ground which must ever henceforward be very dear to me, and my heart hungers for the sound of her voice and the sight of her kindly face. But I cannot doubt that for her it is "far better," so I will not stoop to self-pity.

And, after all, there is not a streak of grey in the picture I have to reproduce. As I live over again those few last days of companionship I feel the curtains to be drawn back from the windows of my soul; I experience the freshness of a heaven-born zephyr. I find myself smiling as one only smiles when memory is pleasing and there is deep content, and I say to myself: "Thank God, it was indeed 'sunset and evening star' and there was no 'moaning of the bar' when the spirit of the gentle motherkin 'put out to sea,' and she went forth to meet her 'Pilot face to face.'"

I think the shock of Sar'-Ann's death upset her, for, like her Master, she was easily touched with the feeling of other people's infirmities, and though outwardly she was unexcited I knew that the deeps within her were stirred.

We always slept together now, for I was uneasy when I was not with her. For months past my cottage had been rarely used except as a bedroom, but now I abandoned it altogether and had my bed brought into Mother Hubbard's cottage and placed in the living-room, quite near to her own, so that I could hear her breathing. Far into the night I would lie awake and watch the dying embers on the hearth, and the light growing fainter upon the walls, and listen for any sound of change.

Each morning she rose at the same hour, dressed with the same care, and sought to follow the old, familiar routine; but she did not demur when I placed her in her chair and assumed the air and authority of commander-in-chief.

"I must work while it is day, love," she said, smiling up at me in the way which always provoked a caress.

"Martha, Martha," I always replied, "thou art anxious and troubled about many things: but one thing is needful, and that in your case is rest."

She drew my head on to her breast one day as I said this for the hundredth time—I had knelt down upon the rug, and mockingly held her prisoner—and she said very, very softly:

"Grace love, I am going to give in. The voice within tells me you are right, and I do not fret. 'In quietness and in confidence shall be your strength.' It is because I am so strong in spirit that I do not recognise how weak I am in body; but I think, love, I am beginning to realise it now. And as I have you to look after me I have much to thank God for. Do you know, Grace love, I am sure the Lord sent you to Windyridge for my sake. It is wonderful how He makes things work together for the good of many. He knew this poor old Martha would soon need somebody to pet her and look after her, so he sent you to be an angel of comfort."

"Well," I said, as cheerfully as I could with my spirit in chains, "He has paid me good wages, and I have a royal reward. Why, my own cup is filled to overflowing, 'good measure, pressed down, running over'—isn't that the correct quotation? I wouldn't have missed these twelve months of Mother-Hubbardism for a king's ransom."

She pressed my head still more closely to her. "Are you very busy this morning, love?" she asked. "I feel that I can talk to you just now if you have time to listen, and it will do me good to speak."

It had come at last, and I braced myself to meet it. "What have you got to say to me, motherkin? Speak on. I am very comfy, and my work will wait."

"Yes, love," she said—and it was so unlike her to acquiesce so readily that my heart grew heavier still—"work can wait, but the tide of life waits for no man, and there is something I want to say before the flood bears me away."

"Are you feeling worse, dear?" I asked; "would you like me to ask Dr. Trempest to call? I can telephone from the Hall."

"No, love," the gentle voice replied, "I am past his aid. I shall slip away some day without pain; that is borne in upon me, and I am thankful, for your sake as well as for my own. The doctor will just call to see me in the usual way, but you will not have to send for him. No; I just want to discuss one or two things with you, love, whilst my mind is clear and my strength sufficient. And you are going to be my own cheerful, business-like Grace, aren't you, love?"

"Yes," I said, swallowing my lump, and summoning my resources.

"Well, now, love, I want to make my will, and you shall do it for me when we have talked about it. I have neither chick nor child, and if I have relatives I don't know them, and once over I thought of leaving all I have to you, love, for you have been more than a daughter to me; but after thinking it over I am not going to do so."

"It was sweet of you to think of it, dear," I said, "but I really do not need it, and I am glad you have changed your mind. Tell me."

She stroked my face with a slow, patting movement as she continued: "You won't need it, love. You have a little of your own, and you are young and can work; but I would have added my little to yours if that had been all, but I *know* you will not need it, and I am glad. But you will like to have something which I have valued, and you shall have whatever I hold most dear."

She paused a moment or two, but I knew she would not wish me to speak just then.

"There are three things, love, which are very precious to me," she continued; "one is the ring which Matthew gave me when he asked me to be his wife. I have never worn it since he died, but it is in the little silver box in my cap drawer. I want you to wear it, love, in remembrance of me. Then there is the little box itself. Besides the ring, it contains my class tickets—tickets of membership, you know, love; I have them all from the very first, and Matthew bought the little box for me to put them in, and he called it my 'Ark.' I am so pleased to think that you will have it, but I would like the tickets to be buried with me."

She broke off and laughed. "That sounds silly, love, doesn't it? It looks as if I thought the tickets would help me to the next world; but, of course, I didn't mean that. They are just bits of printed paper, but I don't want them to be burned or thrown into the rubbish heap, that's all.

"Last and dearest of all, there's my Bible. It wouldn't fetch a penny anywhere, for it's old and yellow and thumbed, and the back is loose; but its value to me, love, is just priceless, and I should hardly die happy unless someone had it who would love it too. Now that's your share."

I drew her hand to my lips and kissed it; she knew what I was feeling.

"Give Reuben the old grandfather's clock. It is oak and will match his furniture, and he can give his mahogany one to Ben. Reuben has always admired the clock, and he will be pleased I remembered him. Let my clothes go to any of the neighbours who are poor and need them. And the lamp which his scholars gave Matthew when his health failed and he had to give up teaching——"

She paused, and I held my peace. It was a chaste and artistic production in brass, which had always seemed to me rather out of place amid its homely surroundings, and I should not have been sorry if it had been amongst the treasures to be bequeathed to me ...

"Yes, dear," I said at length, "the lamp?"

"I want you to ask Mr. Derwent, love, to accept the lamp. He admired it very much, and he has been so very nice to me; and give him the china, too.

"You will not live here alone, Grace, when I am gone. Mr. Evans will want you, and you will not have to deny him then as you have done previously for my sake. These old eyes have seen more, love, than you have realised, and I am very grateful. The Lord bless you!

"Both the cottages are mine. I bought this one when Matthew died, and Reuben sold me the other one, just as it stands, whilst you were away, and we arranged to keep it a secret for a while. Then there will be about £1,500 in the bank and Building Society when everything has been paid. I have thought a great deal about what to do with it, and I am going to leave both the cottages, with all the furniture, for the use of poor widows who otherwise might have to go to the workhouse; and the interest on the money will keep them from want.

"I haven't much head for business, but a lawyer will work it out all right. You see, love, I was left comfortably off by Matthew, and I think the Lord would like me to remember that all widows are not so fortunate; and I don't want to forget that it is His money I have to dispose of."

The tears came into my eyes now and I could not speak. The sun was shining brightly outside, but within that humble room there was a radiance that outshone that of the sun, even the reflected splendour of heaven.

After a while she continued: "I want you and Reuben to decide who are to live in the cottages, but I should like Ginty's mother to have the first offer, love, and I think she will not refuse for my sake; and you must arrange about the other. You will see Lawyer Simpson in Fawkshill, love, and tell him all this. Go this afternoon, for I shall be restless now until all is done. And now let me tell you what no lawyer need know."

Again she rested for a while and then continued:

"They are sure to want a service at the chapel, for I am the oldest member, and a class leader. But I do so dislike doleful singing, so I have been thinking it over and I have put down on a paper which you will find in my Bible the hymns which I should like to have sung. Ask them to sing first 'My God, the spring of all my joys,' to the tune of 'Lydia.' You won't know the tune, love, for it is a very old-fashioned one, but I have always liked it, and it goes with a rare swing. Then I *must* have 'Jesu, Lover of my soul' to 'Hollingside,' for that is the hymn of my experience; and to conclude with let them sing a child's hymn. I'm afraid you will laugh at me, Grace, but I would like to have 'There is a better world, they say.' I think these will be sufficient, and they are all very cheerful hymns and tunes."

"And the minister?" I asked, for her calmness was infectious.

"Oh, either of them, love," she said; "they are both good men, and they must arrange to suit their own convenience. Now give me a kiss. I am so glad to have got this done, and though I am tired I feel ever so much better."

I saw the lawyer in the afternoon, and he called with the draft on the following day, and by the next it had been signed, witnessed and completed.

Mother Hubbard did not go to chapel on the Sunday, but on the Thursday she expressed her fixed determination to take her class. I protested in vain; the motherkin had made up her mind.

"I must, love; it is laid upon me, and I am not at all excited."

"But, dear," I urged, "I shall worry terribly whilst you are out of my care. You are not fit to go—you are not strong enough."

"It is only a step, love," she replied, "and the evening is warm; why need you worry when you can come with me?"

She had never suggested this before—indeed, when I had laughingly suggested it she had been visibly alarmed, and I admit that the idea was not attractive. Somehow or other I distrusted the Methodist class meeting. But my love for the class leader prevailed.

"Very well," I said; "if you go, I go too."

We went together and found eight or nine women of various ages assembled in the little vestry. Mother Hubbard took her seat at the table, and I sat next to Widow Smithies, who moved up to make room for me.

We sang a hymn, and then Mother Hubbard prayed—prayed in a gentle voice which had much humility in it, but an assured confidence which showed her to be on intimate terms with her Lord; and when she had finished I read the 103rd Psalm at her request, and we sang again.

Then she spoke, and her voice gathered strength as she proceeded. I cannot write down all she said, but some of the sentences are burned into my memory, though the connections have escaped me.

"We will not have an experience meeting to-night, my friends, because I want to speak to you, and God has given me strength to do so. I am weak in body, but my spirit was never stronger. It is the spirit which is the real life, so I was never more alive. I have thought a good deal lately on those words:

"'Even the youths shall faint and be weary, and the young men shall utterly fall. But they that wait upon the Lord shall renew their strength: they shall mount up with wings as eagles; they shall run and not be weary; they shall walk and not faint.'

"'They that wait upon the Lord' shall do this. Not just the strong and powerful, but poor, weak old women like me; aye, those weaker still who are helpless on sick-beds; the paralysed and lame who cannot walk at all— all these shall 'renew their strength.' They are unable even to totter to the old pew in the house of God, so weak and shaky is their poor human frame; aye, but they shall 'mount up with wings as eagles.' The eagle is a strong bird; it makes its nest on the cliffs of high mountains, it soars up and up into the clouds, and it can carry sheep in its talons, so great is its strength. And, do you realise it? they that wait upon the Lord are like that. Weak and worn in body but

"'Strong in the strength which God supplies
    Through His Eternal Son.'

"My friends, I thank God that in that sense I am strong to-night; and do you think that when I am so strong I am going to die? Never! Life is going to be fuller, richer, more abundant."

I gazed upon Mother Hubbard in astonishment. She was not excited, but she was exalted. No earthly light was in her eyes, no earthly strength was in those triumphant tones. Death had laid his hand upon her but she shook him off and spoke like a conqueror. I looked at her members, and saw that every eye was fixed upon her, and that reverential fear held them immovable. There was a clock over the mantelpiece, and it ticked away slowly, solemnly, but no other sound disturbed the stillness.

"I have heard some of you speak often of your crosses, and God knows how heavy some of them have been, and how I have pitied and tried to help you. You will not think I am boasting when I say that I have had crosses to carry, too, but I have always endeavoured to make light of them, and I am so glad of that to-night. Because, dear friends, I realise very clearly now that to carry a cross that is laid upon us is to help the Master. I think Simon was a strong, kindly man, who was glad to carry the cross for Christ's sake. I like to think of him as pushing his way through the crowd and saying: 'Let me help the Master: I will gladly carry it for Him.' And I want to say this: that all through my life when I have tried to carry my cross cheerfully the Master has always taken the heavier end—always!

"You will go on having crosses to carry so long as ever you love the Lord Jesus Christ; but remember this—all troubles are not crosses. God has nothing to do with lots of our troubles. Indeed, I am not sure that what we call a trouble is ever a cross. That only is a cross which we carry for His sake. It is a privilege to carry a cross, and we ought to be glad when we are selected.

"'But suppose we fall under it?' some of you may say. Listen: 'They that wait upon the Lord shall renew their strength.' You forgot that. 'When I am weak then I am strong.' Why? Because the good Lord never asks us to carry a cross without giving us strength for the burden. His grace is always sufficient for us. Never forget my words—they are perhaps the last I shall speak as your leader, and oh, my dear friends, how my heart yearns over you! how very dear to me is your truest welfare!—no trouble need ever o'erwhelm you, no temptation need ever cause you to fall, no weakness of the body need ever affect the strength of the soul, no darkness of earth need ever shut out the light of heaven, because—listen, 'Lo, I am with you always, even unto the end of the world'!"

She paused, and the women, unaccustomed to self-control, were sobbing audibly into their handkerchiefs, and Mother Hubbard noticed it.

"We will not sing a closing hymn," she said; "let us pray."

The women knelt; but she merely leaned forward, with her hands clasped on the table in front of her, and commended them all to God. She prayed for each of them individually, using their Christian names, and remembering all their families and family difficulties. She prayed for the absent ones, for the toilworn and the sick; and she prayed for me—and may God in His mercy answer that prayer, then shall my life be blessed indeed.

When she had pronounced the benediction in a very low voice we rose from our knees, and saw her with her face uplifted to heaven, and the calm of heaven spread over it, like the clear golden calm of a cloudless sunset. Then, slowly, the head dropped upon her hands; and when at length we tried to rouse her we found that she was beyond our call.

CHAPTER TWENTY-EIGHT

IN THE
CRUCIBLE

DESPITE THE SQUIRE'S protests I remained in my own cottage until the Monday when Mother Hubbard's frail body was laid to rest in the little graveyard. There was nothing to fear, and I felt that I could not leave her there alone. She would have rebuked me, I know, and would have read me the lesson of the cocoon and the butterfly; but I am most contented when I trust implicitly to my instincts, and my Inner Self bade me stay.

Practically all the village turned out to the funeral, and the chapel was crowded to its utmost capacity. It was a cheerful service, too, in spite of our tears, for the ministers and members had caught her spirit, and "Lydia" was sung with a vigour and heartiness which I should have liked the dear old lady to witness. Perhaps she did: who knows?

The squire and I occupied the position of chief mourners, but the entire village sorrowed, as those only sorrow who have lost a friend that cannot be replaced. There is no other Mother Hubbard here, and how much she will be missed when trouble sits by the hearths of the people only time can make known.

When all was over I went straight to my new home at the Hall, and entered into possession of the lovely room which had been prepared for me. Every morning and afternoon I go to my work at the studio, but without the zest which makes duty a delight. The squire would like me to abandon the studio altogether and do my regular work at the Hall, but I cannot quite reconcile myself to the idea. After all, the studio is there, and as the weeks go by I shall lose the sense of desolation which is now associated with the place, and which hangs like lead upon the wings of my spirit.

Yet what cause for gratitude is mine! Though I have lost one true friend another is here to comfort and cheer me with never-failing insight and sympathy. How I enjoy these long evenings in the library, the quiet talks in the firelight, the hour which follows the lighting of the lamp, when I read aloud from the squire's favourite authors or the learned quarterlies; and best of all, the comments and discussions which enable me to plumb the depths of his mind and make me marvel at the extent of his knowledge. He likes me to sit on a stool at his feet as I did, ages ago, at Zermatt, resting my arm or book upon his knee and within easy reach of his caressing hand. Whatever I may have lost by coming to Windyridge I have certainly found affection, and I am woman enough to value it above all my losses.

So far, Mr. Derwent has come down each week-end and has remained at the Hall over the Sunday. For some reason which he does not explain the squire seems rather amused with him just now, and indulges occasionally in a mild form of banter which leaves the younger man quite unruffled. He asks him how he can possibly tear himself away so often from the attractions and duties of the metropolis; and I cannot help thinking that he suspects the existence of an attractive force there. I wonder if the Cynic has told him anything of Rose. For myself, I am not surprised that he comes to Broadbeck for the week-ends, because the habit is ingrained in him, and bachelors of his age do not readily abandon old customs.

We had a very interesting evening on Saturday. The vicar is away on a stone-hunt of some kind, so his wife came to dinner, and gave spice to the conversation, as she invariably does. I am always delighted when she forms one of the company that includes the Cynic, for she is refreshingly blunt and frank with him, and he does not get all his own way. And at the same time he seems to enjoy drawing her out—I suppose he would say "pulling her leg," if she were not a lady.

On this particular occasion she attacked him the moment we were comfortably settled in the library, and for a long time the battle was a mere duel of wits. She was extremely scornful because he had chosen to remain a bachelor, and he defended himself with more than his usual cynicism.

Something had been said about the growing spirit of brotherhood, when she broke in:

"Bah! don't talk to me about your altruism or any other 'ism. In these days you men make high-sounding phrases take the place of principle. If I know anything of the meaning of words altruism is the very opposite of selfishness—and who is more selfish than your bachelor?"

The Cynic blew a thin column of smoke towards the ceiling and spoke languidly:

"Stevenson says—I mean R. L., of course—that if you wish the pick of men and women you must take a good bachelor and a good wife."

"Stuff and nonsense!" replied the vicar's wife; "if there were such a thing as a good bachelor I should say that he got amongst the pick of men only when he took to himself a good wife. But who ever yet saw or knew a 'good' bachelor? It's a contradiction of terms. Mind you, I don't call boys bachelors; bachelors are men who might be married if they would, but they won't. Good men are unselfish, and bachelors are brazenly self-centred, and usually unbearably conceited. And you are as bad as any of them, Philip."

"Veritatis simplex oratio est," muttered the Cynic.

"Didn't I say so?" ejaculated the vicar's wife triumphantly. "It is a sure sign of conceit when a man hurls a bit of school Latin at his ignorant opponent and so scores a paltry advantage." She pursed her lips in scorn.

"I beg your pardon," replied the Cynic calmly; "I got the quotation from a cyclopædia, but I will substitute a line from an English poet which accurately expresses the same meaning:

"'How sweet the words of truth, breathed from the lips of love!'

"But is there no excuse for me and others in like case? Are we unmarried men sinners above all the rest? Granted that we are selfish, conceited, corrupt and vile, is there yet no place for us in the universe? no lonely corner in the vineyard where we can work with profit to the State?"

"I suppose you think you work 'with profit to the State,'" returned the vicar's wife with a curl of the lip, "when you persuade one of His Majesty's judges to send some poor wretch to gaol, where he will be provided for at the country's expense whilst his wife and children are left to starve. You would be of far more use to it, let me tell you, if you became the father of a family and——"

The Cynic held up his hand: "The prey of some conceited bachelor who should wickedly persuade one of His Majesty's judges to send me to gaol, whilst my wife and children were left to starve. The reasoning does not seem very clear. If I had remained a bachelor I might have become a wretch, and I might have suffered imprisonment, but at least my sins would not have been visited upon the innocent heads of wife and children. And then it occurs to me that I have known bachelors to be sent to gaol at the instance of married men who persuaded the judges to send them there. No, no, madam, you are too deep for me! I give it up!"

"Rubbish!" snorted the vicar's wife, "you evade the issue, which is simple enough. Are—bachelors— selfish—or—are—they—not?"

The Cynic shook his head mournfully. "They are more to be pitied than blamed, believe me. They are too often the sport of cruel Fate— tossed here and there upon the wave of Circumstance—unable, alas! and not unwilling to find safety in the Harbour of Matrimony. Their lot is indeed a sad one. Don't call them hard names, but drop for them—and me—the silent tear of sympathy."

"Oh, of course," broke in the vicar's wife, "I knew that dodge was sure to be employed sooner or later. I was on the watch for it. It is the old excuse that there is nobody to marry. The wave of Circumstance does not toss you into the arms of some captivating nymph, and so you remain all at sea—more ornamental, perhaps, but hardly more useful than a cork on the ocean. If you really wanted to get into the Harbour of Matrimony, let me tell you, you would turn about and swim there, instead of blaming Fate for not rolling you in on the crest of a wave."

We laughed, and the Cynic said: "After all, madam, selfishness is not confined to those who have no intention of marrying. When your good husband took to himself the most charming of her sex he doubtless grudged every smile that was thrown to his rivals. Altruism, as you very sagaciously remarked a moment or two ago, is the very antithesis of selfishness, and hence it is unpopular except as an ideal for others. The popular altruist is he who denies himself to minister to my selfishness. We are all selfish, with certain rare exceptions—to be found, fortunately, within the circle of my friends."

"I am sure I am selfish," I interjected; "I wonder if that is because I am unmarried."

"My dear," said the vicar's wife, "your case is not on all fours with Philip's and other bachelors'. *You* are the sport of Fate, and not these men who can easily find some woman silly enough to have them, but who prefer their own selfish ease and comfort, and then entreat sympathy, forsooth! When women are unmarried it is rarely their own fault."

"All this is very puzzling," drawled the Cynic. "I am groping in the darkness with a sincere desire to find light, and no success rewards my patient efforts. I hear that it is silliness on the women's part to accept our offers, and still we are blamed for saving them from themselves. No doubt you are right, but to me it seems inconsistent."

"Bother your casuistry!" replied the vicar's wife, dismissing him with a wave of the hand. "Philip, you make me tired. What makes you sure you are selfish, dear? I have seen no signs of it."

The question was addressed to me, and I answered: "I am beginning to think it was selfishness that brought me here, and I am not sure that it is not selfishness which keeps me here. At the same time I have no wish to leave, and the question arises, Is it only the disagreeable which is right? Is selfishness never excusable?"

"In other words," remarked the Cynic, whose eyes were closed, "is not vice, after all, and at any rate sometimes, a modified form of virtue?"

"Listen to him!" exclaimed the vicar's wife; "the embodiment of selfishness is about to proclaim himself the apostle of morality. The unfettered lord of creation will expound to a slave of circumstance the ethical order of the universe, for the instruction of her mind and the good of her soul."

"The fact is," continued the Cynic, without heeding the interruption, "Miss Holden, like many other sensitive people of both sexes, has a faulty conception of what selfishness is. There are many people who imagine

that it is sinful to be happy, and a sign of grace to be miserable, which is
about as sensible as to believe that it is an indication of good health when
you are irritable and out of sorts. To be selfish is to be careless of the
interests of others, and Miss Holden is certainly not that."

"It is good of you to say so," I said, "but I sometimes wonder if I am
not shirking duty and evading responsibility by enjoying myself here."

The squire gave my hand an affectionate squeeze, but only his eyes
spoke; and the vicar's wife turned to me.

"What brought you up here, dear? I don't think I ever knew."

"I am sure I don't," I replied, and before I had time to continue the
Cynic leaned forward and looked at me.

"I know," he said.

"You once promised to explain me to myself," I said, smiling. "Is this
the day and the hour?"

"That is for you to say," he replied. "You may object to analysis in
public. True, there are some advantages from your point of view. You will
have one of your own sex to hold a brief for you, and a very partial judge
to guarantee fair play."

"I do not mind," I replied; and the squire smiled contentedly.

The Cynic threw his cigarette into the fire and began: "As I understand
the case, before you left London your duties kept your hands busily
employed during working hours, but allowed you ample opportunity for
the consideration of those social problems in which for the previous year
or two you had been deeply interested, and a certain portion of your leisure
was devoted to social and philanthropic work?"

I assented with a nod.

"Very well. Yielding to what appeared to be a sudden impulse, but to
what was in reality the well-considered action of your subconscious self,
you bound your burden of cares upon your back and fled from your City
of Destruction."

"Like a coward," I interposed, "afraid to play the game of life because
of its hazards. I might have remained and faced the problems and helped
to fight the foe I loathed."

"I will come to that shortly," he said, and every trace of irony had left
his voice; "at present I am considering why your subconscious self decided

upon this line of action. The world's sorrows were oppressing you like a nightmare. Do you know that few of us can meet sorrow face to face and day by day and retain our strength, and particularly if we seek to meet it unprepared, unschooled? One of two things usually happens: we become hardened, or we go mad. From these alternatives it is sometimes wise to flee, and then flight is not cowardice, but prudence."

"I certainly obeyed my Inner Self," I said, "but is there not such a thing as a false conscience?"

"Your 'Inner Self' did not betray you," he continued. "Unwittingly you sought, not oblivion, but enlightenment and preparation. All earnest reformers are driven of the Spirit into the wilderness."

"Yes, but for what purpose, Derwent?" interposed the squire; "to be tempted of the devil?"

"To face the tempter, sir. To test their own armour in private conflict before they go forth to strike down the public foe. To discover the devil's strength, his powers and his limitations, before they match themselves against legions. To discover their own strength and limitations, too. The first essential in successful warfare is to know yourself and your enemy, and you gain that knowledge in solitude. It was so with Jesus, with Paul, with Savonarola, with scores of other reformers. Miss Holden was driven into the wilderness—if you care to put it so—for a similar purpose."

"But ought one to avoid opportunities of usefulness?" I urged. "I was in the fray and I withdrew from it."

"A raw soldier, invalided home, though you did not know it," he continued, "and sent into the country for rest and renewal, and quiet preparation for effective service. Here you have gained your perspective. You survey the field of battle from the heights, and yet you have come in contact with the enemy at close quarters, too, and you know his tactics. You will face the problems of sin and suffering and social injustice again, but with new heart and less of despair."

"You are too generous, I fear. I should like to think that my motives were so pure, but——"

"What is motive? Motive is what excites to action. Your motive was not less pure because it was intuitive and unrecognised. But let me ask you: What idea are you disposed to think you left unaccomplished? What object ought you to have pursued?"

I thought a moment before I replied: "It seems to me that when there is so much sin and suffering in the world we should try to alleviate it, and to remedy the wrongs from which so much of it springs. And from these things I fled, though I knew that the labourers were few."

"You fled from the devil, did you? And you found Windyridge a Paradise from which he was barred!"

I remained silent.

"London has no monopoly of sin and suffering. Evil has not a merely local habitation. If it was a wile of the devil to remove you out of his way it has been singularly unsuccessful, I conclude, for I understand you have found him vigorously at work here all the time. Have you then discovered no opportunities of service and usefulness in the wilderness?"

"If happiness is gained by administering it to others," said the squire with some emotion; "if to break up the hard ground of the heart and sow in it the seed of peace is to defeat the devil and his aims, then has Miss Holden reached her ideal and earned her happiness. I told her a year ago that the devil was a familiar presence in this village, but I thank God, as others do and have done, that she has helped to thwart him."

Perhaps I ought not to write all this down, for it has the savour of vanity and conceit, but I do not see how I can well avoid doing so. There are times when the heart speaks rather than the judgment, and the squire's heart is very warm towards me; and though I would not doubt his sincerity it is certain that he is not impartial where I am concerned.

The Cynic looked pleased. "I quite agree, sir," he said; "Miss Holden has used her opportunities—not simply those which presented themselves, but those which she has sought and found, which is higher service. Hence, I conclude that the policy of her subconscious self has been justified, and that she is absolved from any charge of selfishness."

"Really, Philip!" said the vicar's wife, "your eloquence has almost deprived me of the power of speech, which you will acknowledge is no mean achievement. I thought *I* was appointed counsel for the defence and that you were to prefer the indictment and prove Miss Holden guilty of some heinous crime. *My* office has been a sinecure, for a better piece of special pleading for the defence I have never listened to."

"I must be fair at all costs," he replied; "Miss Holden had no misgivings, I imagine, when she came here at first. Doubts arose, as they so often do with the conscientious, when the venture prospered. The martyr spirit distrusts itself when there is no sign of rack and faggot. I seek now to reveal Miss Holden to herself."

"You are wonderfully sure of yourself," returned his opponent, "but let us be fair to our pretensions. If you are for the defence let me be for the prosecution. Does one serve his country better when he leaves the thick of the fray to study maps and tactics? If one has the opportunity to live is it sufficient to vegetate? For every opportunity of usefulness that Windyridge can offer London can provide a score, and Miss Holden's lot was cast in London. Is she living her life? That, I take it, is her problem."

"Yes," I said, "it is something like that."

"I accept your challenge," replied the Cynic, "and I agree that it is not what we do but what we are capable of doing that counts. But the most effective workman is not he who undertakes the largest variety of jobs, but he who puts himself into his work. You speak of vegetating, and you ask if Miss Holden is living her life. What is life? The man who rises early and retires late, and spends the intervening hours in one unceasing rush does not know the meaning of life; whereas the farmer who goes slowly and steadily along the track of the hours, or the student who devotes only a portion of his time to his books and spends the rest in recreation, or the business man who declines to sacrifice himself upon the altar of Mammon—these men live. And it is the man who lives who benefits his fellows. To visit the sick, to clothe the naked, to dole out sympathy and charity to the poor is noble work, but it is not necessarily the most effective way of helping them. The man who sits down to study the problem of prevention—the root causes of misery and injustice—and who discovers and publishes the remedy, is the truer and more valuable friend, though he never enter a slum or do volunteer work in a soup kitchen."

"And whilst we are diagnosing the conditions rather than the case the patient dies," said the vicar's wife. "We stop our sick visiting and our soup kitchens, and bid the people suffer and starve in patience whilst we retire into our studies to theorise over causes."

"To refer to your illustration of a moment ago, my dear madam, the battle need not stop because one or two men of insight retire to serve their country by studying maps and tactics. We need not chain up the Good Samaritan, but we shall be of far greater service to humanity if, instead of forming a league for the supply of oil and wine and plasters, we inaugurate measures to clear the road of robbers. 'This ought ye to do and not to leave the other undone.'"

"You admit, then, that some may find their opportunity of service in work of this baser sort?"

"No work is base which is done with a pure motive and done well. All I contend for is that when instinct bids any of us withdraw for a time, or even altogether, it is wise to trust our instincts. If Miss Holden had devoted herself to a life of pleasure and selfish isolation she might have been charged with cowardly flight from duty. We all know she has done nothing of the kind, and therefore I say her intuition was trustworthy, and she must not accuse herself of selfishness."

"I agree with all my heart," said the vicar's wife; "but the problems which she left unsolved are no nearer solution."

"How do you know that?" he asked. "The war may be nearer its end because your unheroic soldier sheathed his sword and put on his thinking-cap. That unsoldier-like action may have saved the lives of thousands and brought about an honourable peace. I do not know that Miss Holden has done much to solve the general problem, but I dare assert that she views it more clearly, and could face it more confidently than she could have done a year ago—that is to say, she has solved her own problem."

"There is some truth in that," I said. "Windyridge has given me clearer vision, and I am more optimistic on that account. Mr. Evans told me on the occasion of our first meeting that I should find human nature the same here as elsewhere, and that is so. But the type is larger in the village than it is in the town, and I can read and understand it better. Yet one thing town and country alike have proved to me, and that is what you, Mr. Evans, asserted so confidently—that selfishness is the root of sin. How are we to conquer that?"

"Only by patient effort," replied the squire. "Shallow reformers are eager to try hasty and ill-considered measures. Zealous converts, whose eyes have been suddenly opened to the anomalies and injustices of society, are angry and impatient because the wheels of progress revolve so slowly, and they become rebellious and sometimes anarchical. And their discontent is a sign of life, and it is good in its way, but ordinarily it is ineffective. You may blow up the Council House in Jericho because the councillors have not done their duty, and you may shoot the robbers because they have wounded the traveller, and the zealous reformer will commend you and say: 'Now we are beginning to make things move!' But the man who goes to work to destroy the seeds of greed and selfishness, so that men will no longer either need or covet the possessions of others, is the real reformer; but reformation is a plant of slow growth. Yet every-one who sows the antidote to selfishness in the heart of his neighbour is to be accounted a reformer."

The vicar's carriage was announced at that moment and the conversation was interrupted.

"We will continue it next week, sir," said the Cynic, "if you will allow me to pay you another visit. I cannot be here until the evening of Saturday; may I stay the week-end?"

"Certainly," said the squire with a smile, "if your engagements permit. I think we must all realise that you seek to carry your theory of life into practice."

That was on Saturday. The Cynic left by the early train this morning, and he had no sooner gone than the post brought me a letter from Rose. It was short and sweet—very sweet indeed.

"MY DEAR GRACE,

"Congratulate me! I am engaged to be married to the best of men, *not excepting your Cynic*. You will blame me for keeping it quiet, but how can I tell what is going to happen beforehand? Besides, you don't tell me!

"I am to marry my chief, who is henceforward to be known to you and me as 'Stephen.' He is two or three years older than I am;

good-looking, of course, or he wouldn't have appealed to me, and over head and ears in love with

"Your very affectionate and somewhat intoxicated

"ROSE.

"PS.—He has known your Cynic for years, but he (I mean your Cynic) is too good a sportsman to spoil the fun.

"PPS.—It is a beautiful ring—diamonds!"

I am delighted to think that Rose is so happy, and can excuse the brevity of the communication under the circumstances. But I *am* surprised. I never dreamed that her chief was young and unmarried. Why she should always say "your" Cynic, however, and underline it, too, I cannot understand. I wish . . .

CHAPTER TWENTY-NINE

THE
GREAT STORM

MY BOOK IS nearly full, and I do not think I shall begin another, for my time is likely to be fully occupied now. But I must set down the events of the last week-end and tell of the wonderful climacteric that I have passed through. Then the curtain may be allowed to fall on my unimportant experiences.

They have not been unimportant to me, and my recent adventures have provided sufficient excitement to keep the tongues of the villagers busy for months.

Incidentally I have discovered that Windyridge does not belie its name, but that the storm fiend makes it the stage for some of his most outrageous escapades.

We had samples of all the different kinds of weather England provides last week—rain, snow, sleet, light breezes, fleecy clouds sailing slowly across the blue, dull and threatening times when the skies were leaden.

Saturday was the gloomiest day of all. It was gusty from the beginning, but until the afternoon the wind was only sportive, and contented itself with rude schoolboy pranks. By five o'clock, however, its mood had changed and its force increased fourfold, and by six o'clock it had cast off all restraint and become a tempest.

Whilst I remained in the Hall I hardly realised its fury, for the house is well built and shielded from the full force of the northerly winds. It was when I ventured out to visit Martha Treffit soon after dinner that I became aware of it.

The squire had left the table with a severe headache, and retired to his own room where, with drawn blinds and absolute quietude, he usually finds ease, and I was left to my own devices and the tender mercies of the Cynic, when he should arrive.

But his train was not due until eight, and it would take him a good thirty minutes to walk from the station, so I had more than an hour at my disposal, and I was anxious to find out how little Lucy was progressing. She had been under the care of the doctor for several days, and was still in bed and very feverish.

I put on my ulster, wound a wrap about my head, and stepped out on to the drive, and it was then that I became aware of the raging elements around me.

The wind blew bitingly from the north, charged with smarting pellets of sleet. I had known strong winds before, but never anything like this. It howled and roared, it hissed and shrieked; it was as much as I could do to force my way forward against the pressure of its onrush; but though my head was bent I saw that every bush and shrub was shaken as by some gigantic Titan, and that the tall and naked trees swayed towards me with groans that sounded human and ominous.

On the topmost branches, black bundles which I knew to be deserted nests were rocked violently to and fro, like anchored boats in the trough of a storm-lashed sea. The night was grim and black, save when for a brief moment the full moon gleamed down upon the angry scene from the torn rifts of the scurrying clouds.

The thought crossed my mind that it might be wiser to return, but Fate or Providence urged me forward, and I laughed at my fears and set my shoulder to the storm.

Phew! if it was a gale along the drive it was a hurricane in the village street, and a hot-headed, impetuous hurricane, too. Pausing for a second in its mad rush it leaped upon one the next moment with a sudden fury that seemed almost devilish and was well-nigh irresistible. Twice I was flung against the wall, but as I was hugging it pretty closely I suffered no harm. As I struggled onward the wind was in my teeth; a dozen steps farther and it leaped the wall on my right with a roar, like a pack of hounds in full cry, and tore down the fields with reckless velocity to hurl itself into the black mystery of the wood.

Not a soul was to be seen, but the clatter of a dislodged slate upon the pavement brought a frightened woman to the door of one of the cottages, and I stepped inside for a moment's breathing-space.

"Lord! Miss 'Olden, is it you?" she said. "I don't know how you dare stir out. I'm a'most flayed to death to stay in t' 'ouse by myself, but my master is off wi' most o' t' other men to Gordon's farm to give 'em a hand."

"What is the matter there?" I inquired.

"Ye 'aven't 'eard, then? They say 'at t' wind's uprooted t' big sycamore an' flung it again' one o' t' barns, or summat, an' it's like to fall in, so they've gone to see what can be done."

I did my best to encourage her and then made what haste I could to the house of Roger Treffit, which stood lank and dark against the black sky. As it was Saturday night I hoped that Roger would be away, but it was his voice that bade me enter, and the dog rose to give me welcome.

The fire roared up the chimney and the wind met it there with answering roar. Roger was sitting with his feet stretched out to the blaze, one arm resting upon the table and encircling a half-empty whiskey bottle. In his right hand he held a tumbler nearly full of spirits. I saw at a glance that he was very drunk, but I believed him to be harmless.

"Is Mrs. Treffit upstairs? may I go to her at once?" I asked.

"Quite all right, ma'am, quite all right. Show lady . . . way, Miss T'ry. . . . Missis ill . . . kid ill . . . Miss T'ry ill . . . ev'yb'dy ill. Doctor says mus' keep kid quiet, mus'n' disturb 'er. Won't let 'em disturb 'er, I won't. . . . Go forw'd, ma'am."

He rose steadily enough, and held the door open for me to pass through, and I heard him mutter as he returned to his chair:

"Won't let 'em disturb 'er, I won't."

Martha greeted me in her usual sadly-cordial fashion, and motioned me to a chair near the bed where the little one lay, flushed and asleep.

"She's a bit better," she whispered, "but she's to be kept quiet; an' whatever I do I haven't to miss 'er med'cine every hour. But he says wi' care an' good nursin' she'll pull through."

"And how is your cough?" I asked.

"Oh, about as usual," she replied indifferently. "I have to cough into my apron when Lucy's asleep, but I should soon be right enough if I'd nought to worrit about. It's yon chap downstairs 'at 'll be t' death of us both."

"Has he no engagement to-night? I thought he was never free on Saturdays."

"It's t' dog. She's poorly again, an' he can't work her. My opinion is 'at t' poor brute's about done, an' I believe Roger knows it an' it's drivin' 'im mad. He drinks t' day through, an' in a bit there'll be nought for us but t' work'us, for I can't keep 'im i' whiskey; an' whativver's goin' to come o' our poor little Lucy I don't know. I've been lookin' at her as she lay there, Miss 'Olden, so sweet an' pretty, like a little angel, an' I a'most asked the Lord to take 'er out of all t' trouble, but I couldn't bide to lose 'er."

The overwrought woman buried her face in her apron and sobbed convulsively—deep-drawn, quiet sobs which told of her soul's agony. A solitary candle was burning upon the dressing-table, and the room looked eerie in the half darkness. Outside the storm was at its height, and in the stillness which neither of us broke I heard it shriek with the shrillness which one associates with spirits in torment.

But it was the savage thrust of the wind that frightened me most, and the heavy and repeated thuds which struck the end of the house like the battering blows of a heavy ram. It is no exaggeration to say that the house rocked, and I began to fear lest it should collapse. I remembered what a shaky, decrepit structure it was, and I turned to Martha to see if she shared my alarm.

She caught the question in my eyes: "I think it's safe enough," she said; "it allus rocks a bit in a 'igh wind. I've got while I take no notice of it."

Poor woman! There was a storm within her breast which dwarfed the tempest outside into insignificance; but I held my breath again and again, and tried in vain to stay the tumultuous beatings of my heart as the mad wind rained blow after blow upon the quivering walls with a persistency and ever growing fury which seemed to make disaster inevitable.

By and by I could stand it no longer. "Are you sure the house is safe, Martha?" I asked. "Listen to the wind now; it makes me shudder to hear it, and the wall on yonder side absolutely heaves. Had we not better wrap Lucy up well, and take her downstairs?"

"You aren't used to it, Miss 'Olden, an' it's gettin' on your nerves. You needn't fear. I've seen it like this oft enough afore. But you ought to be gettin' back 'ome, for it's hardly a fit night for you to be out."

I was reluctant to leave, and yet I saw that I was likely to do more harm than good if I remained, so I said good-night and left her; but at the foot of the narrow staircase I found my way blocked and the door barred. Angry voices came from within the room, and my knocks were unheard or unheeded. Roger's back appeared to be against the door, and I put my ear to it and listened.

They were mostly women's voices, and their angry tone convinced me that they had been protesting in vain.

"Don't be a fool, Roger! I tell you t' stack 'll fall in another minute, an' where 'll you all be then? Oppen t' door, an' let's bring your Martha an' Lucy out, or ye'll all be killed!"

"Ye shan't disturb 'er," said the maudlin voice on the other side of the door; "doct'r said mus'n' disturb 'er . . . keep 'er quiet . . . won't let anyb'dy disturb 'er."

"Can't you understand, you gawmless fool," shouted another woman, "'at t' chimley's rockin' an' swayin', an' is bound to come down on t' top on us all while we're standin' 'ere ? Oppen t' door, you drunken beggar, an' let your missis an' child come out!"

"I'll shoot anyb'dy 'at disturbs 'er," stuttered Roger; "hang me if I don't. Doct'r said mus'n' be disturbed . . . won't have 'er disturbed. Clear, all of ye!"

There was a sound of sudden movement, and I gathered that Roger had raised his weapon. Sick at heart I groped my way upstairs again and discussed the situation with Martha.

She was alarmed in good earnest now, as much for my sake as for Lucy's, and we went down and battered the door in vain. We could hear voices faintly, but the crowd was evidently in the road, and Roger was still guarding the door.

We returned to the bedroom, and Martha flung herself upon her knees and broke into fervent prayer to God.

What happened afterwards has been told me since. Afraid of the tottering chimney-stack, and cowed by Roger's revolver, the group of women and boys had fallen back into the road, when Barjona appeared upon the scene with his cart.

With one accord the women rushed up to him and explained the peril of Roger and his family, and the drunken man's insane refusal of help and warning.

A glance above showed Barjona that their fears were only too well founded, and—let me say it to his credit—he did not hesitate for a moment. "Can only die once," he muttered, and without another word he seized his whip and strode towards the house. As he entered the door Roger covered him with his weapon and defied him to advance, but with a hoarse growl the sturdy old man flung himself forward, lashed his whip around the legs of the drunken man, and as the revolver discharged itself harmlessly into the air, he seized his opponent round the waist, and with superhuman strength hurled him into the corner, where he lay stupefied, if not senseless.

The faithful dog sprang at his master's assailant, but he kicked it quickly aside. It was the work of a moment to draw back the heavy bolt and rush up the creaking stairs.

"Out with you!" he cried . . . "Out at once! . . . no time to lose . . . t' chimney's fallin' . . . Bring Lucy, Martha . . . I'll go down an' watch Roger. 'Urry up, now!"

We needed no second admonition. Barjona hurried down the steps, and Martha darted to the bed, seized her child and a blanket, and followed him. I had almost reached the foot of the stairs when I remembered the medicine on which so much depended, and I ran back to fetch it. As I did so I thought I heard a warning cry from the street, and fear gave wings to my feet. But it was too late.

Just as I reached the dressing-table there came a fearful crash, and through an opening in the roof an avalanche of stones and tiles and mortar descended with terrific force. Then, to the accompaniment of an awful roar, a dark and heavy mass hurled itself through the gap, and the crunch of broken beam and splintered wood told where it had disappeared into the room below. A pit opened almost at my feet, and there came up a blinding, suffocating mist of dust, like the breath of a smouldering volcano.

One whole end of the house fell over into the field, and I felt the floor slope away beneath me as I made an agonised clutch at the framework of the bed. Loosened stones fell upon and around me in showers, but I was conscious of no pain. Choked and terrified, however, and certain that my last hour had come, I lost my senses and fell upon the littered bed in a swoon.

I came back to semi-consciousness in a land of shadows. I thought I was in Egypt, lying among the ruins of the great Nile temples about which I had been reading to the squire only a day or two before. Overhead the moon was looking down, full orbed, and tattered clouds were racing along the path of the skies. The jagged piles of masonry were the giant walls of Philae, and the roar of the wind was the rush of waters over the great dam. It was not unpleasant to lie there and dream, and listen to the spirit voices which came indistinctly from the pillared courts.

Then the figure of a man bent over me and an arm was placed beneath my neck, and a familiar voice whispered in tones that sounded anguished, and oh! so distant:

"Grace, my darling! Speak to me!"

I tried to speak, but could only smile and lean upon his arm in deep content, and the figure bent over me and placed his cheek against my lips, and laid a hand upon my heart, and seemed to cry for help; but the cry was faint and indistinct, like that of a distant echo.

Then another form appeared—taller and more stalwart—and I felt myself raised from the ground and carried to the top of the masonry, where formless hands grasped me, and I sank—sank—with a feeling that I was descending into the bowels of the earth—into oblivion again.

When I next awoke my mind was clearer, but I was still dazed. I half opened my eyes and found myself in my own bed, with the housekeeper seated at my side, and Dr. Trempest and the squire talking together in quiet tones by the fire.

"How in thunder did they get her down?" the doctor was asking.

"Derwent heard the story as he got to the Hall and he fetched a short ladder and climbed up as far as he could, and did some wonderful gymnastics," replied the squire; "but Goodenough's sons came hurrying up with longer ladders, and they lashed three together side by side, and managed in that way. Derwent couldn't lift her, but Ben Goodenough has the strength of an ox. But it was a tough job in a high wind on a rickety floor."

"Well, it's a miracle, that's all I can say. I must go see Martha Treffit's child now, but I'll look in to-morrow, early on."

"You are sure there is no cause for anxiety?" inquired the squire anxiously; "she will come round all right?"

"As right as a bobbin," replied the doctor cheerfully. "There's only the least bit of concussion. She was more frightened than hurt. I'll send her up a bottle when I get back."

"You needn't trouble," I ejaculated; "it won't be mixed with faith this time."

"She'll do!" chuckled the doctor, and he turned to me: "Go to sleep now and behave yourself."

CHAPTER THIRTY

CALM
AFTER STORM

OF COURSE THE Cynic had to explain, because he did not realise at first how shadowy the whole occurrence had been to me. You see, I really was not fully conscious at the time, and might easily have concluded that I had dreamt it.

However, he is *my* Cynic now, really, so I can talk quite freely to him; and I tell him that after he called me "darling" and whilst he was trying to make sure that I still breathed, he kissed me; but he says that convinces him that I really was dreaming. But we have agreed not to quarrel about it, as one more or less doesn't much matter.

His professional duties must be pretty elastic, for it is now Wednesday and he has not gone back; though, to be sure, he has done a fair amount of pleading in a local court and has won the first part of his case and seems likely to be successful in the next. A remarkable thing about these bachelors who have waited so long is that they cannot afford to wait the least bit longer. They are no sooner engaged than they must be married. But in this instance things are going to be done decently and in order. The squire says we do not know each other well enough yet, and suggests two years as the term of our engagement, but I think we shall compromise on four months.

"What about my studio, Philip?" I asked this morning. "I have not seen it for days, and it is as dear to me as a lover."

"Is it?" he said; "can you bear to walk as far?"

"Why, of course," I replied; "I'm all right now."

"You'll have to take my arm," he remarked; "you are only shaky yet."

It was merely an excuse, but I did it to please him. Of course all the village knows what has happened, and a dozen friendly folk nodded, or smiled or shouted their congratulations according to the measure of their intimacy or reserve.

When we came in sight of my cottage the studio was nowhere to be seen, and, greatly surprised, I turned to the Cynic for an explanation, but he merely pressed my arm and said:

"Farmer Goodenough is there. He will tell you all about it."

I held my peace until we entered the field and stood by my late landlord's side. Explanation was unnecessary, for the field was still littered with splintered wood and broken glass, though much of it had been cleared away.

"So you're about again, miss! Well, I'm downright glad to see you." Then, indicating the *débris* with an inclination of the head: "I've sorted out all 'at seemed to be worth ought. All t' glass pictures 'at weren't reight smashed I've put into a box an' ta'en into t' 'ouse. But there isn't much left. Them 'at saw it say 'at t' stewdio cut up t' paddock like a hairyplane, an' it must ha' collapsed in t' same way."

"It knew it was doomed," remarked the Cynic, "supplanted—and it promptly put an end to itself."

"Well, never mind, miss," put in Reuben, "there's nought to fret about. 'Off wi' the old love an' on with the new!' I'd nearly put that down to t' Owd Book, but I should ha' been mista'en. However, ye've made a good swop, an' I don't know which on ye's got t' best o' t' bargain."

"I have, Reuben," said the Cynic heartily.

I wasn't going to contradict him, of course, though I know he is "mista'en."

"I was just thinkin', miss, if it's all t' same to you," continued the farmer, "'at it 'ud be a charity to let Martha an' her little lass have your cottage. You see——"

"But you forget they are only for widows, Mr. Goodenough," I interrupted.

He glanced quickly at Philip. "They haven't told you then, miss? Well, it's out now. Martha *is* a widow. Barjona got clear by t' skin of his teeth, but Roger an' t' dog were killed on t' spot; an' though it sounds a 'ard sayin', it's no loss to Martha an' Lucy. Are we to let 'em have t' cottage, think ye?"

I agreed, of course; but the tragic death of Roger had saddened me, and as usual Reuben noticed my clouded expression.

"Now don't you take on, miss. You'll 'ave to leave these things to them above. After all, as t' Owd Book says, 'It's an ill wind 'at blows nobody any good,' an' t' storm has blown you two into one another's arms an' Martha into t' cottage, in a manner o' speakin'; so we must look on t' cheerful side. However, I must be stirring."

He raised his cap and left us, and I turned to the Cynic.

"Philip," I said, and I know the tears filled my eyes, "the sight of the cottage brings back to me sweet memories of dear old Mother Hubbard. How delighted she would have been to welcome us! How pleased she would have been if she had known!"

"She did know, Grace," he replied. "I called to see her when you were away, and the good soul spoke to me about you in such loving terms that I could not help making her my confidante; and do you know, she asked if she might kiss me before I left. She hoped to live to see the consummation, but if that were denied her she bade me tell you how earnestly she had prayed for our happiness, and how fervently she had longed to see us united."

Now I have reached the very last line in my book. How could I end it better than with Mother Hubbard's blessing?

THE END

Lightning Source UK Ltd.
Milton Keynes UK
UKOW06f0706210216

268752UK00001B/9/P